The Way You Love Me

C.E. KNIGHT

authorHOUSE®

AuthorHouse™
1663 Liberty Drive
Bloomington, IN 47403
www.authorhouse.com
Phone: 833-262-8899

Published by AuthorHouse 12/13/2024

ISBN: 979-8-8230-3411-1 (sc)
ISBN: 979-8-8230-3412-8 (e)

Library of Congress Control Number: 2024919840

Print information available on the last page.

Chapter

1

Marcus Jordan stared out the large window that overlooked Main Street from his booth at Juliano's, a popular Italian restaurant. He sipped the vintage scotch, not noticing the growing evening shadow as the streets slowly emptied. The night life in Philadelphia was waking up as the workday was ending. Marcus had spent the past three hours brokering a business deal with Marco and Luca, owners of the restaurant. As Marcus assessed the full scope of the business arrangement, he knew that the lucrative deal would be beneficial to his company. The brothers had two businesses in town, and with Marcus's partnership, they were now moving forward with plans for another restaurant. Within the next twelve months, they planned to open a more upscale restaurant at the Harbors, an area of town that catered to the wealthier clientele.

Marcus quietly contemplated his life. The feeling of emptiness invaded his thoughts as he reflected on his personal life. Sheree, his latest girlfriend, a fashion model for an elite modeling agency, was the subject of this thoughts. She was gorgeous; most men would love to have such a beautiful woman in their lives. He should have been meeting his girl later and celebrating—but the idea made him feel like champagne with no fizz. He had no desire to call her. He was quickly losing interest in their almost two-year-old relationship. Although neither of them had agreed to a monogamous relationship, he felt that Sheree wanted it to be. Over the past few months, Sheree's increasing bouts of jealousy usually ended their nights out with an argument.

The constant conflict with Sheree was playing havoc with his peace of mind. This further demonstrated to him how unmatched they were for each other. He never gave her reason to be jealous; he always showed her the utmost respect. He was far from conceited, although he was a very handsome, striking man. He stood six feet four, with wavy black hair that just brushed his shoulders. His light-brown skin was a perfect contrast to his hair. He was a product of mixed heritage—Indian and African American. He had all the trimmings—wealth, charm, and good looks—but still, he was unable to avoid the emptiness in his life.

Marcus became irritated with his thoughts and muttered to himself. He took a long swallow of his scotch, draining the glass; then he stood, straightening his jacket, preparing to leave.

Luca's wife, Marcella, noticed Marcus getting up from his seat and hurried over to speak with him. They were joined a few minutes later by both Marco and Luca, as they all shared a joke and reminisced about old times.

"Sorry, Marcus, it got kinda busy in here. Do you have to leave so soon?" Marcella asked.

Marcus smiled, then replied, "Afraid so. I think Luca knows I have designs on you, and he knows how dangerous I am around a beautiful woman." They all laughed as he and Luca exchanged exaggerated swings at each other. "As much as it pains me to say this, Luca is the better man, Marcella—but you can outcook him any day of the week. The food tonight was awesome, as usual. Gonna have to have my next office meeting here and let my staff get a taste of Marcella's magic in the kitchen."

They all smiled, as Marco and Luca both extended a hand to Marcus, only to be pulled into a bear hug. The brothers always treated him like part of the family.

Marcus had a good feeling about doing business with them. He headed out the door with promises to be in touch soon.

A few blocks away, Jillian Weston stepped from her car and slammed the door. The car's engine was dead—she had barely made it into town before it gave its last sputter of life. Jill looked around at the empty streets and then at her car. She gave the tire a quick kick, only to yell out in pain. She bent over to grasp her throbbing foot, and a few colorful words escaped her lips. Her immediate future looked bleak. She had traveled for ten hours from her hometown of Claremont, Virginia, to Philadelphia, hoping that the job interview would pan out and she could stay put. Her longtime friend had advised her to choose this city. The decision for making her hurried move was due to family problems.

Philadelphia was listed as one of the more successful cities for the career minded. Jill had not yet thought about what that career would be, but she needed a new outlook to help change her old karma, which was only keeping her down. Claremont was no longer home for her. She'd had her last knock-down-drag-out with her mother. Her father had pleaded with her to give her mother another chance, but Jill could not live with her mother anymore. The abuse had gone on for most of her life. She felt that her mother did not love her, so in order to spare herself the constant feeling of hurt, leaving was the best thing.

Jill opened the car door to retrieve her purse and then locked the car. Everything she owned was inside her car. She gave it a last look before walking down the street in search of a phone or service station. She felt nervous over just the thought of what the repairs might cost her, depleting her cash on hand.

She walked for a few minutes, thinking about her run of bad luck, which had her frustrated and close to tears. She was now in an area with a few stores, but they looked as if they were near closing time. There was a clothing store with only a few customers and a restaurant across the street that specialized in Italian food, as well as a few other miscellaneous small stores. Suddenly, a woman screamed. Jill looked up ahead of her, and only a half block away, she saw a man throw a woman to the ground and walk away. The woman quickly scrambled to her feet and lunged at him. The man again threw the woman to the ground, but this time he knelt over her and landed several blows to her face with his fist.

Jill looked around to see if anyone would help the woman, but the street was empty. She heard the woman's tearful, pleading voice, calling for help. Jill took off running to the woman's side, completely forgetting about her own dilemma. When Jill was only a few steps away from the woman, she heard the woman's plea to let her babies go—and Jill's mind registered the babies' cries. Jill asked the woman if she was ok, but the woman only gestured toward the man, who was hunting for something as the babies continued to cry. She saw the babies in their car seats as the woman continued to yell.

"Please! Save my babies!" the woman cried. "Please! Help me!"

Jill instantly saw red. The man picked up what looked like keys off the street near the car where the babies were and proceeded to get in. Jill—not thinking, just reacting—ran to the car, leaping onto the man. Her small purse went flying, and her things inside it scattered in all directions. She immediately started pounding on his head. He yelled at her but dropped the keys. Jill was a plus-size woman, and the momentum of her leap and her weight, along with his struggling to get her off him, caused her to tumble onto the passenger seat, halfway on the floor and halfway on the seat. She hit her head on the door with a thud. The man pummeled her with his fists. She tried to block his blows, but her attempts were unsuccessful.

Across the street, Marcus had just stepped outside the restaurant into the warm May evening when he heard a woman screaming and pleading for help—and he took off in the direction of the screams. He reached her in seconds. The woman's face was bruised and bleeding slightly. She grabbed Marcus's arm, pleading with him to stop the man from taking her babies. Marcus suddenly realized that the sound of babies' crying were coming from the car. He then saw the man in the car, repeatedly swinging his fists. Marcus felt the adrenaline rush, as rage took over at the thought of kids being beaten. He rushed from the woman and quickly grabbed the man's bloodied fist as he was about to deliver another blow. Marcus bent the man's arm backward, and the man yelled out in pain, as Marcus applied pressure to the arm and dragged the man out of the car and onto the street. The man's body hit the ground, but he immediately stood up, his fists ready to swing. Marcus blocked his punch and quickly threw a series of punches before laying a final chop to the back of the man's neck. The man dropped to the street, face first and unconscious. Marcus briefly stared at the man and then looked back to where the woman had been lying on the street.

She had crawled over to the car and was motioning to him. "Please! Please! Sir, can you help her? She needs some medical attention. She's not moving, and blood is everywhere! That thug threw my phone, and God only knows where. Can you call an ambulance?"

Marcus stared blankly at the woman and then he saw another woman, half on the seat and half on the floor, with blood everywhere. His heart fell to his feet as he climbed on to the front seat and felt for a pulse; he found one. He pulled out his phone and called 911. Soon, he heard sirens, and a police car turned the corner, followed by an ambulance. The ambulance carried away the badly beaten woman, and the thug was taken away to lockup.

Marcus noticed a purse near the front wheel of the car. He picked up the purse, but it was empty. Then he saw two receipts on the street, which he was able to pick up before they blew away. He also found a small amount of money, a tube of Chapstick, and a card from a hotel but nothing else.

A detective walked up to speak to the mother while she was sitting in the car, trying to calm the two babies.

Marcus approached the detective and handed him the items he'd found. "This may belong to one of the two women. There's no ID in the purse; it may have blown away like some other stuff I saw going down the street."

"Well, that's not good because it probably belongs to the victim. I gather you don't know her."

"No, I've never seen her before," Marcus said.

"Mrs. Spellings said the same thing. Seems the victim was just trying to help. So sad, but she—and you—likely saved the lives of two children. The woman who was beaten got the short end of the stick, but she might have played a big part in helping to get that piece of trash off the streets. Now I think you should meet the woman who is incredibly happy that you were here. By the way, I'm Detective Johnathan Harold, and you are Marcus Jordan, correct?"

Marcus nodded. "Yes."

"Nice to meet you, Mr. Jordan. I thought I recognized you. You have done some great things for the city and today's heroic effort can be added to that list. Follow me because I need to speak with you and Mrs. Spellings. I don't know if you are aware, but Naomi Spellings is the mayor's sister."

"No, I was not aware that she is the mayor's sister."

Marcus followed the detective to where Naomi Spellings now sat with her kids in the back of the car as she talked with a police officer. The detective asked both Marcus and Naomi to come to the station to make a formal statement.

After giving a statement downtown, Marcus and Naomi were free to go. Naomi thanked the detective profusely but stressed her concern for the woman who had put her life on the line for her and her children.

As Marcus walked out of the police station, Naomi called out, "Mr. Jordan?"

He stopped and then walked in her direction; she limped a few more steps closer to him.

"Call me Marcus," he said.

"I was wondering if you could call me if you find out anything about the woman's condition. I know I'm asking a lot, but the detective said that they were still looking for her ID. I want to make sure she has whatever she needs."

Marcus noticed a man getting out of a car and rushing over to them.

Naomi turned embraced him; she then introduced her husband Jeremy to Marcus.

Marcus shook hands with the man, who also offered Marcus his thanks.

"Well, I told the detective that I would stand as her guardian for the moment until they locate her relatives. Hopefully, she is local so someone will see it on the news."

"That is mighty thoughtful of you," Naomi and her husband said in unison.

"If it wasn't for the carjacker beating her so much—" Naomi became emotional and couldn't finish her sentence.

"Don't worry," Marcus said. "I'll check on the woman." Marcus nodded his head as Naomi's husband wrapped his arms around her, giving her support. "Tell you what, Naomi. Knowing that you and your kids are safe makes us all feel good. You sure you don't want a doctor to look at your face or your leg?"

"No, I'm fine right now. It's just some scratches. If it feels worse in the morning, I'll see my doctor. I have to leave my car because they are still dusting for prints and taking pictures of the inside for evidence. The detective said he will call when we can pick it up. My babies were so worn out from all that crying that they fell asleep. I called my nanny to come and get them at the station because I thought we would be here for a while. I guess we will head home now. Thanks, Marcus, for all you have done." As she and her husband headed toward their car, she called out, "Thanks again, Marcus!"

When Marcus left the police station, he headed to the hospital. He called his folks and his assistant, hoping they had not heard about what had happened from the news yet. When he arrived, he checked with the emergency room staff and found that a young woman who was beaten in a carjacking was taken to the fourth floor. Marcus found the nurses' station, where a young nurse recognized him.

"You're Marcus Jordan!" the nurse said with a huge smile.

Marcus nodded but looked around, wanting to check on the woman who was injured.

"Oh, you're the biggest hero in this town right now, along with that poor woman in there."

"I'm no hero," Marcus insisted. "That woman who put her life on the line is the hero. Can you tell—"

"The story has been all over the news. Speaking as a mother myself, I think that the two of you need a commendation from the mayor. Thugs like that need to be put under the jail. It's amazing how you just judo chopped that guy right into the sidewalk."

Marcus smiled. "Ah, it wasn't exactly—"

"Boy, was Mrs. Spellings lucky you came along," the nurse said. "I bet that thug feels pretty silly about now. You know what? I gotta—"

"Sorry, Mrs. ...?"

"I'm Carrie," the nurse said.

"Yes, Carrie. I need the room number of the young woman brought in from the attempted carjacking. I was appointed her guardian by the authorities," Marcus interjected. "I'd like to see how she's doing, if that's Ok."

"Sorry, but the doc ordered some strong meds for her. She was in quite a bit of pain and was very anxious. The meds helped to calm her, but she has been sleeping ever since. He left instructions to call him if anyone came to visit her. If you'll hang on a minute, I'll have him paged."

Marcus nodded his understanding and walked over to the waiting area, where he stood with his back to the nurse as he looked out the window.

After the nurse paged the doctor, she came back to Marcus and lightly touched his arm. "Mr. Jordan, I forgot to mention that the police were here earlier, but because she was in so much pain, the doc asked them to save their questioning for tomorrow. The doctor did try to find out if she had any relatives. She only said there was none and started crying. I felt so bad for her. It's just so sad for anyone to be alone, especially after such a traumatic experience. I am so glad Jill has you."

A surprised expression crossed Marcus's face. "You said *Jill?*"

"Yes, that's the name she gave us. Is something wrong, Mr. Jordan?"

"No, I wasn't sure if you said Jill or something else, that's all," Marcus said, trying to cover up the fact that he didn't know the victim's name.

"Ah no, I meant Jill," said the nurse.

Marcus nodded in understanding, although he had no clue as to her name.

"The police wanted her side of the story and to let her know the criminal was captured," the nurse said. "They also wanted to find her next of kin. The doctor didn't see the urgency for the questioning since they have the suspect. He'll be here momentarily and give you an update on her condition."

The nurse directed Marcus to a room just off the waiting room where there were also vending machines and coffee. It was some minutes later that a tall man in a white jacket, with salt-and-pepper hair, approached Marcus, who was looking out the window.

"Excuse me, Mr. Jordan?"

Marcus turned around. "Yes?"

"I am Dr. Franklin. I understand you are inquiring about the patient who was brought in from the attempted carjacking."

"Yes, Doctor. I'm standing as a temporary guardian until the authorities can locate her nearest relative. She and I rushed to the aid of a mother of two who was being carjacked. It was unfortunate that Jill got there before I did. She sacrificed herself for the safety of those two children—pretty incredible." Marcus spoke quietly, as if speaking to himself, but the doctor nodded in understanding. "I think standing up for her is the least that I can do."

"That's a very generous thing for you to do, especially not knowing the person," the doctor replied thoughtfully.

"I just believe in doing my part, and that's what I am doing."

"Earlier, she told me that she has no relatives," the doctor said, shaking his head.

"Wow, that's really unfortunate. Nevertheless, I intend to help in any way I can."

"Good! Well, she has been through quite an ordeal. She's had x-rays, and labs were run. I've ordered several tests for first thing in the morning. I'm concerned with the huge lump on the back of her head. It was hard to rule out a concussion because she was not very coherent during the examination—she kept going in and out of consciousness. I think once her swelling goes down and her headache subsides, we will be able to determine if there is more severe trauma than initially noted. She has some intense bruising on her shoulder and her arms. Her left eye is pretty banged up—some broken blood vessels, possibly, as the area was so swollen. She will be in a lot of pain and have soreness by the morning. She is sound asleep now. I have sedated her because of the pain. I want her to get good rest so that she can be ready for those tests I ordered in the morning. For now, Mr. Jordan, we will wait and see how things look tomorrow. I will tell you this, though—any man who hits a woman in the way that young lady was beaten needs to be punished to the full extent of the law."

"I agree with you, Doctor. I would have loved to have given him just what he deserved right there on the street," Marcus said quietly.

"What you did, Mr. Jordan—you saved not only her life but the lives of those two babies. Now, tell me about your hand. Does it hurt?"

Marcus looked at his hand, seeing the dried blood on his knuckles for the first time. "Oh, nah. It's fine. Just broke the skin a little on it, that's all. I'm fine."

"You sure? That will be sore in the morning. Make sure you put some ice on it to help with the swelling and a little Neosporin or some antibiotic cream to help with any infection."

"Yeah, but I'm fine. Thanks, Doc," Marcus said with a slight smile.

The doctor nodded and said, "Ok, but for now, get some rest because you've had a tough day as well. We'll talk more tomorrow. No need for you to hang around here because I am quite sure she's asleep for the night."

"Ok, Doctor, I'll drop in on her tomorrow. I have her personal effects so if she wakes up and is anxious about it, I'll leave my phone number with the nurse, and she can get in touch with me."

The doctor smiled. "Good idea. I think my patient is in good hands with you, Mr. Jordan."

"Thanks, Dr. Franklin. When I come back tomorrow, should I bring anything? What do you think she'll need?" Marcus asked.

"To start, the best thing would be all the support she can get. Anything else will work itself out. Now I must get back to my rounds. Any other questions?"

"No, I am good for now."

"Well, if you need me, just tell the charge nurse to page me."

"Ok, Doc, thanks."

"You are welcome."

They shook hands, and both men walked away in different directions.

Marcus was almost home when his cell phone rang. He saw it was Sheree's phone number, so he answered. "Hey!"

"Hey yourself, Mr. Caped Crusader!" she replied.

"I gather you heard the news of the day," Marcus said.

"Yes, I did! Trey just told me about it. The whole shoot is buzzing about it, especially since my boyfriend is the hero. They now call you Superman," Sheree said with a laugh.

"Great. The last thing I want is attention from the media. The real heroine is lying in a hospital bed, badly beaten. She is the true hero."

"Marcus Jordan, if it were not for you, she and the mother would be in even worse shape, and the kids would be God knows where. The silly girl needs her head examined. She put you all in danger. What if this criminal had a gun? You could have been shot or worse. I am so glad you are ok. Stop treating your part in the event so lightly."

"Sheree, I am not treating it lightly. She stalled, him long enough for help to come, and that was heroic because she risked her life. How about we change the subject? Are you back in town yet?" Marcus was irritated that Sheree had treated Jill's role in the incident as if it was nothing.

"Marcus, you give people too much credit, and I think—"

"It's really not a good time for me, Sheree." Marcus didn't feel like going around and around with her, like always. "Maybe another time. It's been a long day, and I'm headed home. I'll talk with you later, ok?"

"Marcus, are you cutting me off? You seem upset."

"Just a little worn out, Sheree. It's been one of those kinda days, ya know?"

"Ok, babe. Get some rest. Sweet dreams, sweetie! I'll call you tomorrow. Good night." She ended the call before Marcus could reply.

He felt guilty that he'd been short with her but was relieved that she was not back in town from her photo shoot. He didn't feel like dealing with her drama right now. His mind kept playing images over and over of the girl named Jill, and he wanted it to stop—or did he?

Moments later, he stopped at the guard's gate at the entrance to his luxury condo when he was flagged by one of the guards.

"Hello, Mr. Jordan," the guard said. "That was a mighty fine thing you did for Mrs. Spellings and those kids. You and that young lady deserve a commendation from the mayor."

Marcus smiled at the tall, slender, older gentleman who had been part of the team that guarded this gated community for some time. Henry was retired but worked two days a week as part of security monitoring, and he worked for Marcus three days a week, running errands or doing whatever was needed.

"Thanks, Henry, but I did nothing more than what you would have done."

The older man saluted Marcus as he pulled through the gate.

Marcus pulled into the garage, noticing that his repairman had brought Jill's car.

"Yeah, Marcus, you are all in on this one," he said aloud. He had surprised himself with how he had just jumped in, taking on the responsibility of Jill. He shook his head, at the wonder of it all as he locked his car. Marcus entered his condo and headed directly to the shower.

Later, as he sat in his study, he realized that he had been there for over two hours, and all he could seem to do was think about Jill. He needed to get a handle on his thoughts. Maybe seeing her being beaten had taken a bigger toll on him than he'd thought. He got up, walked over to the bar, and poured himself some scotch. He slowly sipped it, then swallowed the rest of it in one gulp. He set the glass down and headed to bed. He was somewhat anxious to see what tomorrow would bring.

The next morning, Marcus was at the office early; he planned to go to the hospital as soon as visiting hours started. His staff fielded calls from the media about the carjacking, and by eleven o'clock, he was walking through the doors of the hospital. When he reached Jill's floor, he went to the nurses' station. He did not see the nurse named Carrie, with whom he'd spoken with yesterday. Today, Jill was assigned a nurse by the name of Nadene, an amazon-like woman who spoke with a heavy accent. And if he were to guess, he'd say Jamaican.

"Well, Mr. Jordan, your little lady has been in and out of it pretty much all morning. Dr. Franklin came in about seven this morning to see her. Her vitals were better, and she even managed to smile, which made the doc's day. You'd better be careful; that one is truly a heartbreaker," Nadene said with a smile and a wink.

Marcus smiled and placed a hand over his heart. "I will make sure my heart is protected."

"Well, Mr. Knight in Shining Armor, let's see if Sleeping Beauty is awake."

He followed the nurse into Jill's room. She appeared asleep, but after a few seconds, her eyelids began to flutter and slowly opened.

Marcus came around the bed and just watched her. The nurse spoke to Jill, and Jill turned her head in the nurse's direction. Her head was mostly bandaged, with the exception of one eye. That eye looked from the nurse to him. She struggled to sit up after hearing the nurse's greeting. Nurse Nadene immediately assisted her; Marcus stood there feeling very much out of place.

"Why, hello, Princess! I think I found your prince or would that be your knight in shining armor?" the nurse said with a big smile as she nodded toward Marcus.

Marcus felt Jill's gaze upon him, causing a tingle to go through him—it was like a magnetic charge. Her one good eye examined him. The nurse gave him a big smile, inviting him to come closer, and then she left the room. He felt the warmth of Jill's gaze upon him. Her nicely shaped lips struggled to form the word *hi*. The few strands of her hair that had escaped the bandage were dark brown. She looked at him with a guarded expression, and he thought that he should be the first to clear the air.

"Hi. My name is Marcus Jordan." He approached the side of her bed.

She tried to sit up further in bed, but the movement seemed to cause pain. Marcus tried to assist, but she looked so fragile that he thought if he touched her, it would probably cause her more pain.

"No! No, don't move on my account." He said feeling helpless. She continued to have pain, and he felt useless. "Ah, is there anything I can do? Maybe get you a nurse?" He moved to leave, but she reached out to grab his arm, and he saw her shake her head. He exhaled slowly before speaking. "Ok, you don't want me to get a nurse, but I feel like a fool just standing here while you are in pain. I wish I could get rid of the pain for you, but I have no experience in this type of thing."

Her lips quivered. She spoke slowly, and her voice was hoarse. "I could see you as the Superman type."

Her comment caught Marcus off guard. Her attempt to smile through the pain was very inspiring. She held it long enough for him to see it, and he smiled back. She was so strong, he thought. He was amazed that she could be in so much pain yet still show good spirits.

"And Superman always had his Lois Lane—or even better, Wonder Woman," he said with a wink.

A small sound which seemed like a giggle escaped her lips but was quickly replaced by a grimace. He found himself apologizing for making her laugh. It took her a few minutes to recover from the onslaught of pain; but recover she did. Heroically, she tried again to put on a smile for him. Marcus did not know what was taking place, but suddenly, he felt strange, as if something was about to happen.

Jill felt totally lost and delirious at the same time as her one good eye feasted on the gorgeous man who stood at her bedside. He was perfect, from his wavy head of glorious hair to his expensive clothing. She could tell from the way his shirt fit him—not tight but as if it was made for him. The word *hunk* easily came to her mind. The nurse hadn't been lying when she'd called him a knight in shining armor. What girl wouldn't want to be rescued by him? She suddenly felt awkward as he seemed to study her, making his own assessment.

She spoke again, hoping to shatter the awkwardness. "Thank you for what you did." To her utter embarrassment, her voice came out more like a croak. She turned her face away from him.

He thought that his visit might be too much for her to deal with right now. "You sure, you're ok?" he asked. "Maybe my being here is not helping you. The last thing I want to do is make you feel worse. I will leave and come back when it's better for you. Get some rest, and we will talk another time." Marcus turned to leave but stopped when he heard her speak.

"Don't! I'll be fine. I'm glad to finally meet the man who saved me and those kids." She paused, as if to steady herself as she tried to sit up slowly. When she finally got into a better sitting position where she could see him, she exhaled loudly.

He was nicely surprised by the tone of her voice. The hoarseness was no longer evident.

"You're the one they told me about who came out from nowhere and used kung fu on the bad guy."

Marcus gave a short laugh and shook his head. "There have been so many spins put on what happened. I initially was congratulated for using judo on the guy, and the next response I got was that I had used kung fu on him." Marcus said.

Jill looked confused. "Huh?"

"No, it's just that people are making it more than what it was. I did some simple rounds on the guy and a chop to his back—that's all."

"Simple? I don't think so. If I remember correctly, the man was huge. I owe you a big thank-you for jumping in the way you did. I'm sorry I didn't witness it. I really wish I could repay you in some way, but I just moved to town, and I don't have a job yet." Her bright attitude suddenly seemed to grow dimmer, and she tried to control her trembling lips. "What a beginning, huh?"

Marcus was curious about her situation. He pulled up a chair and sat at her bedside, still watching her as she explained the reason for her being downtown that evening. She expressed concern for her car and the belongings in it.

"Hey, don't worry about your car," he said cheerfully. "It's safely stored in my garage, and you have my word that it's safe and will remain so until you are able to get around."

The more she talked, the more he learned about her—she had a lot of pride as well as having had hard times. It was the latter that brought out his protective side. Was it her attempts at smiling or that something quiet and gentle seemed to be her aura? He didn't know, but something about her made him feel comfortable. Her appeal was fresh and down-to-earth, making him want to linger. There was something going on that caused quite a reaction inside of him, and he didn't want the feeling to end; it felt so good. He came out of his thoughts to hear her speaking.

"My sorry attempt to stop a car thief failed. It was ridiculous, actually." She looked down at her hands, which were clasped in her lap.

"Actually, that 'ridiculous' thing you did allowed enough time for help to come," Marcus said.

"I know, but it doesn't stop me from feeling stupid. My fighting that big guy was so ridiculous."

"No! You just did what you thought you had to do to help the mother of those kids. I spoke with the mother; she said that whatever you need will be taken care of, no matter what. She intends to come to see you tomorrow. Sorry, but you never told me your name."

"Oh! Sorry, it's Jillian Weston."

"Ms. Weston, you risked your life for people you didn't even know, and you went up against a notorious bad guy—one with a long history of committing crimes, I might add," Marcus told her.

"Yeah! Well, if my mother knew what I did, she would say, 'I always knew that girl of mine has rocks for brains.'"

Marcus listened with a slight smile as she tried to make light of it.

When she started to laugh again, she clutched her head and then her side. "Oo-oh! Ummm! Jeeezus!"

Marcus jumped up as she laid her head back on the pillow and pressed her lips tightly together.

"Hey! Are you ok? I really think I should call a nurse," Marcus said.

Jill raised her hand, gesturing for him to sit down.

Marcus was still not comfortable with not calling the nurse, but he sat back down.

When she had gotten the pain under control, she slowly opened her eyes and looked right at him, making him again experience the impact of her gaze.

"Sorry about that," she said. "I guess laughing is not the best thing for these ribs right now. It makes them hurt like crazy." She continued to gaze at him but with a more subdued smile, as opposed to the full wattage she'd presented earlier. "Tell you what, Mr. Jordan. I like *Jill* better than *Ms. Weston*. Besides, I'm not an old maid yet, and there is probably not a lot of difference in our ages. I'm twenty-six, and I'd say you are around that age yourself, right?"

When he saw the devilment in her eyes, he spoke up. "Very good. I'm twenty-seven, and I prefer *Marcus* to *Mr. Jordan*, since I don't think I need a walker just yet either." Marcus continued to watch her closely. "Are you sure you don't need something for the pain?" He got up again, just a little worried, and leaned over the bed to look closer at her.

Jill found it suddenly hard to breathe as she inhaled the scent of his cologne. She began to experience other feelings besides the ones from the injuries; and rushed to respond. "No, I will be fine. It usually settles down after a few minutes."

"Well, back to what happened with the carjacker. Jill, that woman is the mayor's sister, and the two babies in the back of the car are his niece and nephew. Your deed probably won't be overlooked, not by a long shot, by the top heads in this city."

When Jill realized that he was not kidding, a shocked expression spread across her face.

That reaction was to be expected, but Marcus felt something else was going on. "Something wrong Jill? What you did saved lives and captured a notorious criminal, at the risk of your own life. That's pretty amazing. This town loves you right now, so I'd say your beginning has some perks!"

Jill tried to roll her eyes, but this effort caused her great pain. She placed a hand on either side of her temples. "I don't have a problem with that, if it were true. Just face it, Marcus—if you hadn't stepped in, there might have been three casualties. I am not the hero; you are."

"How about this: it was a team effort. Don't worry about a thing. Relax and get well. We will have you settled in no time." When he noticed her still grimacing, he got up and said, "You need something for that pain. I can't stand to see you suffering any longer, I'll be right back—and no arguments, young lady." He left before she could think about stopping him.

Just for a second, Jill thought that it felt really good to be cared for.

Marcus found Nadene, the nurse, who rushed in, to check on Jill and decided that Jill needed to rest. She left after checking Jill but returned with pain meds. Marcus stayed long enough for Jill to get her meds, and then he took his leave, telling her he would be back to see her the next day.

Marcus decided to make some phone calls. He needed to call Mrs. Spellings and give her an update on Jillian. One thought kept running through his mind—Jillian was not alone; she'd mentioned her mother. So why did she tell the police that she had no one? He aimed to find out exactly what she was hiding or from whom she was hiding. Then he asked himself why he needed to know. What business was it of his? The feeling of needing to know all about her kept nagging at him. His thoughts were interrupted by the ringing of his phone; he answered and found it was his brother on the other end of the line.

The next morning when Jillian awoke, she felt as if she had been hit by a train. There wasn't a place on her body that did not feel sore.

The medicine helped to numb the pain, but she did not want to take too much of it because she wanted to be awake when Marcus came to visit. The thought of him made her want to smile. The brother was so fine, and he had a great sense of humor. He was the in-charge type, the kind of man who a woman would love to have taking care of her. She wanted to find out more about him, but who could she ask? The nurses all adored him. She knew this because when they came into her room to change the monitors, and they thought she was sound asleep, they talked about him. It seemed he had a girlfriend, and he was very rich. But that was all Jill could make out from their whispering.

She could hardly blame them; he was a walking dream. She hadn't thought of another man this way since Phillip. The thought shocked her after all she had been through with Phillip, her ex. She didn't think she would be thinking of another—at least not in that way. She once thought Phillip was the only one; and look how that had turned out. Jill groaned out loud. *What was I thinking? I'm not even in Marcus's league.* She thought he would want a model-like woman hanging on his arm, and she was no model type. She was overweight and broke. Her spirits began to dive as she thought about her life. She needed a job and a place to live. She had no transportation because her car had just died. Jill felt that tears were not far away when the door opened. There in the doorway stood a very thin woman of medium height with a halo of blonde hair that was worn in a neat bob. She wore a big smile as she asked, "Jillian?"

"Yes?"

"I'm Naomi Spellings, and this is my husband, Jeremy. Is it ok for us to come in?"

Jill hadn't initially noticed the man behind her. He was only slightly taller and had a nice smile. "Yes! Come in."

"We had to check on you and also wanted to tell you how grateful we both are for your help in saving our children." Naomi smiled at Jill.

"Thank you, but it's not necessary. I would do it all again if I had to save those children from that maniac," Jill said with conviction.

"We are so grateful you were there," Jeremy said. "The kids are safe and happy, as are their parents. As my wife said, we are very thankful that you came along."

"Jillian, is there anything we can get for you?" Naomi asked with a concerned look.

"Ah, no, I will be fine. Thanks for asking."

There was another knock on her door, and Marcus walked in, dressed in a gray suit, with a big smile on his face. He was followed by another man with dark hair, wearing a brown suit; he was also smiling.

"Good morning, Jillian," he said cheerfully and then winked at her. He was carrying a shopping bag in each hand, which he placed in the corner. Then he turned around to greet the Spellings, before referring to the man behind him. "Jillian, I'd like you to meet our esteemed mayor, Thomas Thornton, Mrs. Spellings's brother."

The mayor extended his hand, and it closed around Jill's. "How do you do, Ms. Weston?"

"I'm better, Mayor Thornton. Thank you for asking." Jill felt overwhelmed at being the center of attention

"Well, we're all very happy that you are doing better," the mayor said with a radiant smile. "Let me just say that not only is my family in your debt, but the whole city is, given the criminal that you helped us to catch. He had been on a crime spree around the city, and until he ran into you and Naomi, he seemed unstoppable. It's unfortunate that your meeting up with him landed you in the hospital, but we are so very thankful that you survived the ordeal. Now, your bill with the hospital will be taken care of. Is there anything else you need?" When Jill shook her head, he said, "My office will be in contact with both you and Mr. Jordan. If something should come up, we will take care of it. You know, those two children are my family, and anyone who did what you did has my total support. I won't tire you out. The nurse gave us a stern warning about time limits. I just wanted you to have my personal thank-you. We are so grateful. You take care, and if you need anything, just call." He handed Jill his card. "Ok, I will take my leave now. Don't worry about anything. We owe you so very much. Thanks again, and I wish you a speedy recovery."

"Thank you, sir. I appreciate all that you have done," Jill replied.

"That goes for us too, Jillian," Mrs. Spellings said. "We will leave now too because we were only supposed to be in here for fifteen minutes at the most. I'm sure the nurse will be back in to remind us—it's in your best interest. As my brother said, if you need anything—anything at all—don't hesitate to call us." They all left, and Marcus followed them out.

Jill felt a little down when she saw Marcus leaving with them. She closed her one good eye and tried to convince herself that she was not interested in him. She also tried not to pity her situation.

There was a brief knock at the door, and she was shocked when she saw Marcus enter the room.

"What? You going to sleep on me now? Am I that boring?" Marcus teased, rolling his eyes and then smiling.

She smiled back and said hesitantly, "I thought you had left with the others."

"Nope! What a start to your day, young lady. Who else gets the mayor's attention first thing in the morning? You are now part of the celebrity list of this town. How are you doing this morning?"

"Grateful to be alive," Jill said and exhaled a deep breath, trying to expel the shock of seeing him again so soon.

"Now that's what I want to hear. I took the liberty of doing a little shopping this morning. Those hospital gowns can't be comfortable." He retrieved the big bag from the corner of the room.

"This morning? The stores aren't open yet. Are they?"

Marcus raised an eyebrow at her inquiry. "Oh, baby girl, you don't know who you are dealing with. Special connections can get you just about anything you want, my dear. I wanted to make sure you had all that you need for your stay in here."

"All this stuff—it's not hot, is it?"

He frowned at her and then gave a short laugh as he resumed emptying the bags. "No, these things I got for you are not hot, my dear. I bought them in a department store, not out of someone's trunk in a parking lot! Jeez, the girl only met me ten minutes ago, and already she's imagining the worst of me! Now that we have that all cleared up, I got you some fashionable nightgowns and some body scents, lotions, and other skin care products—you know, all that stuff women love. I didn't know what scents you liked, so I picked what I liked. I had a clerk assist me with that, and he seemed to know his job very well. So, I hope everything fits. If not, we can fix that too." He looked up when he heard her slight laugh. "What?"

"An image of you and the … ah … clerk just came to my mind; that's all." She could barely conceal her smile.

"Oh yeah, and it made you smile. How come?" When she hunched her shoulders but still looked as if she would burst with laughter at any time, he again asked, "What?" but with a more serious look. When her shoulders began to shake, his curiosity got the best of him. "Ok, Jillian, tell me what's got you so tickled."

"You probably wouldn't like it, so I'll keep it to myself." She was failing at trying to hold back her laughter.

"Ah! No, don't do that! Anything but that. I hate when someone says that! Come on! You have to tell me, Jill." He had a pleading quality to his voice.

Suddenly, her laughter died out, and she just looked at him. He was glad she could laugh without the pain she'd had yesterday. As their gazes locked there was a feeling of something in the room that was moving at a slower speed, and although it was hard to describe, both of them felt its force. Then, in the next second, it was gone.

When he'd said her name, the way it came out—kind of soft and smooth, like a caress—she loved the way it sounded. She did not know what it was, but it felt different. The sound just seemed to wrap around her like an embrace, and the feeling stunned her in that moment. When she looked up and found him staring at her, she had to say something to fill the quiet. She decided to explain. "Ok, when you were pulling stuff out of those bags, I could easily see you with a store clerk who was assisting you in the women's department, a scarf tied around his neck—or was it your neck?" Jill smiled before continuing. "And you were snapping your fingers." She tried to hold back her laughter, but it exploded at the expression on his face and then she started to groan in pain.

"See what happens when you start being a bad girl?" Marcus said. "'God don't like ugly'—that's what my mother used to tell my brother and me when we were bad." He winked to let her know he wasn't serious. "Speaking of mothers, you said yesterday that if your mother knew what you had done, she would have ordered you back home. Would you like me to call her and let her know that you are doing better? We haven't contacted any of your relatives, but that's no problem; just give me the information, and I'll make the call, or I can have them—"

"No! Marcus, there is no one to contact.," Jill said without looking at him.

He noticed that her smile was completely gone. "Why not? Surely, they will be concerned when they don't hear from you."

"It's not that way for me."

The room became quiet. Jill's fingers absently twisted the bed covers. He wanted so badly to know what she was hiding, but he knew he needed to back off.

He quietly changed the subject. "You said that you were job hunting. Have you had any leads?"

Jill hesitated. She just wanted the questions to stop, but she knew that if she were in his position, she would be just as curious. She took a deep breath. "No, not really. Before I arrived in town, I sent my résumé to a company called Rogers, Huffman, and Berg, an advertising agency here in town. I received a notice from Mr. Rogers that he was interested in bringing me in for an interview. I talked with him about a week ago, and he knew that I was making plans to move here. He seemed to like my résumé. He told me that interviews would start soon and that I was sure to be one of the applicants he called." When Marcus looked surprised, she said, "What?"

"That's pretty adventurous to make such a big move before knowing if you had the job," he said gently. "You said the other day that you were from …?" He looked at her in search of an answer, noting her hesitation before she spoke.

"Claremont."

"You drove all the way from Claremont, not knowing if this was a dead end? Your man must be going crazy with you making such a big move." He asked because he wanted to know the answer.

She was not comfortable revealing the personal chaos in her life, so she tried to make light of his question. "I always wanted to see what Philadelphia was like, and with my love for the arts, what better place? A lot of great musicians have come from this city. Besides, a reliable source told me that this place is filled with opportunity." She had kept her eyes averted from his but stole a quick glance.

"And the other part to my question?" Marcus asked quietly, still looking at her.

"What other part?" she asked, trying to avoid answering.

"Isn't your husband or boyfriend worried about your being so far away?"

"There is neither in my life," she said, focusing her eyes on a spot on the wall behind him.

"I find that hard to believe—or do you just not want to tell me?"

"Jeez! You are like a dog with a bone." A few minutes passed without either of them saying anything; then Jill said, "Sorry, that was rude of me. I don't have a man in my life."

He didn't respond immediately; he only watched her. Then he replied, "Why do I get the feeling that there's more to your story?"

She visibly took a deep breath. Jill felt she had to say something more about her situation, but her next words were more than she had intended to reveal. "Well, truthfully, I have hit some rough patches that hurt like hell, so I'm seeking some time to heal. That's as far as I'm going with the truth, Mr. Jordan." She still found it hard to look him in the eye.

Marcus kept staring at her, and he could feel her anxiety. *Whatever she's running from must have hurt her intensely*, he thought. "Ok, I won't dig for anything that you don't want to tell me. I understand the opportunity part, but what if the interview didn't happen? What then?" When she didn't answer, he asked, "I know it is none of my business, but I'm sure you have a backup plan."

Jill didn't have an answer to his sensible inquiry, and she suddenly realized that she had traveled thousands of miles on a whim—and sheer stupidity. She felt tears gathering at the back of her eyes and tried desperately to stop the flow before the dam broke. She tried to focus on anything in the room but Marcus. She could not help it when her one good eye made contact with his. The gentleness she saw there made her long for the security of his arms. It was crazy, but more than anything, she wanted to feel his arms wrapped securely around her—but that was a ridiculous thought. The feeling of loneliness was back, making her want to give in to a good, hard cry, but this was not the time. Something about him had her wanting to open up and confide in him.

"Sorry, I don't mean to be rude, but when I left home, I was not on good terms with my family. I am a victim of my own stupidity. You've made me realize that now. I have to make the best of things. I do *not* want my family contacted. I appreciate all you've done for me, but you have done enough, Mr. Jordan. I certainly won't take up any more of your time." She glanced at him, then looked away.

Marcus tried to lighten things up. "It's Marcus. The *Mr. Jordan* part belongs to my father, Ok?"

"Ok. I really appreciate Mrs. Spellings paying for my hospital stay, but I cannot keep taking handouts."

Marcus heard the anxiety and frustration in her voice and decided to let the subject drop for now. He pulled a tissue from the box and waved it in the air.

Jill held back for a few minutes before a smile appeared. "What are you doing?" she asked with a slight frown.

"Surrendering," he said as he waved a tissue from the box.

"Why?" she asked as her smile broadened.

"Not going to frustrate you anymore. You can take control of how you want things to go."

He loved her smile; it caused amazing reactions within him. If he could always make her smile like that, then—quickly a red flag came up. He had to shut his mind down because his thoughts were going in a totally different direction. He surfaced in time to hear her response.

"Thanks, I appreciate that, but I do appreciate all that you have done. It's just hard for me to accept help from other people."

A few seconds passed in silence. Then she shook her head as she smiled at him. "Ya know, you are quite the negotiator, Mr. Jordan."

"Thank you, Mrs. Weston, but why do you say that?"

"It's actually *miss*, remember?"

"I stand corrected, Miss Weston." He felt relieved just knowing that, but he had no clue why he felt that way.

The nurse came in then, so he never got the answer to his question.

"Sorry to interrupt. This young lady has a date with an MRI," she said. An orderly with a wheelchair followed behind her.

Marcus stood up. "I had better get out of the way. Jillian, call me if you need anything, Ok?"

"I will. Thanks, Marcus," she said quietly.

The nurse frowned when she looked over at Marcus, and he noticed the look the nurse gave him before he left the room. He raised his eyebrows; he had no clue about the sudden change in Jill's demeanor. It was like she became so sad. *Maybe she's nervous about the testing she's about to have*, he thought. It baffled him.

When he stepped into the elevator, he fought the feeling to turn around and go back. He wanted to be with her, but he was unsure if she wanted him there. She seemed all alone, and that did not sit well with him. *work will help to settle my mind*, he thought.

After being at work for two hours, his mind was still on Jill.

Joseph Freeman, Marcus's assistant, entered Marcus's office. "Hey, man. You sure you're alright? Every time I come in here, you're daydreaming. Maybe you need to go home and catch a nap or something." He grinned. "Maybe your job as a superhero is finally catching up to you."

Marcus looked at Joseph and replied, "Joseph, you need to take your show on the road. You are way too funny, man. But I think I will go home and get some rest. I can't seem to get myself in the routine today. Guess I am still tired."

"Ok, tell ya what. Everything is going kinda slow today, so why not go home get some rest?"

"I guess you're right. I think I'll follow that suggestion and get some sleep. If you need anything, you know where to find me."

"Ok, man, see you in the morning!" Joseph said before walking back to his own office.

Marcus found that he had left at a good time—there was no traffic. He figured by now everyone had made it to their destinations, and he was soon on the outskirts of town without the hindrance of heavy traffic. He saw the abundance of trees and knew the city was behind him. The drive home always was relaxing for him. He enjoyed the freshness of the air, which helped to clear his mind. To his surprise, he saw a fawn grazing near the edge of the road. He slowed his car because he knew how unpredictable deer were—they tended to take off running in any direction. The scene was calming; that's why he chose this area to live.

A few other small animals scurried away as he passed by, almost out of the wooded area. His subdivision was just a half mile away.

A minute later, he approached the gated community and greeted the guards. He drove around the huge man-made lake and then took the final turn into his driveway and parked in his garage. He grabbed his briefcase and headed inside.

His attempt to sleep had him tossing and turning, and after a short time, he gave up. He didn't know why he couldn't seem to settle down. He made himself some coffee, and about thirty minutes later, he got a call from Eddie, his mechanic, who was checking out Jillian's car.

"Hey, Marcus, this car you told me to check out really wants to commit suicide. It needs just about everything. The immediate need is the wheel bearings and brakes, and there is an electrical problem going on."

"Ok, Eddie fix whatever problems you find and put it on my tab."

"Sure, if that's what you want."

"It's exactly what I want. Thanks, Eddie."

"No problem. It'll take me a while, but I'll ring you when I'm done."

"Ok, that will work." Marcus replied.

"Catch ya later," Eddie said before ending the call.

After Marcus hung up, he grabbed his keys, hoping that Jill was through with her test because she was about to get some company.

When he walked into her room, she appeared to be sleeping, but she must have heard him come in because her eyes opened.

"Marcus?" She said sounding unsure.

He slowly turned around with a huge smile. "Hey, I didn't want to disturb you. Just checking to see how everything went after I left."

"I don't have anything to report. The doc hasn't made an appearance yet. You didn't have to make the trip all the way back here just for the doc's report. I could have called you."

"Would you have called me, Jillian?"

She suddenly became interested in straightening the covers.

He placed his hand over hers and asked again. "Would you have called me?"

She looked up at him with eyes that were completely innocent, then shrugged her shoulders. "No, probably not." Not wanting to hurt his feelings, she quickly inserted, "You see, Marcus, I am not your responsibility. I got myself into this mess, and I don't need to burden you with my problems. Understand?"

He turned away, running his hands through his hair as he walked to the window. He stared out for a few minutes, remaining silent.

Jill, fearing she had hurt his feelings, tried to get his attention. "Marcus? I hope I haven't hurt your feelings." He turned around to look at her, but she still couldn't gauge how he felt.

"And if I say that you have, what then?" He did feel some type of way, only he didn't know why. He only knew that he felt more alive when he was around her. She'd already had an effect on him, but he had no clue how that happened.

"I would say, I'm sorry, and it was not intended to hurt you," she said.

"And if that's not enough?" he asked.

"Then I'd say, what can I possibly do to make it up to you?" She had no idea what else to say.

"Tell you what, Jill. How about if we barter?"

"Barter?" she asked, as if she was not clear about what he meant.

"Yeah, like an exchange of goods for services"

She struggled to sit up in the bed. "*Excuse me*? I am sorry, Marcus, but I do not service men! Just because you're rich and … and … very good-looking does not mean that I am easy—at least not *that* easy! I am not that kind of girl. If that's what you think this is, then I suggest you leave right now. I can make it on my own." She flopped back down against her pillow, closing her eyes and muttering to herself.

"Unbelievable!" Marcus snorted.

Jill opened her eyes when she heard him laughing—laughter that seemed to envelope him. She watched him for a few seconds and then said, "What's so funny, Marcus Jordan?"

It took a few moments before he could sober up, but then he looked over at her, shaking his head. "You are, sweetheart," he said with a grin. "Where did you get the idea that I wanted sex from you?"

She looked back at him, and in an instant, she knew she had arrived at the wrong conclusion. *I wish this bed would just swallow me up*, she thought. *Trading favors for sex is not what he meant.* Since the fiasco with Phillip, she seemed to assume that all men wanted a quick romp in bed—something in which she lacked experience. She felt so embarrassed to have assumed that of Marcus. *Who am I kidding?* she thought. The fact that she couldn't hold on to a man back in Claremont was a sharp reminder of how unattractive she was as a woman.

She sighed heavily. "On top of the fact that I am the one-eyed monster, I have the gall to think that you are coming on to me. I am such an idiot. Of course you weren't propositioning me. I want to apologize for what I said and was thinking."

His expression became softer. "It's ok," he said, offering a slight smile. "No apology needed, especially given the things you have been up against. All I meant to say is that since you hate *owing* people, bartering seems a fair way to cover any expenses, if you really feel you need to pay me back. I welcome good cooking any time. You tell me what skills you have, if that makes you feel better, and we can go from there."

"I've been told that I'm a good cook. I can type and take shorthand. I have taught music and dance. My sewing ability is very good. I think that's about the extent of my bartering abilities."

"We definitely have something to work with, especially the cooking. Now, will you allow me to get you set up here? You know, just until you are back on your feet again?" When Jill looked as if she might refuse, he said. "Don't tell me you are still doubtful, when I was getting my taste buds revved up for that good cooking that you mentioned. Give a brother a break."

The expression of frustration on his face finally won her over. "Ok! Ok! I'll accept any help you can give me for the time being—on one condition."

A weary look crossed his face as he answered. "What might that condition be?"

"I need you to be totally honest with me. Are you attached or living with someone?" It was hard for her to look directly at him, but she wanted to gauge his reaction.

He immediately responded. "What does that have to do with anything? But no. I am not married or living with someone, but I've been seeing someone for the past year or so. I am not in a committed relationship, meaning I have not made promises to anyone."

"Look, Marcus, you have been exceptionally kind to me. I don't want to cause any trouble. I would rather just recuperate in some place on my own. I hope you understand."

"I will find you a place to recuperate," Marcus said, "but the doctor doesn't want you to try being on your own just yet. We will figure something out." He made notes on his smartphone.

"It's agreed, then." He asked as she nodded her head.

Marcus's face broke out in a big smile. His expression showed his approval and satisfaction. "Outstanding! Now, I need information, and then we will decide on your place of recovery until you're able to take charge of things again. See? That wasn't so hard."

Marcus punched in some numbers on his phone to get things rolling for her after her discharge from the hospital. He had no idea why he was jumping in with both feet to provide for this woman, who was a stranger to him. She seemed to bring out his charitable side, even though she initially did not welcome offers of help. She reacted as if kindness was a rare thing for her, and this did not sit well with him.

Once he had informed a person on his staff, someone named Sidney, about a place for Jill, he ended the call.

"What about my end of the deal?" Jill asked. "Are you sure that cooking will repay you for all that you are planning to do for me?"

Marcus stopped making notes on his phone and looked over at her with a slight smile. "I think we could barter a deal with your cooking skills, and the music lessons would go great with the kids at the community center, which a friend of mine manages. I help out there sometimes." He returned his attention to his phone.

"You know, Mr. Jordan—I mean, Marcus—you are quite amazing. A black belt by night and quite the organizer by day—what more could a girl ask for?"

Marcus again stopped making entries to look at her, as he thought he'd detected a note of sarcasm in her voice. He smiled, then winked at her. "I don't know about that, Jill. I'm not anyone's knight, but I was thinking about that one-eyed–monster thing. Maybe a brother could get used to that."

She stuck her tongue out at him, and he shook with laughter.

"I'm sure you'd do the same thing for me, if I was in your place," he said, winking at her, before getting back to his task of making notes.

Marcus and Jill made plans for her new start in Philadelphia, and they got to know one another in the process.

Over the next few days, Jill was put through a battery of tests, which indicated that her injuries were less extensive than was originally thought. She had some broken ribs and an eye contusion, which would take a little more time to heal. The doctor removed the large bandage that was wrapped around her head and replaced it with an eye patch. She was given medicated eye drops and a referral to an eye specialist. The doctor also advised her that the cuts and bruising to her head were healing nicely, but since she had a concussion, she would have to be cautious about moving around. She was released at the end of the week and was given a referral to a doctor's office for a follow-up.

On the morning that Jill was discharged from the hospital, she was waiting for Marcus's administrative assistant to come into her room. Instead, Marcus walked through the door, clad in a nice pair of jeans and a casual burgundy shirt, the top two buttons of which were undone, giving her a glimpse of his sexy chest. His scent made her brain freeze, and she tried to recover quickly before he noticed. The man oozed sex appeal, no matter what he wore. He was simply a fantastic male form.

When he had to repeat his question a second time, Jill realized that it was obvious that she was mesmerized by him, but she played it off. "What a surprise! What happened to your assistant?" Jill said, trying to hide the happiness in her voice. *Don't want to give him the wrong impression*, she thought.

"I felt bad about handing you over to someone else on your first day home," he said. "I would have wondered all day if you were satisfied with everything that was put together."

"Marcus, I am sure anything will be fine," she said with a smile.

He studied her for a moment before turning to the two bags that were packed. "Ready?"

"Yes, I just have to stop by Patient Accounting to get my bill and make arrangements. You know, let them know where to send the bill once I have an address." She knew she'd overdone it with the explaining.

"There is no need for you to go to accounting. Your account is taken care of, remember? So, now, baby girl, you are in good hands. Just relax and enjoy recuperating."

She seemed to take a nervous swallow, followed by a brief speechlessness; then she said quietly, "It's so hard to get used to everyone being so nice to me when I'm a stranger to them."

"Well, get used to it because in this town, there are a lot of good people. Your bill is being forwarded to a victim's fund, which will take care of any medical fees because of what that goon did to you."

"Really?" She looked up at Marcus.

"Yes, really. The mayor put it all in motion. Just relax. No worries."

"Will I have to go to court?" she said in a quiet voice, not looking at him.

"There's a possibility that you may have to testify, but we will cross that bridge when we get there. First, let's concentrate on your recovery," he said in a reassuring tone.

"*We*? Marcus, I can't take advantage of your generosity anymore. You have been amazing."

He exhaled slowly before he spoke. "Jillian, let me decide if you are taking advantage of me. Just so you know, I am enjoying this knight thing that everyone wants to label me with, so relax and enjoy me in my new role—although I call it 'hospitality, Philly-style,' baby girl." He winked at her and reached for her bags.

"I'm Jill to all my friends. I would like it very much if you'd consider yourself one."

He gave her a smile. "Jill, I am honored—"

He was interrupted as the door opened, and the nurse walked in with a wheelchair.

They took the elevator to the first floor and headed through the front doors. Marcus's SUV was waiting at the hospital entrance. The nurse held on to Jill as she slowly stood. Marcus opened the passenger door, then quickly swooped up Jill, catching her by surprise and causing her to clutch him. He gently sat her inside the huge vehicle.

Everything this man does is grand, she thought. She waved to the nurse, who winked at her. *When that nurse gets back to the floor, Marcus will become the man of every girl's dream.*

Marcus reached over and grabbed the seat belt to buckle her in. This put him once again in close proximity to her. Jill inhaled his scent, and when their eyes met, she gave a timid smile. He winked before stepping back to close the door. He walked round to his side, put on his seat belt, and started the powerful engine.

She glanced at Marcus, whose attention was on the traffic. *He's aware of the attention he draws*, she realized, *but seems to overlook it as something women naturally do.* "You do realize that you will be all the rave on the fourth floor when the nurse gets back upstairs," Jill said with a smile.

"All I did was assist you into your seat in a truck that's too high for you to be jumping into. I should have driven the car. What was I thinking?"

Jill looked around the big, luxurious truck, thinking about how some people lived. Her car was a joke compared to this monster of luxury. "Whatever you say, Marcus, but the grapevine will be in full force. Just wanted you to be aware, my dear."

"Yes, Grandma, I pay that stuff no attention." He glanced over at her and then turned his attention back to the traffic.

They soon pulled up in front of the apartments where Jill would be staying. He helped her down once again, and she held onto his arm as they walked to the building.

The apartment building looked very nice. She wanted to know the cost but felt too embarrassed to ask. *This is only temporary*, she told herself. *Why not enjoy a little luxury, if only for now?* She would find out all that she owed him once she got gainfully employed.

It was a one-bedroom with balconies leading off the living room and the bedroom. The living room had a fireplace, which made the room so cozy, and the ceiling had skylights. *It would be perfect for a romantic evening*, Jill thought—but she quickly shut off her mind to those thoughts. She could easily imagine living a happy life here, but dreams like that were not for her; they were fairy tales. She didn't have her strength back yet, so she tried her best to not be overly exuberant, as that feeling would take a plunge when he left.

Moments after entering the apartment, she heard Marcus swearing.

"What's wrong?" Jill asked.

"What the hell? There is no electricity in this place." He walked through to the kitchen and swore again. "I'll be damned! No water, either. You cannot stay here like this." He pulled out his cell phone, called a number, and then spoke into the phone. "Mrs. T? Is Gracie there? Can I speak to her, please?" He drummed his fingers on the wall as he waited for Gracie. Then, he said in an angry tone, "Gracie, I am standing in the apartment. Can you tell me why no one bothered to let me know that the place is not ready? There is no electricity and no water. This is unacceptable. The place has not been aired out. It looks unfit! ... He *what*? No! That sorry son of a—no, I will call him. No, Gracie, I'm telling you there are no lights and no water, and it doesn't look as if the maid has been here either. I thought you had checked it out. ... So, he told you the place would be ready by yesterday? We should have checked it out and not taken his word for it. It is your job to make sure that when we hire people, they do the job we pay them for. We should have made sure because, apparently, we cannot count on him. I'm going to call him right now."

Marcus ended the call, muttering to himself as he punched in another number. "Floyd Davies, please. Tell him Marcus Jordan needs to speak to him." Marcus resumed drumming his fingers as he waited. "Floyd, I am standing in my apartment. What happened here with the electricity and water? More importantly, why didn't you tell me or my staff that it would not be ready today?"

Marcus paused as he listened to Floyd's response, though he was clearly still fuming. "*What?* This is unacceptable. I left instructions with my office manager, and if you could not get this place up to standards, it was your responsibility to call her or me." Marcus listened again and then replied, "You told my manager that you would handle everything and would call me if it could not be ready. Floyd, I got no phone call. I do not pay you, as the caretaker, to leave work undone. If there was a problem, you should have called me."

Marcus released a breath, as he listened to the caretaker. Trying to speak calmly, he said, "Tell you what, Floyd. I do not have time to labor over what should have been or your problems. I will talk with you at the office. Be there at eleven tomorrow morning. I will see you then." Marcus ended the call with a loud swear word. He leaned on the counter, running his hands over his face and through his hair. A few minutes later, he suddenly seemed to realize that Jill was standing there.

"Jill, I'm sorry. My supposed caretaker really messed up. The apartment, as you can see, is not ready, so we will have to switch to an alternate plan."

"It's Ok, Marcus. I can find a hotel. It's not your problem. Can you drop me off at a hotel? I think we passed a few on our way here."

He continued leaning on the counter, just staring at her for a few minutes, which made her feel uncomfortable. "You've got to be kidding, right?"

She had turned away from his staring eyes, but his comment made her turn around to face him. "Kidding? No, I am not. You've done more than enough already." She tried to be strong because she had no idea where the nearest hotel was or even if she could carry anything, much less herself. Because of the caretaker debacle, she realized that Marcus was not in the best mood.

"Thinking you can manage on your own. The doctor does not want you to lift anything that weighs more than a toothbrush for at least a week. Besides, you are about done in right now, so stop trying to hide it. I am taking you home with me."

She shook her head. "What? Now *you* are kidding, right?"

"Nope, I smile when I am joking around, and right now, after this craziness with Floyd, I feel like I could smash something. But you wanna know something? Hearing, 'Yes, Marcus, I will come and recuperate at your place for now,' would be such a nice way of soothing my ruffled feathers." He had spoken in a high-pitched voice, imitating the response he would like to hear from her as he looked at her expectantly. Although he tried to look threatening, it only made Jill smile at his facial expression and the way he'd sounded. He was totally amazed by the appearance of dimples with her smile for the first time. "What? You are not scared of me, woman?" he asked, frowning with one eyebrow raised.

"Actually, no, and I am so sorry, but I don't even feel a twinge of fear, Marcus Jordan," she said, still trying to hold back a smile.

He winked at her as a smile began to appear on his face.

"All jokes aside, Marcus, I don't think it's wise to bring another woman to stay with you when you have a girlfriend. I think you should take my advice on this. Most girls would be livid if their boyfriends did such a thing. Since I am starting to have such deep affection and devotion for you, I cannot impose on you like that. It could have major consequences."

He smiled broadly. "Deep devotion, huh? And here I was thinking a dog is man's best friend."

Jill's mouth fell open at his remark.

He burst out laughing at her reaction to his comment. "What? I'm just saying."

"You know what I mean, Marcus."

"Let me worry about those consequences. It's like you said—you are devoted to me, and that's how friends should be. What kind of friend would I be to leave you like this? So, yes, you will come to my place to recuperate, no ifs, ands, or buts about it, baby girl. Besides, I have more bedrooms than I can sleep in, so I insist." He looked at her, trying to hold a stern look.

"I guess I will take pity on you since you're having such a hard time with your employees. I won't cause you any more problems. I'll comply but only for a short time. Don't get used to my giving in. Understand, old buddy?" She raised an eyebrow, trying to appear braver than she felt.

He smiled at her. "You are so much fun, but I understand, and I appreciate your giving in, Ms. Weston. Now, let's get you settled in. You've been up on your feet far too long." He stood with his hands on his hips as he watched her.

"I'm fine, Marcus. You're worse than a mother hen." Jill got up from the barstool.

"Well, let's head to the henhouse, so I can take better care of my baby chick. I'll carry you if you feel the walk is too much for you."

"No, I can make it under my own steam. Jeez, man! I hope your girlfriend won't mind."

"It's none of her business. Besides, I've made no promises to her, nor she to me."

"So, you have an open relationship?"

He chuckled, and the sound was so pleasant to Jill's ears. "Sheree would have a fit if I mentioned having an open relationship with her. Although we are not in the committed stage, I sense that she would like it to be; For me, it's not there."

"Oh, I see. I certainly hope she knows this. There is nothing worse than two people who are not on the same page."

"Yes, I agree. The situation with her is complicated right now. But my relationship with you is none of her business."

"I see," Jill said, sounding doubtful. "Well, she has nothing to worry about from me. I am not a threat to her whatsoever."

Jill walked slowly out ahead of him. Marcus stood there for a moment, thinking about what Jill had just said. A smile suddenly appeared on his face as he walked out behind her and locked the door.

They had only driven about twenty minutes when Marcus entered a gate after being waved through by security. They drove past beautifully maintained lawns and what Jill assumed was a man-made lake, which was lined with garden benches here and there. A beautiful array of flowers highlighted the flawless landscaping, giving the place a comfortable and serene setting. The only word that came to mind for Jill was *nice*.

Soon, they pulled into his garage and from there entered his condo. Jill walked ahead of Marcus into the house. There was an entryway that went either left or right. The left side of it led to a living room with huge floor-to-ceiling windows that overlooked the man-made lake. The view of the lake was simply breathtaking, and Jill admired the view.

The right side of the entryway a few feet away were steps that led to the upper level, into the kitchen and other rooms. Jill took the stairs at a slow pace, but after only a few steps, she had to take a moment to rest, which caused Marcus to once again swoop her up into his arms. He took her to the top of the stairs and placed her in a chair in the kitchen.

She said a quiet thank-you, as she felt totally exhausted. She looked around as he pointed out features in the kitchen.

"This is incredible," she said, looking at the totally equipped kitchen. The high-tech refrigerator had her smiling as Marcus demonstrated its internet capability, along with a few other things, like the glass door.

Jill was totally amazed. "Your kitchen is a chef's dream," she told him.

"Thanks, but the windows downstairs that overlook the lake sold me on the place. The lake lights up at night, and when there's a full moon, it's quite amazing! I'll take you to your room now so that you can rest. We can continue the tour later, if you're up to it." He looked at her as if he'd thought better of the tour idea.

"Who wouldn't feel reenergized with a place like this," she said with a smile. "Let's finish it now. Lead the way!"

Marcus could see she was faking it, but he did not push the idea of rest. He showed her the game room, complete with a pool table, bar, full-size refrigerator, and flat-screen TV. There also were plenty of video games and a shelf that held the various game systems.

"My brother plays with the kids on these systems when we bring them over from the community center. He thinks he is a gamer, until the kids beat him," Marcus said.

"From the smile on your face, you two must have an amazing relationship."

"Yeah, we do. How about you? Any brothers or sisters?" He watched her demeanor turn from soft and warm to closed and nervous.

She looked away from him, as if she suddenly had an interest in the games on the shelves. "Two sisters, but we are not close. I think I'll go lie down now if the tour is finished," she said, looking over her shoulder.

"Yeah, the tour is done. There is only the Jacuzzi room, which is on the first floor before you walk out on the terrace. Your bedroom door is a few steps down this hallway—the second door to the right. You have your own bathroom. Jill, feel free to move about as you like, but if you feel dizzy or light-headed, let me know. While you're resting, I'll be in my office just down the hall, catching up on some work. We can have lunch when you wake up, if that's sounds good to you."

"Yes, that's fine. And thank you again, Marcus. I'm off to take a nap." She headed down the hallway.

"Sure! No problem at all. Oh! I almost forgot about your bags in the Escalade. Go lie down, and I'll get your things."

He went back out to the truck, and when he returned, he knocked on her door before entering. He put the suitcase down, then stood watching her as she sat on the side of the bed, looking totally wiped out.

"I think the nap idea is a good thing," Marcus said. "Let me help you with your shoes, and let's put your legs up." Before she could stop him, he was kneeling down, taking her shoes off, and lifting her more securely on the bed. "Now how is that?"

"That's good," she said, her eyes almost closed.

He knew she was exhausted because usually she would have fussed about him doing too much. "Remember I'll be in my office," Marcus said. "When you wake up, Esther will probably be here with our meal." When she nodded her head in answer, he noticed she was having a hard time keeping her eyes open. "Sweet dreams, Jill," he said as he placed a blanket over her. Then he walked out, closing the door.

Jill felt herself drifting as sleep overcame her.

Marcus spent the rest of the morning making phone calls and catching up on work. Every now and then, his mind would drift to the woman sleeping just down the hall. He wondered what had happened to make her pack up all her things and drive away from her home. She took a chance, with no job and—from what his mechanic had told him—with a car that was on its last legs. *How could her family just let her go like that? Maybe she was the problem, and maybe that was why she dodged talking about her family—because she was a troublemaker.* The more Marcus thought about it, something inside told him that Jill seemed more like someone who had a hard life and that things had not come easy.

Jill had been sleeping for a couple of hours. He hated to wake her. Esther Wilson, who worked for him, cooking a few times a week, was bringing over a home-cooked meal for them, and he was starving. At the chiming of the doorbell, he got up from his desk and went to the front door. As he got there, he heard Esther's key opening the door. Marcus relieved her of the bags she was carrying and led the way to the kitchen; she followed him.

"Esther, I am so happy you could do this for me. There is nothing like your home cooking to heal the sick. Hmm! This food smells great! I certainly hope Jill wakes up soon. I am starving!" Marcus opened the bags, and the aroma filled his nostrils.

"I hopes she likes what I have prepared," Esther said, smiling at Marcus's appreciation of the food.

"I'm sure I'll love it," Jill said.

Both Esther and Marcus turned their heads to see Jill standing at the entrance to the kitchen. They both smiled at her, and Marcus hurriedly pulled out a chair as he made the introductions.

"It's nice to meet you, ma'am," Jill said. "I'm sure I'll enjoy every mouthful, judging by the aroma that is coming out of this kitchen."

"Oh, honey, I love to feed appetites. Marcus, she has won my heart already, and Jill, the name is Esther. I heard about what happened to you and the mother of those children. You were very brave and such a hero; those babies are safe." As the older woman sang Jill's praises, her smile was full of warmth.

Marcus leaned against the counter, silently watching the two women as they chatted.

"Mrs.—ah, Esther—that's a very kind thing for you to say, but I did nothing. It was Marcus who saved the day and those kids."

"Oh no! No! You were very much a part of it. Most people would not have gotten involved, but you did not think about your own safety. God will bless you, child, for your unselfish act. Now, I have said enough. I'll get this table set so you two can eat. Marcus is hungry. I can tell his gills have gone all blue." She gave a hearty laugh and then busied herself with setting up everything.

Jill could tell from the way that Esther looked at Marcus that she adored him; and he seemed to feel the same way about the elderly lady. They teased each other, and every now and then, Esther would give a shout of laughter.

"Ah, Esther, you have done so much already. Can I help?" Jill offered.

"Nonsense. You are recuperating and should be waited on, hand and foot," Esther said.

Jill looked over at Marcus, who only smiled. "I know you are enjoying this, aren't you?" she whispered.

"Every second."

After Esther had seen to their every need, she wished them a good night with a promise to check in on Jill the next day.

"Wow, she really is a great cook," Jill said. "I really would have felt better if I could have helped her, though."

"As if she would let you. The one thing I have learned about Esther is that she loves to wait on people. I think since her kids have grown up and now live so far away, she seldom gets to spoil anyone. It's just her and Wilson now. I let her have her way with my kitchen, but I will not have her cleaningup after me. I wash the dishes, and Wilson comes in once or twice a week to do some light housekeeping," Marcus explained.

"Really?"

"Yes, and that's all I need. Had a bad experience once with the maid thing."

"Oh yeah?"

"Yeah, I'll have to tell you about it sometime."

"So, is he like your butler?" Jill asked.

"Kinda, maybe. He actually works for me only a few days a week, and the rest of the time he does security at the gate here. My mother introduced Esther to me, and I also met Wilson at the same time. He was looking to pick up a few more hours a week so I hired him for around here. They are such a good fit for me. It has worked out very well."

Their dinner conversation flowed between them very smoothly. He told her about the town and some things that might interest her. He would not allow her to help him with the dishes. "Just keep me company with conversation," he said.

When the doorbell rang, Marcus found Louis Brooks, the company's attorney and his friend, on the doorstep. After the introductions, the two men excused themselves and went to Marcus's office.

Jill decided to look for something to read. She found a book called *The Myth of Winnie Abigail* and from the synopsis, she found it interesting. She decided to take it to her room and read a little before going to bed. She didn't want to interrupt Marcus's meeting with his attorney, so she left him a note on the table.

By the time Louis left, it was almost eleven o'clock. Marcus locked up and checked in on Jill, finding her fast asleep. After closing her door, he took a shower before going to bed himself.

The next morning, Jill woke up still feeling the pain in her ribs, as well as a headache with movement, so she gingerly got up and headed for the bathroom. Afterward, she tried on another comfortable outfit that Marcus had bought for her—light-green lounging pants and matching top. It was very pretty, and the fabric felt so soft. By the time she had finished dressing, she was starving so she headed slowly toward the kitchen. She stopped short when she saw Marcus sitting at the table with a cup of coffee, reading the newspaper. He looked up when he heard her and found Jill standing there, totally surprised.

"Hey! Come join me. Esther left you a special breakfast."

"She was here already? She didn't have to do that, but it's a very nice thing to do," Jill said with a smile. She was glad she didn't have to fix something to eat because her head was going crazy this morning.

"I guess you made it into her fan club. She left it in the warming dish."

Jill tried to cover her nervousness. "I see. Um, oh, I thought I was alone here. I thought you had gone to work, so I was a little surprised to see you."

"I didn't want to leave for work while you were still sleeping. I was just catching up on the news, the stock market," he said, watching her.

"I don't want to interrupt your schedule," she said, trying to think of something else to say. "So, what's happening in the news?"

"Well, the stock market is holding its own for now. It looks like you made the front page of the Philly *Observer*, along with yours truly. The mayor took time out from his busy schedule to tell our fair city how everyday citizens can help to keep our streets safe. It seems he is also planning a small parade and celebration, along with other political stuff. He is inviting both you and me to attend—he wants to present us with the key to the city. My office has already taken a slew of phone calls from the media, wanting to interview us."

He noticed that Jill was leaning against the counter, as if she needed support. She looked like she did not feel well. He could see the weariness in her eyes, and she seemed to wince, when she moved. He got up from the table, concerned. "Are you in pain?" he asked.

She waved off his inquiry with her hand. "Oh, I'll be ok."

Marcus opened a cabinet door and took out a pill bottle.

Jill tried to distract him from her pain issue. "Never thought I'd make the news. The city must be really dull if the media is seeking me out," she said, but the pain was so bad in her temples that she was having a hard time focusing. "Marcus, I agreed to stay here but not to complicate your life in any way. You really do not need to babysit me. I will be all right here. I don't want to delay you getting to work."

Marcus seemed to ignore her words. "Here, take these. The doc said 'as needed for pain.' If your pain is more frequent, you are to take them every four hours." He shook the pills into her hand and gave her a glass of water. "Jill, everything is fine. Stop thinking that you are going to upset the normal running of my life. I'd suggest you enjoy your food. Esther would be heartbroken if she thought I wasn't taking good care of you, per her instructions." He looked down at her.

She swallowed the pills. He then walked over to the table and held out a chair. Jill, not wanting to seem contrary, took her seat. She watched him remove the food from the warming dish. The aroma made Jill's stomach growl, but seeing Marcus took away her appetite for food. He wore a black-and-gray–striped silk shirt with gray pleated slacks. The clothes only emphasized his toned body. She closed her eyes—and closed her mind to the direction in which it was headed—and when she opened her eyes again, she found Marcus staring at her oddly. She reassured him that she was feeling fine enough to be left on her own.

He finally agreed to go to work but left numbers where he could be reached. He told her the fridge was fully stocked and then went in search of his briefcase. He was about to leave when she called out to him.

"I'll try not to bother you any more than necessary," she said.

He looked back at her. "You could never bother me. Besides, if you happened to not feel well and didn't call me, I would feel so guilty. Jill, call me no matter what." He smiled at her, and she smiled back as he went out the door.

"That man is so dreamy!" she said aloud. She finished eating and then took her dishes to the sink. Every day that week went much the same. Esther would drop off food for them to eat for breakfast and dinner. Jill had mentioned to Esther that she would like to contribute by at least cooking dinner. The older woman had only tutted as she closed the oven door. She turned to smile at Jill and said in a soothing voice, "Now, my dear, you are still healing. I would feel bad if I let you take on such a chore too soon. There will be plenty of time for that. Mark old Esther's words."

"I'll be leaving here in a few weeks, and I just want Marcus to know how much I appreciate everything he has done—and you, too." Jill smiled at Esther but noticed a gleam in the older woman's eye.

"Pardon me for saying so, Jillian, but I think Mr. Marcus would be a fool to let you go so easily."

As Esther turned away, Jill was sure she heard Esther mutter, "and he ain't no fool." When Esther turned back around, the gleam was still in her eyes, which made Jill wonder what was going on in the woman's mind.

Later that evening, Jill thought about how easily conversation flowed between her and Marcus. She listened to him talk about his day when he came home from work. It helped her to have something else to concentrate on besides her life. Marcus was also very funny, but Jill was curious about his not having a date or that his elusive girlfriend had not shown up to kick her out. So far, there were no signs of her. At least, Marcus didn't act as if he had somewhere to go.

Jill's injuries healed quickly, and the only indication of the altercation was the bruising that still had not completely faded. The doctor removed the bandage from her eye two weeks later, and to Jill's relief, her vision was almost normal. The headaches had gone away, and the doctor seemed to think her vision would continue to improve.

She had built up a comfort zone with Marcus. It felt very natural for him to come along with her to see the doctor. After her last visit to the eye surgeon, Marcus took her to lunch, which was a nice surprise for her. Afterward, he dropped her off at the condo before going back to work.

The following week, she had started doing some of the housework, like washing the clothes and cooking. Marcus disapproved, but she told him she felt so much better. Being able to chip in just a little bit made her feel like she was paying him back in some way, and he finally gave in.

By the end of June, they had fallen into a routine, and it seemed quite natural for her to have dinner ready by the time he got home.

On the morning of the Fourth of July, Jill woke up and just laid in bed, listening to the quiet of the house. She felt so alone, especially now, because Marcus had been out of town all week. Although he had called almost every day, she really missed his being around. *I need to get him out of my mind*, she thought. She knew he would be spending the holiday with his girlfriend.

"And he should be, Jillian," she admonished herself out loud. She thought of him way too much, and she knew she had to stop those thoughts. As she got up, she pushed thoughts of him to the back of her mind and decided to go to the workout room and get on the treadmill. She put on some old shorts and a tank top, then made her way to the room with all the equipment.

She was standing at the treadmill, making adjustments to the machine, when she heard the front door alert system announce that the door was opening. She went to the door of the workout room, thinking it might be Mr. Wilson or Esther. As she waited to greet them, she was totally shocked to see Marcus coming up the steps.

"Good morning, sunshine," he said with a tired smile, setting his suitcase down.

"Morning, Marcus! I didn't think you'd be back so soon," she said, frowning.

"Oh yeah? Why is that?" he asked, looking her over.

"Well, I thought you'd be spending the holiday with your girlfriend—a logical assumption." Jill said. Her words had seemed to trickle out because of the way he was looking at her. He was making her nervous, and the temperature in the room suddenly seemed to have gotten warmer.

"No, I visited Sheree on assignment in Miami. We had dinner, and then Sheree and her entourage went to a party. I was not in the party mood, so I came home." He looked around the room and not at Jill.

"Oh," Jill said. Her brain couldn't think of anything else as a response.

"My first stop was California, where I took a look at some real estate for a possible purchase, and then I visited an old buddy in Minnesota. I then had to fly to New York for a meeting at the new office. After the meeting in New York, I took a flight to Miami, my last stop before coming home. So now, I'm experiencing jet lag," he said as his attention focused back on her.

"You look really tired. Do you want me to cook you some breakfast?"

"I appreciate the offer, but all I want right now is my bed."

"Ok. I'm going to hop on the treadmill, but if you change your mind, just holler."

"Thanks, Jill. I just want to go to sleep. And be careful on that thing—you're still recovering, remember?" He looked back at her before he headed to his room, his bag in hand.

Is he tired from being out with Sheree or from traveling? she wondered. *Either way, it's none of my business.*

After her workout, she did a little light cleaning. She made a sandwich for lunch and sat down with her book to read for a while. Later, she watered Marcus's plants on the terrace, and that's where he found her around four that afternoon. She was standing on a stepladder, trying to reach the last plant that was hanging from the wrought-iron Strip above. He startled her, when he called her name and she lost her balance.

Marcus caught her to him and held onto her. It seemed as though they were stuck together as the heat radiated between their two bodies. He slowly let her body slide down his, which started a fire that affected both of them. When her feet were firmly on the floor, he stepped back and stood there, looking at her.

Jill tried to ignore the electricity that had surrounded them. She searched frantically for something to say to erase the awkwardness. "Thanks. I was totally in my own world, enjoying these beautiful plants. Your voice startled me. Sorry!" She looked up at him.

He was still at first, but then, as if he had been taken off pause, he exhaled loudly. "That was a close call. Girl, you need to be careful. Getting up on that stepladder is not safe. But I'm glad you're ok. You almost gave me a heart attack when I walked in here and saw you on that old thing. I should have thrown it away a long time ago. I'll show you where a better stepladder is, but I'd rather that you wait 'til I'm around to water the plants up there."

"But Marcus, I'm just watering plants. I don't need to bother you with something so trivial."

"It's not trivial if you take a fall! Jill, it's too soon, after all you've been through."

"I'm not glass," she insisted. "I can water the plants. That's so sim—" Her words came to an abrupt halt when she saw the look in his eyes. "Ok, I'll wait for you before doing the stepladder thing again. Happy now?" She folded her arms across her chest.

"Immensely!" he said with a smile, loving the way she pouted. "Now, I'm getting the grill out. How does a nice thick steak sound to you?"

"It sounds great, but who is going to cook it?" she asked teasingly but with a straight face.

"Me, of course! I'm giving you the night off. I will grill the steaks."

"You sure about that?" she said with an uncertain look.

"What? Why are you looking at me like that? Girl, your friend Marcus does a mean steak on the grill."

She started to laugh, and looking at his expression made her laugh even harder.

"You think I'm kidding?

"I swear I didn't think you could boil an egg," she said, still smiling.

"Oh! It's on now, Jillian! If you don't mind, would you get out the potato salad that Esther left? If you'd rather have one of those garden salads in the fridge, get it out too. I got the steaks. When you've finished eating my work of art, an apology would be nice because I can tell from your expression that you doubt my ability." He strutted off, winking at her, which only made her smile more.

"Jeez! The attitude!" she teased as he walked away.

A little later, they ate on the terrace, and Jill was amazed at how good the steaks were. The atmosphere was pleasant as they talked and watched the neighbors taking walks around the lake. Some threw Frisbees to their dogs; others were out being sociable. Marcus had brought out beer to have with the steaks. Jill tried a small amount, which proved to be refreshing because it was cold.

Marcus's friend Fonze had tried to get Marcus to come out to an event at the community center, but Marcus told him that he was still tired from hopping planes.

Jill was very happy that he stayed there with her. She would mark this day in her memories as unforgettable. Once the daylight began to fade, people gathered around the man-made lake to watch the fireworks from somewhere in town. Marcus and Jill easily saw the display from where they sat on the terrace. Jill noticed that some of the residents had stretched out on blankets to take in the beautiful explosions of color. Someone played music in the distance, and the evening held a nice ambiance.

A week later, Jill received a call from the advertising firm Rogers, Huffman, and Berg, where she had applied for a job before coming to town. She was scheduled for an interview at the end of the week, and when the call ended, she felt as if her heart would jump out of her chest. She had to go in for a typing test, but this was the closest she had come to getting the job since applying so long ago, and that made her smile. In her excitement, Jill reached for the phone to call Marcus, who picked up right away. When she told him she'd had a call for the interview, it was hard to contain her excitement. He expressed his happiness for her, and they talked a little more before she ended the call. Once she was off the phone, still bubbling with excitement, she went in search of something to wear to the interview.

Four months later, Jill hurried off the elevator, thinking that she had forgotten something in her mad rush to get to the office on time. She had just walked through the doors of the office when she heard Sarah Fischer, the receptionist, call out to her in greeting.

"Good morning. You need a hand with that?" Sarah saw that Jill had entered the office with both hands and arms loaded with files and a briefcase, and she gripped her bag lunch between her teeth. Jill mumbled and gestured with her eyes and head, and Sarah rushed to open the door to the secretarial pool. After Jill got through the door and had placed most of what she carried on her desk, she went back out to greet Sarah.

"Hey, Sarah. Thanks, girl. I feel like I have lockjaw from clenching that bag with my teeth."

The two women laughed as they shared their Monday ritual of telling who did what over the weekend. Sarah was married and spent all her spare time with her two beautiful girls and hubby of eight years. Jill wanted a family life with kids and a husband, like Sarah, whose face glowed when she talked about her family—although it often wore her down.

"*So*, what about you?" Sarah asked. "Did you share any interesting moments with tall, fine, and loaded this weekend?"

Jill shook her head. "No, but I did run into him when I went into the market on Saturday afternoon."

"So, was he with, ah, you know? Ah, the model girl—what's her name?" Sarah frowned, trying to think of the name.

Jill shook her head again. "You mean Sheree, and no, he was not with her."

Sarah's eyes got bigger as she touched Jill's arm. "What? Who was she? Did, um, did he introduce you?" When Jill nodded, Sarah waited for more information.

"Yes, Sarah. Girl, you should have seen me. Marcus introduced her. I believe her name is Antonia something-or-other. They were strolling down the street, coming from the Tea Room. They were casually dressed but designer casual, I'm sure. There I was, coming out the front door of the market with my arms full of catfish, wearing my old sweats that I use to clean the house and a baseball cap on my head. It was humiliating, to say the least."

They both giggled, but then Sarah groaned.

"Ugh! Don't you just hate it when you are at your worst, and you see people you don't want to see?"

Jill just waved her hand in the air and nodded. "Well, he's such a great guy. He didn't remark on my raggedy old clothes, and get this—he even offered to carry my smelly fish to the car for me. I quickly said, 'No thanks, but I appreciate the offer.' He seemed to be in no hurry and acted like he had plenty of time to talk. I told them I had to run, and I think *she* was very relieved by it, although she stood patiently by his side."

"Who wouldn't wait for that man?" Sarah asked. "He's simply gorgeous personified!"

Suddenly, they both turned their heads as someone entered the office, which they realized when they heard him clear his throat.

"Morning, ladies. I don't want to interrupt, but I thought it would be rude of me to stand here and eavesdrop as the two of you salivated over some poor guy." Marcus had a sparkle in his eyes, letting Jill know that he was in a playful mood. He did notice the shocked looks on their faces before Jill hid her expression. He also was aware that both women got quiet. Jill recovered first, as Sarah tried to hide her embarrassment.

"Hi, Marcus. No one was salivating here. Sarah's a happily married woman, and I, Marcus Jordan, do not salivate over any man!" Jill replied, but a slight smile crept onto her face.

Sarah's reaction to Jill's comment was to make a funny sound—to Jill's dismay. Jill quickly changed the subject and tried to hide that familiar feeling of warmth that she experienced whenever he came around. She tried hard to ignore the sensation, wondering if Marcus had heard all of her conversation with Sarah. He seemed to be studying her closely—or was it her overactive brain at work after being caught. Jill hoped he didn't know they'd been talking about him. She tried to distract him as Sarah tried to come up for air.

"So, what brings the top exec of Jordan Enterprises to our office so early in the morning?"

Marcus lifted the box in his hands, and Jill was able to see an assortment of pastries.

"Mmm! Those smell wonderful!" Jill exclaimed.

"Blanche, down at the pastry shop, prepared a tray for an early meeting we had in the office this morning. We had too much, and I know how you love the apple fritters that she makes, so I stopped by to bring you some. There are enough in there for Sarah also." He looked at Jill and asked, "So how are things working out for you? Everything Ok? Do you need anything?""

"I'm doing good, actually, but thanks," Jill answered.

"Good, good. I'm glad to hear that." He winked at Jill before turning toward Sarah on his way out and treating her to a thousand-watt smile.

Sarah blushed and was speechless. She continued to stare as Marcus took his leave. Jill looked at Sarah and could only shake her head. She understood the effect Marcus had on her friend.

Suddenly, Sarah came out of her coma. "Why didn't the earth just open up and swallow me so I wouldn't have sat here all stupid-looking, instead of responding intelligently. He has to be *the* finest thing that ever graced a pair of pants," Sarah murmured, partly to herself.

Jill laughed at her friend's reaction. She then realized it was time she got to work, so she headed to her workstation but called over her shoulder at Sarah, "Yeah, ditto for me too, girlfriend. Guess I'd better get back to work before everyone thinks I'm getting special treatment or kissing up to the boss. We have dessert for our lunch, so don't be late, Sarah."

It was just another routine Monday at the advertising firm, located in downtown Philadelphia. A jazzy tune blanketed the atmosphere of the office, filtering out the sound of fingers making a clacking sound on keyboards and the steady hum of the fax machine. Jill had been employed at Rogers, Huffman, and Berg for nearly three months, not long after coming to town in May. She was hoping to go from the general typing pool to advertising accounts. But for now, she was happy to have a job and a nice view of Commerce Street, which she could see from her desk in the typing pool. The room was huge with long floor-to-ceiling windows.

Jill took nothing for granted and was grateful for her job as one of the many secretaries for the service reps. She hated being the center of attention, and her connection with Marcus had caused her all sorts of problems where other people were concerned. She endured the envious looks whenever he sought her out. The spiteful remarks had her seething on more than one occasion; all were bad, but the worst one was that he felt sorry for her. Jill hated hearing it, although sometimes she felt it was true. She tried without success to distance herself from Marcus, but it only seemed to make him come around more. She really loved having him around, but there was no use in dreaming. He was out of her league. She tried to believe that there was good in all people, but that idea left her open to hurt on many occasions.

Her view of herself could be attributed to the fact that when she was growing up, she was always compared to her younger sisters—a comparison that was most often unfavorable from her mother. The put-downs she frequently received from her sisters had an even bigger effect when her mother added hers to the pile. It affected the friendships she made, as well as her accomplishments. Her father was totally devoted to his oldest daughter. Through all the years Jill lived at home, her father was her saving grace. He made life more bearable.

She was unaware of her beauty, and it was not until she had the love of some good friends that she grew stronger and became more confident. Jill was an average height, a plus-size woman who carried it well; from the male point of view, she would be described as being healthy where it counted.

To her true friends, she was one of a kind. She often felt her life drew a parallel to that of Cinderella's but without the prince. Her sisters constantly left her out of social activities. She would hear things like, "Men don't take big women for their wives, at least not the successful ones." Her mother seemed to pound that thought into her quite often. Being told that she would be lucky to get any man's attention made it easy to keep to herself. Jill began to believe the constant put-downs from her mother and sisters. She often didn't attend parties or social gatherings for fear of sticking out like a sore thumb or, worse, being the one that people whispered about.

Her shoestring budget prevented her from dressing to the nines, like most of the people in her office. Her dresses usually came from the local thrift store, and she felt that a few of the snobs who worked in the secretarial pool looked down on her because of it. The women in the secretarial pool gave her the name "Thrift Store Queen." She felt self-conscious at times when talking to Marcus, wondering what he saw in her and if he saw what the others did. Instead of looking down his nose at her, however, he made her feel as though she could give anyone a run for their money. His attention to her when she was in his company did not seem to waver, and that did amazing things toward rebuilding her ego.

The snide comments she overheard from time to time used to make her mad, but she learned to handle the nasty remarks. She overheard two of her coworkers discussing Marcus after he visited her one day at the office.

"I wonder what he sees in her."

"He probably feels sorry for her. Look at her—she wears such old-looking dresses."

"Yep, definitely from the thrift store."

Jill could hear them laughing as they walked away. Such statements often caused her to avoid putting herself on display.

As time went on, she began to step out of the shell she had created for herself. The slow metamorphosis was brought about primarily because of her new friends and, of course, Marcus, which helped to bring out a stronger side of her character that had always lain dormant.

Marcus Graham Jordan, president and CEO of Jordan Enterprises, Inc., was a very influential figure in the business world. He was a land-development mogul who bought and sold prime real estate all over the country. Jordan Enterprises was a diverse company that was well known for its charitable contributions and its involvement in community affairs. Marcus had made the list of the top twenty most successful men in the country.

Upon reflection, Jill realized that her initial thoughts of him had been of a sexual nature. It was after their friendship developed that she saw beyond his physical attributes. She found that he was a very smart and down-to-earth person. His popularity greatly stemmed from his warm, caring, and charismatic nature, but he could also turn on the charm. Their friendship seemed to sprout vines and grow since their initial meeting. If she had a religious mindset, she might call it *divine intervention*. The carjacking incident seemed to have served multiple purposes, as it brought two people together who both needed a change in their lives, and it had created such a friendship.

Chapter

2

Jill had just returned to her desk and set down the files she was carrying. She reached for her purse, took out her ChapStick, then placed her purse on the stand next to her desk; she saw a note left for her. It read, *Give Yvonne a call.* She thought about how she'd first met her friends. She had been working for the advertising firm for a few weeks when she met the three girls. On her second day on the job, she went across the street to get something quick for lunch. One of the supervisors had recommended a burger shop called Sammy's, so that was her choice for lunch that day. Everyone raved about it having the best burgers; it also had quick service, as well as being inexpensive. Jill found the place was packed with people, and after getting her food, Jill couldn't find an empty seat in the place. She contemplated getting it bagged and taking it back to the office when a woman walked up to her. She was of average height and slender build, brown-skinned, and wore her long, dark-brown hair in a ponytail.

"Hi. My name is Yvonne Sinclaire," the woman said.

"Hi, Yvonne. I'm Jill."

They smiled at each other.

Yvonne looked around and said, "The place is jammed, but there's space at our table if you would like to join us."

"Are you sure?" Jill asked.

"Ah, girl, come on. We'd love to have you sit with us."

Jill got good vibes from the woman, who had a friendly smile, so she agreed and followed her to the table, where two other young ladies sat. Jill felt warmth and acceptance emanating from the table as they all welcomed her and smiled. As Jill took her seat, she noticed how the girls joked with each other. Jill immediately felt something inside her want to break out and laugh too—they all acted as if they had known her for some time. She remembered having the same feeling when she met her best friend back home.

She was introduced to the other two girls, Cynthia Cruz and Jazmin Daniels. Cynthia was a plus-size, like Jill. She was lighter-skinned and wore her light-brown hair twisted into a French roll. Jasmine was mixed—Jill guessed perhaps Hispanic and black. She had long, wavy black hair and a slender build. Her brown eyes were warm and welcoming as she offered Jill a seat beside her.

Jill found herself hanging out regularly with the girls as they got to know each other. They became so close that it seemed they had formed their own sisterhood.

A month later they all joined a fitness club, and each made a vow that she would be dedicated to self-improvement.

Jill initially had tried joining an aerobics class but became unhappy with her progress. She found it hard to listen to the class instructor, who was much bigger than anyone in the class. To top it off, one day Jill caught the instructor eating a powdered doughnut and drinking a Coke before class. Jill thought, *What a hypocrite she is, talking to us about nutrition and what we should and should not do, when she is a junk-food junkie herself.* Jill walked out of class that day and never returned.

Once she and her new friends began to work out together, she found she looked forward to the workouts more.

On her way to work one Monday morning, Jill had no luck in suppressing the butterflies in her stomach. It was her first day as a junior ad assistant. She had been called into Mr. Rogers's office on Friday, and to her surprise, he offered her a promotion. She knew it was partly because the person who previously held that position was suddenly fired. Jill was surprised by Mr. Rogers's offer—she had not been working for the company long, not even a year, and to be offered a promotion was amazing.

Jill had felt so anxious that she had dialed Marcus's number before leaving her place, but she only got his answering service. Jill hung up without leaving a message, thinking she would try later or the next day. She wanted to thank him for all his help on Friday night, but she felt it should be delivered personally. Her wanting to see him face-to-face was not only to express her gratitude but also because of her attraction to him.

Earlier that morning, she'd showered and then grabbed a cup of coffee but took only a few sips, feeling too nervous to eat anything for breakfast. She emptied her cup in the sink and then decided to head for work.

As she locked her apartment door, she thought about how good it felt to be on her own. She had rented her apartment only a few weeks ago, after finally making Marcus see sense that she wanted to find something affordable and to stop She hoped that someday, she would be able to have the things that she had dreamed about all her life. Things like a family's love, a good man and to visit the Maldives. These were just a few on her list. She pushed it far back in her mind, not wanting anything to cloud this day, but she remained hopeful. She put on a smile and hummed a few bars of her favorite tune. The humming was her way of conjuring up inner peace and removing any bad vibes or thoughts as she considered what lay ahead for her with the new job.

She got into her old gold Nissan and exhaled slowly before backing out of the driveway. She sent a prayer of thanks up to the heavens that her car was cooperating. Moments later, she was preparing to turn onto the exit that would take her to downtown Philadelphia but noticed a car up ahead on the side of the ramp and a man leaning over the bonnet of the car. When he looked up, Jill saw that it was Marcus. She remembered reading the society section of the newspaper over the weekend; there was a review of the Mayor's Ball, and Marcus was mentioned in the article. She'd read that Marcus Graham Jordan was interviewed, along with his current girlfriend, Sheree Davis, a well-known model. It was rumored that Sheree had held Marcus's attention longer than all the others, and maybe she was the one.

Jill pulled the car over to the side of the road and rolled her window down as he approached her side of the car. Her heart rate increased as he bent down, bringing his eyes level with hers. She looked straight into his gorgeous face, feeling that familiar feeling, as if she had died and gone to heaven.

"Good morning," she said with a big smile, before dropping her eyes from his extremely handsome face. *Just imagine being lucky enough to wake up to that face every morning*, she thought.

His voice interrupted those thoughts. "Hey! Good morning, Jill. My car seems to have quit on me, and in rushing around this morning, I left my cell phone at home. I can't even call a tow truck. You wouldn't happen to have a phone, would you?"

Her voice seemed to have failed her as it came out breathless when she replied, "Um, no, I sure don't have a cell phone, but I can give you a ride."

He pushed himself away from the car and replied, "Hey, that will work just as good for now." He looked at his watch. "I'm due at a meeting in about twenty minutes."

Jill reached over to open the passenger door and smiled at him. "Well, come on; get in. Maybe this will help in some small way to reduce the tab I have with you, huh?"

"I haven't given that a thought. All I care about is getting to that meeting." He rushed back to his car to retrieve a briefcase, and they were soon on their way.

"I'm really glad you came by. Everything going ok with you?" he asked, looking over at her.

"It's going good. The training is quite intense! There is so much to learn. Mr. Rogers seems to be impressed with my work, and the apartment is great. I tried to call you earlier, and now I know why you didn't answer. Do you think it's something minor with your car?" She glanced at him before turning her attention back to the highway.

"Not really sure. I had some work done on it a few weeks ago, but now I think a sensor or something like that has gone out. I'll have my mechanic check it out."

"Why don't you just use a limousine service instead of driving your own personal car?" Jill asked. "You know, all the rich folks I see are usually getting out of one or being picked up by one as they move about town."

"I do have my own limousine driver and limo for special occasions, but I also have a service I use when I'm out of town. When it comes to my daily routine—home and office or jetting around town to look at sites—I love driving my own ride."

"By the way, I read about you in the newspaper." When he looked as if he didn't understand, she continued. "The article talked about some glorious ball you went to over the weekend." Jill glanced over at him to see his reaction.

Marcus grunted as he gazed out of the window. He thought of the terrible argument that he and Sheree had gotten into when he took her home. He was totally pissed with Sheree because she had gotten into it with the mayor's daughter.

"Believe me, I would rather forget about that night." He was not interested in the media's opinion, but he asked, "So what did the article have to say about me?"

"Oh, just that the lady you were with could be the potential Mrs. Marcus Graham Jordan, being that you have been dating her longer than the 'others.'"

Marcus snorted and said, "You should not believe everything you read. The media is always printing what they think people want to hear instead of the truth. I wonder why people read that stuff? What is the fascination?" Marcus gave her a baffled look.

"Well, speaking as a reader of the trash media, we like to know how the other half lives. You know, the lives of the rich and famous are always a matter of public interest. Besides, everyone likes to dabble in a little what-if fantasy from time to time. Although it's old hat to you, everyone loves to dream."

"I don't blame anyone for dreaming." A few seconds lapsed before he looked at her and asked quietly, "So what does Jill dream about?"

She could feel herself blushing. The sudden change in his tone did things to Jill, and she found herself unable to look at him before she spoke. "Lots of things, like a successful job, my own family, a nice house, and I'd like to travel a little. I don't have to be on the go all the time, but I'd love to visit the Maldives—I so love being near the water—and maybe some historic places, and maybe even go to Paris one day."

"Those are nice dreams, and I'm sure you will do them all. Just don't believe everything you read in the newspapers. It can be full of trash, so be careful of what you read and hear, especially about me."

"Yes, I agree with you, and I guess your status just comes with its own dark horse, ya know?"

"You might have a point there. *So*, Miss Weston, today you start your new position, huh?"

Jill looked at him. "This is my first day working for Rogers, Huffman, and Berg as a junior advertising assistant—*yes!*" Her reply held a little more confidence than when she first woke up that morning.

"I am happy for you, Jill. I knew you wouldn't stay long in the secretarial pool. You know, Garrett called me. He'd already decided to give you that promotion. Impressing Garrett was all done by you."

When she looked at him skeptically, he shook his head.

"Yes, the fact that he was in the process of conducting interviews for additional staff was one of the things he brought up in the conversation we had. He told me that someone left him short-handed and that was his decision. He told me that his decision was because of how you just seemed to jump into a project with such dedication, and your creativity really wowed him. I simply said that I already knew that, and he just laughed. I often talk to him during the week—you know this. We play golf at the same club all the time, so our business relationship and friendship has developed over the years. I'm in and out of his office quite a bit, as he is in mine. We have become connected as friends, and we collaborate in our mutual businesses.

"He told me that he was searching for creative and independent ad execs who were willing to work hard, someone with the potential to move up the ladder because his business was really booming. So, the end of story is, you got this position on your own merit. Nothing to do with me at all. I know you thought it had something to do with me, but sorry, baby girl, it's all you," Marcus admitted.

"I'm curious—what do you think of me?" Jill asked, suddenly needing to know.

"You know, if I thought you were not capable of doing the job, I would have told Garrett what I thought right away, especially since he asked. But from the time I met you, I saw that strong will. You are so smart and such a people-person. That all bodes well for a position in dealing with the public."

"I just wanted you to know I'm a hard worker and that I appreciate everything you have done for me," she said. "Besides, I am everything that you said—smart, intelligent, and personable, and never would I disappoint a business magnate such as yourself," she said, teasing him, and they both laughed.

"Disappoint? Never! But pretty, yes!" He noted her nervous smile; she seemed lost for words and a quietness fell over the car.

After the awkward silence, Jill had a hard time finding a way to change the subject, but she asked, "So, do you really like what you do? You know, all the wheeling and dealing stuff? You've said the business was handed down to you, but does that mean you would have chosen something else?"

"Yeah, initially the family business was not my dream. It was scary at first because my father got sick, all of a sudden. I was living in Atlanta, where I had just graduated, and had made plans to pursue my dreams of going pro for basketball. I majored in engineering with a minor in business, but the NBA was my dream. When Dad collapsed, it shook my world, and someone had to take up the slack. My brother, Brice, was carrying heavy responsibilities with his job on the border patrol, so I was the only choice. Mom knew very little about running the business, and Dad needed her with him anyway, so I was the only viable choice at the time.

"I was really scared that I would ruin my family's business, which Dad had built from scratch." He grunted. "But everyone had such faith in me. They stood behind me 100 percent. My mother said, 'Marcus, this has been too much on your father for far too long. It's time he took a break. You or Brice must step in because this is the only way your father will step down; otherwise, the doctor said the stress will kill him.' Jill, when I found out how hard my father had been pushing himself, my dreams of pro basketball did not seem all that important anymore. It was then I poured my heart and soul into the family business to show my father that he could depend on me. I was green at first, but I learned fast. My father's right-hand man took me under his wing and showed me the ropes and how Dad worked the business. When he retired, I promoted Joe from the PR Department to being my assistant. I built my own team, and we all worked well together and made even stronger connections. The board was happy with the progress the company was making. When my father came back only to announce he was taking a back seat, the board voted me to move from interim head to the CEO of Jordan Enterprises.

"My father only comes in a couple of days a week now, just to check on our progress, and his health is much better. Slowly, I began to feel that I was in the right place, and the more I went around with my dad, the more it became second nature to me. Folks started asking for my opinion, forcing me to step out from dad's shadow. Before I knew it, I began to feel like the CEO. Brice and I just decided that we will do whatever it takes. So that's my story, baby girl."

They were soon driving onto the parking deck of the huge building. They boarded the elevator to their respective floors.

"That was an amazing story, Marcus. I would have never known that business was not your first choice as a career."

The conversation was interrupted by the ding of the bell to announce the arrival of the next floor. *Jill's floor*, Marcus thought, *unfortunately.*

She stepped out of the elevator, only to lean back in and with a big smile. "It was a fun ride to work, Marcus. If you need a ride home, you know where to find me. Good luck with your meeting. Thanks for keeping my thoughts off my new assignment. I was kind of worked up about it." This time she winked before turning away to walk to her office.

"Hey, Jill!"

She stopped when she heard her name and turned around to face him once again.

"You have nothing to worry about," Marcus assured her. "Hiring you is the best thing Rogers has done in a long time." He leaned casually against the elevator door, smiling at her, then pushed the button and winked at her.

Jill smiled to herself; she had such a giddy feeling after her morning ride with him. "What a way to start the day," she said, still smiling as she hurried to her workplace.

———

Marcus walked into his office, set his briefcase on his desk, and fell into his chair. He swiveled it around to the window and stared at the morning view of the city. His mind raced back to the elevator as he stood watching Jill. He highly approved of the way her skirt swirled around her shapely legs—that image became fixated in his brain. His intercom buzzer sounded, briefly interrupting his thoughts. Marcus found that even though he was sitting in his office, he still could smell her freshly showered scent. What was ordinary on most folks seemed amazing on her, and her scent seemed to stay in his head.

She was different from any of the ladies he had dated. Jill was heavier—*Probably a plus-size*, he guessed—but she carried herself very well. Something about her curves had him taking a second look. Her wardrobe could use a little updating; he knew so many judged her by body image instead of the person inside. She was easy to be with; her personality was another bonus to the whole package.

The continued buzzing of his intercom finally brought Marcus out of his contemplations. He frowned at the unwanted interruption as his secretary's voice flowed into the office, alerting him that the meeting would begin within ten minutes. He quickly reached for his desk phone and called his mechanic to tow his car to the shop, explaining what happened. He ended the call and took a deep breath before shifting his brain into gear. He gathered his files for the meeting and headed to the conference room.

Chapter

3

Jill was happy with the progress she was making. It would take time, and though she received many compliments, it was the compliment from Marcus that gave her self-esteem a really big lift. This happened one day when she was waiting for the elevator. Jill's back was turned, watching the elevator's slow descent, when suddenly she felt the hair rise on her skin.

Marcus appeared at her side, leaned over, and quietly said, "Coming back from lunch?"

Jill turned around with a smile as she recognized his voice. "Yes, I am. How are you, Marcus?"

"I'm doing good."

"The elevator is so slow"—Jill frowned—"and the stairs are definitely out of the picture."

"Oh yeah, with the number of floors, it would not be a good choice," he advised.

"Well, that and the fact that I'm feeling the effects of all the working out I've been doing," she said with a slight laugh.

"Oh, I see what you mean. Working out can make movement kinda difficult, but once you get into a regular routine, that will all go away."

"Believe me, I cannot wait until that time comes."

"I can see it's paying off. You look really great," Marcus said. "Are you enjoying Philly?"

"So far, so good. I've met some really nice ladies, and we all go to the same fitness club. Maybe you know them—Yvonne Sinclaire, Cynthia Cruz, and Jasmine Daniels. There is also a popular club here that we are planning to go to called—oh shoot! I forgot the name of it. They say a lot of the people who work in this building go to it. Um …" Jill racked her brain for the name when Marcus jumped in.

"Do you mean Exclusive Company?" he asked.

"Yeah! That's the one. Is it as nice as they say?"

"I would definitely say yes. A good friend of mine runs the place. His name is Rudolph Lancey, but we call him Rudy. I go there quite a lot. The disc jockey is very good; he plays the best music. It's a pretty big place. You can dine there as well. The food is pretty good. They rent their conference rooms to companies for events. Sheree reserved one of the rooms for a birthday party for me this year. It's supposed to be the second weekend in November. It's unbelievable how busy the place is on the weekends, but on the holidays, people usually make reservations because it's that busy. So do you plan on checking it out anytime soon?"

"I'm not sure exactly when I will go, but I think the girls are trying to plan for something soon," Jill said.

"Maybe I'll see you if I stop by the club sometime."

"Sounds good. I'm definitely looking forward to going, especially if the music is as good as you say it is. Are you looking forward to your birthday party?"

Marcus shrugged. "Yes and no. Since I've had nothing to do with the plans, I won't offer any opinions on it. I would prefer something more private with close friends, but since that is out of my hands, I'm just going with the flow. The music at the club, though—I can assure you it's first class. I like to dance, so I guess that's one of the reasons I go there so often. My mother used to make us go to dance classes, and so I got into it. My brother makes up dance steps as he goes," he said, laughing.

"Now, that's funny. I did the dance class thing too. I also love to dance."

The elevator finally pinged its arrival, and Marcus and Jill prepared to get on.

"Earlier you mentioned someone named Yvonne," Marcus said.

"Did you say her last name is Sinclaire?" he asked as he pushed the button for their respective floors, and the door slowly closed.

"Yes, it would be."

"It's a small world. Yvonne and my assistant have been seeing each other off and on for quite some time. I like her and think she's good for him."

"Joseph Freeman is your assistant?"

Marcus nodded. "Yes, the one and only."

"I've never met him, but she does talk about him a lot, and she has this almost dreamy look when she does," Jill said, laughing.

In that moment, Marcus thought that Jill had the prettiest smile, which seemed to cause certain reactions within him. "Did I tell you how amazing you look today?"

Jill felt uncomfortable under his scrutiny but said, "Yes, I believe so. Compliments like that keep me dedicated to my goals." She hoped he would change the subject and stop looking her over.

"You are welcome. Do you have some time left before going back to work?" When he noticed her slight hesitation, he rushed on. "There's something I want to show you—if you have a few minutes. I wanted to take you on a tour of my office so that you would have a better idea of what I do—or at least what Jordan Enterprises does. What do you say?" He looked expectantly at her.

"I have thirty minutes left on my lunch hour."

"That will work. I can do better than that and have you back in no time."

"Ok," Jill agreed.

Marcus seemed happy that she agreed as he reached over, pressing the button for the twenty-fifth floor again, but luckily, the elevator arrived, and the doors opened. "Ok, let's go." He then stepped back, allowing her to precede him.

Two men entered the elevator. They greeted Marcus and found a place to stand.

"This building is huge," Jill said. "My first week, I had a hard time remembering exactly what floor I needed, let alone directing clients to meet the reps in the office. I had told a guy who had a meeting with one of the reps that we were on the seventh floor. When he finally got to the meeting, he was over forty-five minutes late, but he laughed it off because our company saved him a lot of money, so he was happy." She and Marcus both laughed about it.

"The mistakes help you to learn," Marcus said. "Now, you look back and feel comfortable with it. Aren't you glad the newness has worn off?"

"Yes, I am!"

The dinging of the elevator brought their attention back to the arrival at their floor. Marcus waited for Jill to precede him off the elevator.

"The entire twenty-fifth floor houses Jordan Enterprises," Marcus said. "This is the home office, where we handle all types of real estate contracts, new developments, and charity foundation projects. The newest venture is the redevelopment of target areas in the city, battling housing issues. We have a giant project currently going on downtown. We've already torn down some of the condemned factory buildings, and we are on schedule to put in apartments and some single-family homes. We also have some city projects currently under contract. We have smaller offices in three other cities, so that's one reason I'm out of town a lot."

Marcus opened a door, allowing Jill to precede him. They took the hallway that led to the right, which was the financial side of the business. The left side was the developmental side of the business, which included research. Jill noticed that all the offices were elaborately furnished. Oak and brass finishes were in some areas; others had cherry wood and brass. It was quite a substantial difference from the other offices that Jill had been in since her job started.

They came to the double door, which denoted the left side of the hallway; it had a waiting area situated across from it. Jill glanced up to see the name *Jordan Enterprises* directly above her head. Marcus reached around her, opened one of the double doors, and ushered Jill inside. Directly in front of her was a large antique desk. Seated behind it was an older lady with salt-and-pepper hair, styled short but fashionably. The friendly face and warm eyes smiled at Jill.

"Hey there, Mrs. Thomas," Marcus greeted the woman. "I have someone I'd like you to meet. This is Jillian Weston. She works in

Garrett's office. Jill, this is Mrs. Thomas, my brain most of the time. She keeps me on top of things."

Both ladies exchanged greetings. Mrs. Thomas was easy to talk to, and she and Jill conversed very well as Marcus quickly looked over some papers that had come in via the fax machine.

"Jill, how is it working for Garrett? He never hesitates to help me when Marcus needs something at the last minute, and I can't figure out what to do."

Marcus groaned a few feet away, and Mrs. Thomas winked at Jill and continued to tease him.

Jill liked the lady after knowing her for only a few minutes. She enjoyed watching the good-natured banter between Marcus and his secretary.

"Come on, Mrs. Thomas. I'm not that bad. Besides, you are not supposed to air our dirty laundry to our guest," Marcus said, looking over his shoulder with a smile.

Jill could tell from the easy way they interacted that it was admiration.

"Now to finish my tour before she gives you the wrong impression of how I run things around here. I'll show you where the real genius work is created." He winked at Jill as he saluted Mrs. Thomas.

"Watch him, Jill. If you need rescuing, just yell, and I'll be in with my yardstick," Mrs. Thomas said, not looking up from the papers on her desk, as Marcus chuckled in response to her comment.

Marcus led Jill through a set of double doors, which opened to reveal a huge desk. Behind it was windows from floor to ceiling, with a complete view of Commerce Street and beyond.

Jill marveled at the amazing view as Marcus closed the door behind them. "This view is fantastic! I'm getting the impression that you like windows, Mr. Jordan."

"Yes, I do. I was definitely sold on this office, for sure."

"The view just grabs your attention beyond all else," she quietly said, still looking out the huge window. She didn't notice how he was watching her.

"Yeah, something like that," Marcus replied distractedly.

She then turned, catching him watching her intently. Jill suddenly felt nervous, realizing how alone they were. She slowly brought her gaze back to the room with its decadent and plush furniture—the huge oak desk, the walls decorated with various displays of art, and outdoor activity featuring different boats. She also noticed a drawing desk farther away in front of the window. It held a drawing of a blueprint, and opposite that area were shelves of books on all forms of architecture and engineering research. There was also a shorter set of shelves that held what looked like maps. A table by the window displayed photos of Marcus on a sailboat, along with someone who resembled him. The table was flanked by two chairs, like a sitting area.

Jill pointed to the photos. "This guy has to be a relative because you resemble each other."

Marcus came toward her, peering over her shoulder at the photo. "Oh, yeah, that's a relative all right. That is the infamous Brice Jordan, my one and only big brother." Marcus smiled.

"Where is he now?" she asked.

"He lives and works in Texas."

"Do you get together often?

"He comes to town at least once a month, if he has the time. He is one of the captains with the border agents. He wants to retire in five years and settle down, but until that time, he calls himself a dedicated playboy."

"Like his brother, no doubt," Jill said quietly as she slowly moved around the room.

She saw a picture of an older version of Marcus and Brice and two other people, whom she assumed were their parents. All four had their arms around each other at some type of cookout. Their smiles revealed such happiness, a feeling she had never felt with her family. This thought had Jill gazing at her watch. She didn't want Marcus to see the sadness she was feeling as thoughts of her family situation weighed down on her. She wanted her family to look at each other in that same loving way; but knew that was impossible. She avoided his watchful eyes. She felt suddenly ashamed by the feelings of envy she experienced after gazing at Marcus's family pictures.

"I once would have agreed with you about being a playboy, but not anymore. Now I want a different kind of life," he said, looking directly at her, but she quickly looked away.

"Oh, Lord! I've only eight minutes to get back to work. I enjoyed the tour, Marcus, thanks." She had moved toward the door and was grabbing the handle when his cell phone rang.

"I'll see you later," he said to her. "If Garrett says anything, tell him that I asked you up here and have him give me a call."

Jill nodded as he answered his phone. As he began talking, he walked over to the window, already in business mode. She watched him a moment longer before closing the door. She took a minute to gather her thoughts, berating herself for being jealous of Marcus's happy family. The picture of him with his family seemed to have opened old wounds for her. She stood quietly, trying to compose herself. She suddenly pushed all her hurt and disappointment to the back of her mind and walked down the hallway toward the reception area.

She stopped as she heard a man talking to Mrs. T. She called the man *Joe*. Jill thought that maybe this was Marcus's assistant, and the man Yvonne liked. When she reached the reception area, she saw Mrs. Thomas staring at paperwork that the man named Joe was placing before her. They didn't see Jill, as their backs were turned, but she hesitated, not wanting to interrupt but wanting to say goodbye to Mrs. T. She was shocked by what she overheard.

"My meeting with Beelman was not successful. Is Marcus in his office?"

"Yes, Joe, but he has someone in there right now," Mrs. Thomas said.

"Who?"

"Her name is Jill, and she works downstairs for Garrett. She seems nice. She's a friend of Marcus's."

Before Mrs. Thomas could say more, Joe said loudly, "Is she browned-skinned, kinda heavyset, and wears hand-me-downs?"

"Now, Joseph! Keep your voice down and behave yourself. That's not nice at all."

"I hope he doesn't go picking up charity cases. I mean, I know they saved those kids and were given the key to the city, but uh-uh. No! No, *no*! She's not in his class and certainly isn't the type that he should have on his arm, especially when he gets into the political arena. You know the rumor mill has it that he only took pity on her. Don't get me wrong, Mrs. T. You know it doesn't bother me if he has his fun, with her behind closed doors. I'm sure he'll return to his high-maintenance chicks—that's Marcus's forte. You sure that's who is in there with him?"

When she didn't answer, he continued. "The homey-looking new girl from downstairs—what does he see in her, I wonder? Why is he showing her around? He needs to think about his image. Marcus and his big heart can't pass up a stray, can he? Patronizing some downtrodden woman who probably already has a crush on him—it's too much. She's not his type! He needs to cool it with pitying the less fortunate. Too much can make even a dog sick. He's being positioned to run for the office of mayor someday, not being the local poster boy for the thrift store addicts!"

They both turned as Jill walked past them to the door.

"Jill! Wait!" Mrs. Thomas called out as she rushed around the desk. "Please don't run off. I guess you overheard our conversation, and I am so sorry. Joseph can be a bit harsh in his assessment of people sometimes."

"Mrs. Thomas," Jill said before the older lady could ask Joe to apologize, "it was nice meeting you, and I am so thankful that not all people look down on others as if they were a piece of dirt on a shoe. I am thankful that you are one of the nicer few I've met since starting work here. Have a good day, Mrs. Thomas." Jill didn't glance at Joe before closing the door behind her.

"Hey! Wait!" Joe said. "I didn't mean to—"

The door closed on Joe as he stood there, wishing the floor would open up and swallow him. Mrs. Thomas gave him a thunderous look before she turned away when her phone buzzed.

"Mrs. Thomas, did I hear Joe out there?" Marcus asked.

"Yes, he is right here."

"Can you send him in here? I need to ask him about his meeting with Mr. Beelman."

"Sure." Mrs. Thomas then relayed the message to Joe without looking at him, which only made him feel much worse.

"Sorry, Mrs. T. Guess I put my foot in it again. I didn't know the girl was standing behind us," Joe said, as if his excuse was justifiable.

Mrs. Thomas finally stopped shuffling papers and looked at him with a seething expression. "Regardless of whether you knew she was there; it was an awfully bad thing to say about someone!" Joe finally looked ashamed, but she still did not excuse him. "I met Jill, and it is my opinion—as well as some others—that she is an original. She is genuinely a nice person, which is more than what I can say for some folks! Joseph, Marcus is waiting." She turned to pick up a file and took it to the cabinet.

Joe realized that he had just been dismissed. "I'm sorry, Mrs. Thomas." She did not turn around.

He strode into Marcus's office, and when he entered, he just leaned on the door for a few minutes before walking to the desk.

Marcus hung up the phone and asked, "Hey, Joe. How did things go?" Joe shook his head as he approached Marcus's desk. Marcus found it odd that the normally talkative Joe was so quiet. "Everything ok?"

"No, but I have the papers you wanted."

Marcus watched him closely.

"Beelman didn't like the workup. He said the figures were wrong, and he wants to speak to you about it," Joe muttered.

"Why? Couldn't you answer his questions?"

"Yeah, I did, but he didn't like the answers. The man wants a bigger discount, and I told him that was the lowest we could go unless we go back to the drawing board and have a new workup done, which would call for lower-quality products. He thinks he can get more for less money. I said that our offer is reasonable. My guess is he wants to see if he can speak to you and throw on the charm."

Marcus studied Joe as he spoke, but Joe never made eye contact with Marcus. Marcus took the file Joe handed him, never taking his eyes off Joe. "So, you want to talk about it?" Marcus asked.

"No, I'm pretty sure he wants a lower price, but he wants to hear it from you."

Marcus frowned, then said, "I'm not talking about Beelman. I'm talking about whatever is eating you. You seem distracted."

"I might as well tell you before the fallout gets worse."

Marcus put his pen down, leaned back in his chair, and gave Joe his undivided attention. "Let's have it," Marcus said.

Joe took too long, and Marcus did not like the vibes that were bouncing off Joe. "Mrs. Thomas—man, she is pissed with me right now, and I know she's going to give it to me with both barrels. I think she's just waiting until she calms down. I got her upset, and she unloaded a little bit, but I don't think she is finished with me. I really put my foot in it this time. I probably will get sued for slander. Ah man, you've always said my mouth can get out of control. Why can't I keep it shut for once?"

Marcus sighed impatiently. "I don't know, Joe. Why did you put your foot in it again? And with whom this time?" When Joe only kept shaking his head without speaking, Marcus said, "Look, man, if you need an attorney, Lester the fence man can hook you up with one of his ex-con in-laws who moonlights as an attorney." Marcus smiled, trying to lighten Joe's mood.

"Marcus, this ain't funny! Ok? We will see if you find it funny after you hear who it involves. A few minutes ago, I told Mrs. Thomas that I needed to give you this report, but she said someone was in here with you. When she told me who it was, I started going on about stuff that I had heard—ya know, around. It was gossip that gets tossed around. I heard that the ladies in Garrett's secretarial pool have an ongoing bet that this Jill person will give herself to you. The rumor has it that you will take it, just to make her feel better, and then you'll toss her to the side—your usual MO. But that's as far as it will go with you because your chicks run along the line of high society and high maintenance. Jill walked in on me repeating those things I had heard, and she also heard me say that I thought she was homely, not in your class, and that you had a knack for charity cases. I said that I hoped you'd get over it soon because you are in position to run a political camp—"

"*What. The. Hell!* You are kidding, right?" Marcus scowled at Joe and then pushed away from his desk. He walked over to the window, then walked back to his desk, staring at Joe. "What the hell? Tell me you're just pulling my leg."

When Joe kept quiet and only slowly looked back at him, Marcus saw the look in his eyes and knew Joe was not kidding. "Ah, Joe, man! What is wrong with you? What right do any of you have to say those things about her? Do you even know her personally?" When Joe only shook his head, Marcus shouted, "Exactly! *Dammit*, Joe! That was foul man! Really bad! I thought you had gotten better about listening to the gossip bullshit in this building. If you remember, this ain't the first time you got involved in this office grapevine stuff. It turned out badly for you that time as well. What gives you the right to run off at the mouth like that and not give a good goddamn about anyone's feelings?"

"I know, I know, Marcus! I guess I was still upset about not getting Beelman's signature to go ahead with the deal that I—"

"*Uh-uh!*" Marcus interrupted. "Please do not blame this on Beelman. You have to take responsibility for your own actions. You know this because you told me this on one of the first accounts that I blew and tried to blame it on something else."

A few moments passed by, and Joe stood up and paced as he rubbed his face and cursed in frustration. He stopped walking, then looked over at Marcus.

"I told you before that I don't live my life according to anyone else," Marcus said. "It's on my terms. That lady is my friend, or at least I was hoping she would be. She is one of the few women who tells me exactly what is on her mind and doesn't bother buttering me up to make sure old Marcus is pleased with it first. She is one of the few people I know who is for real. I enjoy her company, and if she lets me, I will keep on being her friend without your or anybody else's permission. If you paid less attention to the damn grapevine, you'd be better off, my friend. I am not the only one you should be concerned about. If you are still interested in Yvonne—she and Jill have become very good friends. Yvonne values her friends for who they are, and she values Jill. You should take notes because from what I know, she would not like this either."

Marcus walked over to the window again, taking a deep breath, then paced back to his desk. He picked up the phone, dialed a number, then hung up and dialed again.

"Hey, Garrett, it's Marcus."

"Hey, Marcus, how are things going?"

"I'm trying to reach Jill, but her phone just rings. Has she come back to the office?"

"No, I haven't seen her," Garrett replied.

"She left here a little bit ago, and I remembered something I had to ask her."

"Hold a moment. I'll ask Sara if she's returned." A few seconds later, Garrett was back on the line. "Apparently, she's not back yet. Oops! Speak of the devil—I just saw her walk in and go to her office. Want me to get her for you?"

"No, I'll call her once she has time to settle back at her desk. Thanks. Talk to you later."

"Ok, Marcus, don't forget the greens on Sunday."

"Oh, I won't just bring cash!"

The other man's laughter came across the phone. "I won't need it. Got my lucky rabbit's foot."

"You mean the same one that Pete fished out of the pond a few months ago when you completely missed the eighteenth hole, or was that the first hole? I can't seem to remember, but I know that old rabbit's foot took a swim," Marcus said, and they both laughed.

"I'll let you have that one for now. Just wait 'til Sunday, my friend. Let's see who is fishing what out of where." Garrett said, laughing as they ended the call.

Marcus hung up and dialed Jill's number; again, there was no answer. Marcus continued to call but finally slammed the phone down after the fifth time trying to reach her.

"Look, man," Joe said. "I'm sorry. I was wrong. You are right. I don't even know the girl. My intentions were good; it's just that I didn't check out the facts. I was honestly looking out for you. You know, gossip has ruined many people in the public eye."

Marcus didn't speak; he gazed out the window with his back turned toward Joe. When he did speak, he uttered the words quietly, but the effect was as menacing as if he had raised his voice. "Intentions? The road to hell is paved with good intentions, or so the saying goes. And, Joseph, those expectations of my running for public office—well, let's just say that's still up in the air. Honestly, Joe! I don't care about gossip or the public's designer pics of who I should have as my friend. I like who I like for whatever reasons I like them. No one is going to pick and choose my friends for me. I value our relationship in both the business and personal sense. You have always been someone I could trust, and nothing is going to change that, but your opinion here is way off the mark!" Marcus paused before going on. "Give the girl a chance. She'll surprise you, Joe."

Joe nodded in understanding. "I guess I've been a total idiot on this one, huh? I know the answer from the look on your face, but you aren't the only one. Mrs. T has already given me the cold shoulder. You know the way she rolls her eyes at ya when she is mad; it's pretty scary." Joe noticed Marcus's slight smile. "But I know I deserved it. I guess you're right. I really do apologize for my behavior. I was out of line."

"I'm not the one you need to apologize to." Marcus raised an eyebrow and crossed his arms over his chest.

"Yeah, I guess I'll start with Mrs. T," Joe said. "Should we go over the original proposal again? I tried to find out what changes he wanted, but he said he was still working on it. I think he wanted to meet with you all along because I could never get him to tell me exactly what price line he was looking for. He just kept saying the proposal was too high."

"If the original quote is not what he wants, we will see how close we can get the figures without being on the losing end of the deal. We will wait it out if he delivers a new proposal with what he wants, and if it's reasonable and not too much trouble without too much of a price change, then we can go with it. First, I just want to see what he comes up with. He could be checking out other contractors, but we will wait and see his next move. If he does not get back in a week, I'll give him a call, touch base, and see if I can figure out what's going on with him. If he and I can't knock the problem out over the phone, I'll get our folks in research to iron it out. I think, for now, since you'll only be waiting around, you should take the rest of the afternoon off. You'll need it to mend some fences."

Joe nodded his head and walked to the door, then stopped and turned to look at Marcus. "Guess I'll get out of here and tend to those fences."

"Just see that you do, Joe. I don't want her hurt."

Joe nodded again before heading out the door.

"Joe, what have you done?" Marcus whispered to himself. He hoped that Jill didn't believe what she'd heard Joe say or that at least she would hear him out. He picked up his phone to dial her desk again.

Jill got back to her desk, clocking in ten minutes late, from lunch. Rhonda, one of the girls who rarely spoke to Jill, eyed her suspiciously.

What's that look all about? Jill wondered. She felt that she could worry about that later; right now, she had other worries on her mind. Jill was still trying to calm herself after leaving Marcus's office hours earlier. She kept telling herself that it really didn't matter, but deep down, she knew it did. It was a little later when her phone buzzed; it was Garrett, asking her to come to his office.

Once there, he handed Jill some incomplete files before showing her to her new office. "Oh, by the way, Marcus called for you earlier. Did he reach you?" Garrett asked as he handed her a key to her office.

"No, I haven't heard from him, but I haven't checked my messages yet either. I'll give him a call."

Garrett nodded and headed out the door.

The rest of the day was so busy that it helped to distract her from the scene in Marcus's office. She had been working on an assignment that Garrett had given her when she recognized silly mistakes in her work and realized she was letting that scene affect her concentration. Finally, she closed her mind to the ugly things Joe had said and focused on her work. She had heard insulting things said about her before, but the hurt did not get any easier to handle. When quitting time came around, Jill packed up the assignments she was working on and took them to her new office. She was glad she decided to move her stuff at the end of the day because the later she left, the less likely it was that she would run into Joe or Marcus. Ninety minutes later, she had cleared out her old desk and felt that now was a better time to get out of there. The rest she could do in the morning.

She spoke to Garrett before quietly leaving the office. She went out the back of the building, which led out to an alleyway. She chose a bus stop that was a couple of blocks away, making sure she did not run into anyone. She knew she would not be able to avoid Marcus for long, but for right now, she wanted to avoid any conversation about what happened in his office. When she got home, she found several messages from Marcus and one from Joe, both asking her to return the calls. She cut off the answering machine and took a shower. She was too upset to eat, but she drank some water and tried to read notes—only to give in to tears. She fell asleep, feeling emotionally spent.

The next day she made it to lunch hour without running into anyone.

She decided to go out for lunch instead of choosing someplace popular with the staff. *Go out the back way, just to be safe,* she told herself. She had almost made it out of the building when someone tapped her on her shoulder, and she turned to see Marcus.

"Are you in a hurry?" he asked

"Yeah, I have lots of errands that I need to run before lunch is over. I'll catch you later," she said as she turned away.

"Why are you going out the back way? The parking lot is this way." He indicated the opposite direction from where she was headed.

"Ah, I don't have my car today so I—"

"What do you mean, you don't have your car?"

"It wouldn't start this morning, so I caught the bus. I'll have it checked out this evening."

"I see. I can drive you wherever you need to go."

"Marcus, that is so not necessary!"

"I insist. No arguments. Come on!" He placed a hand behind her back and steered her to the entrance to the parking deck.

Although she tried to change his mind, it proved difficult. "Wait! Marcus! Will you stop! I don't need you to take me to run errands."

"You will use less time if we go by car."

By the time they got to his car, Jill was completely out of arguments. He steered her to the passenger's side of the huge SUV, opened the door, and helped her inside. She felt like a fish out of water as she waited for him to climb in on his side.

Once he was behind the wheel, instead of pressing the ignition button, he sat quietly, staring ahead instead of looking at her. Then, quietly, he asked, "Why are you avoiding me?"

"Who said I—"

"Stop, Jill!" He turned to look at her. "You know you were. You haven't answered my calls, and I have been calling you since yesterday afternoon. A few minutes ago, you were sneaking out the back of the building, and you jumped like a scared rabbit when I tapped you on the shoulder." It got really quiet in the car, then he took a deep breath. "Why are you avoiding me?" he asked, this time giving her a direct look.

She struggled to answer. It took her a few seconds to get herself together before looking over at him. She released a deep breath because all she could think about was the way Joe had talked about her to Mrs. Thomas. The horrible scene kept playing over and over in her mind, and she just wanted to run away; she felt so hurt.

"Look, Jill, I know about what happened after you left my office." He watched as she released another breath. "I am sorry about what happened, with Joe. He regrets what he said. Joe's mouth tends to speak sometimes before his brain can catch up. He is sorry he hurt your feelings."

Once again, she felt the pain. It was as if the door to all her life's hurts was about to fly open. She bit down on her lip, feeling a good cry coming on, but she fought the temptation and stifled those feelings. It took her a few minutes before she could speak. "It's embarrassing." Her voice was barely a whisper as she fought through the emotions inside her. "You know, Marcus, the bad part is that he was telling the truth. I mean about how he and some others feel about me or how they see me. And no matter how you or anyone else sugarcoats it, it won't change a thing."

Marcus listened, and he did not like the sound of her voice. It was wobbly and very nervous. She sounded like someone all alone, and he did not like it one bit. Her quietness and the defeat he heard in her voice vibrated within him, and it made him feel out of sorts. He could hear the sadness and wanted it to stop. The loneliness was like her aura, and he hated it because as long as he had breath in his body, she would never be alone. He ran his hand over his hair. "It's not like that! Look, Jill, honestly, I don't want you to think that I'm trying to make excuses for Joe or that I am trying to soothe your ego or even that I think the same way as the narrow minds do, because I don't."

"I appreciate your thinking about my feelings, but I don't need anyone's pity. I'm doing fine. I will always be grateful for all the help you have given me. I'm pretty much used to people like Joe. He's not the first person who has said nasty things, and I dare say he will not be the last." Her voice cracked as she said, "Don't worry about it." She looked out the window, trying so hard not to let him see the hurt she felt.

He placed his hand under her chin, gently turning her face to look at him. "I do not pity you. I just wanted to make sure you were ok and that you didn't feel bad about the opinions of only a few people. What you heard is not the way most people feel about you, and that includes me. Well, that is if I have any credibility with you."

The simple act of his finger holding her chin caused all kinds of sensations, so she moved slightly away.

It was a movement that he noted, and he said, "I know you are hurt right now, but you cannot pay any attention to what he said."

"Joe just said what probably a lot of other people are too chicken to say to my face. But the only problem is, he didn't even say it to my face; I walked in on the conversation. No, actually, he did not know I was standing there." Jill tried hard to keep her composure but failed miserably; a tear escaped.

He quickly reached over and wiped it away with the pad of his finger. "Jill ..."

She heard the strained whisper of his voice as he spoke her name. When he reached over to wipe away another tear, she quickly wiped the tear away before he could touch her again. "Honestly, Marcus, you worry too much. I'm not going to shut down 'cause a few people say that I'm homely or that I'm out of your league. I know I'm not part of the upper crust, and neither am I trying to be. But I will tell you this; just make sure you keep that moron away from me, and I'll be fine. It's funny, though, how people in your social sphere do not appreciate my ingratiating myself with you, even with us being just friends."

A dark frown played across Marcus's face. "I don't give a damn about other people or their opinions."

"Don't start swearing. It turns you into a monster, and I don't like monsters," Jill said suddenly, seeing the humor in his reaction as he exhaled heavily before a glimpse of a smile appeared.

"I swear, you and Joe may be the end of me. One is calling me a monster, and the other can't keep his mouth shut!" He looked at her for a moment and then said, "If I like you and you like me, that is all that matters. Quite frankly, Jill, I'm not in the babysitting business, but I did tell Joe that I was disappointed in him. When he told me some crap about my image and other people's perception, I told him that I was not—nor will I ever be—anyone's puppet. I call my own shots, and that means I do what pleases me. Everyone thinks they know me, and what really pisses me off is that no one thinks I'm capable of making my own choices in my personal life. Image isn't everything, and I just wanted you to know that I have a different point of view. I wish you would only listen to me and trust me. I like you, and I could not care less about where you come from, your bank account, or where you shop." Marcus ran his hand over his hair again, which made Jill aware of its silkiness, making her want to touch it.

Feeling awkward, she tried to lighten the mood. "You sure about that? You know I'm broke, right? You're not afraid I'll take advantage of you?" When he only looked at her with a serious look, she tried a different strategy. "Look at us, we shouldn't be doing this. Joe is the one I should be strangling, not wrestling with you."

"I guess I need to take you to get those errands done. I just wanted you to know that whatever anyone thinks or says about you and me doesn't matter as far as I'm concerned. But I thought you already knew that." He sighed.

"That's awfully nice of you, but you didn't have to do that. I don't want you to worry about me. I don't know what I did to deserve a friend like you, but I really appreciate this gesture. It seems to have made something shift back into place; I think. At least I feel better. Thank you, Marcus." She treated him to a smile, and he reciprocated.

"Sure, anytime. I guess the mother hen in me had to make sure my baby chick was ok." He winked at her, and she nodded her head as she looked back at him.

"I guess I'd better not hold you up any longer. I can run errands later. I'll see you around." Jill reached for the door handle.

"Since we're already in the car, how about if we grab something at the Burger Barn? You gotta eat, right?"

She hesitated momentarily before smiling and agreeing. He then pushed the ignition button, told her to buckle up, and they went on their way.

They ate lunch outside under the umbrellas at the Burger Barn and then headed back to the office. They both enjoyed themselves after they had cleared the air. Jill could not remember ever enjoying herself like she did when she was with Marcus.

The rest of the day went quickly, and since it was Friday, the weekend was here.

On Monday, when Jill arrived at work, she came to a stop when she saw the door to her office was open, and Rhonda was standing at her desk, looking at something. When Jill got closer to her door, she saw a huge bouquet of flowers on her desk; Rhonda, the office gossip, was trying to read the card, but it was in an envelope.

"Can I help you, Rhonda?" Jill set her bag down as she watched the surprised expression on the woman's face.

Rhonda placed a hand on her chest, looking around with a guilty face. "Oh! Jill, you shouldn't sneak up on people like that. Girl, you scared the life out of me," Rhonda exclaimed.

"I guess since this is my office, there is no need for me to apologize, but you still have not answered my question. What is of interest to you on my desk? Certainly not my flowers, I'm sure." Jill glared at the other woman.

"I was just admiring them—real pretty. Everyone is talking about them and, um, wondering whether Garrett sent them because you got hired for the new position, or, ah, for something else."

Jill reached over and took the envelope out of Rhonda's hand. "I'll find out who sent them soon enough. Is there anything else, Rhonda?"

The woman's eyebrows shot up, but she walked out of the room, saying over her shoulder, "Let me get back to my work."

"Don't let me stop you," Jill said, equally as loudly. A smile spread across her face as she shook her head. *Oh, that felt good, and it's gonna kill her, not knowing who sent the flowers.* Jill opened the card, thinking it must be from Marcus.

When she read the bold handwriting on the card, she was shocked. She could not believe the nerve of him to send flowers. *Like that, will make it all better.*

The card read,

Dear Jill,

Please accept the flowers as my effort to redeem myself. I now realize that I misunderstood you in a big way. I hope you will give me the chance to make up for my misguided opinions.

Yours truly,
Joseph

Jill thought all morning about the flowers and that rat's cheap explanation all day. Shortly after lunch, Jill came up with an idea on what to do with Joseph's flowers. When the mail steward arrived, she told him that she had a delivery for Joseph Freeman at Jordan Enterprises on the twenty-fifth floor.

The steward looked at Jill curiously. "I'll have to make a special trip for such a large item," he said. "I'll be back."

Jill refrained from commenting, not wanting to stir up office gossip. She later found herself laughing as she composed a note to go with the returned flowers. *This should give Joe an idea that I don't take his actions lightly*, she thought. *It's not so easy for him to earn my forgiveness.*

She spent the rest of the afternoon finishing the paperwork on her desk. She was glad of the end to a long day and hoped that tomorrow would be less chaotic. Jill was dropping off some financial paperwork for one of the reps when she saw Marcus going into the print shop. Although she only got a glimpse of him, her body suddenly became very warm.

Jill still found it hard to put the incident with Joe completely out of her mind. Marcus seemed more concerned about her feelings. He was very attentive, but although it felt great to have his attention, she did not fool herself; he was out of her league. She would sometimes find him staring at her whenever she was near him in the building or the few times when she would walk pass him in conversation with other people. His eyes seemed to burn a hole right through her, and she felt the heat, wondering if it was her imagination.

The rest of the week went by quickly, and on Friday afternoon when Jill looked at the clock, she was surprised to see it was already two thirty. She wondered if Marcus was in town because she hadn't seen him since earlier in the week. She tried her best to turn her mind back to her work; she had only two hours to go before it was officially the weekend again.

———

Marcus returned to the office just before four, when everyone was straightening up, bringing the day to an end. He and Joe had planned to work for at least another couple of hours on some accounts that needed fixing. Marcus headed straight for his desk to pull out files that he needed. A few minutes later, Mrs. Thomas knocked and then entered. They went over the schedule for Monday, and he then bid her a good evening. When the other staff had left, the office became so quiet that Marcus could hear the slightest sound. Joe suddenly swearing out loud had Marcus going to Joe's office to see what was wrong.

"Hey! Hey! What's the problem, Joe?"

Joe sat at his desk, holding his head, and pointing to a side table as he held a note. Marcus saw the huge bouquet of flowers on the table. He took the note from Joe, read it, and burst out laughing.

'Joseph Freeman? Do I know you? Why would you send me flowers?

Did I do something to be awarded such a gift? If so, tell me what, because if you were the guy I overheard talking about my clothes and me as a person by labeling me not good enough, not good enough for what? Or whom? You presumed to know me, and you and I have yet to have a conversation. You talk about me as if you know me, but you don't, and with Gods help you never will. I would not waste my time with you and I pray for any woman who does. Flowers are meant for someone you care about not for someone you obviously despise, so do not waste my time with trivial measures to ease your guilty conscience.

Peace

The Thrift Store Queen

Joe only shook his head. "No doubt you are enjoying this! Why is it that I feel like I have just been told to kiss her ass but in a totally clean sort of way? I feel like she has cussed me out without even saying, the words. How does she do it?" When Marcus looked at him strangely, Joe frowned and said, "I feel like a damned fool. Why is that? My intentions were honest. I'm a nice guy. I guess I really pissed her off, huh?"

"Oh-ho! My man, she just chewed you up and spit you out. I'm really surprised at you, Joseph, not recognizing a strong black sister. You have misjudged her, and you know that as black men, we have to recognize, my brother. She is a woman of great untapped potential—and I thought you were good at interpreting people. I feel we haven't even scratched the surface with this woman. I think the rest of us are in for a big surprise. She is just getting started, my friend." Marcus tossed the note onto Joe's desk.

Joe threw up his hands, then looked over at Marcus. "*So,* since you seem to know her so well, what am I supposed to do next?"

Marcus placed his hand under his chin as he thought over Joe's question. "I would say that whenever you see her, just be very humble. Just be sincere in your apology and don't overdo it. In general, women can sense when a man is faking it. She would see right through you. That, my brother, is about all you can do, except remember never to judge a book by its cover." Marcus smiled.

"Oh! I'm straight on that one. Man! You can see that she sent the flowers back. Most would have at least kept those. I don't want to get caught up in this again; besides, you were pretty pissed off with me. I know I'm always giving you a hard time when it comes to Sheree, but you were different this time. I am truly sorry for what I said about your friend. But I still stand by my opinion—that you would be good for this city. But I've decided not to push you anymore. Whatever you want is how we will play this out. No more positioning you for public office. Agreed?"

"Agreed." Marcus nodded and bumped fists with Joe. Marcus had turned to go back to his office when Joe spoke again.

"So, Marcus what's with you and Jill? I mean, I've never known you to get your back up when I crack on Sheree the way I do."

Marcus shrugged his shoulders, trying to figure out the answer to that himself. "Honestly, man, I really don't know. Sheree is always aggravating somebody so when you give her back just as good as she gives, it doesn't bother me. Jill is different in so many ways from Sheree. She doesn't put people down like Sheree does. Jill is easy to be with; she tells me like it is and doesn't seem to fear losing our friendship. She likes me for me and doesn't care who my family is—and that impresses the hell out of me. She's fun to be with, and we have this funny connection. I really don't know how to put it, but I value it for what it is. End of story. I'm seeing Sheree right now, and Jill is making a life for herself here. That is that."

Joe nodded his understanding. "I don't understand why you put up with Sheree, especially when there are so many others who want to be with you."

Marcus just shook his head and threw his hands up in the air. "Joseph, we have been down this road before; let's just leave it. How about the requisition, along with the file for the Norton project? Can you bring them into my office? After we decide what to do with that, we'll call it quits for today."

Joe agreed as he got up to look for the file.

———

Marcus had entered his office but had barely sat down when he heard a rustling sound in the reception area. He went to the reception area and was surprised to see Jill unloading mail onto Mrs. Thomas's desk.

"Hey, Marcus. I thought everyone had gone home," Jill said, not looking directly at him. She busied herself with unloading the bin before putting it back on the small cart.

Marcus thought maybe she was still trying to avoid Joe; he greeted her trying to get rid of some of the stress he could see as she hardly looked him in the eyes.

"Jill, what are you doing here?" Marcus said in greeting.

Jill looked down at the cart with the now-empty mail bin on it.

"The mail guy, Rodney, had an emergency and forgot this box of mail in our office. Sarah left early today so I was appointed errand girl. I didn't want to wait in case there was something someone needed right away. I already delivered to a few offices; yours was my last drop-off."

"You didn't have to do that, but I'm glad you did. Why don't you come in for a few minutes? I only got back to the office thirty minutes ago," Marcus said.

Jill followed him into his office. "Thanks, but I need to—"

Before she could finish, Joe walked into the office, but he didn't notice Jill. "Marcus, man, you've been burning the candle at both ends lately, and now that things have settled down some, why don't you take tomorrow morning off and get yourself a massage and—" Joe suddenly saw Jill standing there. "Oh, man. I'm sorry. I didn't know you had someone in your office. Hi, Jill," Joe managed to say before releasing a breath.

Marcus's eyes never left Jill's face. He saw the look that passed across her face—as if she wanted to be anyplace but there at that moment.

Jill returned Joe's greeting, and then the room became quiet.

Marcus tried to alleviate an uncomfortable situation by initiating conversation. "Joe, Jill was kind enough to go out of her way and bring our mail that Rodney left behind. I was thanking her. I was also trying to get her to have a seat and chill a minute, but it appears she needs to leave. It is, after all, the end of her day—but not ours, huh?" Marcus said as Joe joined in with Marcus,

"Lucky girl, but the clock is still running for us. That being said, I hope she can spare me just a few minutes. I have something important I'd like to talk to her about. I promise not to keep you long. Give me five minutes, please!" Joe begged, giving her a pleading look.

Jill released a breath before nodding her head at Joe. He held the door open, allowing her to walk through the door to his office first. He followed her, closing the door behind him, and then told her which door off the hallway was his office.

Marcus noticed the solemn expression on Jill's face as she walked over to where Joe held the door. She looked like she was bracing herself for an unpleasant experience as she left the room.

Once Joe had closed his office door behind them, he immediately said, "As you can see, I received the flowers you sent back." Joe gestured toward the flowers on the side table.

Jill looked at him and shook her head before taking a few steps toward the door. Then she stopped, turned around, and approached his desk. She seemed to be weighing her words carefully. She stepped closer to his desk and gave him an exasperated look. "Joseph, I have already thanked you for the gesture, but I could not accept them." Her smile seemed to lack warmth, almost as if it could lower the temperature in the room.

"First let me say I am truly sorry for what I said," Joe replied. "Second, the flowers were sent with good intentions I deserved your scorn, but can you give a brother a break—please?" Joe acted as if his life depended on this apology.

"For crying out loud!" Jillian said. "I told you in the letter that you didn't need to send me flowers. It not only didn't impress me, but it fed the grapevine around here. Everyone likely thinks that you and I have something going on or that we did the dirty deed. Your big advertisement with the flowers was a bad move! Why would I be pleased about your flowers when my best friend could find out that you sent them to me?" Jill crossed her arms and stared at him across the desk.

"Damn! Jill, I didn't think anyone would see it that way. Now everyone will think that I'm a two-timer."

Jill burst out laughing. "I can't believe you. You talked about me to Mrs. Thomas. You hurt my feelings and embarrassed Mrs. Thomas. Then you have this bright idea to send flowers, which only gave the grapevine something to talk about. The only—*only*—thing you seem to worry about is your reputation. What about Yvonne's feelings? I don't give a crap about what they say about me—so much has been said already—but Yvonne doesn't deserve the fallout from the idiotic things you say and do! You sent flowers and think it was such a great thing."

"It's done so get over it, Jill! You really take the cake. How did you get this job anyway? Not by thinking ability, I'd bet!"

She took a minute to calm down and then said, "Look, I gotta get out of here. This is a joke." Jill started walking to the door but stopped when he called her name.

"Jill, please! I'm sorry for what I was thinking. I didn't say I was perfect. This apologizing thing—I'm not any good at it, so give me just a tiny break. Please? I'm not all that bad. It's just that sometimes, I get my foot stuck in my mouth, and I make a total fool of myself."

Jill sighed heavily. She turned to look at him, and when his expression became a very dopey looking one, Jill fought hard to keep a straight face.

"Come on, have mercy on me," Joe begged.

"Tell you what—we'll wipe the slate clean. If anyone asks me about the flowers, I'll just say they were sent to the wrong office. I think you need to give them to that lady friend of yours before she hears something different elsewhere."

Joe came round the desk with a grin on his face. "You really surprise me, lady. I initially thought you were mousy and probably would run and hide, but you came out slugging. Marcus said that's the kind of person you were, but you don't show that side of yourself. Why?"

"I'm tired of having to defend myself with the people around here. If you don't dress in designer clothes, you quickly become an outcast; it's really unfair. It was not the first time I've heard about how I look or how I dress. But you didn't even know me, and that caught me off guard. I felt so bad that Mrs. Thomas heard it also; it was embarrassing. So, I struck back at you."

"I was very nasty to you, and for that I'm truly sorry. I have learned my lesson. Hopefully, we can turn this around and be friends." Joe looked in her eyes and shook his head. "I'm sorry for misjudging you. It will never happen again. If you can find a way, please forgive me."

Jill smiled slightly to make her next words not so harsh. "I don't know about the friend part, but let's just see how things go from here."

Joe nodded in agreement; he was satisfied with her answer.

"I need to be going. See you around, Joe." Jill walked out, but before she closed the door, she stuck her head back in the office and said, "Joe, thanks for feeling that you needed to make things right between us."

"Sure, thanks for understanding," Joe replied.

Just then, Jill heard someone walk past her to Marcus's office, and she turned to see, a tall, slender woman with perfectly tanned skin and long dark brown hair. The woman was beautiful, but her look was so cold. She just stared at Jill without speaking. Jill gave the woman one last look, wondering if she'd mistaken the woman's look as cold, but the same look was on her face as the woman turned before closing the door. The vibes

Jill picked up from the woman were not good. Jill decided to leave through the door leading to the receptionist's desk. She gathered up the mail cart and pushed it out into the hallway, heading for the elevator.

Marcus realized that he would get little work done tonight due to Sheree's unannounced visit, as well as her whining. He buzzed Joe. "You are still alive in there?" Marcus asked.

"Yes, I'm fine. Things went well. Jill just left. I'll tell you about it in a minute. I'll be—"

"I will check with you later about that," Marcus interjected. "How about we cancel the workload tonight. Sheree is here, so I'm going to get out of here and spend some time with her. We can pick up in the morning where we left off, Ok?"

"That's Ok with me, Marcus."

"Besides, we'll have to come in on Saturday anyway to close those other two accounts. I'll see you in the morning, probably around ten o'clock. Can you lock- up for me? Get some rest, and I'll see you tomorrow."

"All right, Marcus. Later," Joe agreed.

Sheree came around Marcus's desk, wrapped her arms around his neck, and rained kisses on his face and neck. "Finally, I get you all to myself. Oh baby! It's been too long."

When she tried to undo his necktie, Marcus put his hand over hers to halt her progress. "Whoa! Baby, slow down. Joe might walk in on us," Marcus said and stopped her from sitting on his lap. "Just let me gather up these files and put them in the tray, and then we can get out of here to somewhere more private, and you can show me how you have missed me." Marcus winked at her, although he was not feeling like himself tonight. It was the oddest thing because usually he would be eager to have sex with her when she came back from a modeling shoot, especially when it had been a while.

Maybe by the time they got out of the office he would feel more in the mood. He also felt disappointed that Jill had not come back to his office after speaking with Joe. He hoped that things had gone well. He wanted to know firsthand how she felt. But now that Sheree was here, his hands were tied. Marcus decided he could stall no longer; he held the door for Sheree as she walked out of the office.

Chapter

4

The advertising reps were working long hours due to short staffing. Garrett held interviews for the positions that had been vacated. Jill found herself becoming very familiar with the more intricate details of advertising because of working long hours and the issue of trying to cut down on the workload. She was very comfortable with the new assignment, and she liked what she did. She was given more freedom until she could handle the whole account by herself. She did all the research and the final workups in preparing accounts for presentation to the clients.

Jill's work with the advertising execs did not go unnoticed by Garrett. By the fall of that year, he wanted her to take on even more responsibility. Garrett told Jill that he was considering promoting her from junior advertising assistant to the position of advertising representative. She was shocked by the offer, and knowing that he was considering her for that position boosted her confidence even more. She thought this raise would get her closer to being more stable financially. She knew that when she was formally offered the job, she would accept.

Every Saturday morning, she and the girls would meet at the gym, committed to getting into better shape. They all wanted to prepare for various social events coming up for the holidays. One Saturday morning in November, as Jill walked to her car, the fall air felt chilly, and her light jacket offered little comfort. Jill met her friends at the health club promptly at ten o'clock. Two hours later, they all sat at a local pub, drinking iced tea and trying unsuccessfully to avoid anything on the menu that was high in fat.

"I thought that I would see more results than this. Shoot, I'm beginning to think that these love handles are here to stay, or maybe they're just a birth defect," Cyn said, shaking her head, as the others voiced similar complaints.

"Cyn, think of them as grippers, large enough for a man's hands," Yvonne said.

Everyone chimed in, enjoying the humor of it all.

Cyn shook her head before joining in the lighthearted fun. "You know what else? If you had to deal with these ..." Cyn picked up her ample breasts and let them drop with a bounce, and they all squealed with laughter. "They feel like I'm carrying bricks around, especially when they're excited, like when I see someone who turns me on."

"I hope that someone is of the male gender," Jasmine said, "because if it ain't, we're gonna cancel girls' night out at your place, Cyn!"

They all continued to laugh, unaware of the attention they were getting from across the room.

A few minutes later, their waiter came to the table with a message. "Good afternoon, ladies. The gentlemen at the corner table have just ordered you all another round of whatever drinks you desire. Those were their exact words. I swear."

Yvonne looked for the waiter's name tag. "Eric? Tell those gentlemen thank you; it's just what we needed after a long workout."

Eric left to convey the message.

"Well, girls, what do you think? Any takers in the corner?" Yvonne asked.

The table became quiet before anyone answered.

"I don't know, Yvonne," Jasmine mumbled. "They look married to me." She looked over at Jill.

"Yeah, I think so too," Cyn agreed. "Why are they in a corner, looking like a can of sardines? They're so close to each other. Bet you they've got something to hide. What do you think Jill?"

Jill hunched her shoulders, then said, sounding unsure, "They look nice enough, I guess, but you guys, I'm not a good judge when it comes to a man. What do I know? But they offered free drinks so why don't we have them come over to our table? We can find out what's up with them. What do you say, ladies?"

"Let's do it!" Cyn said eagerly.

Yvonne summoned the waiter to carry a message over, and soon all three guys headed toward the girls' table.

"Hi, ladies," one of them said. "I'm Mitchell, and this is Leo and Bruce."

They all exchanged greetings, and the waiter brought more chairs as they began to get acquainted.

"You ladies are looking in fine form. Is this a favorite spot for you?" Mitchell asked.

"Yes, it is. We all just came from the gym." Cyn said "You know a woman has to keep herself in shape, not only for the health benefit but to keep you guys on your toes."

The guys all agreed as they looked around at the women sitting at the table. Cyn's comment seemed to be an ice breaker, as Leo and Bruce, who had been quiet, started in with questions.

All three guys worked for the same IT consulting firm downtown. Leo and Bruce were from Philly, but Mitchell was a transplant from Washington, DC. They shared lot of laughs and before long, they were requesting another round of drinks.

Later, as the girls prepared to leave, they promised to hang out with the guys at the club the next Saturday. Mitchell gave his phone number to Cyn and asked her to call him if that plan changed.

It was Thursday evening, prior to the girls meeting up with the guys at the club, when Jill called Yvonne. "Hey, girl, everything still on for Saturday night?" Jill asked.

"Sure, girl, as far as I know. Cyn plans to touch base with Mitchell tomorrow evening just to make sure. So where have you been the last two days? I came over on Tuesday, but Sarah said you were out running errands. And Wednesday you had left work early. Everything Ok?"

"Yes, I'm fine. I was trying to get some things done that I can't do on the weekend, and I'm still getting to know Philly. I've been trying to get my hands on some jazz tickets for the upcoming show for the first weekend in December. I'd really like to go, but you know how that is—all the seats are sold out so I guess I will have to wait for the next show. Can you believe how fast the year is going?"

"I know what you mean, girl," Yvonne said. "Time has really flown by. I am already hearing that the concert is sold out for Thanksgiving weekend. I hope the weather will be nice, but then again, there will be more concerts. There always are, so don't worry if you miss this one. You know, Jill, meeting those guys at the club on Saturday is Ok, but I'm working on this relationship or possible renewed relationship with Joe, you know? I'll hang out with you all, but I'm not trying to get hooked up with any of those guys. I'm just trying to see where this thing with Joe goes, you know what I mean?"

"Yeah, I do," Jill said.

"Joe and I have been on again and off again so many times. I would really like to know this time around if I should keep spending my time on us. So far, it's good. He works for Jordan Enterprises, you know, and it's going pretty well for him there. We have this sizzle, or I guess you could say it is like a slow burn."

Yvonne didn't seem to notice that Jill had become quiet. Jill wondered whether she should tell her friend how she'd met Joe. She finally decided that Joe should be the one to tell her. Jill suddenly realized that she had missed much of what Yvonne had said. Jill made little comments to cover up the lapse in her responses, but Yvonne continued to talk, never noticing Jill's lack of attention.

"Like, for instance, the other day when I was in the break room at the snack machine. He came in, and somehow, I knew it was him without turning my head." Yvonne sighed dreamily.

"Sounds like some pretty strong energy you two have going," Jill said.

"I don't know. Sometimes I feel so unsure around him, as if I'm going to really blow it, but once we start to talk, everything seems to flow so naturally. Girl, when I turned around and he was standing there,

I just wanted all my clothes to fall off—it got so hot so fast." Both girls burst out laughing. "His eyes told me that he was just as hot as I was. He asked me if he could share my treats, and I was speechless. He started laughing at me and it sort of broke the ice, but that man—I'm telling you; he just makes everything stop for me, and the feeling is just so exciting. We talked for a few minutes, and then I had to get back to work. He asked me to go to the opening of the comedy club with him. I was supposed to be hanging out with my girls. Do you think anyone will mind if I hang out with him on Saturday night? I could come by afterward. What do you think?"

"I'd say go for it, and you know the rest of the girls would say yes as well."

"Yeah, I knew you would say that, so when Joe calls me on Thursday night, I'll tell him I will go with him. I think it's really good that it worked out this way—we all can have someone to chill with. You know what I mean?"

"Well, I don't plan to set myself up with one of those guys or anyone else right now. They seem to be nice guys, but I just want to have some fun. A little dancing is all I want. I want to take my time and enjoy myself for the first time in my life."

"I can understand where you're coming from. Sounds good to me," Yvonne said. "I guess I'd better let you go. I'll talk to you tomorrow."

"See ya." Jill turned back to her work and then did some errands for her boss before going out to grab a bite to eat.

———

The following Monday, Jill was entering the building after lunch when she saw Marcus walking toward her. He was accompanied by the same woman who had scowled at her when she'd left Joe's office after his apology. The woman was gazing at Marcus as if she would devour him at any moment. Jill didn't want to deal with the off-putting woman, so she decided to just speak in passing and keep walking. Unfortunately, what she wanted to happen and what actually happened were two different things.

Marcus stopped walking as he got near her, much to the woman's displeasure, especially if the look on her face was anything to go by. Jill easily smiled at Marcus but when she looked at the woman, it became very hard to keep her smile in place. The look in the woman's eyes could have chilled boiling water. When Marcus stopped to speak, Jill felt, like being a little devil as she gave him a huge smile.

"Hey, Jill, how is it going?" Marcus said, smiling down at her.

"Hey, Marcus, it's going really well. Are you off to lunch?"

"Yes, we are. Sheree and I are going to have a late lunch. By the way, have you met Sheree?"

"I don't believe I have," Jill replied. She looked at the woman standing by Marcus's side. She had that same stone-faced look, as if she was extremely bored. Jill extended her hand as Marcus made the introductions, but Sheree completely ignored the extended hand and just grunted a reply.

Marcus gave Sheree a look that spoke of dissatisfaction. Then he turned back to Jill. "So is Garrett behaving himself?" Marcus asked.

Sheree misunderstood the relationship between Jill and Garrett and jumped to the wrong conclusion. "*So, Garrett's your man?*" She jabbed her elbow into Marcus's arm as a smile broke out on her face. "Why, Marcus! Why didn't you tell me this was Garrett's, um, girl?" Sheree's face had gone from pure stone to a big wide smile, showing perfectly white and even teeth. She beamed at Jill mischievously.

Marcus frowned, but before he could say anything, Jill jumped in for the save with an overly sweet response.

"Oh, sweetie, no, no! You've got it all wrong. Garrett is my boss." Jill placed a finger on her chin as if she was contemplating the thought. Then she giggled as she spoke. "Lordy! I can't even imagine that thought. My taste in men runs a little younger than that, wouldn't you say, Marcus, darling?" Jill put a little drawl to her words as she watched Marcus trying to hide his smile. "Although Garrett is a sweetheart, I prefer him as a boss. Oh, girlfriend, you do say the funniest things. Can you imagine that, Marcus?" Jill kept smiling as if it was the funniest thing she had ever heard. She bid them goodbye and walked toward the elevator, still shaking her head. Jill added a little extra roll to her hips, exhibiting a sexy walk.

Marcus's eyes were glued to her body in motion. Sheree fumed as she watched the direction of Marcus's gaze.

When the doors opened, Jill immediately stepped onto the elevator, only looking in their direction as the doors closed. She saw that Marcus was still smiling as he ushered a somewhat indignant Sheree out of the building.

"What's so funny?" Sheree asked as she and Marcus headed for the parking deck.

"You are," Marcus said.

Sheree stopped walking and looked directly at him. "I honestly thought the girl was Garrett's lady. I think, given the conversation and your inquiry about Garrett, that my assumption was a reasonable one."

Marcus looked at Sheree and shook his head. "First of all, you know Garrett is a married man. Sheree, you can't go around making that kind of assumption. It could cause serious problems."

Sheree shook her head and pointed out her reasoning again. "Exactly my point! She looks just like a homewrecker, with those doe eyes and that bad impression of a Southern drawl, along with the shy routine when she is anything but. Ump! And girlfriend claims she prefers her men younger. I think she had better go for whatever she can get! She is kind of on the thick side." Sheree swung her arms around her derriere, further demonstrating how she saw Jill. "A workout regimen sure wouldn't hurt, wouldn't you agree? We know what you like, and thick is not your preference. I believe I know." Sheree kissed his cheek and whispered, "Just like the other night. Remember, honey?"

Marcus ushered her to the car before he spoke. "In reference to your comment on thickness, guys love the curves. You are being really ugly, Sheree. You don't even know the girl!" He had the same smile as when he'd watched Jill, walk away, and that irritated Sheree even more.

"My intuition tells me she could be a troublemaker."

"Come on! That's an unfair assumption. After all she was my partner in crime when we took down that carjacker."

"So what? If not for you, that could have ended very badly. But that was then. Now that she knows the lay of the land, she looks pretty tricky to me."

Marcus shrugged as he opened the car door for her. She got inside, still watching him; she didn't like the way he'd responded to Jill, but she would find out more.

Two weeks later on a Friday evening, Jill walked down to the video store to rent a couple of movies to pass the night away. Her friends had invited her to the club, but she decided to stay home, especially since her car was not sounding too good. She didn't want to risk it stalling at night and didn't want to ask someone for a ride to the club, even though her friends would not mind. She didn't feel up to any company, so she decided to have a quiet evening at home.

She arrived at the video store, and the employees there greeted her, as she had become a regular customer, always renting movies, as well as a DVD player. Jill had taken an old western off the shelf and was reading its cover when someone whispered in her ear.

"That one is Ok, but if you really like westerns, this one is better."

Jill turned to see Marcus smiling at her with a movie in his hand.

"Marcus! Hi! You're movie-hunting too?"

He leaned against the shelf. "Yeah, a quiet evening at home is on my agenda, so I decided to add a movie. What about you? I didn't see your car outside when I pulled up."

"Believe it or not, I had the same thought. I didn't want to do the club thing. Since my car does not sound too good, I walked over here. Besides, it's a warm night, although after tonight, the cold begins right on time for the holidays."

"Yeah, I guess we should enjoy it while we can. It was so warm I thought we were back in springtime. Let me show you this western that I liked a lot. It's called *Silverado.* Stay right here. I'll be right back."

"I won't move a muscle," Jill promised. She smiled as she watched Marcus peruse the shelves. She noticed he had changed out of his usual business attire and now wore a pair of faded blue jeans that hung off his muscular hips as if he was born that way. His dark T-shirt defined how muscular his chest and biceps were and hinted at washboard abs. He wore a blue-and-white bandanna tied over his wavy hair. She was brought out of her contemplations as he returned.

"One *Silverado* for the lady."

Jill groaned aloud as she read the names of the actors in the movie. "Oh, Marcus! My goodness, Sam Elliott? Wyatt Earp? This has to be good."

Marcus nodded. "It is. I guarantee it."

"Thanks! What have you got there?"

"A few of my favorite comedians doing stand-up comedy. Do you like any of these? I have rented this tape so many times, but I laugh so hard no matter how many times I see it." He read the performers' names on the back of the DVD cover. "So, you like westerns and comedies. What other types of movies do you like?" he asked.

"I like action and adventure movies."

"I'll bet you like the romance and tear-jerker kind of stuff," he said with a raised eyebrow.

"It has to be really good for me to check it out, but I would rather see an action movie. But there's nothing like a cowboy in chaps," she said, smiling."

He raised an eyebrow again and shook his head at the look on her face as she talked about cowboys. A few seconds elapsed as they watched other people come and go while they stood there.

"I guess I'd better head back home," Jill said. "It's almost six thirty. Thanks for the tip on the movie. See you later, Marcus." Jill was walking away when she felt Marcus's hand on her arm.

"Jill, are you expecting company tonight?" When she looked at him, frowning, he quickly said, "What I mean is, if you're watching your movies alone, well, so am I. Why don't we watch them together? It's better that way, don't you think? We could go back to my place, where the delivery guy is supposed to bring a pizza in about twenty minutes. That is, if you like beef topping and the best pepperoni drowned in cheese. It's the best pizza your mouth probably will ever taste."

Jill looked directly into his face. "You're asking me to watch movies with you at your place?"

He smiled and looked around before answering her. "Yep—that is, if you have no other plans. I promise I'll be on my best behavior. My reputation far exceeds the real Marcus so remember that before you pass judgment on me, like you did when we first met."

"Touché! Touché! I made a mistake," she said, continuing to walk toward the checkout counter.

"So, are we eating pizza and watching movies?"

Jill placed her movie on the counter and looked at Marcus. "I can't drive out to your place—my car, remember?"

"I can take you and bring you back."

"Ok, if you're sure. You got a deal—but only if, next time, I make the pizza. I guarantee that your palate has never tasted pizza as good as what I can make. What do you say?"

"Homemade pizza, you say? Ok, baby girl, I can't wait for that treat!" Marcus winked at her as the clerk appeared to assist them with checking out. Marcus placed his card and the movies in the clerk's hand before Jill could present her card. He shook his head at the look Jill gave him. "This is my treat. The next time you can treat me, if that will make you feel better."

Jill agreed, and Marcus paid the clerk. They walked out the door with tapes in hand. Once they got outside, Marcus strolled over to a Harley and placed the movies in his saddlebag.

Jill looked around. "Where is your car?"

"I'm on the bike tonight."

"I see. Well maybe another time, then." She turned to walk away.

"Hey! Where are you going?"

Jill turned at the sound of Marcus's voice. "Well, um, I was thinking that since my car is broke down, no need for you to run me all the way back to my place." She tried to avoid looking at him. Marcus walked up to her, but Jill took a step back. *I hope he's not expecting me to get on that thing,* she thought, *let alone to ride with him in such close proximity.*

He frowned. "I told you I would take you and bring you back, so what's wrong?"

"Nothing!"

When he gave her a disbelieving look, she released a tightly held breath.

"It's a nice night, and we could save time by riding together on the hog here." Marcus then noticed the fear in her eyes and realized the problem was the bike; she just stared at it.

Jill took another deep breath, then swallowed hard before she spoke. When she did, her voice sounded a little hoarse. "I had a cousin who was badly injured when riding one of those things. I guess I have a fear of them, so I have never ridden one. And you only have one helmet. We can't break the law, you know."

Marcus grabbed her hand and drew her back to where the motorcycle was parked. To Jill's dismay, he opened another compartment and pulled out another helmet.

Great—he would have a spare, she thought.

"First, let me say this: it's not safe at all for a woman to walk the streets after dark alone. Second, if you have problems with your car, all you have to do is call me, no matter what. Remember that, Jillian. Third, there is nothing to be afraid of when riding a motorcycle. It's lots of fun; as a matter of fact, it's the coolest ride. It makes me feel carefree. It helps to release stress. It's really relaxing. I'm not kidding you." When she looked unconvinced, he said, "Tell you what—we'll ride a little way, and if you still don't like it, I'll call a cab to take you to my place, and after the movies, I'll drive you home in my car. But for now, we need to pick up our pace cause the pizza guy will be at my place soon. *So*, you ready, baby girl?"

Jill nodded her head, "Ok, Marcus, lets' do it." She wasn't sure that she'd sounded 100 percent more positive than she felt, but she managed to present a reassuring smile.

"That's my girl. Here let me put this on you, and then I'll show you what you need to know about the fantastic ride you are about to embark on."

Once Marcus had given Jill instructions, they hopped on the Harley and exited the video store parking lot. Marcus took it easy, and after about five minutes of riding, Jill gave him the thumbs-up sign when they stopped at a red light.

"Jill, you, Ok?"

"It's really not that bad; I kinda like it."

He turned his head, smiling at her, feeling happy that she liked it. There was something about her arms wrapped around him that made him feel *so* good. "Baby girl, that is good to hear. Want to step it up just a notch?"

"Sure, why not? I think I could become a Harley babe."

Marcus laughed. He could see her dressed in all leather—one of those vests that women wear. He had to stop his thoughts, which were headed in the wrong direction, so he concentrated on the ride. He picked up the pace just a little to give her a better feel of how nice it was to speed down the highway with the freedom that the bike allowed. Marcus took several turns, heading toward the back portion of the huge complex, and avoided the speed bumps. He finally pulled into his garage, his exclusive parking area.

Jill climbed off the bike at Marcus's instruction and waited as he pulled down the kickstand and switched the engine off. After the bike was secured, they grabbed the movies and went inside. Jill loved Marcus's place—the big rooms, the huge windows, the view. She looked out at the man-made lake with the moon illuminating it. She marveled at the luxuriousness of it all.

"Your place is so beautiful," Jill said as she followed Marcus up the steps to the kitchen. "How are the plants doing?"

"I have no clue." He opened the cabinet doors and pulled out a big bowl.

"What?" she exclaimed.

"Yeah, sorry, that's Henry's department. He keeps all the greenery around here popping. I'm no good at that stuff."

"So how did you get the plants anyway? They're gorgeous and a nice variety, especially for your patio."

"When I moved here, one of my agents from the office and my mother put together the finishing touches, like the plants and household items. I did the rest of it."

"The plants are gorgeous. I've always thought that plants complement any home. Mr. Henry does a great job. He must have a green thumb."

"I didn't know you were into plants like that."

"Yeah, it's very relaxing. So, anything I can help you with?"

"This bowl is for popcorn. Do you want any other snacks, like chips or vegetables and dip? What do you want to drink?"

"The popcorn will be enough for me, and whatever you have for the drink is fine, even water."

"I think I can do better than water. Let's see what's in here," Marcus said as he walked over to the fridge.

When the doorbell rang, Marcus hurried downstairs to answer it. A few minutes later, he came up the stairs with a huge box in his hand.

"Wow, that's a huge pizza for one person. You were gonna eat all that?" Jill asked, frowning.

"Sure, I was starving, and besides, I'm a growing boy." He grinned at her.

"Honestly, Jordan, I have no comeback for that." She shook her head, and they both laughed. The atmosphere seemed so cozy. Jill always had this feeling when she was with him; it felt so good that she just wanted to wrap herself in it like a blanket.

"Time to eat this masterpiece because it's calling my name," Marcus said. "You grab the glasses, and I'll take the pizza downstairs and then come back for the plates and napkins. We can eat while we watch these movies. The little fridge at the bar has a variety of drinks so get what you want.

"Marcus, you got brownies too?" Jill exclaimed.

"Yep, you know I always do dessert, girl. There are some with nuts on top and some without them."

"Oh, they look so delicious."

"Believe me, they are. You have to try them," Marcus said. "I think we have everything; except I need to get this TV ready."

"While you do that, I can put some pizza on your plate, if you want me to. You've done everything else."

"Sounds like a plan. Go for it!"

Jill put two huge slices on his plate, and seconds later, they were both eating their food as the movie began.

When the movies were over, Marcus turned the TV off, and through the voice control his stereo system played his favorite songs. When a song by Hall and Oates played, he heard Jill humming along as she organized the stuff on the table. He started to sing and walked over to her, grabbed her hand, and pulled her close. She laughed at him, but when she looked into his eyes, her laughter died away. Their movement turned into a slow dance as he continued to sing to her.

Jill looked up at Marcus, liking the sound of his voice as he pulled her even closer. Their bodies swayed from side to side. When their bodies touched, his voice faded away as their gazes locked. Before Jill knew it, she was enveloped in his embrace. The electricity slammed into her body with such an effect that she broke the embrace and stepped back. Quickly, she turned away, totally at a loss for what to say or do.

Then, suddenly, Jill exclaimed, "Oh! Marcus, look at the time. Let me help you clean this stuff up so that you can take me home. I hate keeping you up so late." Jill rushed over to the table and picked up the plates and some of their trash.

Marcus watched as she busied herself and just left him standing there. He tried to figure out what had happened to change the mood. "Tomorrow is Saturday, Jill. I have no plans first thing in the morning so there is no hurry."

She didn't look at him. "Yeah, but still it's getting late. You don't need to be running up and down the road this late at night for me. I should've just, ah, taken a raincheck, and I got, um, carried away in the moment. I'm, um, sorry." She headed to the kitchen, both hands full.

Marcus stood there, trying to figure out what had just happened; then he slowly walked upstairs to the kitchen.

When she saw him, she held up the napkins. "Do you want me to put these in the washer?" she asked, still not looking at him, trying to focus on anything else.

Marcus walked over to her and saw her tense up. "Hey, slow down. This stuff doesn't matter. Let's talk about why you ran away from me. Look, I'm sorry if I made you uncomfortable. The truth is, Jill, I thought everyone liked my singing. Listen, I won't do that to you again. Next time I'll just hum softly." Marcus tried to look pitiful and not smile.

Jill suddenly looked up at him. "Huh? What?"

"You ran away from my bad singing. You probably didn't want to hurt my feelings; that's why you stopped dancing with me and rushed to clean up so that I could take you home. That's ok, Jill. I understand."

When her face went from a frown to a burst of laughter, he also frowned and then laughed. He felt better that she was smiling instead of looking as if she had committed a federal offense.

"Marcus, I'm sorry. I'm not laughing at you, not at all. Believe me, you wouldn't understand." Jill said, sobering up from the laughter.

"Will you tell me what I wouldn't understand?" he asked

"Maybe another time."

"Ok! I guess I had better get you home. You sure you don't want to take some pizza home?"

"Oh no, I'll have to work twice as hard at the gym tomorrow."

"Ok, then, more for me. I'll just put the pizza away and then we can leave."

When the clearing up was completed, Jill gathered her belongings and followed Marcus out the front door. Instead of approaching the Harley, he headed for a two-door, sleek black sports car.

Wow, Jill thought.

The ride home went too quickly for Marcus. He'd had a good time tonight. They shared many of the same interests. If there was any one thing that he didn't have a handle on yet, it was her shyness when anything between them even hinted at intimacy. He could not remember any girl he had been out with who still blushed at the slightest reference to anything sexual, even a kiss. This was different, and it made him feel as if he couldn't get enough of being around her. Her shyness was a refreshing experience for him.

Whatever this feeling is, you'd better shake it real fast, he told himself, *before you get yourself into deep trouble.* He came out of his thoughts as he made the turn onto her street.

Jill watched people standing out on the street, talking as if it was the middle of the day. "Why do people love to hang out on the streets all night long?" she asked. "Don't they ever get tired?"

"It's a way of life for them. Many of them probably are jobless or their ambitions are not what you would call ambitious."

Jill agreed with Marcus as he pulled into a parking space.

He walked her to the door, and when she invited him in, he stayed only long enough to make sure everything inside was ok. Then he headed to the front door, saying, "I'll be in touch." Suddenly, he turned around with a smile on his face. "And by the way, the next movie night, I am very much looking forward to that homemade pizza, so don't try to back out."

"Now why would I do that after having such a fetching date?" she said.

"Oh yeah? I like that! Good night, baby girl."

"Night, Marcus," Jill said as she closed the door behind him. She walked over to her balcony window, watching as he got into his car and slowly backed out of the parking lot. She couldn't seem to hide from her feelings for him. Earlier, when he was singing to her, she wanted to be in his arms, but the feelings of attraction were so strong that she knew where things were headed. She wanted him—he had to know, but he respected her and let her out of the embarrassing situation by saying it was his singing. She felt he knew all along what was happening between them. She wanted to be with him, but he had someone, and that was why she had to stop herself. But she loved how he played it off to get them out of the awkward moment and back on the right footing.

She exhaled slowly as a smile spread across her face. She wondered how the girls would react if they knew that she had spent the evening with Marcus. Although it wasn't in an obvious way, it was sort of intimate in an important way. It was a way that told her he really was a respectable man, and he thought a lot of their friendship to want to spend that type of evening with her. Marcus Jordan, a sexy and intelligent man of means, was truly her friend; that alone made her feel less lonely and more confident in herself.

One evening, after leaving work late and heading home, Jill noticed her car making a strange noise after only traveling a few miles on the expressway. The car sputtered and then seemed to lose power. Jill managed to get it to the side of the road. After several attempts to restart it with no success, Jill realized it was useless. She tried to decide on her next move. She tried her cell phone, but the call didn't go through—she seemed to be in a dead spot.

"Great, Jillian, that's what you get for buying a cheap phone!" Jill raged as she dropped it back into her purse.

She decided to walk to the nearest exit, find a station or store where she could call a wrecker. Thirty minutes later, Jill was still sitting in her car, trying to suppress her fear of walking on the expressway alone. She imagined all kinds of things that she'd heard on the news had happened to people. Jill realized that sitting there could be just as dangerous as walking, so she took her chances, got out of the car, locked the door, and started walking.

Jill had walked only a little away from her car when she heard the sound of another car. She thought it would slow down and pass by. She became alarmed when it pulled to the side of the road just in front of her. It was a sleek, black, foreign-looking sports car, the kind that exemplified the expensive tastes of the rich. Why would someone driving a car like that stop to pick her up? Maybe it was a crazed lunatic or some person out to get their jollies. Jill again felt the panic.

As the feelings of panic got stronger, Jill turned around and quickly retraced her steps to her car. *If I can get there*, she thought, *I'll lock myself in the car.* Just as she tried to put the key in the lock, she heard her name and looked up to see Marcus rushing toward her. He had put on his flashing emergency signal.

"Jill! Are you Ok?"

Looking directly into those hazel eyes, Jill smiled with relief and clutched her chest; her heart was beating rapidly. "Oh, Marcus! You scared the life out of me, but I'm so glad to see you. My car just quit on me, and it won't start."

"I could tell you were scared. You looked as if you were running for your life, and it's definitely not safe out here. Where is your cell phone?"

"It's in my purse, but I might as well not have one. The stupid thing says it can't make any connections out here."

"Well, that's definitely not good," he said, and she agreed. "Tell you what—put your key in the ignition, and let's see what's going on."

Jill hopped inside and turned the key, but nothing happened.

"Are any of your lights on your dashboard on?" he asked

"Yes."

"Try to start it again."

She tried it with no success.

"Well, I guess it could be an alternator issue, but the battery has power. That may rule out a battery problem. I'll get my mechanic to come out with his wrecker, haul it back in, and put it on the machine so that we can be sure it's not anything that's really problematic. It's not safe to leave the car out here."

"Can you give me a ride home?"

"Sure, where are your things? I'll store them in my trunk and call my mechanic to get your car towed off the road and to his shop. Now let's see if there really is no reception out here for cell phones." He pulled out his phone and called a number. He spoke to his mechanic, giving him the location of Jill's car.

"I guess my convenience-store phone is not doing its job," Jill said, sounding weary.

"It will be ok, Jill. Let's get you in my car."

Marcus helped Jill into his car, then slid behind the wheel, and they got back on the expressway. Marcus gave a short laugh, and Jill looked at him questioningly.

"I was just thinking about how you scurried back to your car as if I was the highway rapist or something evil. But it's lucky for you it was just your friend, come to save the day."

"Yes, but excuse me; I do not scurry, Marcus. Besides, who knows what lurks out here? I was just being cautious." When he looked over at her, she agreed and said, "ok, I was in somewhat of a hurry to get in my car until I knew who had stopped."

"Good. I'm glad you kept your wits about you, especially in a place that is so isolated."

"Honestly, Marcus, I was scared, so I may have been scurrying back to my car, especially with all kinds of thoughts going through my head." She laughed, and he joined in but then suddenly stopped.

"Anyone ever tell you that your laugh is very nice?" he asked.

Her laughter stopped as she turned her head, looking directly into his gaze as he smiled at her.

"Oh yeah, I'm serious. You know that type of laugh where it makes you feel like laughing? Whether you know what a person is laughing at or not, it makes you want to laugh. Your laugh is like that, and it has a nice sound to it."

Jill sobered with Marcus's words. "Marcus, that's sweet, I have never been complimented on my laugh. Thanks."

"So did your car troubles spoil your plans for the night?" he asked.

"No, I was only planning to go home, cook dinner, and relax. I was so far on the outskirts of town because Jaz wanted me to check out a fabric shop where she saw material for the dress she wants me to make for her. She didn't know if it would work with her pattern. But because I never got there, I'll have to make another trip—maybe this weekend. Otherwise, I had no plans for tonight."

"I'm glad to hear that because I would like to ask a favor of you. I'm due at a business dinner, which happens to be at a restaurant. Would you mind joining me?" Before she could answer, he added, "I am hoping you will agree to join me since it's a business meeting with dinner included, and it would look good for me to arrive somewhat on time. Would you mind going straight to the meeting now? You can also think about it this way: now you won't have to cook."

She smiled and said, "I'm ok with it as long as there are no hitches to your plan. I think I can handle it, especially since I owe you for coming to my rescue, among all the other times."

"Great! It'll be a blast with you there with me. And I promise, no hitches," he said, smiling at her. "Well, Miss Weston, let the adventure begin." He turned his focus back to his driving. They rode quietly for a few minutes before she spoke again.

"I didn't recognize this car when you were backing up, but now I remember it was the one we rode in the night I watched movies at your place."

"Yes, this is the one. But I am glad you were cautious." Marcus turned his attention back to his driving, letting the powerful engine take over the road.

Marcus bought Jill up to speed about the business dinner at Henry's Steak and Seafood Tavern, which was located on the outskirts of town. The restaurant, Marcus said, had a lot of troubles in the past, but with a little restructuring and some updates, as well as remodeling and the fact that Henry had a one-on-one with Jordan's marketing advisers, the company was thriving. The dinner was basically an update for Marcus to see how things were going and to find out if there was any negative feedback from Henry.

After the introductions, they were led to a secluded area of the restaurant, where a large fountain with lights enhanced the restaurant's skylights and gave it an atmosphere. Olivia, Henry's wife, entertained Jill while the gentlemen completed their business.

When the gentlemen had concluded their business, they all enjoyed a superb meal. Marcus felt that both the meeting and the dinner had worked out well. Jill seemed to be having a good time as well, laughing as Henry and Olivia talked very animatedly about their life before deciding to go into the restaurant business.

Marcus came out of his private thoughts to hear Henry say, "A strong and powerful man like you, Marcus, needs a woman who is positive and gentle, with just a little sternness thrown in to keep you motivated and your success thriving. The true spark behind a strong man is a good woman."

Marcus glanced in Jill's direction and hoped she was not embarrassed by Henry's frankness.

Olivia came to their defense. "Oh, Henry, you are embarrassing them," she said with a frown. "How about some coffee or even cake? It's quite decadent but I will let you be the judge. Olivia smiled at both Marcus and Jill.

"Oh, no cake for me, Olivia. I've already overdone it tonight with this fabulous food," Jill said, smiling at the older woman, "but some coffee would be nice."

"Tell you what," Marcus said. "Olivia, I will take a slice of that cake but bring me two forks." Henry and Olivia laughed at Marcus's silent challenge to Jill. "I cannot pass up dessert and especially not Olivia's. She makes the best cake that I have ever tasted."

Olivia beamed, always happy when someone had enthusiasm for her food. Marcus's ability to indulge Olivia pleased Henry as well.

Shortly afterward, Henry and Olivia bid them good night, and Marcus and Jill walked out of the restaurant.

The drive home was filled with a relaxing tone of conversation. Jill inquired about Henry and Olivia, wanting to know more about the nice couple. He filled her in on how he met them and told her what he missed most in his busy life. He did not like the inability to see a lot of the people who were once just business associates but had become friends. They laughed about different comments or expressions that Henry or Olivia made about their supposed impending matrimony.

Marcus suddenly fell silent, and Jill studied his profile in the darkness of the car. "Jill, I'm sorry I had to get you into this charade, but if you like, I can tell Henry that we are not a couple."

"I think it was sort of assumed—you know, like a visual thing with no one coming out and saying. I don't think an explanation is necessary."

"Point taken, and I agree. You're pretty smart, and you give sound advice," he said as he experienced a warm feeling again. Marcus turned his attention back to the highway but glanced at her again.

"Yeah, but not smart enough to realize that you set me up with that extra-fork thing," Jill said.

"That worked beautifully, didn't it? There you were, 'Oh, I couldn't eat another bite, but some coffee would be nice, Olivia,' but as soon as she set that cake in front of me, I saw your eyes, and I read your mind," Marcus said. He laughed as he looked over at Jill and saw a small smile that was about to grow into a huge grin. "As soon as I picked up my fork and looked over at you and that look that said, 'Oh God, that looks so delicious,' the next thing I knew you said, 'Oh, give me that fork, boy.' I knew what I was doing when I asked for two forks. Henry laughed so hard and so did Olivia. They loved it and so did I."

"Yes, you got one over on me, smarty-pants," Jill said, watching him. He was full of laughter, and soon, she joined in; this seemed to be pretty much how their time together always ended.

They arrived too soon at her street, and Marcus pulled the car to a stop in a vacant parking place. He opened the car door for her and thanked her again. Jill tried to tell him that he didn't have to get out, but he just shook his head.

"My mother would probably kill me if I didn't escort a lady to her door and make sure she was safely inside." Jill just smiled. "And always respect a woman—that's what my mama taught me," he said with a Southern drawl as he winked at her.

They discussed a good time for him to pick her up for work as he checked out her place. Afterward, he said good night, went back to his car, and drove away.

Monday came too quickly, and the weekend was a distant memory. Jill looked at some faxes that Sarah had laid on her desk, but her mind continued to drift. She wondered where she would be now if she had never left Claremont. The ringing of her desk phone interrupted her scattered thoughts.

"Advertising. Jillian Weston. Can I help you?" Jill answered.

"Jill, it's Yvonne. What are you doing for lunch?"

Jill was still foggy from her thoughts but then said, "Lunch? I've no idea. What do you have in mind?"

Yvonne picked up on the tone in Jill's voice, "Jill, are you Ok? You sound strange."

Jill grunted, "Oh! I'm fine. My mind was off someplace instead of concentrating on all this work I have in front of me."

"Girl, I know what you mean. Cyn is joining us too, but Jasmine had something to do. So how does the grill sound to you?"

"Sure, that's fine."

"Yeah, at least it will get us out of the building. My morning started with total chaos so getting out of here for lunch will be good for me."

"It's the exact opposite here. I think that's why I was drifting. I'll meet you there at one o'clock sharp. See you then." Jill ended the call and tried to put a little dent in the work before lunchtime. The rest of the morning went by uneventfully, and before she knew it, it was one o'clock. Jill grabbed her purse and rushed out of the office.

Yvonne greeted Jill as she walked up to the table. "Hey, girlfriend, we were beginning to think you had been taken off by aliens or maybe something better. What took you so long?"

"Oh, just work issues," Jill replied as she fell into her seat.

They all ordered lunch, and then Cyn talked about her day. It went from one to the other as the conversation bounced around. After lunch, Jill returned to work, and the rest of the day went by in a blur as the office became very busy.

When it was almost quitting time, a man entered her office, asking for her by name, and told her that he had delivered her car, per Mr. Jordan's instructions. When she asked him about the cost, he waved her inquiry away, saying that it had been taken care of. He handed her the keys and left.

She felt so strange having things taken care of for her. This was a new experience; one she could get used to but dared not. Marcus was someone else's property. She would keep that thought in mind when she phoned him that evening to square up the bill.

She called Marcus when she got home, but her call went to voicemail. The next day, when Yvonne called, she found out that Marcus was out of town for the next two weeks to open a new office in Connecticut. Joseph would be joining him the following week to get the job completed for its opening, but there was no firm date for that as yet.

When Marcus called her back, it was two days later. Jill was distracted as she answered the phone, until she heard his voice.

"Hello?" She forgot to answer the phone with her usual business spiel but realized it too late."

"Jillian?" Marcus asked.

"Oh, hi, Marcus," she said suddenly, as the sound of his voice did strange things to her body. She was so happy to hear from him, only that feeling was not portrayed in her voice.

"Well, your enthusiasm sure can be deflating to a brother's ego."

"Sorry, brother," she said with a little giggle.

"Funny!"

Jill baited him even more. "I could see you as my brother. Couldn't you see me as your sister?"

"Definitely not! I got your message. What's this about your needing to reimburse me for an invoice?"

"For the repair to my car, remember?"

"Oh, that. I thought you were supposed to cook for me to take care of the repairs since you were demanding to pay me back."

"Ah, sure, but you know that tab is way more than cooking you a meal, Marcus Jordan."

"No, in my world nothing trumps food. That's my answer to your paying me back."

"Ok, Marcus. When is the meal to take place?"

"I haven't figured that out yet, but once I get back in town, we can set up a date. And you can surprise me with your culinary skill. Capisce?" he teased.

"*Capisco* [I understand]!" Jill replied with a touch of amusement in her voice.

"Nice comeback. Where did you learn to speak Italian?"

"When I took music lessons, my instructor was very fluent in the language and sometimes, he would say things to me that needed a response. That was one of the few words I could reply to him, but it's amazing how you knew what I was saying. I am light-years from speaking it fluently, but I can read a menu," she admitted, laughing. "So, what about you?"

"I learned just by the people I'm around. I did take Spanish in College, but I was so happy to get out of the class with a 'C'. I hated that class. So, what are your plans for this evening?"

"Jaz wants me, along with Cyn and Yvonne, to go to this nutritional meeting that's happening at the workout station—you know, the place where we go to exercise."

"Yes, I remember the place."

"She's invited us to come along with her, but I think her purpose is to check out the guy who's speaking there tonight. She always manages to find these health geeks, as Cyn calls them, and she dates them for a short time, then breaks up for some reason or another. Tonight, will be our third experiment with one of Jaz's prospective boyfriends," Jill said, laughing.

"I'm surprised that you're going, knowing that she just wants to check out some guy."

"We also wanted to make sure the guy is on the up-and-up—you know what I mean."

"Yes, I do. You all are looking out for your little sister, but remember she is a grown woman. If she really likes him, she may not take advice that doesn't make this guy sound good."

"I know, and that does bother me, but we'll be careful to tread lightly. How are you spending your evening, Marcus?"

"I'll probably work late, then head back to the hotel. Joe will be staying late with me. I have an interview in about forty-five minutes for a manager for this office. Once I choose someone for that position, the rest of the work to get this place up and running will be much easier."

"Who's going to train your new manager?" she asked.

"Sidney, along with two others, will be heading down for that part of the setup. Time is rolling. I'm going to grab a coffee and Danish from the little shop next door. But we will talk later, and you can tell me all about Jaz's health guru." They said good-bye and ended the call.

Jill busied herself with work, although she found herself smiling from time to time as she worked accounts—that was the effect he had on her. Garrett called her to go over some of her accounts. He asked her to come to his office, so Jill grabbed the files and headed there.

Jill and Marcus continued to communicate by phone for the next week. He called her a few times but told her that she could call him anytime. She decided not to do that because he was still seeing Sheree. She didn't want to give herself false hope, so she contented herself with waiting until he called her.

———

Jill had just left the market and was headed home when she noticed her oil light had come on. She pulled into the first car shop she saw, the Double Q Tune and Lube. She had passed the place many times on her way to work. When the technician finished working on her car, he answered her questions—and he seemed to smile at her a lot. Then, before she realized what was happening, he handed her his phone number. Jill accepted it, not wanting to hurt his feelings, but then she left.

As she drove down the highway, Jill did not plan to call him, although he was very funny. He reminded her of stepping back in time, like the brothers in that '70s flick *Car Wash*. Jill had evaded his questions about going on a date by saying she had a new job, and she would have to see how her schedule worked out. Jill thought she was safe because she hadn't given him her number, but a few weeks later, when she walked into her apartment after having dinner with Jasmine, her phone was ringing. She picked up and heard a slightly familiar voice on the other end of the line.

"Hey, Jilly! It's Tyrone from the Double Q. Girl, you are a busy lady. I called you last night, but I got no answer. So I tried again, and this time I got lucky."

"Hi, um, Tyrone. What a surprise. How did you get my number?" *There goes confidentiality out the window*, she thought.

"Girl, you blew my mind so bad that I forgot to ask you for it when we were talking. I knew you wouldn't mind me taking the liberty of getting it from the form you filled out in our office. I mean, I felt the magic between us, girl. I knew it was only a matter of time until I saw you again. I got it bad, girl, for you, so I hope I didn't jump the gun about this."

"I guess it's ok. I've been pretty busy. Ah, how are you?" she asked because of a lack of anything else to say.

"Oh, sugar, I'm feeling pretty good, now that I've caught up with ya."

"Oh!"

"Yeah, when I called last night, the phone just rang and rang, so I assumed you were out on a date or something."

"I have been working a lot. We lost a couple of people so it's the next man up. I have been really exhausted, lately."

"Yeah, I hear that. I know exactly what you mean. I work two jobs, and it wears me out, but I manage."

"Wow, that's some load. That would be hard for me, although sometimes I feel like I already work two jobs."

They both laughed.

"Kinda used to it by now. It hurts the love life, if you know what I mean." Tyrone gave a short laugh and then lowered his voice. "But I'm hoping things will change now."

"I would have thought you would have lots of women to choose from," Jill said rolling her eyes, wondering why she was still talking to him.

"Nah! Girlie, ain't nothing like that. I was hoping that you would be free to hang out with me on Friday night. I liked the way our conversation was flowing the other day, and I said to myself, *Ump! Tyrone, man, you got to see her again.* So, I'm hoping you will take me out of my misery and go out with me."

Jill tried not to laugh at this blatant come-on. She tried to figure out an escape, then she finally came up with an excuse. "I'm really not doing the dating thing right now. I'm just getting over a relationship. I hope you understand what I mean."

"I do, Jilly, but if you fall off a horse, the quickest way to get over it is to jump right back on. I'm not asking for a commitment, just two people enjoying each other's company. How is that?"

"I'll think about it, and if I change my mind, I will let you know, Ok?" Jill said, trying her best to end the call.

"Ok, guess I will have to wait by the phone cause I don't plan to let something as sweet as you get away. *Ciao, bella!*"

She heard the line go dead and quickly hung up the phone. *He does not appeal to me at all*, she thought. She shook with laughter as she silently mouthed the words, *ciao, bella*. Jill thought he had probably got that phrase from the movie *Mahogany* with Diana Ross and Billy Dee Williams, but he was certainly not the Billy Dee type.

The next day at lunch when the girlfriends got together, it seemed that everyone had decided to go to the club on Friday night, except Jill.

"What are your plans if you're not going to hang out with us?" Yvonne asked her. "You aren't keeping tall, bronze, and rich to yourself, are you?"

Before Jill could answer, Cyn beat her to it. "I don't blame her. If I had something that fine, I would keep him to myself too."

All the girls started laughing and Jill joined them.

"No, I do not have a date. I just thought I would stay home and rent a good movie."

"Oh, no. You can't do that! You have plenty of time to be old. Come out with us!" Cyn pleaded.

"Yes, Jill. I was hoping to introduce you to my new man. How about it? Please?" Jasmine said excitedly. They all looked at Jill expectantly.

"What do you mean, your new man? I thought you were getting with the guru from the workout station. That was, like, two months ago." Jill looked surprised.

"Oh, didn't I tell you? He was not so much a health nut as a gigolo. He was using the workout station as a pickup spot. So, I had to kick him to the curb, girlfriend. Now my latest is a businessman, and he is so fine. You got to come out with us and meet him." Jaz winked at Jill.

"You best agree with her, or she will worry you to death," Cyn added, shaking her head.

"Ok, Jaz, count me in," Jill agreed.

Friday night at the club, there were no empty tables. The girls were having a blast, and Jill found she liked Jasmine's new man. The girls were busy on the dance floor, hardly getting a chance to sit down before being asked to dance again. Much to Jill's disappointment, Sheree was there with a full table. Jill had walked off the dance floor once and when she sat down, she looked up to find Sheree staring at her. She said something to one of the women in her group, then they both looked at Jill.

Jill looked away as Yvonne asked her to go to the ladies' room with her. Jill was glad to get away from the staring eyes. Once in the restroom, Jill waited for Yvonne and then decided to freshen her lipstick. As she was looking for it in her purse, she heard the door open but did not look up. Then she heard Sheree's voice.

"So, this is where you ran off to. I know it must be disappointing that Marcus is not here. But you still have plenty of men to whore around with. It's a virtual playing field out there." Sheree then complained to her friend. "Renee, this is the bitch I told you about, always following Marcus around. He is much too nice to tell her to leave him alone, so I guess it's my job!"

"Sheree, if you are going to talk about me, at least tell the truth! Marcus and I are only friends. If you weren't such the jealous type, you'd see—"

"All I see, bitch, is that everywhere my man goes, you are not far away. You need to listen and listen good, or—"

"Or what, bitch?" A voice from the doorway said.

They all turned around to see Jazmin in the doorway, flanked by Cyn.

"Come on, tell us what comes after the *or*, Sheree!" Cyn said. "Because it sounds like something Jaz and I would love to be a part of you know. But let me give you another little bit of information. If you mess with Jill, chickee, you're damn sure gonna mess with us!"

Yvonne came out of the stall and walked to the sink to wash her hands, while keeping an eye on Sheree and her friend. Sheree looked at the three girls who were waiting for a reaction from her.

Sheree laughed. "Oh, I see. So, you are her bodyguards?"

No one said anything; they just stared at Sheree and Renee. "Tell

your girlfriend to stop chasing my man, and everything will be fine!"
Sheree said, glaring at Jill.

"Oh, wait a minute now. You definitely have it all wrong, girl,
because the way we see it, if anybody's doing the chasing, it's definitely
your boyfriend! But wait! What did you call him—your man?" Cyn
started laughing, and Yvonne and Jaz joined in. "You need to check that
'cause I don't think you have the grip that you should have! Everybody
knows that Marcus's nose is wide open lately, and it's not for you!" Cyn
said, then turned her back on Sheree. "Ladies let's get out of here. She
is making us miss all this good music." Cyn turned her head, looking
directly at her friends.

"Good idea! I am so tired of this foolishness!" Jill complained. The
girls waited for her to walk out first, leaving Sheree simmering.

When they got back to the table, everyone was laughing but Jill.

"Can you believe her?" Jasmine said.

"She is so typical," said Yvonne.

"*Desperate* is more like it," Cyn chimed in. "She feels threatened,
and she should feel that way because my boy Marcus is so over her!"

The girls all agreed with Cyn. Jill just looked from one to the other.
The waiter appeared, and they ordered drinks.

"I don't know, girls. I feel so mad that she would act like that," Jill
said. "I met her twice—well, you could say once because the first time
I saw her, she just stared at me. The second time, they were headed to
lunch, and I tried to walk past, but you know Marcus—he had to stop
me and introduce her to me. She was so nasty; she looked down her
nose at me. Now tonight, Marcus is not even here, and she still is acting
as if I ran off with him or something! I am sorry you guys were put in
the middle of this!"

"We enjoyed it," Cyn said. "Furthermore, when it comes to you or
anyone of us, we stick together!"

All the girls agreed with Cyn.

Later that night, Jill kept playing the scene with Sheree over and
over in her head until she finally fell asleep. The next morning, Jill got

up late, ate breakfast, and then cleaned around her place. As she was heading home from the grocery store, she thought that if she dated other people, Sheree would probably stop accusing her of being after Marcus. She remembered how Sheree became all smiles when she thought Jill was dating Garrett, so maybe that kind of distraction would make Sheree back off. Since she had no other prospects, maybe she would take Tyrone up on his offer of going out.

The following week, at lunch on Wednesday, Yvonne brought up the club and asked who was going. All the girls said they were—except Jill.

"I have a date for Friday night," Jill said quietly. They all looked at each other with knowing smiles on their faces. "And no! It isn't with Marcus. I met this guy at the Double Q where I stopped to get my oil changed."

Jasmine sputtered with laughter at the innuendo, and the other girls followed suit.

"No! Oh, my God! Y'all, come on now. I'm being serious. Really, he is a technician there, and we started talking. He is not *all that* by any stretch of the word, but he made me laugh so I thought, why not when he asked me out. I haven't been on any dates since coming to this town, and I thought I should venture out more." Jill looked around the table at faces that had become sober after the laughing had ceased.

"Girl don't pay us any attention," Yvonne said as she patted Jill on the shoulder. "You know we're happy for you. Who knows? Marcus could have some competition!"

The other girls laughed as Cyn chimed in, "Not a chance!"

"This date will give me a chance to get back into dating. It's been a while for me, and I need to meet other people, you know? I just somehow found myself agreeing to go out with him. It's only going to be for Friday night anyway, for right now. He works two jobs, so he stays busy. Who knows? If things don't go well, I might drop in on you guys."

They all agreed with Jill and hoped that the evening would turn out great for her. They talked a few minutes longer before heading back to work.

Chapter

5

On Friday night, Jill dressed very casually in nice jeans and a cream-colored blouse with sleeves that dangled over her hands. She sprayed her hair to make the curls hang down in little spirals. She took a final gaze in her hall mirror before grabbing her keys and heading out to meet Tyrone at the budget cinema.

The budget cinema was located on the east end of town. She had heard that the theater catered to mostly the younger crowd, and it tended to get a little rowdy at times. When she arrived at the theater, people were everywhere on the street, just hanging out. Jill felt a little apprehensive when she noticed that she was under heavy scrutiny by a gang of boys standing farther away from the theater. Then she saw Tyrone; he stood out in the crowd with his yellow flowered silk shirt, yellow slacks, and white shoes. Jill smothered an *Oh my God,* as she prepared to get out of her car and face her date's bright attire. He was standing in front of the ticket booth. When she walked up to him, she noticed that people stared, and some covered their mouths to keep from laughing out loud.

"Hi! I'm not late, am I?" Jill said, smiling.

His eyes took inventory of her body. Tyrone's face suddenly exploded with a huge grin. "Hello! Jill, wow! You're looking really sweet tonight, and no, you are not late. I'm just here a little early because I know this place is usually packed on Friday nights. I've got our tickets, but the show does not start until another hour. You want to go sit on one of the benches, and we can rap and get more acquainted?" Tyrone led Jill to a bench a few feet away.

Jill felt a little strange because he had already gotten the tickets without asking what movie she wanted to see. She felt a little annoyed as they sat down to talk. "So, what's the name of the movie we will be seeing?" She tried to conceal her annoyance with a tight smile.

Tyrone seemed oblivious to her mood. He smiled as he talked about his choice of the movie. "*The Resurrection of Dark Man*," he told her. When Jill frowned, he misread her expression as one of not being familiar with the movie. "It's a scary flick; they're the best. I know you are going to love it." He spoke as if he already knew her.

"I don't really get into horror movies, Tyrone," Jill said gently, suddenly taking an interest in the people passing by.

"Ah, come on, Jilly. If you get scared, we can cuddle. That would be my pleasure." He looked at her as if she was a juicy piece of steak.

Jill felt like kicking herself for agreeing to go out with him. Tyrone slid closer on the bench and placed his arm around Jill, causing her to stiffen.

"Oh, I'm sure I'll be fine," she said as she became more irritated.

"You'll love this movie, girlie. It has some good actors in it. I know how the women love scary movies, cause they get to cuddle with their man, if you know what I mean." He gave a short laugh as he looked at Jill's expression.

Jill leaned away from him. She was irritated by Tyrone's assumption that they would be sharing such intimacy when she hardly knew him. She gradually put some space between them. "Really, Tyrone, is that what they say? I've never heard that before." Jill dreaded the rest of the evening.

"I'm afraid so, Jilly. I catch women staring at me all the time. I don't lift weights, but I manage to keep my body pretty much tight." He began flexing for her benefit, but from where Jill was sitting, she couldn't see any muscle mass that could be construed as part of someone who was built.

"Tyrone, you really amaze me."

At that moment, someone called out to Tyrone. Both Jill and Tyrone turned saw a man crossing the street in a hurry. He was of small statue, a little rough-looking around the edges, and he walked with what was once known as a "pimp" to his stride. When he stopped directly in front of them, Jill could see he had a tooth missing in the front of his mouth, but the others were covered in gold.

He gave Jill a lecherous grin. "Rone! Man, I have been looking all over town for you. So, who have you got here? Not your usual, I see." Before Tyrone could answer, the man turned to Jill and rubbed his hand down the front of his body, keeping his eyes on her. "Hi there, sweet, hot, and fine. I'm Ray, Tyrone's main man. Where did Tyrone find such a fine package like you?"

Jill gazed from Tyrone's sour face to the leering man, and when Tyrone still said nothing, she said, "I'm Jill. I live here in town."

"Well, I'd like to hear more. You see, Tyrone and I share everything, and right now I'm just tickled pink at the prospect of it."

"Dammit, Ray, don't you go there," Tyrone said. "This is my date for the evening, and Dogg, you are overstepping right about now. Don't play me like that, man. This ain't the right time. You know what I mean? You need to get to stepping, if you get my drift."

Ray gave Tyrone a funny look, then turned back to Jill with a grin. "Well, I guess I just got kicked to the curb, so I'll just take myself somewhere that I'm appreciated. But angel, if this fool doesn't treat you right, just give me a holler. I'm in the phonebook under Ray Jones Jr. Ciao, baby." He ignored Tyrone as he walked away.

Even after he'd gone, Jill didn't know what to do or say. She was still in shock from the weird happenings between Tyrone and his friend.

"Jill, baby, I'm sorry you had to see that clown," Tyrone apologized. "I became his friend 'cause I felt sorry for him, and now, whenever he sees me, he gets carried away. I think the movie will be starting soon. Let's go get a good seat."

Tyrone ushered her along, and Jill was glad for the distraction of finding the theater that their film was being shown in, so she wouldn't have to voice her opinion about Tyrone's friend. Tyrone didn't mention the episode with his friend again, so Jill tried to focus on getting through the movie, especially since she hated horror flicks.

Several times during the movie, Tyrone turned to Jill when she jumped during a particularly scary scene, and then he finally opened his arms. It was amazing to her, but Jill felt a lot better with his arms wrapped around her.

After they left the theater, Tyrone teased her about burying herself in his chest. "Ah, Jilly, you are nothing but a scaredy-cat. Do you really think that horror stuff is real? That movie had you so scared that I thought at any time you would just haul ass and leave me sitting right there." Tyrone bent over laughing as they walked toward the parking lot.

Jill rolled her eyes. "Ok, mister 'I ain't scared of anything'. I think that's enough joking at my expense. Next time, I'll pick the movie, and let's see who will have a good time."

Tyrone suddenly stopped and stood there with a smile on his face. Jill turned around to see him standing still; then he slowly walked toward her with a huge grin on his face. When he got closer, he walked right into her personal space and slowly wrapped his arms around her, resting his head against her forehead.

"So, I guess I must have passed the first phase, huh, Jilly? Another date with you is worth sitting through those mushy love scenes. I don't know—maybe it can help me get better at being a lover. Women like it when a man goes all soft. Maybe I can learn how to turn a girl like you on—make you as hot for me as I am for you. Hm, what do you think? I tell you what—hold that thought." Tyrone lowered his head until he had captured her mouth. Jill felt the warmth of his lips and tasted the peanut butter flavor of the candy he had been eating. But it was a wet and sloppy kiss. There was no electric charge or good feeling. She felt more violated than anything else. She had to push him away, as his kiss got too demanding.

"I know, you got to get used to me," he said. "We can take it slowly, but man! I feel it in my bones. *Oh*, girl! This just tells me what I figured all along!"

Jill looked at him with raised eyebrows after wiping her mouth from his assault. "And what was that?" She said as she took a few steps back from him.

"That you and I would be totally explosive together. Girl, I know for a fact that you would be hot in bed—my bed, that is," he said with certainty.

"How can you tell all that from one brief kiss? Are you psychic or something?"

Tyrone smiled as he took a step back, then grabbed her hand as they walked toward her car. "If I were psychic, I would definitely be looking in my little crystal ball to see when we would take that tumble cause, girl, you got the kind of body I like. I like my women with curves." He laughed out loud at the look on Jill's face. "What?"

Jill shook her head at him. "Tyrone, compliments are nice, but this is overkill here. This is only our first date, so slow down, cowboy. All right?"

Tyrone raised both hands as if in surrender. "All right! All right, I can take a hint. I promise to slow down, as long as we can see each other again soon. If it will make you feel better, we can do the public thing again. Say, another movie or a club. You pick. How's that? Let it never be said that old Tyrone is bossy. What you say, Jilly?"

She thought for a few minutes and replied, "I'll think about it and give you a call. Tell me something, Tyrone—do you like to dance?"

"Ah shucks, girl. I love to dance, as long as there is some old school." He showed her his dance moves.

"Great! I'll give you a call if there is anything special going on at this club I like. Maybe we can go there, and you can show me around the dance floor." Jill smiled as he continued to dance.

"Can you do the Popcorn or the Smurf? I won't show you all of my stuff now; you might go home and practice and try to show me up. I'll lay it on you when we go to that club of yours."

"I guess I'd better say good night, Tyrone."

"What about a nightcap? It's still early, only 11:45."

Jill shook her head as she took out her keys and got into her car. "Sorry, Tyrone, but I have an early day tomorrow. I'll have to get a raincheck."

She rolled down her window, and although Tyrone looked a little put out, he finally nodded and leaned in through the window to give her a kiss. Jill had to push away a little because he was pushing her up against her headrest. The kiss caught her totally off guard; she did not like his being so rough.

"Sorry, Tyrone, but I must go. Good night."

"Night, Jilly. You know you can't always run away. I know you want it as badly as I do, but for now, I'll let you have your way. Night." Tyrone stepped away from the car as she revved the engine and put it in gear. Waving, she drove off.

"Oh Lord, I thought I wouldn't get out of there with my clothes on from the look in his eyes!" she exclaimed out loud. "Lord, help me! I like him but I don't feel the attraction he is talking about. I just want to be friends! Why can't men understand that?"

Across town, the activity at the club was on the quiet side. The girls sat at their table, watching Marcus's table, where he sat with Sheree, Joe, and two other women; moments later, another tall and handsome guy joined Marcus's group.

"Oh my, Yvonne. Who is that guy who's just walked over to Marcus's table?" Cyn asked.

"I don't know, but hopefully, he is the husband of one of those women and the disgruntled brother of the other one who's left over," Yvonne said, and the girls all laughed.

"Hey, Yvonne, why don't you go say hi to Joe and inquire because that is something I could go for, if he is single," Cyn said.

Yvonne looked over at the other table and then looked at the girls with a huge smile.

"Uh-oh. I know that look. What are you up to?" Cyn asked.

"Well, maybe I could knock out two birds with one stone," she said, smiling.

"What do you mean?" Jaz asked.

"I could ask Joe who that guy is, but I can also casually throw it out there that Jill is on a date, just to see Marcus's reaction," Yvonne said. "What do you think?"

The girls all laughed.

"I like it—smooth and crafty," said Cyn.

They watched as Yvonne walked over to the other table. It wasn't before Joe looked in her direction as she walked toward them. When she reached the table, Joe stood up."

"Hey, Yvonne! Are you enjoying yourself tonight?"

"We are, but I miss my other buddy. I hope she's enjoying herself." Yvonne spoke loud enough for everyone at the table to hear.

"Your other buddy? Who might that be?" Joe asked.

"Jill. You remember her, don't you?" Yvonne said innocently.

Joe crossed his arms over his chest and said, "Oh yeah! So where is she tonight?"

"She went on a date with some guy she met. We're waiting for her to call us when she is safely back at home. I guess we're like big sisters or something." Yvonne noticed that she now had Marcus's attention. *Bingo*, she thought.

Joe introduced the new guy as one of his old buddies. Sheree's girlfriend was trying hard to monopolize his attention.

When Yvonne turned to walk away, she pulled Joe to the side and whispered, "If I were you, I would warn your buddy about the sharks. See ya later."

Joe smiled as he watched her walk back to her table.

The girls stayed only an hour longer before they left the club. They planned to meet on Saturday for their weekly workout.

The weekend flew by, leaving Jill feeling as if she had only been off for one day. On Monday, it seemed that time just stood still. She felt that Mondays were never short days, and that morning seemed to drag. Jill was sitting at her desk, her mind drifting, when she heard someone walk into her office. She turned her head to find Marcus leaning against the wall near her door, his arms folded, just looking at her.

"Daydreaming are we?" he asked. "Or are we feeling a little tired, perhaps hungover?"

She looked startled as she gathered herself. "No, workload sucks today, that's all. What's up?" she said, sitting up in her chair.

"I thought maybe you would like to go to lunch with me?" he said, coming into her office and closing the door.

"Oh! It's lunchtime already! Great. I've wasted so much time this morning. Sorry, Marcus, I'll have to eat- in today. The workload is crazy."

He hesitated, looking her over. "You sure you're, ok?" he asked.

She frowned. "Yes, I am. Why?"

"How was your date Saturday night?"

Her eyes grew wide as she looked at him. "You mean Friday—wait. How did you know about my date?" she asked as she looked at him.

"Oh, a little bird told me. Well, technically, the bird wasn't talking to me. I just overheard it."

"Ha! So, which one of the girls did you pick for that information?" She tried her best to give him a stern look, which only made him chuckle.

"I feel insulted that you would think I would pick your friends for information on your carryings-on." He gave her the full dramatic effect, with hand over heart.

She rolled her eyes. "Ok, enough with the drama! Besides, you are a lousy actor." She smiled slightly when he feigned hurt feelings again with his hand still over his heart. Then he switched his stance by crossing his arms.

"I will tell you about my date. He is just someone I met while having my oil changed at the Double Q. He asked me out to the movies. End of story. No big deal."

He tried to make light of his snooping. "Sorry if I was getting into your personal business. I just wanted to make sure everything is ok. Why don't I check him out?"

When Jill looked at him, she saw something there that made her heart flutter while at the same time, his look made her nervous. She covered it with a slight smile. "Ah no. It won't be necessary, Father, since I won't be seeing him again."

"Father? I am not trying to be your father. I'm just looking out for you. Guys can be dogs, Jill. But did you say you're not going to see him again. Why? Did he try something?"

She could not help it when a laugh slipped out. "I appreciate that you are looking out for me, but it's not necessary at this point. I am not seeing him again, and no, he did ... uh, anyway, it's nothing. I just didn't feel any chemistry."

Marcus felt relieved, for some crazy reason, but he did notice her hesitation when he asked if her date had tried anything. *I'll let it go*, he thought. *She's not going to see him again anyway.*

Two weeks had passed since Jill's talk with Marcus. She could not say for sure how it happened, but she had agreed to go on another date with Tyrone. *I've got to be out of my mind*, she thought. *I'm definitely leading him on, and that is not what I want to do.* She didn't know if seeing Tyrone again was to get Sheree off her back or to convince herself that what she felt for Marcus was just an attraction. When it came to Tyrone, she found herself laughing at his craziness. He did seem to fill in a tiny portion of her life that was empty—that is, if she were to admit there was something nice about having him in her life.

Since Marcus had been working in the new office, she didn't see him as much. Usually, it was around the office, but he called her often just to see if she was ok. That gesture just allowed her feelings to deepen for him, and she did not want that to happen. Although she missed their time together and felt sad about it, deep down she knew it was better this way. She also read the society pages of the paper, and there was usually some tidbit about him and his girlfriend or some business venture he was embarking on. She also read about the buzz around him as a candidate for future mayor. She definitely had Marcus on the brain and wondered if there was a clinic that could help her get rid of her addiction to him.

Jill's life with Tyrone had gotten into a routine; this kept her busy. Tyrone stood six foot three and slender. He was brown-skinned with lots of hair, which he wore in a huge Afro style when he wasn't wearing a do-rag on his head. He reminded Jill of Huggy Bear, a character on a detective show in the '70s. She often smiled at this thought because Tyrone always seemed to think that women found him irresistible. He once told Jill not to worry if women approached him, 'Just stay calm. I'll handle everything,' he'd said. His unfounded reasoning about the depth of his charm often astounded her. When Jill commented on his out-of-date wardrobe, he responded, "You don't recognize classic style, especially things of the vintage variety."

She got home late from work one evening and found a message from him: "Hey, baby, this is Tyrone. I just called to let you know that I'll be there around seven on the tick-tock. I will bring us some take-out Chinese for dinner—and how about *you* as the dessert? Mm-mm good! Ciao, baby!"

Jill shook her head and walked down the hall for a long soak in the tub before Tyrone arrived. While Jill was in the tub, she thought, *this thing with Tyrone is a waste of time. He wants to have sex with me, but that's the last thing on my mind with him.* Time seemed to have moved very fast, as she realized that she had been dating Tyrone for a few months. *Now that I think about it,* she told herself; *in examining things closely, I've done more laughing* at *him than* with *him.* The thought made Jill feel guilty about being with him.

He spent most of his time admiring himself—*as if he was a natural wonder or something*, Jill thought. At least he made her laugh. Tyrone was a typical wannabe player type, but he lacked certain skills. He was selfish and quick to anger if he didn't get his way. Jill lately suspected him of being dishonest, but she had no proof so far.

Jill got dressed and asked aloud, "Why do I put myself through this? Surely, I can find a man who excites me." Speaking out loud helped her to analyze her question. Her mind conjured up Marcus's face, and warmth spread all over her body, like the effects of a man's hand bringing excitement to a woman's body. Jill swore aloud, trying to steer her mind away from such thoughts. She went to her dressing table, putting more effort into picking out her makeup. She wondered why she was getting dolled up for a man who had such little effect on her. By 7:05 p.m., Jill had finished dressing, but there was no sign of Tyrone.

The phone rang, and Jill rushed to answer it, thinking it was Tyrone—but it was someone selling vacation packages. Jill snapped, "No, thank you," but the persistent telemarketer on the other end of the line refused to hang up—so she angrily hung up the phone. She immediately felt ashamed of her behavior and scolded herself for being so rude.

At nine o'clock, there was still no sign of Tyrone. Jill gave up on him and the Chinese food and made a peanut butter and jelly sandwich. One hour later, she tried to watch TV, but her anger at Tyrone took over, and she cut off the TV. She grabbed a book and went to her bedroom, hoping this would put her to sleep. Thirty minutes later, she was still unable to concentrate on the book, so Jill closed it. She was still so angry with Tyrone that she turned on some music, hoping it would help her calm down enough to fall asleep. It was a restless sleep, as she tossed and turned.

The next morning, Jill was late for work since her alarm never went off. This bad start to her day, after a disastrous night, only contributed to Jill's dark mood—her car would not start, and she had to catch a cab to work. Jill's mood especially singled out the male species; she knew, with all her bad luck, that her car had to be male. Once the cab dropped her at work, she rushed into the building, barely catching the elevator as the doors were closing, but they once again opened and revealed Mr. CEO himself, Marcus Jordan. He stood just inside the elevator, looking right at Jill with a raised eyebrow and a question in his eyes. "Good morning, Jill!" he said, sounding spunky.

The sound of his chipper voice only added fuel to her irritation. The smile she gave him was not so friendly, nor did it reach her eyes as she muttered something unintelligible. She took in the other occupants of the elevator but avoided looking at Marcus—although her eyes were hungry for the sight of him.

Marcus was annoyed by her brief nod in his direction. He refused to be ignored so he tried again, lowering his voice to a quiet tone but looking directly at her as he leaned in closer. "Hey, is everything ok?" Marcus stared steadily at Jill, waiting for her answer. As he studied her, he could have sworn she was counting. Was she counting to ten before speaking to him? What had he done?

Jill released a long sigh. "Everything is just fine, Marcus." She had replied as if the words were being pushed out, and she continued to avoid looking at him. When the elevator reached another floor, other people crammed into the small space, pushing her closer to Marcus. She felt that she was like a ticking time bomb. She was wound up so tightly, and she thought, *all these feelings can't be because Tyrone stood me up.* Maybe it had triggered something because she had not seen Marcus in a while and she needed a fix, but that would mess up her plan of trying to stay away. The emotions she felt were driving her crazy. She knew that deep down in her core, all she wanted to do was block out the world and just be in his arms at that moment. That was all her mind could think of. It further irritated her that she could not shut off those thoughts of Marcus. Jill could feel his eyes still on her, and although she turned her back to him as he spoke, she could hear the cheerfulness in his voice.

"Wow, my radar is picking up on some negative vibes. I have some research to do," he mumbled.

Jill could not believe he was having fun at her expense. She shook her head and what he saw in her eyes was suddenly put into words. "I don't think anything can help me at this point, but thanks for trying. Later, Marcus," she said, sounding annoyed.

Two seconds later she got off on her floor and noticed the other occupants on the elevator were watching her and Marcus. She inwardly grimaced. *That's all I need*, she thought; *In addition to everything else, to be part of the gossip.* What would the office grapevine conjure up next about Jill and Marcus's relationship? It would probably be something to top the charts. *Oh well!* Jill thought. *Who cares what the latest rumor will be?* She just wanted to feel not so agitated because the day was already underway. "Thanks, Tyrone," she muttered as she headed to her office.

An hour later, Jill had just left Mr. Rogers's office, arms loaded with files, when she noticed Sarah staring off into space. Jill took the files to her office and then went to Sarah's desk to say hello and to pick up any messages Sarah had for her.

Jill leaned against the corner of the desk and smiled at Sarah. "How has your morning been, Sarah?"

Sarah rolled her eyes in answer. "Jill, you don't want to know. First thing this morning, Mr. Rogers came in like a bull in a China shop. He, um, just caused havoc all over the place with all these changes, sending everyone off in all directions. It was not until Marcus came in that he settled down and began to act like a human again. I don't know what Marcus said to him, but they were in his office for a while. Whatever it was, it worked."

Jill became curious. "So, Marcus Jordan was here this morning?"

"Yes," replied Sarah. "Oh, and before I forget, he went into your office, hoping to see you. I told him you were in a meeting with financials, and then you would be meeting with Mr. Rogers. He said he'd call you later. I swear, looking at him helped me to get over Mr. Rogers's tirade. Oh boy! He smelled so good, not to mention that he took time to tell me not to worry about Garrett. He's fine now, and it's nothing that I did. I did manage a thank-you, and I didn't freeze like I always do. He nodded and smiled when I said thank you. Then he was out the door. I wish I worked for him."

Jill laughed at Sarah's reaction to Marcus. "I'll talk to you later," Jill told her. "I have to get some work done before the meeting."

She returned to her office and closed the door. Her phone started ringing, and she rushed over and picked up, on the third ring. "Good morning. Jillian Weston speaking."

"Good. At least you sound better than you did earlier. I came down to your office, but you were in a meeting. What time will you be free for lunch?"

Marcus's voice caught her off guard. "Well, um, Marcus, I'm working through lunch and leaving at two o'clock today to find out why my car wouldn't start this morning. Sorry, maybe some other time. I really appreciate the offer."

The other end of the line became so quiet that Jill wondered if he had hung up. Then he said, "Jill, you have to eat, and if your car hasn't been checked out yet, I can have my mechanic do that. He's familiar with your car."

"Marcus, I can't put you to that trouble. I owe you enough as it is. Besides, it's asking way too much of you. I mean, it's not your job to keep saving me. Eventually, it will put a strain on our friendship." Once Jill began to speak, she could not seem to stop. She could almost see his expression as he spoke.

"Tell you what—let him check it out to give you an idea of the cost and what's wrong with it. We can go from there, ok?"

Jill exhaled slowly. It was useless to argue with him, so she gave in. "I guess so, Marcus, but I want to pay for the repairs."

"Fine with me. Now, what else has you down? Yes, I'm being nosy. What else are friends for?"

"Marcus, there is no problem. I just woke up late and then the car thing."

"I see. We'll go someplace relaxing for lunch, and when you come back, everything will be fine. By the way, I hope you're starving because I missed breakfast. I'm twice as hungry as I was this morning. Are you game?"

"Ok, but nothing fancy. Where are we going, or haven't you planned that far ahead yet?"

"I think I'll surprise you. I have the place. I just need to see your lovely face downstairs 'round one o'clock. Is that good for you?" he asked.

"Sounds good," she answered.

"And our destination will be a surprise for now. Later, Jill."

Before she could reply, he got off the line. Jill still sat there, holding the receiver, minutes later. *This is the effect Marcus always seems to have on me.* She stared straight ahead with an incredible feeling running through her body and with a smile on her face. She was hardly ever shy around him as long as things did not get too personal. Something about the way he handled her made her more confident.

Jill contemplated their conversation for a few minutes and then realized that she was in a much better mood than earlier that morning. Marcus was responsible for her change in mood. He always seemed to take her away from whatever had brought her down and somehow made her look at things in an entirely different way. Yes, she was a lucky girl to have a friend like him. She looked upward and said, "Thank you," and then turned back to the work at hand.

A few minutes after one o'clock, Jill exited the elevator and glanced around the lobby in search of Marcus, but he was not there. She walked over to the large glass windows and stood there, looking out.

Marcus quietly came up behind her. He was becoming aware that every time he saw her, something inside of him seemed to settle down and become calm. The feeling, whatever it was, scared him because it had never happened before her. He didn't know exactly how it happened or what to do about it. He leaned around her and said softly, trying not to startle her, "I hope I didn't keep you waiting too long. It seems like whenever I'm about to leave, everybody wants to talk to me about something." He put his hand on her back and gently guided Jill toward the exit doors to the employee parking deck. Marcus kept his hand casually on the center of her back and opened his car door for her.

She sat down inside, and he admired her shapely legs as her skirt slid up slightly. He closed the door and took a deep breath to settle his body from the effect she had on him. Then he walked around to his side of the car and got in.

"Well, Mr. Jordan, CEO extraordinaire, that's what your title implies—just ask Marcus." She smiled at him.

Marcus looked at her, and the feelings came to life inside him from just watching her speak. It had been so long since they had shared any time together, and he'd missed it. The way you say my name along with the title, makes my job sounds much bigger than I feel it is. Maybe I missed something. I think that with such a title, I need someone to schedule all these people who demand my time. I need to hire you. Imagine—I can see it now—your being at my beck and call," he said, then watched her reaction before he started to laugh.

Jill rolled her eyes. "You wish, Jordan! The line is too long, and I already have a job, Mr. Smarty-Pants. Too bad you didn't think of that way back when, but it's too late now. You missed your opportunity." She smiled, but his next words took the smile off her face and replaced it with shock.

"I know, and it's not like me to miss opportunities. I must not have been on my A-game that day! But the way I see it, someone like you needs a strong hand. It's like breaking a horse that's never been tamed. You go at it strong and steady to let it know who's the boss right away!" he said seriously, frowning. He found it hard to hold the frown when she stuck her tongue out at him.

"Sounds like a control freak!" she said and watched as his shoulders shook with laughter. She fell victim to the sound and burst out laughing.

"See? This is what I miss. You, my friend, are in your own special place."

When Jill looked over at him, his smile seemed to have died away completely, and she met the totally intense look in his eyes. She knew instantly that she was getting into deep water with him—and she didn't have a quick comeback, so she faked interest in the control panel of the car.

"What's wrong? Cat got your pretty little tongue. Actually, I may be on to something. That remark wiped the smile clean off your face." Marcus was the one smiling now.

"Oh, shush! You know I blush easily. Besides, I'm already on your girlfriend's hit list, so I thought I'd be the bigger person and quit while I am ahead. There is no need for me to completely blow your mind with all my smarts. You would be ruined, I tell ya!"

When she heard his laughter, she could not hold off any longer. It was so infectious that suddenly, she joined in.

"I have really missed this kind of talk between us. It's always so much fun. Girl, you make me laugh like nobody else." He looked at her, and she felt the atmosphere change—the same way it always did with them.

She tried once again to get them on safer ground. "So where is our destination for lunch?"

He gave her a slow smile. "The Ship's Cabin on Pier 23. Heard of it?"

Jill's face exploded into a huge grin. "You're kidding me, aren't you?" She bounced in her seat with excitement.

"No."

"Food is one thing, but the Ship's Cabin is another thing altogether, Marcus, my friend."

"How would you know? You're always telling me that you don't go out much. You also said you'd never been anywhere fancy in this town."

"I've never been there, but I heard that it is *the* joint. Yvonne has been there, and she goes on and on about the place. Cyn has been planning to check it out, but it's way off my budget. Do you go there a lot?"

"I haven't been there much lately, but the food is always great. I think you will like it. The dinner shows are the best. Maybe we can go one night when the workload isn't too hectic."

"That would be great, Marcus; just let me know when. Oh, no—I'm not dressed for that place. I can't go in there looking like …" She looked down at her black silk jumpsuit. It buttoned from the waist up, but she had three of the top buttons undone, hinting at her cleavage, above that a black choker adorned her neck.

"You look very nice to me. Your outfit its very fitting for the restaurant, so no further argument. We are going to have an outstanding lunch and enjoy ourselves."

They looked at each other, and she could feel his reassurance. She smiled and nodded her head.

Marcus found an empty parking spot. He shut off the engine, and they went inside the popular eatery. The maître d' greeted Marcus and immediately showed them to a table; he wanted Marcus's approval. Marcus had phoned ahead for a reservation, and they seemed to be seated at one of the best tables in the house. They had a panoramic view of a coastal inlet. Marcus marveled at Jill's appreciation for everything.

"Marcus, this place lives up to its reputation so far. Thank you for not letting my stubbornness get in the way of such a great surprise."

"Glad you are enjoying it." He smiled at her, then his face took on a serious look. "I don't worry so much about your stubbornness. It's when the conversation becomes more personal between us that you always find a way to change the subject." He watched her reaction.

"Marcus, I don't! You just get a little heavy sometimes, and I try to lighten things up."

"No, you try to avoid certain subjects." When she gave him an incredulous look, he said, "Let me explain. Whenever you feel unsure of something or maybe afraid that I am getting too personal, you try to laugh things off, hoping you can get me off the subject." He paused briefly before saying, "Anyway, you don't need to hide anything from me. I am your friend … always. I feel comfortable with you." When he finished speaking, he looked at her for a response.

Jill felt like she was back in the elevator from earlier and all the feelings were just waiting to attack as they cornered her. When she spoke, she felt bare, as if she had exposed herself, and she was not ready to reveal any part of her deeper feelings to him. Still, she knew she had to say something to explain her behavior. She didn't want to make him feel that she was ignoring his feelings.

"You are easy to be with," she told him, "And I feel so, so comfortable and safe with you in the most unimaginable way. You don't have to impress me with words. I like you for who you are—and not the size of your wallet either, although that does have its perks." She offered a nervous smile, and after a few seconds, he responded with a thoughtful look and a smile of his own. "I've never had a friend like you, so forgive me if sometimes I act a little weird. I'm not shutting you out when things get a little personal; it's just that I'm respecting our friendship, and I would never do anything to cause problems in your personal life. So, if I have made you feel that you are overstepping in any way, then I'm sorry; it was not intentional. You have made my life so much better just by knowing you. So now are we cool?"

"We always have been, baby girl. You think we connect in the most unimaginable way, huh? I like that. I like that a lot. But I wanna know why you were in such a mood this morning. I'm not buying the car breaking down or the alarm clock issue, so come clean, Jillian. I'm taking advantage of my clout as your very good friend. Now spill." He looked at her intently.

A few moments went by before she spoke. Unconsciously, she played with the stem on her water glass. "Well, you know a couple of weeks ago when you came to my office, and I told you that I had decided not to pursue a relationship with Tyrone—that's the guy's name. Somehow, I never got around to breaking it off, and I'm still seeing him. There's no chemistry between us—ah, well, I mean in a sexual way," she said with a short laugh. "I am not attracted to him, but he does make me laugh. I feel bad because I find myself laughing *at* him more than *with* him. It seems every time I try to break it off, something happens, and now, I just find myself going with the flow. But he has this tendency to stand me up or not even call to say he can't make it. Last night, he was supposed to come over and bring dinner, but he never showed or called. I should be used to it by now because it's happened before. It's almost as though he thinks I will accept whatever way he treats me. I ate a peanut butter and jelly sandwich and went to bed, totally pissed! This morning, I woke up late with a headache—I guess from all my inner anger. When he calls this time, I will tell him it's not working for me. So now you have the real reason I had a case this morning"

He was quiet for what seemed like a long time, but it was only a minute. "You are sure you don't have feelings for this guy?" he said, looking at her intently.

"No, not at all. Unfortunately, I have let it drag on for this long, and now I just want to be done with him." She leaned back in her chair.

"Jill, I can't tell you what to do because when I have in the past, you tell me to butt out. I could have checked him out for you, but you said you could handle it. So, I have done my best just to respect your wishes. But if you ever need me to check him out, just say the word."

"No, I'm Ok. Thanks for the offer, though. I guess if I had invested a lot of time in the relationship, then maybe, but now there is no need. Let's get back to our lunch and this fabulous restaurant," she said, smiling at him.

"If you are sure."

"I am," she said, hoping he would change the subject.

"Good, something smells so good in here, and my stomach is about to disappear." Marcus looked at her smile, and his eyes gave her the once-over, as if she were part of the menu. He then switched his attention to the menu, and they decided on lunch.

Later, over dessert—Marcus's favorite—the conversation was filled with one laugh after another. Marcus shared stories with Jill about playing with his basketball league and how his brother once had joined in with the cheerleaders during a game. He thought her laugh was so sexy; he couldn't get enough of hearing it.

Marcus asked Jill's opinion on some prospective property that he wanted his company to acquire. At that point, when they were engrossed in conversation, Sheree, accompanied by her best friend, found them.

"Fancy seeing you two here, Marcus. You have the best seat in the house. Is this a working lunch so far away from the office? Why, hello, June! It must be your lucky day to be dining with the best of Philly. I bet that's quite an accomplishment for you, huh, sweetie?" She raised an eyebrow as she stared pointedly at Jill.

Jill looked at Marcus. He shook his head, clearly very displeased with the intrusion. He replied angrily, "Mind your manners, Sheree."

"Oh? Is she working for you now?" Sheree purred in that same smooth tone.

Marcus gave her a look that Jill thought could make water turn into rocks. "Sheree, it's none of your business," he whispered through clenched teeth as he gave her an unflinching stare.

Sheree's friend grabbed her arm, trying to get her to leave, but Sheree snatched her arm from her friend's grip. "I'm not leaving, Renee.

I have more of a right to be here than she does!" Sheree turned to Jill. "My, my, this thing gets around. Here I find you having lunch with my boyfriend and at one of the finest places in Philly. I wonder what is next. Well, I will tell you this, June. Know your place; go back to the other side of the tracks. You are in the wrong zip code. We don't cater to downtown trash here. Take my advice and stay away from Marcus, or I will show you where you should be, and it's not with my man," Sheree said in a quiet tone laced with anger.

Jill decided to leave before the situation got worse. She stood up, and Sheree took a few steps back. Jill grabbed her purse and stared at Sheree for a few seconds more before speaking to Marcus. "I think I will find my own way back to the office, Marcus." Jill turned away but not before Sheree threw in the last barb.

"I think that's a marvelous idea, sweetie, especially since your plan is going nowhere. You see, Marcus is taken. Got that, girlfriend?" Sheree yelled because Jill had already gotten halfway to the exit.

The other customers had begun to whisper as they watched the model go on a tirade.

"Sheree! That's enough!" Marcus barked. "You have gone way too far, and I have had it!" He got up, threw down his napkin, dropped money on the table, and he turned to leave.

"Marcus, where are you going?" Sheree exclaimed, grabbing his arm.

He removed her hand from his arm but only stopped long enough to give her a very frustrated look. "I'm going someplace that you are not." Then he turned his back on her and walked away.

Jill had made it out to the main street when she heard Marcus call her name. She refused to stop; she felt she might explode. When she reached the street beyond the restaurant, he caught up with her, grabbing her arm and turning her around just in time to see the explosive look on her face. To Jill's annoyance, a smile spread across his face.

"What the hell is so funny, Marcus?" That only made him break out into a full grin, and she then replied, "I hope you choke on it, or better yet, go back in there, and you and … and that she-devil can choke on it together." His laughter only got louder. She paused to catch her breath; her high heels hadn't helped her trek go any quicker. "You know, if you hang around with me, I just may soil your reputation. According to Sheree, I'm from the other side of the tracks."

Marcus didn't say anything, and Jill realized that he was just staring at her. His look caused something within her to shift in the most earth-shattering way. The look suddenly was gone but his mood had sobered, and his next words seemed to amplify the look from moments ago.

"You know what I think? You are simply one gorgeous woman, and what comes out of Sheree's mouth is filled with spite and jealousy because she is not half the woman you are. She sees you as a threat, and you don't realize the power you have. See, the problem with you is that you doubt your own worth. You fail to see the thing that scares people like Sheree. You have a beauty to you that is so natural and untouched that it's simply amazing and refreshing. You are my friend because of you and how you make me feel. I think your beauty is just a bonus. Jill, what I said back there in the restaurant has not and never will change. You are the best friend I have ever had. You are even more fun than hanging out with the guys and definitely more fun than Sheree."

Jill looked away, suddenly not ready for him to see how his words were affecting her. A smile came from nowhere and spread over her face. She was not ready to go all soft on him just yet but her emotions got the best of her after his compliments, "You know Jordan, sweet talk may get you somewhere. Why do you waste your time with someone who doesn't hold your attention, hm?"

He rubbed his hand over his face and exhaled. "Ah, Jill, it's sort of been this way for quite a few months now. I'm trying to gently back off from her, but it's proving to be a bit tedious." Looking at Jill, he said, "Do you have any suggestions to help me out?"

Jill grunted. "If I knew the answer to that one, I'd be free of Tyrone. You, my brother, are on your own. I must find a bus, or I will be late getting back to work."

She walked off, but Marcus just stood there watching her walk away. Suddenly he rushed to catch her. After they had walked a few more paces, he looked at her, although she tried to avoid looking at him. In a quiet tone, he offered, "I'll take you back." He touched her arm, and she halted. "Now it's my turn, out of curiosity, Jill. What do you see in this Tyrone?"

Jill released a breath, looked at him, and said thoughtfully, "I guess about the same as what you see in the Barbie doll back there."

Marcus grunted in understanding. Jill just smiled to herself, thinking, *Zero for Marcus; game, set, and match for Jillian.*

Suddenly, it felt like they were back on their usual footing, and they turned around and walked back to the restaurant. When they reached his car, Jill looked around, as if thinking Sheree would materialize, but there was no sign of her. Marcus opened the door for her, stepping back for her to get in; then he closed her door. Once Marcus got behind the wheel and started the engine, he said, "You were really going to walk back to the office?"

"Yeah, I would have. Better than another Sheree altercation," Jill answered.

He then turned his attention to his driving as the engine purred to life, and they left the parking lot and drove through town.

When they got back to the office building, Jill thanked him for lunch.

"You can either stop by my office after work," Marcus said, "or I'll meet you in the lobby and take you home."

She agreed to meet him in the lobby.

<hr/>

Later that day, as Marcus pulled his car into Jill's parking lot, she saw her car and noticed that it looked shiny and clean.

"So, you had them bring my car home?" When he nodded, she said, "Now this is strange. When I left it this morning, my car was dirty, and now it is so clean and shiny. Maybe the fairy stopped by to clean it." She said with a gleam in her eyes; and she saw Marcus looking like the cat that swallowed the canary. "Oh! Marcus, you didn't. No! You did not have my car repaired and cleaned." When he still looked guilty, Jill quickly admonished him. "You were only supposed to have your mechanic look at it and then tell me how much it would cost. I have to budget my money to make allowances for the expenses and—"

Marcus silenced Jill by holding up his hand. "Jill, I left you a message to tell you it was just your starter, but Eddie said he would prefer to put it out of its misery. The repair was done in no time, and Eddie and his crew always detail their customers' cars after the repairs are done. The repairs were not much, under two hundred dollars, labor and parts. If I told you what the repairs would cost, you would probably have put it off for another six months or so and endured riding the city bus." Then, seeming to become frustrated, he muttered, "Jill, just sue me for wanting to make sure you were safe, if that will make you feel any better."

Marcus's words made Jill feel foolish for her outburst, and guilt began to wash over her. She tried to think of a proper apology for her behavior. She cleared her throat and slowly measured her next words. "You know me so well. I feel so small, but you need to understand something. It's not that I am ungrateful. I just don't want you to think I always expect something from you in order to have your friendship. I wonder how I could be so lucky to have you in my life." Smiling, she turned to open her door but then turned back to gauge his reaction to her words. "Whatever I did in another lifetime, I am glad I did it, if it has brought you into my life. I am truly blessed. Thank you, Marcus. Now, what do I owe you?"

A smile broke out on his face, and he acted as if he was contemplating her question. "How about you cook me dinner as a thank-you, and we can call it even. What do you say to that, Jill?"

Jill looked at him in amazement. "Are you serious? You want me to cook for a man who can hire any cook in town or in the country, and he wants me to prepare him a home-cooked meal? Come on, Marcus, get serious. You have any number of available women in town who will do that."

Marcus frowned. "Yeah, maybe, but I am asking you." He looked directly at her.

Jill looked at Marcus as she waved her finger at him. "Ok, but here is the deal. I will not tolerate being attacked by Sheree, like what I experienced at the restaurant. You know what I mean, Marcus?"

Marcus nodded his head and apologized again for Sheree's remarks. Jill agreed to cook for him. Together they walked to her car, and after checking that she was satisfied, Marcus left for a business meeting.

Jill left work late on Friday. When she got off the elevator on the first floor, she saw the evening janitor, whom she'd nicknamed Mr. B (short for Billings), but everyone else called him Stanley, his first name. When he saw Jill coming toward him, his long, slender face broke out in a broad grin. He stopped sweeping and waited for her to reach him. Jill always thought that he was probably a very handsome man in his day, and although he was getting on in age, he still possessed the charm of a much-younger man. He bowed as Jill reached him.

"Well, hello, Mr. B. How are you doing this evening?" she said with a huge grin.

Stanley Billings smiled back at her. "Well, hello, gorgeous! Why is such a lovely lady working late when it is the start of the weekend?"

Jill shrugged. "Well, Mr. B, everyone doesn't have a reason to rush home like you do, so we stay behind and gather all the extra hours we can so when that special someone comes our way, we can go home on time and enjoy that little nest egg."

Mr. B wagged his finger at Jill. "Now listen here, little lady. If you would stop working so hard and get more rest, you could see what's in front of your face. Mm-hm, but Mr. B is not going to say any more on that subject because you are not ready to see what us more mature adults already know, huh, Jillian?" The old man chuckled at the expression on her face.

Jill smiled and said, "Oh, Mr. B, you never give up on your romantic notions. Sometimes I have to look at you twice because you sound just like my daddy." She walked on, waving her hands in the air.

He smiled as he watched her walk toward the door. "You are just like my Ella—stubborn to the bone. Have a nice weekend, and I'll see you later."

Jill replied, "You do the same, and be careful going home."

When Jill arrived at the club, it was already in full swing, and the dance floor was packed. Although the club was private—mostly frequented by those who worked in the Commerce Towers and Commerce Park buildings—it had become one of the hottest spots to hang out in Philly. Jill had become a frequent customer of the club through her friendship with the girls. It was Cyn's favorite because it was known for its privacy, probably because a lot of high rollers who often frequented the club. There was top-notch security, so it was very safe as well. Cyn swore she would meet Mr. Right here. The arrival of Cyn and the others back at the table brought Jill out of her thoughts, and she greeted them with a smile.

"My, my, my, have we been busy out there on the dance floor?" Jill teased.

Cyn replied, "Oh, girl, it felt great after such an awful week with the new intern I've been training. I swear the girl kisses more butt than the reject who was fired before her." They all laughed as she continued. "The place is packed, but I need something to pique my interest, and mostly what I see so far is low on the food chain." She rolled her eyes, and then all the others joined in laughing with her.

Jasmine looked around and nudged Jill. "But there are some repeats that are worth repeating. Looky, looky! Over there is that tall, light-brown, and loaded. He's looking kind of bored with his date, the snobzilla."

Jill and the other girls looked over in Marcus's direction. Jill recognized the look on Marcus's face as being in deep thought, or maybe he was just trying not to hear what his girl was saying. Sheree was sitting so close that she might as well have been in his lap. Sheree's persona oozed high fashion from her head to her perfectly pedicured toes. She seemed to be attempting to spread herself all over Marcus. His best friend and right-hand man, Joe, was in deep conversation with a girl at the opposite end of the table.

I'd give anything to just walk up to that table and take Marcus onto the dance floor, Jill thought. Suddenly, Jill realized that Cyn was speaking to her. "Oh! Sorry about that. I guess I drifted off."

"Yeah, girlfriend, you really did, but I can see why." Cyn smiled and winked at Jill.

Then Jasmine announced, "Yvonne is bringing someone to our table."

Jill recognized the guy from the office building.

"Hey, girls, I want you to meet Rob. He just started this week as one of the processing supervisors, and he's new in town. I've invited him to join our little group tonight." Yvonne made the introductions as everyone gazed at the brown-skinned male of average height. He was very muscular, as if he lived at the gym.

Rob soon fell in with the gang. He answered questions about himself and said that his first week had not gone as planned. Shortly afterward, when Rob excused himself to find the little boys' room, Yvonne and Cyn teased Jill because it seemed that Rob had taken a particular liking to her.

Jill brushed off their teasing, trying to look disinterested, although she found him to be a sweet guy.

"So, Yvonne, what gives with you and Joe?" Cyn asked the question that everyone else was thinking. "I thought you two were hot for each other. What's happening?"

Yvonne glanced over at Joe's table and saw him take the girl out on the floor; she seemed to be occupying all his time that night. "Look at him. He thinks he's a mack daddy or something." Yvonne turned around to talk to the girls. "We had a big fight after I found out that he had said some rotten things about Jill. I told him, 'You're always knocking Sheree, but you and she are made from the same mold—the kind only for the uppity rich folk who live on the high side of town.' The argument only got worse after I told him he was a sell-out. Brother did not like that one bit! To make a long story short, he told me that maybe he needed someone who knew him better, someone who would stand beside him and not judge him for every mistake he made. I told him to go for it, and the rest, as they say, is history." Yvonne reached for her drink as the others digested what she had said.

"Yvonne, I'm sorry," Cyn said. "We really liked Joe, but I understand what you're saying. I'm sure the two of you will find your way back. You and Joe have so much history."

"Well, Cyn, I thought so too until I saw him here tonight, and his date was clinging to him like a vine or something." Yvonne rolled her eyes.

"Yvonne, he only started clinging fifteen minutes ago, when you came in with Rob," Jasmine said.

"Really? Maybe two need to play that game."

"Whatever you do, Yvonne, don't use Rob because we think he's got the hots for Jill," Jasmine said.

"No! He does not!" Jill replied. "Besides, Yvonne, I really feel bad causing trouble for you and Joe. Is there anything I can do to make things better between you?"

"Hey, girlfriend, it's not your fault that Joe tends to run off at the mouth more than what's good for him. Don't worry about it; just enjoy yourself. We've broken up before. It's no big deal. How about we get back to more interesting subjects, like the way Rob has been trying to get your attention since we got here. What do you think about that, Jill?" Yvonne asked.

"I say, let's make this interesting!" Cyn shouted across the table, and she and Jasmine cheered.

"How about this Jill—I will bet you a dance with Marcus that when Rob comes back to the table, he will ask you to dance first before any of us!" Jasmine said excitedly.

"Jasmine! I'm shocked, but I want in. Now, what are the stakes again, or should I say who?" Cyn laughed out loud.

Jill looked at them and shook her head. Then Yvonne just burst out laughing as Jill turned away.

"What? I'm just anticipating you going over there and asking that gorgeous piece of man for a dance with the shark at his side." Yvonne continued to laugh, but Jill put on a front, sticking to her guns that Rob would not ask her to dance first; therefore, she would not have to ask Marcus anything.

But when Rob returned, he was only seated for five minutes before he turned to Jill and asked her to dance, and it seemed that, suddenly, Cyn and Jasmine needed to hurry to the ladies' room.

Yvonne stayed behind to cheer Jill on. "Give the guy a break and dance with him, will ya?"

Jill followed the direction of Yvonne's eyes and realized that Rob was waiting for a reply to his request.

"Don't mind her, Rob," Yvonne said. "The girl works too hard, but she loves to dance, and she's good at it. See for yourself"

Rob again asked Jill for a dance and extended his hand to Jill.

"Oh, of course, I would love to dance," Jill said.

They headed for the floor, unaware that a pair of eyes were watching very closely from another table.

⸻

Marcus noticed Jill from the moment she stood up and was led onto the dance floor. He also noticed her very short caramel-colored dress, which swirled around those wonderful legs of hers. He became aware that if he noticed her in that way, he was not the only one.

Joe motioned to Marcus with his head and said, "Hey, man, isn't that Jill over there with the new guy? You know, the shop manager for Vince Fielding. The ladies have gone wild since he came aboard." Joe continued to make his comments about Jill and her partner's every move. "He's a fast mover with the women, that's for sure. I got to give the brother props for his initiative."

Marcus only grunted, but he didn't take his eyes off the couple on the dance floor. "Yes, I see," Marcus said quietly.

Then Sheree smiled and said, "Oh, they do look good together. Boy, that chick really gets around. Every time I see her, she has some guy with her. Looks like everyone is getting a turn."

"Damn, he's got her smiling as if he is the best thing since—what's that movie about Stella?" Joe said.

Marcus's full attention was focused on Jill and Rob on the dance floor.

"Marcus! Man, you got to give the brother his props. Look, I tell you he's got her eating out of his hands. Her eyes are glued to him, not to mention the way they move together. You know women go for that muscular and all-buffed look," Joe said, continuing to watch his buddy's reaction. The fact that Marcus hadn't taken his eyes off Jill and her dance partner spoke volumes.

Joe almost burst at the seams when Marcus suddenly jumped up, walked over to Sheree, who had gone over to another table and was talking to someone as Marcus walked up to her, and said, "Excuse me, come on, Sheree, let's dance."

"Not really feeling like dancing to that fast song, baby. How about if we wait for a slow one?" She went back to talking to her friend, disregarding his request.

"Ok. We can sit this one out," he said and headed back to the table. He signaled the waitress and ordered another drink and then again watched Jill and the guy on the floor. A few minutes later, the song ended, and they headed back to her table.

Sheree was still talking with her girlfriend, and Joe was now into a conversation with Rudy. Marcus was listening to the guys as he sipped his scotch.

———

Jill sat back down, and Rob headed to the bar once she was seated. The girls all had their eyes on Jill, and then they all smiled.

"Jill, darlin', it's time to pay up on our bet!" Cyn said, hardly able to get the words out.

"I did dance with Rob!" Jill exclaimed.

"Yeah, that part we know, but the bet was, that if he asked you first, then you have to ask Marcus for a dance."

"You guys are kidding, right? Tonight? Now?"

Cyn and the others nodded their heads.

"Yeah," Yvonne chimed in. "Sweetie, a bet is a bet, and now its Marcus's turn."

"You guys are so full of it!" Jill exclaimed, and they responded in unison, "We know!" They all fell out laughing. Jill got up just as Rob was returning to his seat. She slowly walked over to Marcus's table, and as she got closer, his head turned watching her approach.

"Hello, everybody," Jill said, looking quickly at everyone at the table and then back at Marcus.

Sheree's mouth was open, but nothing came out. Marcus and Joe both spoke to Jill.

"Marcus," Jill said, "would you like to dance with me?"

Marcus smiled, and Joe's face exploded in a huge grin.

Sheree became belligerent. "I know she did not ask my man for a dance!" Sheree huffed.

Jill kept her eyes on Marcus, who got up, seemingly pleased.

"Sheree, I asked you earlier, and you turned me down," Marcus said, "so I think I would love to dance with someone who wants to dance with me." Marcus and Jill headed to the dance floor as Bohannon began to play. "I think the night just got better!" Marcus said to Jill with a twinkle in his eyes.

Jill looked up as Marcus moved closer to her. She felt nervous, but the electricity between them soon smothered that feeling. She loved the way he moved, and nobody had the effect on her that he did. Jill matched her steps to his as the deejay pumped up the music. The crowd erupted because the song was a favorite. Everyone seemed to pile onto the dance floor, and space became limited.

"You look like you are enjoying yourself a bit too much!" Jill told him with a huge grin.

"I am, I am! And don't worry, honey; I got your back."

"You better have, because if looks could kill, I would be dead already from the knives that Sheree is throwing at my back" Jill said, looking a little worried.

"No worries, baby girl. I'll mop up the blood and be there to give you a transfusion if you need one. I wouldn't change partners if my life depended on it." He moved closer to her, then took a few side steps and then another, and he came even closer to Jill. She shook and twisted her hips; they complemented each other's dance moves. "You see, Jillian, it has become a known fact that you are a very good dancer. But I am curious—can you hang with an old pro like yours truly? Shall we find out? What harm can that do—or are you chicken?" He saw the answering light in her eyes as she silently took the challenge.

Jill continued to match him. *If you can't beat him, join him,* she thought, and they put on a show for the onlookers.

———

"Oh, Cyn, Yvonne! Do you see what I see? Those two are like poetry in motion!" Jasmine exclaimed.

"Go get 'em, Jill!" Jasmine shouted joyfully.

"Yeah, Jaz, but they are showing us a little something else. They haven't taken their eyes off each other. It's sizzling between them," Cyn said.

"There is a lot of something else between those two," Yvonne said as she studied the couple dancing, hot and heavy, on the floor, as if no one else was around.

"Yeah, look at Sheree over there. I'd say Jill had better be careful because if looks could kill …" Jasmine said.

"With what's happening between those two, Sheree is powerless to all that energy. She just hasn't figured that out yet!" Cyn said, then laughed.

"I felt that something was between those two, and now I know it is. It's just going to take some time for them to figure it out," Yvonne said.

———

Across the room, Joe and Sheree got into an altercation.

"That bitch! I knew she'd be trouble. She has played Little Miss Unfortunate too many times, and I'm sick of it! Joe, what are we going to do? You know how Marcus is with charity cases, and I heard how you gave her an earful. We have to get this wench out of his life. He's dancing with Shirley from *What's Happening*! But she will never have him! Marcus's appetites run along the lines of slender and sleek."

Joe shook his head at Sheree's hateful remarks. He disliked her even more and understood Yvonne's point of view. "Puh-lease! You and I have not seen eye to eye on anything since when? Yeah, uh-huh! Gotcha! Sheree, let me tell you something. You are the type of person who uses people for your own gain. Sorry, chica! I ain't the one! You know something? You could take notes from Jill. She has more of him than you do! Girl, you need to get over yourself. How he has put up with you this long still amazes me. You need to come out of fantasy land. My man Marcus needs a woman—a real woman—not someone who ain't even human. Now, see, if you were more like Jill—"

Sheree angrily hurried away from the table before Joe could finish. Joe laughed at her reaction.

"Man, you came down hard on her," Rudy said as he took a seat.

Joe continued to smile. "Rudy, she was way overdue for that. Marcus has catered to her for too long. It's time somebody took her down a peg or two. You know what I'm saying? I know you do because there has been a time or two that she has given your staff hell! She thinks because

Marcus is a silent partner that she can come in here and treat people however she pleases. But what I'm saying is that she does this wherever she goes! She has embarrassed him countless times. How he does it, I do not know. It's time he enjoyed himself, and if what I see is correct, tonight my boy is doing just that!"

"Yeah, I think his nose is wide open with this lady. When he comes in here, he practically searches her out, always managing to say something to her before the night ends," Rudy said, ending with a laugh as he watched Marcus on the dance floor with Jill.

———

The deejay slowed the music down, and Jill thought that she'd head back to her table, but Marcus grabbed her hand.

"I think it's my turn now. Jill, will you have this dance with me?"

Jill felt thrilled and nervous at the same time but also daring, as she agreed. His eyes never left hers; he slowly pulled her into his arms. The song "Slow Dance" began to play, engulfing them in its melody. Jill thought it was the most soothing feeling to be in Marcus's arms. The music seemed to enclose them in a cocoon as they swayed from side to side. The distance between their two bodies had slowly disappeared. Jill closed her eyes, her body recorded the feel of him for future memories. Jill always thought he would feel so good, and now she knew for sure; it was all she had imagined. She looked up at him. He smiled down into her face, but remained quiet.

"Oh, so now you have nothing to say for yourself?" Jill teased. "I guess that's the effect I have on guys in this town, just shuts them right up, especially the talkative, controlling, playboy types." She smiled.

"I'm wondering how an evening that was slowly turning into a miserable time suddenly became so enjoyable," Marcus said. He raised one eyebrow and looked deeply into Jill's eyes.

"Well, Marcus, when you go from a spoiled brat to a beautiful black queen, that experience can be truly earth-shattering." Then, realizing how catty her remark sounded, she said, "I'm sorry. I should not have said that. It wasn't nice, and after all, she is your girlfriend, and I need to respect that—I think." Jill looked at him shyly, and they both started laughing.

When the song ended, Marcus thanked her for the dance and escorted her back to her table. He saw his brother heading over to his table, and he quickly turned to Jill and said, "Hey, Jill, I have someone I want you to meet. Come with me." He grabbed her hand and pulled her along with him.

"You sure?" she asked and then thought, *I don't want to be in Sheree's vicinity.*

"Yes, positively," he said, ushering her along with him. Jill looked over at his table and saw another man talking to Joe and the manager. His back was turned so Jill couldn't see his face. When she and Marcus got to the table, Marcus called out to Brice, and as he turned around, Jill knew that this must be Marcus's brother. He was tall, with the same jet-black hair only closely cut, broad shoulders, and a nice smile. His voice was deeper than Marcus's. He had dark eyes, which were very assessing as he watched her. He was very handsome, which seemed to be typical of the Jordan men.

"Hey, man! You must have gotten into town late. What a surprise." Marcus said as he hugged his brother.

"Actually, I got in earlier but got hung up talking to the folks. Mom had a million questions. I ended up coming up with an excuse to cut out of there before she got any ideas about having some surprise guests show up." They both laughed as if they were sharing a secret.

"I'm glad you did. I have someone I want you to meet. Jillian, this is Brice, my big brother. Jillian is the new heroine of Philly," Marcus said as Brice extended his hand. Jill placed her hand in his firm grip, only he raised it to his lips, kissing her knuckles, which made Joe laugh.

"Down, boy!" he shouted out from his seat at the table. "Jill, you got to watch—this one is rogue."

"Yeah, he's been rogue for years!" Marcus chimed in, and they all laughed.

"Please ignore the children; they need training," Brice said. "But I have to ask—how long have you been hiding in corners?" Brice winked at Jill. She gave him a big smile but was unsuccessful at hiding her blush. The guys all roared with laughter.

"Also, Jill, have you met Rudy?" Marcus asked as he nodded toward the older man who was sitting at the table.

"We spoke a few weeks ago when I first came to the club, but it's nice to officially meet the man in charge."

"No, the pleasure is all mine, and it's nice seeing you again. But if you will excuse me, one of my servers is looking, this way, so I guess I had better go back to work. Enjoy your evening, and Brice, take it easy on the lady, will yah?" Rudy said laughingly as Marcus shook his head.

"Don't worry, Rudy. I got this. If he doesn't behave, he will have kitchen duty. I'm sure you have dishes back there that need washing."

Rudy turned away, continuing to laugh, as did Joe.

"Pay no attention to those boys, Jill. I am very good at spotting beauty, but somehow, I must have missed a beat," said Brice.

"I've just started coming to the club, so I'm pretty new here."

He nodded his head in understanding. "But I am so baffled—how did such a pretty little thing end up hanging around these clowns? How about we go find a quiet table so that we can continue with some intelligent conversation."

"Marcus, this is your cue. I'm going to handle business I have elsewhere," Joe said. He got up from the table, still smiling, and walked across the room.

"My, my, she sure does get around," Sheree exclaimed, as she came back to the table.

Before Marcus could make a comment to Joe, Sheree's snide remark ticked him off.

"Don't start," Marcus said, sounding annoyed.

"What do you mean, don't start?" Sheree demanded. "Are you afraid I might hurt her feelings or something? Well, too bad. She is rolling in a different class now, so she has to hold her own. Besides, why are you coming to her rescue?"

Marcus tried to contain his anger, but it was not working.

Brice spoke up quickly. "Ok, why don't we find a table. We need to get out of the line of fire."

"Sounds like a good idea," Jill agreed.

"Yeah, Brice, please take out the trash!" Sheree said angrily.

"You will have to excuse Sheree," Brice said. "She's just a bitch most of the time." He glared at Sheree before smiling at Jill, then ushered her over to the bar area.

"I am figuring that out," Jill said. "This is like the GA zillionth time I have had a run-in with her, and every time, I feel that if she could get rid of me, she would. She seems to be the jealous type. I don't know why she sees me as a threat. She's a model, beautiful, and well known. There is no competition here!"

"Wait a minute now! I can see why she would feel threatened by you, and I will explain. Let's find a seat." He steered her to an empty booth.

"I appreciate your trying to make me feel better," Jill said.

"Sure, I want you to feel better, but I am telling you the truth. When I saw you the word 'wow' came to mind. You are pretty, and yes, I can see why Sheree feels threatened, not to mention that my brother can't seem to take his eyes off you. I also noticed when I came in that he was on the dance floor with you, and he seemed happy. *Now* take a look at him."

They both looked over to where Marcus and Sheree were seated, and it was easy to see that he was not pleased and that she was now in make-up mode.

"He really doesn't look happy," Jill admitted quietly.

"No, he is not. He's been that way with her for some time now. He just needs to break it off. They are like oil and water."

"I know how that feels to be in a bad relationship. Been there, done that, too many times myself," Jill admitted.

"Oh? If I'm not being too nosey, what happened?"

Jill saw Brice's sincere expression, and it made her want to open- up to him. She felt comfortable with him, like a confidant. "I caught him cheating with someone close to me." She then took a sip of her drink.

"He must have been a total idiot. Well, darlin', I say, out with the old and in with the new!" Brice said encouragingly.

Brice and Jill continued talking and quickly became good friends. Later, the two went out on the dance floor, and he kept Jill laughing as they danced from one song to another. When she told him it was time to take a break, he escorted her back to the table where her friends were seated. It happened that Brice was part of her circle of friends, so the fun continued, although Jill felt that there was some extra chemistry between Brice and Cyn, and that thought made her very curious.

When a friend of Brice's stopped by the table, he soon left with the guy to go mingle, and Jill nursed her drink as she looked around the club. Thirty minutes later, she watched as Marcus followed Sheree out of the club, and it seemed he took all the life when he left.

Jill was very thankful for the guys who came to ask her friends for a dance because she wanted to put off being questioned about dancing with Marcus earlier. It gave her an opening to escape to the ladies' room, just to get away from it all.

When the deejay took an intermission, the crowd slowly left the dance floor, and everyone took advantage of the break. Jaz noticed that their table was empty and looked through the crowd for Jill. She asked Cyn and Yvonne, "I wonder where Jill has gotten to? I hope she's ok. She looked kind of strange when we left the table."

Cyn gave her a mischievous look before replying. "If any of us had of danced with a man as fine as Marcus in the way that she did, we would be wearing a silly look as well." The others agreed, and Cyn continued. "Remember how shy Jill was when we all first met, and compared to as far back as six months ago, she has made very positive strides in finding that she is stronger than she thinks. Her judgment is still a bit off, especially where that two-bit mechanic is concerned. He has *Player*, with a capital P, written all over him! Everyone seems to know it but Jill."

Yvonne had a different take on the situation. "I don't know if I would say she's not aware of what Tyrone does. Sometimes you do try to overlook someone's faults, but in time, you realize that it will not work anyway. I said it before—she is using him as a cover against Sheree, but I could be wrong, as I have been before."

"No matter what Jill's situation with any other guy, she still has Marcus as a close friend," Jasmine said, "and boy, are they ever close. Jill is incredibly lucky." Jasmine leaned her head on her hands and looked heavenward.

Yvonne spotted Joe making his way toward their table. "Uh-oh, here comes Joe, and there's no sign of the chick who was all over him." She turned on the charm, giving him her most brilliant smile. Both Cyn and Jasmine made themselves scarce to give Yvonne and Joe some privacy.

"Mind if I join you?" Joe asked.

She indicated the chair beside her by nodding her head. "Please do." When he sat down, she remarked, "This place is really jumping tonight, isn't it?"

"Oh yeah. Yvonne, let me start by saying I am sorry for my behavior with Jill. I now know that she is very nice and not anything like the gossips were saying. I regret what I said. Can you forgive me?"

"Yes, it's all water under the bridge, Joe, so you are ok, we are ok, and most importantly, Jill is ok. I'm surprised that you have the time to come over with the way that woman was monopolizing your time. I thought you would have left here by now for a nightcap." Yvonne looked around the room and then at the couples dancing on the floor.

"Definitely nothing like that, but every time I tried to come over here, by the time I was halfway here, you were on the dance floor. Girl, you have been keeping the dance floor hot! I am surprised that you are sitting here alone. When I saw you sitting here, I thought I had better grab the chance to sit with you and talk a little bit. You got all these knuckleheads chasing you. It's so hard for a brother to have a chance with you."

She lowered her voice as she replied, "I never know what you want, Joseph. If I had known that you wanted to dance, I would have kept my dance card open, just for you." Yvonne took a sip from her glass. "I assumed, since you have been wrapped around that redhead all evening, that you had other plans." She raised her eyebrows and gave him a questioning stare. "Or did they fall through?"

He released his breath, then shook his head as he moved closer to her. "Before we take this any further, Yvonne, I am not playing any games, unlike some other people I know. I am very much in control, and as such, I know what I want. Cat-and-mouse isn't my game. I don't have the patience for that kind of thing. But I am sorry for how I treated your friend, and I really do want there to be an *us*. There is no one else. That girl tonight, well, Sheree was just up to her old tricks, trying to put something together, but my heart is right here, where it always has been. I am a man who needs his woman, and that is you and only you. I plan to dance with you, so stop playing hard to get. We both know what we want. We don't need to pretend. You know how combustible we are, so let's start it off tonight with a dance, and right now, I want to dance with you."

Joe gently lifted her hand and placed a kiss on it. He looked in her eyes, slowly stood up, and pulled her up to him, brushing her body against his to send a message of where he was planning to take things. She added fuel to the fire by making even more contact with his body. He led her toward the dance floor, and meaningful looks passed between them.

While Cyn and Jasmine watched Joe and Yvonne from the bar, they also could see through the glass door entrance to the concierge's desk. They saw the bouncer speaking to someone dressed in multiple colors, which was so eye-catching. They knew of only one person who dressed that way—Jill's current beau. Tyrone was a walking advertisement for the '70s. He looked like he had time-traveled, compared to everyone else's mode of dress.

"Wow! Seeing him makes me think the time machine has landed, and it made a mistake and dropped him off in the wrongtimeline." Jasmine said.

Cyn was so amazed at how Tyrone carried himself, like he was the best thing ever created.

Jill exited the ladies' room and was about to enter the area of the club when she heard someone calling her name—and she cringed. She would know that voice anywhere; and it was her current pain-in-the-neck beau, Tyrone. When she turned around, he had formed his hands around his mouth as if it was a megaphone and seemed about to yell her name across the lobby again. Jill quickly waved to him, even though at that moment, she wished the floor would open up and swallow her. Everyone was staring at Tyrone as if he was an alien. Tyrone was loving the attention, thinking he was *all that*. Jill put a smile on her face but thought he needed a reality check.

When Tyrone walked up to Jill, her smile dimmed, and she said in a serious tone, "Tyrone, did you have to be so loud and practice your Tarzan call here?"

"Ah, Jilly, I had to get your attention. I can't help it, but people just love to watch me when I enter a room. Everyone can't be fortunate to be born with such good looks and stylish tastes as I have." He winked at her and extended his arm to escort her back into the club. "Oh yeah, you got to go over there where those two big gorillas are and sign me in. They would not believe me when I said I was your guest."

Jill nodded, and they walked over to the counter where the bouncers were still watching Tyrone. Once Jill verified him, they headed into the club.

"So, sweet thing, just enjoy the ride and imagine how many ladies would love to be where you are—the lady on Tyrone's arm."

"I didn't know you were coming here tonight. How did you know where I was? Besides, what happened to you the other night? You were supposed to come over but no Tyrone, no Chinese food!" Jill said, getting mad all over again.

"I apologize for that, Jilly. My boss had an emergency, and who else would he call but Tyrone. So don't be too mad with me. I apologize for not letting you know what happened. I kinda figured you'd be here. I been calling you all evening. It's all good. We're here together; let's enjoy our night." He seemed to disregard any arguments she might have.

Jill and Tyrone approached the table as Yvonne and Joe were just sitting down. Upon seeing Jill and Tyrone approach the table, the whole gang greeted him and moved the chairs around in order to accommodate everyone. Joe and Tyrone soon were engaged in conversation, and Yvonne used this time to whisper to Jill that they needed to get together and have some real girl talk, preferably before the weekend was over. Jill agreed but knew that it was probably about Tyrone. This seemed to satisfy Yvonne, so the rest of their conversation drifted from the different dances that people were doing on the floor to the food, until they noticed Tyrone ordering drinks but getting a little upset when they did not have his favorite drink, Mad Dog 20/20.

A little later, the club was busier than ever; the crowd seemed to grow. Tyrone had been up dancing for a while but only danced with Jill twice. She sat at the table while everyone was on the floor, dancing, even Tyrone. Suddenly, Marcus and Brice appeared at her table.

"I know you are not sitting here letting all this good music go to waste."

Jill looked up into Marcus's smiling face as he extended his hand to her. Brice saluted her before going over to another table to find a dance partner, just as a funky tune by the Fatback Band played. The song had people shouting on the dance floor. The club was in full swing.

"Shall we show these folks how it's done?" Marcus asked.

Jill thought about Tyrone for a moment, but since he was already having fun, it was only fair that she did likewise. "Why, of course!" she said, smiling.

Marcus did a short bow. "Lead the way." He followed her onto the very crowded dance floor, where everyone was having a good time. They had to dance close, given the space, but the deejay just kept playing great tunes, one after another. Jill and Marcus had a great time. She once again felt the happiness that he always seemed to bring when she was around him. He was totally focused on her, but she found it hard to hold his gaze at times. When she looked away, somehow she knew he was still watching her. It made her feel so sexy because when her eyes moved back to him, he winked at her as if he knew what she was thinking. She had almost forgotten about Tyrone. She and Marcus had been on the dance floor so long that she felt energized. The deejay finally slowed it down, and she turned to leave the dance floor, but Marcus grabbed her and brought her into his arms.

"You know this will not help your situation with Sheree," she told him.

"Probably not, but she has gone home sulking. She always pouts and thinks she will get her way, but I'm so tired of that. I just want to have a good time and not argue with anyone."

"I understand. Tyrone is here—at least, I think he is still here. He has been constantly dancing with other women while I sit. He thinks I'm stuck-up."

"He needs to meet Sheree." Marcus said, and they both laughed.

"What the hell is this?" Both Marcus and Jill turned at the loud voice booming behind them.

"Hey, Tyrone," Jill said with a smile before turning back to Marcus.

"What do you mean, 'Hey Tyrone'?" Tyrone said, mimicking Jill's voice.

Marcus stopped dancing and watched Tyrone.

"I am dancing right now. I will meet you back at the table," Jill said. Her smile had dimmed as she picked up on the tension.

"The hell you will!" Tyrone reached for her arm, but Marcus stepped between them. "Listen, dog, this ain't about you. It's between me and my lady, so I'm asking you nicely—step off," Tyrone told Marcus.

"Well, *dog*," Marcus said, exaggerating his words to duplicate Tyrone's, "the lady is dancing with me right now, so do like she told you, and go sit down!"

"Listen here, pretty boy, you don't know me, and I don't take orders from you or anybody else," Tyrone said loudly. "This is my woman, so for your benefit, you need to stay out of my business!"

"Well, dog, as you put it, she is my friend, and it seems you haven't been treating her right tonight, so I don't think she needs to go anywhere with you," Marcus said, still standing between Jill and Tyrone.

"Who died and made you king? This is my woman, and she will leave when I tell her to."

Jill touched Marcus on the arm. "Marcus don't worry about it. It's ok," Jill murmured, but Marcus continued to stare down Tyrone.

"That's right, little Marcus. Go back to the playground where all the pretty boys play cause this is a woman—my woman—and I don't think you are ready for grown women yet. You still got milk around your mouth."

"This is my *playground*, and if you think you are dealing with a boy, why don't you test this boy? If you are not going to respect her, then you need to bounce, man!"

Jill had never heard Marcus, sound so mad before, and she was more afraid for Tyrone. Then again, he deserved everything he got for ignoring her and embarrassing her.

"You know what your problem is, pretty boy? It's that you are used to everyone letting you have your way, but not tonight. I got something for you!" Tyrone shouted.

"Well, bring it if you got it cause I can't wait to beat your ass!" Marcus said menacingly as he stepped closer to Tyrone. Neither man backed down.

Jill begged for Tyrone to go back to their table. "Come on, guys. People are looking," Jill said.

Brice jumped in between the two men, lending his support to Jill. "Hey, fellas. How about we calm down, Marcus?"

"Oh, he gonna calm down all right when I put my foot to his cute ass!" Tyrone stepped away from Brice and took a swing at Marcus; both Brice and Marcus ducked. Tyrone turned around and tried to rush up on Marcus, but with the second swing, Marcus grabbed his arm and flipped him to the floor, then stepped away. Tyrone tried to get back up, and as he did, the bouncers walked up, telling him to leave the premises. He then looked over at Jill and told her to get her coat. When she just stood there, he shouted at her.

Jill physically jumped in fear, as his intense anger rattled her. Jill turned to go, but Marcus touched her lightly on the arm, shaking his head and halting her movement.

"What the hell is wrong with you, girl? I told you to get your coat. He ain't running nothing, so do what I say now, dammit!" Tyrone yelled at Jill as he tried to get to his feet.

The bouncers stepped up and grabbed Tyrone by the arms. Jill was relieved when she noticed there was only a handful of people left. She watched as Tyrone was led out of the club, grumbling and cursing his way through the building. Jill started to walk back to her table, but Marcus quietly asked her to follow him. They walked down the hallway leading to Rudy's office. Marcus closed the door behind them and just leaned against it.

Jill took a seat on the sofa. "I am so sorry for all that out there. It was so embarrassing! I never thought Tyrone would come after you like that."

"You have nothing to apologize for. I'm just glad I was here to handle him."

The room was quiet for a few minutes; then Marcus pushed away from the door, walked over to the bar situated in the corner of the room, and poured himself a drink. He emptied the glass in one gulp and then set it back on the bar. "You need to leave him alone, Jill. He is way too crazy for you to mix with. He takes running after other men's women as if it were a game, while you sit on the sidelines and look on. It's a big thrill for him. He loves power-tripping" He angrily started pacing again, then turned back to look at her.

She seemed so tense as she released her breath, not looking at him. "He never has treated me as badly as tonight. I never thought, You think he is—what's power-tripping?" she asked, looking as if she was having trouble getting herself together.

"He is one of those guys who gets off on controlling people, especially women," Marcus answered.

"You know, now that I think about it, you are right. He's not happy unless he gets his way. I have been telling myself I need to break it off with him for some time now. I guess I just thought he would be someone to hang out with, but now it seems we do more disagreeing than anything else."

"Yeah, I know what you mean; hence, the earlier part of my night," he admitted.

"I wasn't looking for anything serious, but now I have someone, and all we seem to do is argue—and he gets kicked out of the club for being stupid!" Jill said, her voice wobbling.

"You got me if you want to hang out, but that clown thinks he is a player, and everyone knows it. Look, Jill, not trying to come down on you hard or anything, and it's certainly your decision to make, but if you value my opinion, stay away from him. I care about you, and I do not want anything to happen to you. But I have to say, if you continue to hang around him, you will be gambling away your happiness or worse."

"I really appreciate all your support, Marcus, but Sheree wants to scratch my eyes out, so I don't see you and I hanging out, so much. But I will be fine. I will just have to explain to Tyrone that we cannot see each other anymore. End of story."

"Like I said before, I do not answer to, Sheree, and neither does she to me. I prefer it that way. We are not in a committed relationship, although she would love nothing better. I don't think I'm ready for that, at least not with her. She is a very jealous woman, and her jealousy has caused a lot of problems. She tells me she is over it, but I think she is only pretending to my face."

"Well, I think someone needs to tell her because whenever you and I are in the same vicinity, homegirl is like a mama bear, and I am the trespasser."

"Sheree could never come between what you and I have, baby girl. Just remember that."

"Yeah, I hear what you are saying, but tonight I am a little to blame for getting her riled up because I lost a bet."

"What?" he said with a frown. "You lost me there."

She smiled somewhat timidly before answering him. "The girls were teasing me a bit about the new guy. I guess he has a thing for me, but I said that he didn't, so Jaz started this bet at the table that when he returned from the bathroom, he would ask me to dance before he asked anyone else. I said no, but the girls said that he would, and if he did, afterward I would have to walk over to your table and ask you to dance. So that's how that happened. I really did not want to upset Sheree, but a bet is a bet, yah know."

"Yeah, it is, but now my ego is hurt. I thought you really wanted to dance with me," he said; hand over his heart.

"Oh, no! I love dancing with … um …" Her words faded as she realized what she was about to reveal.

He looked at her intently. He smiled, and she smiled too but wasn't able to hold his look as he winked at her. He walked back to the minibar, where he poured himself another shot, threw his head back, and then placed the glass back on the bar.

"You know, you may have a point about the trespassing thing. I had better do a good check of your place. How about we get out of here and get you home. I want to make sure old Tyrone is not lurking around your place," he said as he preceded her out the office. When they walked back out into the club area, only a few people were still partying, but Jill's table was still very much alive. All her friends were laughing and some still dancing. Even Rudy and Mable were sitting at the table, much to her and Marcus's surprise.

"Well! It's about time you two got back. Come on—let's shut the club down," Rudy said. "It's still too early for me to cut the lights. What do you say, Marcus? The doors are locked, and it's just our private party. No one can get in, and the bouncers are still on duty by the door. Jill, help your good old friend Rudy shut the place down." Rudy smiled at her as he waited for an answer.

Jill caught Rudy's wink, and then she looked back at Marcus. "I guess if we leave now, that would be rude, and we can't let our friend Rudy down, now, can we?" She smiled at Marcus.

"Ah, no, we can't," Marcus answered.

"Ok, Rudy, we're in!" She smiled as Marcus led her onto the dance floor, joining the others.

They all had such a good time. The earlier drama with Tyrone Was a faraway thought as Jill and Marcus danced the danced the night away. She was given no time to give Tyrone a thought as the two brothers kept her busy. Her friends were happy that Jill wasn't bothered by the scene Tyrone made earlier.

"I am so glad Tyrone was kicked out of the club tonight. Now look at her, out on the floor with Marcus," Yvonne said.

They all watched as the two danced to a slow dance and chatted away.

"What in the world does Jill see in that clown Tyrone anyway?" Joe asked. "He is a major embarrassment. I tell you, Yvonne, I wanted to knock the hell out of him two or three times tonight. He is a worthless pimp. You know that don't you? He will never be faithful to Jill, and everyone knows that."

Yvonne nodded her head in agreement with Joe. "Everyone knows that but Jill, and then again, having Tyrone around is a useful tool for her in the war against Sheree."

Joe suddenly realized what she was implying. "Marcus? You think she is using Tyrone to protect herself from Marcus? Come on, Yvonne, why would she need to do that? They are the best of friends with a little chemistry thrown in. All she has to do is reach for it, and my man Marcus will more than meet her halfway, I'm sure. The problem is that neither one of them will make a move on it."

"Sheree is a large part, if not all, of this problem."

Joe's expression indicated that he had never thought of that idea. "You know you are on to something."

Yvonne nodded her head, feeling quite sure. "Marcus and Jill get along so well. You can even see them watching each other but trying not to let others see them doing it. Sheree knows it, and she is so out of control because she cannot seem to stop the inevitable. Jill is very guarded about what she says about him, but I know she has a thing for him," Yvonne said.

"So, what do we do now? Because I know for a fact that Marcus was not enjoying himself tonight until he got on the dance floor with

Jill," Joe said. "Sheree was stretching his nerves a bit thin, and I threw a monkey wrench in Sheree's plans by not agreeing to cause trouble for Jill. But you know, Yvonne, now that I really think about it, when we all sit around the table together, it's as if they are the only ones there. I know I said some really bad things about her, but now that I know her and see her more, I realize that she and Marcus have more in common than any of the girls that he's dated. Sometimes, when I think about what I did, I might have ruined a good thing. I really feel bad about the things I said about her. Marcus did not like my impression of Jill. He protected her like a knight protects the queen—something like that."

"Yes, I get what you're saying. The only problem is that Sheree has caught Jill and Marcus out a time or two, and she has accused Jill of trying to take Marcus from her. Sheree calls the girl all sorts of names and has even tried to embarrass her in front of him. Marcus is a class act because he stops Sheree by telling her to back off. I'm afraid there have also been times when he wasn't around, and Sheree let Jill have it. I've even had to jump in, and Jasmine—well, you know Jasmine—we had to hold her back from slapping Sheree after we walked in on Sheree loud-talking Jill in the ladies' room. I think that's why Jill uses her relationship with Tyrone to make Sheree think that she is not interested in our boy Marcus."

"Well, let me tell you this—Marcus is at the end of his patience with Sheree and with Tyrone. I think the breakup is coming soon for him and Sheree. I also think that fight tonight, is something Marcus wanted to happen. Yvonne, I tell you right now—Marcus does not even need a reason to whoop his ass! But enough about them. How about we show Jill and Marcus that they are not the only ones who can dance?" They both smiled as Joe led her onto the dance floor.

A little while later, Cyn and Jaz made their way to their separate homes. Yvonne and Joe left the club and headed to Joe's place as a cozy ending to the evening. When Marcus took Jill home, it was four in the morning, but he still would not leave her there alone, for fear that Tyrone would turn up. Jill felt relieved with his being there, so she brought him a pillow and a blanket and set up her couch for him to sleep on.

She cooked breakfast for him, to his delight, and not long afterward, he left to spend time with his brother, telling her he would call her later.

Chapter

6

That next day, Jaz treated Jill to a movie, and afterward, they stopped by Cyn's place to drink wine and have girl talk. Yvonne came by a little later and joined in the fun.

"Yvonne, I'm surprised to see you here tonight. I would have thought you and Joe would be having a romantic evening, especially after last night. It seemed you two were closer than ever," Cyn said as they all carried plates with different hors d'oeuvres prepared by Cyn. Jaz refilled everyone's wine glasses, and the girls got more comfortable on the sofa.

"Well, Brice is in town, so the fellas are hanging out. They played golf earlier, and tonight, it's shooting pool at Joe's place. They even have the grill out, as cold as it is. Joe and Marcus were cooking some beer hot dogs, while Brice and Fonze were grilling the steaks. They were having a ball, trash talking. Before the night is done, they will probably pull out the card table, and then it really will be on. I did my escape thing to be with my girls," Yvonne said with a smile.

"We are so glad you came, girl. Jaz and I came over on the spur of the moment after going to the movies, and we were lucky Cyn didn't have a hot date, so we parked it here, and now that you are here, it's perfect!" Jill said as the other two girls agreed.

"Perfect! How was the movie?" Yvonne asked.

"We saw that new Gloria Hawn movie, *The Choir*. It wasn't as good as we thought it would be, but it was ok," Jaz said.

"Yeah, I have heard a few people say that it was not worth the hype! Man! Cyn, these shrimps are incredible! What did you do to them?" Yvonne asked.

"I found this marinade and from the reviews, I had to try it. I liked it so much; thought I would try it on you girls," Cyn explained

"Yes, it's awesome!" Jaz and Jill both added.

"So, you gonna try this on Brice?" Yvonne asked, smiling.

"Are you kidding me? Brice is not paying any attention to me," Cyn admitted.

"I don't know if I agree with that. I detected some serious vibes the other night when he was at the table," Jill said as she went to get some more snacks from the table. The other girls spoke up as well.

"No, y'all, I'm serious. That man is too busy playing the field to concentrate on one woman," Cyn insisted.

"We all know how Brice is, but it seems when you two are around each other, we can feel something," Yvonne said.

"Yes, Cyn, I noticed that the other night when we walked back to the table. He was different around you," Jill agreed.

"Well, that's not the vibe I get, so until he makes a move, I will just wait and see. But on to a different subject. Jill, give us the 411 on crazy-ass Tyrone," Cyn said, and the others turned to Jill.

"Yeah, last night got quite lethal with him and Marcus pushing up on each other," Jaz said.

"Yeah, but my boy Marcus held that drunken fool in check. How dare he boss you around for dancing without his permission, when that's all he did most of the night!" Cyn exclaimed.

"Yeah! Girl, what gives with you and him? Please tell me you are not going to still see him?" Yvonne said.

When the girls all looked Jill's way, she knew she could not lie. She sat back on the couch, adjusted a pillow, and then said, "I did get a call last night, but I turned the phone off so Marcus—" Jill stopped suddenly, realizing she was about to reveal that Marcus had slept over at her place. But her realization came too late.

Cyn broke the silence that blanketed the room. "Ah! Jillian, repeat that! I mean, are you saying that you were with Marcus all night?"

Jill took a deep breath and then reached for her glass, suddenly needing something to do.

"OK, missy, that's enough stalling. Spill the beans." Yvonne demanded.

Jill took a sip and then put the glass down and shrugged her shoulders nonchalantly, as if it was no big deal. "Marcus thought Tyrone might try to come over to my place, and he was worried that Tyrone might not have cooled down, so he stayed at my place. But he slept on the couch; nothing happened between us. He left early this morning, after breakfast. So, y'all, it was nothing!" Jill still felt uncomfortable about revealing so much, knowing how her friends were hoping for so much more between her and Marcus.

"Nothing?" Cyn asked.

"Nothing," Jill answered.

Yvonne just shook her head. "You know we were so hoping."

"Yeah, I know. But he does have a girlfriend. I don't intend to cross that line."

"So, what about Tyrone? Have you heard from him since last night?" Jaz asked with a worried look.

"No, there was a hang-up on my answering system but nothing else. If he had called, I would not have answered or returned his call. I do not think I want to continue with Tyrone."

"I think that's a good idea," Yvonne said, and the others chimed in their agreement.

"The sad part about it is that I was never interested in Tyrone in a romantic kind of way. It was mainly to keep Sheree off my back about Marcus. I do feel guilty for using him in that way, though." Jill said somberly.

"I knew it!" Yvonne exclaimed. "I knew there was no way in hell that you would be attracted to someone like that ... that '70s reject!"

"What are you gonna do if he persists, Jill? He doesn't seem like he deals very much with reality. I mean, what are you gonna do when Marcus is not around? I don't think Tyrone will take *no* easily, especially as he sees Marcus as competition."

Jill shook her head. "I told him that Marcus is just a friend and that he has a girlfriend. I think he will get tired of the hassle, and it will all be over."

"Girl, I hope you are right. We all want to see him out of your life," Cyn said, looking not so sure about Jill's reasoning.

"Me too. It would be great if he stayed away. So, ladies, on a better note—Miss Jasmine, how did your date with what's-his-name—Narojic—go?" Yvonne asked.

Jaz laughed at Yvonne's mispronunciation of her date's name. "It's pronounced *Na-re-jor-ic*, but girl, don't even waste your time. Narie, as I call him, was a big fat zero. He told me he had a technique for measuring body fat. He wanted to try it out on me. He told me all I needed to do was take off all my clothes so that he would be able to accurately measure my body-fat ratio. If my ratio was too great, then he would put me on his diet plan. I gave him what-for in answer to his ratio-finding pursuit! I kicked him out!"

The girls rolled with laughter.

"Oh, Jasmine, where do you find these guys?" Yvonne said laughingly.

They spent the rest of the evening going from one topic to the next as the laughs kept coming.

The rest of that week went by quickly, and the following Saturday, Jill spent time powerwalking in a nearby park. Most of the day, she expected to hear from one of the girls, but no one had any plans. Later, she noticed her message light flashing—the message was from Tyrone. Jill exhaled slowly, not wanting to deal with him. Tyrone left a message almost every day, but she had not returned his calls. She was not in the mood to talk to him.

The following day, she held off, as long as she could before finally calling him back. He seemed quiet and not himself, which further caused Jill to feel bad. She found it hard to end it with him, as he kept pleading with her over and over, so she agreed to meet him at a small diner across town at one o'clock on Saturday afternoon. Jill dreaded the meeting, but when the day came, she headed out to meet him.

He was carrying flowers when they met at the restaurant, which he immediately handed to her. After he made another long apology, she did her best to appear that all was forgotten, although she still had a nagging feeling inside. Tyrone was on his best behavior; he even managed to make her laugh—something that should have been hard to do, considering the problems he had caused. She also noticed that he was not demanding or being selfish like his old self. Once they were through eating, she decided to end the meeting before he asked her something that she was not ready for; she felt that he wanted more.

Jill told him that she had to leave to take care of some errands. She was surprised when he did not try to persuade her to stay. She thought maybe he had taken a good look at himself and was making efforts to be a better person. If so, she was impressed with his efforts. He asked her about having dinner the following week, and once again, she agreed, which surprised her. But it was hard for her to hurt anyone. She thought maybe she would let things fade away—at least, that was her plan.

———

Monday had been busy, and Jill didn't realize until later in the day that she had a message to which she hadn't listened to and it was from Marcus. It was nice to hear his voice. She really missed him. He had called to let her know he would be out of town for the rest of the week—something had come up at one of his construction sites—but he would call her when things settled.

She decided that she would not tell Marcus about seeing Tyrone. She did not want to upset him. It was nice not having to deal with any drama from Tyrone or Sheree. She had to admit that the last few weeks had been quiet, just like she liked it. During the week, she had her nose to the grindstone and was happy to see that she had made lots of progress in getting her work caught up. When Friday came, she was mentally exhausted and was not looking forward to spending any time with Tyrone.

Tyrone had to work late, so their lunch became dinner. Jill was ready when he arrived at seven. They headed to a restaurant a few blocks from her place. To Jill's dismay there was a waiting list, and she did not want to wait another hour. Tyrone made it up to her by taking her to Winky's, one of his favorite nightspots. Once there, she realized it was a dive; back home, they would call places like this a *hole in the wall* or *beer garden*. It was a small place compared to Exclusive Company. A few customers were sitting at the bar, and farther back in the room, near a small, square dance floor, the deejay was setting up.

They took a seat near the dance floor. Menus were on the table. Tyrone handed her one, and they both took their time in checking it out.

"Well, well, look at old Tyrone," the bartender said to a gentleman sitting at the bar. He handed him a beer, and the patron was surprised to see the girl who his buddy seemed to have a thing for.

"Now how in the world did he manage to get with something like that? She must be a cokehead or something," the bartender said as they watched the two take a seat at a table.

"Nah, D. I know that lady, and she ain't no hood rat or cokehead. What you see there is a very nice woman who is definitely out of her element," the patron said.

"We need to upgrade the place, and she gets my vote!" the bartender said before walking away to attend to another customer.

Jill never noticed the man watching her from the bar. She felt a bit overdressed compared to the other women in the club. The crowd inside slowly increased as it got later in the evening. Jill was apprehensive, but since Tyrone seemed to know everyone, his explanation was that he sometimes worked here after he was let go by the car wash to help his cash flow.

"Ya know, Jilly, I still think you and I have all sorts of possibilities with this thang between us. I'm truly sorry for what happened at the club that night. I guess my head got a little too tight. I now know that ... that guy you know, the rich boy, is not in your league. He deals with those high-dollar women, and they party on yachts and fly their private planes to the Bahamas and shit, whenever they want. I know that night it was more about just dancing and having fun."

A little while later, Tyrone told her he had to speak with the manager about getting some more hours, and he would be back. When thirty minutes had gone by, Jill wondered what was keeping him so long. Then someone asked her to dance, and she agreed. Tyrone still had not come back by the time she had finished her dance. Twenty minutes later, he still had not shown up, and she began to worry. The music turned up as more people went onto the dance floor, and the club got into full swing. Jill's back was turned to the entrance, so she never saw the police officers come into the club, speak to the bartender, and then head to the back.

"Hey, Fonze, man, you need to get your friend and get out of here," the bartender said.

"Why? What's happening?" He looked at the bartender, who looked around before turning back to him.

"I don't know, man, but five-0 just asked for Mike, and I know Tyrone is in Mike's office. I tried to call Mike, but his line just rings, so he might be back in the room with Tyrone. You know what Tyrone does around here so I'm thinking it's not legal."

"Say no more, man, but if Josh comes around, send him home. I don't want him caught up. Thanks, man!"

Jill got up to pick up her sweater from the floor, only to stop when several cops entered the restaurant and spoke to the bartender, then went to the back of the building. She then realized that was the same direction Tyrone had gone, and a nervous feeling invaded her gut.

"Excuse me, but isn't your name Jill?"

Jill looked up to see a tall, slender man, whose face looked familiar. "Yes."

"My name is Fonze. I'm a friend of Marcus Jordan. We met at his place once."

Jill nodded. "Yes! I do remember you. It was when I first came to town."

"Yes, that's right! But I gotta tell you—there is something going down, and you need to get out of here because there are already several cops in the manager's office, and some more are headed in here."

"But my friend who I came here with, he—"

"Yeah, he is part of the action that is kicking off back there, I'm sure. You definitely need to get yourself out of this situation with him. We need to clear out of here."

"Are you serious?"

Fonze nodded his head.

"I came here with him. I don't have my car."

Just then, more sirens were heard.

"No worries, I can take you home, but we need to go *now!*" he whispered. He motioned with his hand for Jill to follow him. She immediately got up, looked back in the direction where Tyrone had gone, then hurried to catch up with Fonze. Once they were outside, they noticed the patrol cars heading toward the back of the club.

Fonze turned to her quickly, asking, "Are you alright?" When she nodded her head, he said, "Sorry I had to rush you out like this, but my car is over there. Let's go before it gets crazier." He led her to a black Mustang with a soft top and opened the door for her. Just after they pulled away from the club, two more police cars came around the corner at high speed with flashing lights. He turned to her again, trying to calm the situation. "That was close, but at least we are away from all that mayhem."

"I can't believe this is happening. So, you are a friend of Marcus's. How did you meet?"

"Well, like I said earlier, we are good friends. We grew up together—different sides of town. His family always looked out for us here downtown. His father was always working with the community center, and he would bring Brice and Marcus along, and that's how we met. We have been friends since middle school. Marcus always preferred the community center, and the activities there as opposed to the private school and its activities. Yes, he is a good guy. What happened back there, I wouldn't worry too much about it. Tyrone is used to this kind of thing, so I'm told," Fonze said.

Jill was still in shock about all that had just happened. After Jill gave Fonze directions to her place, she leaned her head back on the headrest.

Fonze turned his head slightly, looking over at her before speaking. "I seriously do not think that this is the type of club for a classy girl like you."

Jill answered in a defensive tone. "How do you know that I'm a classy girl? Scratch that, I was being rude, sorry. Yeah, the things I get myself into. I should have never come here tonight. I wish I could just rewind my whole evening and erase my date with Tyrone. I am just so glad you were here. I had no clue as to what was going on in there. He said he was going to talk to the manager about getting more hours, but he was gone, such a long time. Thank you for getting me out of there and driving me home, Mr. Fonze."

"You are welcome! But call me Fonze."

Fonze was very nice, and he had her laughing, which helped her to not dwell on how close she had come to trouble again from being with Tyrone. He soon turned his car onto Jill's Street and stopped in front of the apartments where she lived.

"Mr., ah, I mean, Fonze, how much do I owe you?"

He shook his head. "Nothing, Miss Jill. I was just glad to be able to help. I hope you will take my advice and stay away from Winky's. It's definitely not a place for a classy woman like you."

Jill then blinked and hesitated before speaking. "I am Jill to my friends; the *miss* is not necessary; but thank you for everything."

He nodded.

"Well, thanks again and good night." She entered her building, thinking only later that she should have told Fonze not to mention what had happened to anyone, especially Marcus.

———

A few cities away, while attending a dinner at John Jacobs's home, an old client of Jordan Enterprises, Marcus suddenly became aware of a peculiar feeling that something was wrong. Although he tried to shake it, the feeling kept returning. He left the dinner early, telling John that he had to pack for an early flight, but he would be back in a few days to check on their ongoing project. When Marcus arrived back at the hotel, he picked up his messages and headed to his room to pack. He took a shower. He still felt wound up after his shower, still unable to rid himself of this feeling, he called his parents. He hung up after feeling reassured that they were ok. He returned Sheree's call, with her reminding him to make sure he was back in town for his birthday party, as he promised her that he would take an early flight out the next day, which was Friday. After he reassured her, he hung up and packed his suitcase. He checked his other messages as he looked over his calendar, seeing Thanksgiving and calculating the number of days he would have to complete the part of the project he wanted done before the holiday.

Later, he poured himself a drink from the wet bar, hoping this would help him to relax. Finally, he was able to sleep.

On Saturday morning, Jill got up early to join the girls at the gym; then, later, she would run some errands and maybe do some cleaning around the apartment. She felt on edge, not knowing what had happened to Tyrone last night—or why? He had promised to be better, but the feeling that he was doing something illegal hovered in her brain all day. She was not sure if he was in jail.

Thanksgiving was coming up soon, and it seemed likely that her holiday would be to enjoy a frozen meal alone in front of the TV. She thought of Marcus and wondered whether he had gotten back in town yet because his party was tonight. Jill got an idea about a present for Marcus, and on Sarah's recommendation, she found a store that had a good selection of desk pens with a holder. She could get the engraving done there as well. She purchased a set of moderately expensive pens and left them to be engraved. She reminded herself to pick up his gift to carry with her when she went to the club, just in case she ran into him. She knew it was probably wishful thinking, but she would take the gift anyway.

After the gym, everyone went their separate ways in preparation for meeting up at the club that night. Jill picked up Marcus's pens at the engravers on her way home. She felt good about the work that was done; it looked very professional. *Marcus will be so surprised*, she thought. *I hope he likes them, although he probably already has a lot of pe*ns. Now she thought that her present would probably be dull in comparison to his girlfriend's gift.

When Jill got home, she picked out the black cocktail dress that she had bought a while back for a special function; she would wear it that night to the club. She was amazed at how much better the dress fit her now. The crisscross bodice hung slightly off her shoulders and outlined her cleavage. Her body had become so much firmer since the workouts. The skirt flared out slightly and swished appealingly around her shapely legs. When she saw herself in the mirror, she was very pleased—her hourglass figure was on full display. Although she wasn't thin, the weight loss was doing wonders for her self-esteem. She felt that she could probably handle some of the snide comments her sisters used to make about her being overweight. She had never looked or felt this good in her life.

When Jill arrived at the club, she signed in and showed her employee pass. She went into a large ballroom that had a bar and tables scattered throughout. The rooms were divided by frosted glass on one side of the room, slightly separating the dining area from the club side. The tables were oval for the club and square for the dining area. There were also small booths for two people. The tables were covered with white linen tablecloths and adorned with a bowl of fresh roses and small candles. The ceiling lighting was turned down low, giving the room a very cozy yet classy atmosphere. Jill had heard that different celebrities often frequented the club, which, she thought, was probably how it got the name Excusive Company.

The sound that filled the room was like smooth jazz or some type of ballad. A few couples were on the dance floor, moving slowly to the smooth tune. It was early, so the club was not yet full. Jill found two of her friends, Jasmine and Cyn, who were seated at one of the round tables, waving to her.

"Jill, girl, you look amazing!" Cyn said. "Those workouts are paying off. Don't you think, Jaz?"

"Yeah, see the guy in the gray silk shirt at the bar? He has not taken his eyes off you since you walked in. You look great, girl."

"Thanks, guys. I need all the compliments I can get. I do feel good, though. You two are looking great as well," Jill said, looking from one to the other.

"Thanks, girl," Cyn said. "After all our hard work, compliments help to keep us focused."

A gentleman walked up and asked Cyn for a dance. For the next hour or so, the girls barely had time to catch their breath before there was another request for a dance. Later in the evening, Jill was coming from the ladies' room, and as she was reaching for the door to go back inside, she heard her name called. When she turned around, she saw Marcus standing on the other side of the lobby, and he started to walk in her direction. When he reached her, she also noticed Joe standing to the side as a tray was wheeled out, loaded with ice.

"Marcus? Happy Birthday! What are you doing here?" Jill said excitedly. She gave him a hug, and he returned, her embrace, which lasted longer than she expected. When they drew apart, her eyes feasted on his fine form in a blue suit, crisp white shirt adorned with cufflinks, and dress shoes to complement his attire.

"Thank you. I just got back in town for my party but after that I will be returning to New York. I'm trying to get as much done with this project as I can before the holidays. You look really nice in that dress. Is it something new?"

Jill had goose bumps from the way he looked at her. "Ah, no, it's been in my closet, but yes because this is the first time I've felt comfortable enough to wear it. The workouts have done wonders for me." She still felt nervous, as the electric charge between the two of them seemed to ramp up.

"Well, you look incredible in it. I wish I could stick around to have a few dances with you, but the ice machine quit working in the conference room. I sent someone over to pick up the order, but they needed a signature, and Rudy wasn't available at the time so here I am. But the club is really rocking. I bet you've been burning up the dance floor."

"Yeah, I guess you could say that. But before I forget—I have something for you." Jill opened her purse and pulled out a small gift-wrapped box.

"Hold on a minute," he said, looking around. "We'll take this where there are no prying eyes. Follow me. I don't want any trouble I make for myself to touch you." He led her inside the club, away from the tables, and down a hall to the left. They stopped at the door marked MANAGER and went inside.

Once inside Jill pulled out the small gift box again and handed it to him.

He gave her a huge smile as he tore off the wrapping paper and then opened the box. "I know you are going to find this hard to believe, but no one has ever given me engraved pens before. You would think I'd have a desk full, but I don't. Jill, I will treasure these, especially since they came from you. Thank you." He stepped closer and wrapped his arms around her, pulling her closer and kissing her on the cheek.

The sensation of his lips on her skin did crazy things to Jill. Everything seemed to stop, and the room was so quiet. She heard him release a breath; she didn't realize she was holding her breath until her lungs seemed to burn.

He stepped away, looking at her still. "Oh, how I wish that I was in this club tonight, but ..."

"That's ok, Marcus. You are where you should be."

He stared directly into her eyes. "Maybe for now. Well, I guess I should get back to the party," he said without enthusiasm.

"Yes, of course, but I'm glad I was able to give you your gift. I'll see you another time, Marcus." Jill walked toward the door, and Marcus hurried to open it for her.

"Until next time," Marcus said. "Hey, don't have too much fun without me, ok?"

Suddenly, Jill felt the butterflies in her stomach start to dance. She blushed, both from what he'd said and from the intense look in his eyes.

"I'll try not to," she said as she walked out the door ahead of him.

The girls were still dancing when Jill sat down. Soon, Jill was asked to dance, but he kept getting too close, which proved annoying for Jill. When the song ended, he preceded to annoy her by sitting down at her table, trying to talk her into going on a date. She declined the offer and was relieved when he left the table. She felt less in the mood for dancing or for having to deal with such an obnoxious guy, so she told the girls that she was going home alone.

———

Jill did not hear from Marcus for the rest of the weekend. By Tuesday, she was really missing him and wondering if he had gotten back in town for Thanksgiving. She was sure he would be occupied with Sheree and his family, so she really did not expect to hear from him.

Just as she put thoughts of Marcus away, the phone rang. She was uneasy, thinking it might be Tyrone. She let the answering machine get it, but when she heard Marcus's voice, she quickly grabbed the phone. "Marcus!" she said eagerly

"Hey, Jill."

She found it hard to keep the smile out of her voice as she responded happily, "Are you back in town?"

"No, I wish, but I am still in New York." He longed to be on the other side of the phone call with her. He missed her more than he realized. "It's nice to hear your voice." He sounded kind of quiet, and she felt her body react to the sound of him.

When she became quiet, Marcus said, "Jill, are you still there? Jill?"

Jill fought a battle of not letting her need for him be heard in her voice, but she was failing fast. She cleared her throat and then said, "Yes! So, tell me, how is everything going?" She tried to sound normal.

"Very slow, but I'm sure things will get back to normal soon. I had to go to a dinner party last night, and I guess with all that I'm trying to do here, it was hard for me to really get into the party. I did make some really great contacts, though."

"That's good. Does the traveling back and forth so often bother you?"

"Ah, sometimes. But if it's a really good project, without many conflicts, it is very enjoyable. Besides, I get to meet some extraordinary people. Now, this project has been a pain, in my side. When I got here yesterday, we managed to iron out a lot of the issues, and the client was very happy. When I got back to the hotel at, like, ten o'clock last night, I was worn out."

"Maybe you are getting burned out. You really need to get someone to help you with the workload. You are quite the workhorse."

"Who? Me? I don't think so."

"You are. Marcus, sweetie, listen. When you are here in town, you have a big office, and you get to delegate a lot of stuff because you have plenty of staff. But now you are on the road, where you have to do a lot more instead of delegating some of that workload."

"Um, 'sweetie'—that has a good ring to it."

"I'm serious, Marcus!"

"Ok, I see what you meant. I think you have a point because I find myself so frustrated because things I need done can't be done right away."

"See? Told yah! I know you like, a book. You need to pay me an adviser fee," she said with a short laugh.

"Ok, so how about you come here and work with me?"

She laughed in response. "You wish, Jordan!"

"Yeah, I do. But I am so wanting to get this wrapped up as soon as possible and get on a plane to head home."

"Guess you are missing me already, huh?" Jill realized what she had said and wished the words back.

Marcus beat her to the punch by quietly responding, "Yeah, I really do. I was sorry I missed dancing with you the other night. You were gorgeous. I really liked that dress. So how did you hold the fellas off? Did you stay out of trouble?"

She sighed heavily into the phone. "Funny you should mention trouble, but I will fill you in later. So, tell me, how is New York at this time of year?"

"Oh no, you're not getting off that easily. Tell me what is going on."

Jill, trying to minimize what she had let slip, said, "Marcus, it is so funny, and now I am thinking that I'd rather tell you when you are here so that I can watch you crack up just like I did."

Marcus sighed. "Uh-huh. Why do I get the feeling it will not be as funny to me?"

"Oh, Marcus, you will find this really funny. Trust me."

"Ok, I will wait but not willingly."

Jill tried to change the subject. "Tell me, did you have to beat them off with a stick?"

He gave a short laugh before answering. "No, not really, but you do have an active imagination."

"Excuse me if I say I do not believe you."

He got quiet for a minute or two.

Then Jill said, "My, my, does my question require this much thought?"

"Nope, no sticks needed," he admitted.

"Will you be back any time soon?"

"Yeah, but not to stay. I don't have the space to work, but since I am right here on-site, I just work from a small table in the trailer. The guys are all pretty cool, and it's really not so bad. So, besides the news you want me to wait to hear, anything else going on?"

"My life is dull and boring. I still think you need to have Joe come and help you or get one of your many assistants to help you."

"Right now, at the office is where I need him most. The problem here is nothing that I can't handle. If I can't, then I will call in the reinforcements, but I figure in a few trips, it will all be better soon. The coming holidays will slow things up a bit, but it will get done."

"I sure hope so, Marcus," she replied quietly.

"Why? Are you missing me, woman?"

Jill was caught off guard by the question and didn't know how to answer, so she just gave him the truth. "As a matter of fact, I do miss my buddy." She added the buddy part to lighten things up because she could feel the electricity, even being so far away.

"Oh, I like the part about you missing me. At least I know I'm not forgotten," he said quietly. He heard her soft laugh, and it was like the softest touch that spread heat all over him. He knew that he needed to end the call before he said something silly. "Well, I guess I'd better end this call and get ready for bed. I have another long day tomorrow." Shortly afterward, he ended the call.

When Jill hung up the phone, she felt sad and knew it was because she wished he were there with her and not so far away. She got ready for bed wearing a smile, as she thought about the phone call. Her last thought was how he made her feel, just from a phone call. Her new life had brought this man into her life, and no matter what, she was so thankful to experience real love, and that's exactly what she felt for him.

Marcus thought back over his phone conversation with Jill and realized it would be hard for him to spend three more days in New York. He knew he would work fast to get it all done in as few days as possible so he could get home by Thanksgiving. Jill hadn't mentioned Tyrone, and Marcus hoped that he was not back in her life. He smiled to himself, not believing he just equated Jill with home, but it did feel good.

The next few days, Jill managed to stay busy. Mr. Rogers was away on business, so Jill was assigned many appointments, which kept her away from the office on Monday and Tuesday, but by Wednesday, business had come to a halt. It was the last workday before Thanksgiving. The office was almost empty; there was only Jill, the receptionist, and two other people in the secretarial pool. The building was so quiet, especially since the phones hardly rang. She had a video conference at one o'clock, and then she was off work until Monday. Her conference call was with Drucker Foods, an old client of Mr. Rogers. He wanted her to personally take care of the account.

Jill was happy that it went nicely. The client wanted a new complete workup of advertisement for his online ordering. She was just shutting down her computer when Sarah peeped into the office to wish her a happy Thanksgiving. Jill grabbed her bag and made sure everything was locked up before heading out the door. She was just putting in the security code, and when she turned around, she stopped short when she saw Marcus walking up. She instantly smiled and before she knew it, she was wrapping her arms around him, and he did likewise. It felt very natural for them.

"Marcus! Oh my gosh! I didn't think I would see you so soon. When did you get back?"

"Oh, I like this kind of welcome."

She laughed to cover her blushing.

Then he said, "But I got in about an hour and thirty minutes ago. I stopped by the office, but everyone was in a hurry to get out, which I could understand. It was the same way in New York, so I shut everything down and hopped onto the company plane. I thought I would check on my buddy, but I see you are heading out early too. Any place in particular?"

"Nope, not really. The girls all have family or boyfriend things to do, so I'm just headed home to put my feet up and enjoy the quiet."

He watched her and then smiled. "Since you have no plans, how about joining me for dinner?"

Jill was caught off guard and became flustered. "Dinner? I thought you would have—you know."

"Yes?"

"Well, Sheree, what about her?"

"What about her?"

"Shouldn't you make plans with her?"

"Nah, things are not as they should be so I'd rather have dinner with someone who will not ruin my enjoyment of a good meal. So, what do you say?"

"Ok, then, I accept."

She followed him in her car to a small deli that was a favorite, just a few blocks away.

Dinner was so nice and cozy at the small eatery. They were constantly laughing as he talked how his mother would practice on him with her cooking before Thanksgiving. But in the last few years, because he was usually working, she had to use his father or whoever was around. "Brice always played it smart by not showing up until Thanksgiving Day," he said.

She was still smiling about his stories when he looked over at her and asked about her holidays at home. She hesitated but then began to tell him. "Um, my memories were not as warm and fuzzy as yours. I usually would spend the night before Thanksgiving and most of the day making sure everything was done. I did the cooking while mother invited people over. My sisters got to hang out with their friends, and once everyone had eaten, I cleaned up." She took another sip of her tea.

"You didn't get to go out with your friends?"

"No; and didn't make a fuss about it. I didn't want to upset the normal running of things for Mama."

"Now I know why you are such a good cook, but you needed the time with your friends as well, Jill." He looked as if he had a sour taste in his mouth.

"We didn't have the togetherness that you had going on. The term *togetherness* for my family meant something different."

"Why is that?"

She hesitated again before speaking. "That's something I have never figured out, but maybe one day I will have the answer to why my mother treated me differently. I love the fact that we have been laughing nonstop. This has been great, Marcus." She looked around, not wanting the blemish of her old life to interrupt the good time she was having with him. "The food was so good. I have always loved Jake's Deli. It's very cozy and relaxing."

"Yes, it is."

"I guess we had better get moving. Looks like they are closing."

He saw that some of the chairs were being put on top of the tables. "Yeah, you're right. Are you ready?" They headed out, and he walked her to her car. "Hey, I forgot to ask you—what are your plans for Thanksgiving?" He noticed her hesitation before she replied.

"Oh, I have no big plans, just cooking dinner for my neighbor because I know she will be alone."

"Oh, ok, just making sure you were not alone, although both of you could come and share Thanksgiving with us."

"That's really thoughtful of you, Marcus, but she doesn't like to go far from her home. You know, I think it's a thing with older people, so she is allowing me to take over her kitchen and just do a little something, nothing major."

He nodded his understanding. "If you change your mind, the offer stands."

"Thanks, I appreciate that. I will say happy Thanksgiving, and I'll talk to you later. Thanks for dinner. This was really nice."

He agreed and held her door for her as she got in. "Happy Thanksgiving to you too!" He shut the door and headed to his car.

As Jill pulled out, she saw him as he did the same, ending their evening. She gave a long sigh, and a smile appeared on her face.

———

The next day, Jill slept in—there was no reason to rush to get up; it was the holiday, and she had no plans. She thought that she would check on her neighbor, Mrs. Bishop, because she too was alone. Jill had met Mrs. Bishop a few days after moving into her apartment. She was a little lady with gray hair that she always wore in a bun. She was widowed; her husband of some fifty years had passed away only five years ago. They had no children, and her remaining family lived out of town. Jill grew fond of the old lady, often taking time out just to visit with her or run errands. They had developed a friendship and always looked out for each other. When Jill thought about it, she would certainly place Mrs. Bishop as part of her new family.

She felt bad, having lied to Marcus, but she didn't want to spend the holiday avoiding Sheree's glare or snide remarks if she was at Marcus's parents' house. Two hours later, there was a knock on her door. *That's odd*, she thought. *Everyone I know is either out of town or with their families.* She went to the door. When she called out, the response was from her neighbor. Jill opened the door with a smile and invited the older woman inside.

"Oh, no thank you, dear. My sister and her daughter are next door at my place. They thought they would surprise me and take me to a family dinner at my niece's house. Isn't that wonderful?" Mrs. Bishop said with a radiant smile.

"Oh yes! I'd say that's a very nice thing for them to do. I am so happy for you."

"Yes, I am very happy to see them. You know how I dread holidays, but I'm so glad to go with them. Would you like to come with us? I know you're all alone, and it should not be that way." The older woman frowned at Jill.

"Oh, Mrs. Bishop, I am fine. Marcus invited me to his family dinner, and now that you will be gone, I think I will take him up on it. I think things worked out very well."

The old lady raised an eyebrow before another huge smile broke out on her face. "I knew he was a sweet man. You go with that young man, Jillian. I tell you; you have got yourself a good thing with him. Don't let him get away. Darling, I'm going to head out with my folks now. It's getting on noontime, but I wish you the nicest Thanksgiving."

"And I you, Mrs. Bishop." Jill was quite surprised when suddenly she was engulfed in a firm embrace. Then the old lady walked away, leaving Jill with a smile.

Two hours later, Jill took out a turkey pot pie and placed it on the counter. Then remembered she needed to water her two plants. Suddenly, feeling the quiet start to get to her, she went out on her balcony to look around. Maybe the fresh air, although chilly, would lighten her mood, but she was wrong. She could hear the family downstairs as they shared laughs, and the heavy weight of loneliness seemed to take over her mind. She wrapped her arms around her body as she realized how alone she really was, and the tears started. She felt isolated and suddenly missed her father and his smile. She quickly wiped at the tears. Her father always had the biggest smile for her. She missed him so. She wanted to be with someone, friends, family, and to feel the love. She missed Marcus and the phenomenal feeling that being with him gave her.

Her thoughts got no further, as there was another knock at her door. She thought maybe Mrs. Bishop forgot to tell her something. She wiped at her tear-stained face before she opened the door—only to find Marcus standing there. She simply froze, having been taken totally off guard.

"Hey," he said.

"Ah, hey, Marcus." Jill stood there for a moment and then invited him in. He saw the hesitation, and the look on her face as he walked in, leaving her to close the door.

"So, what's up? I thought you would be busy cooking up a storm or something." He turned around, looking pointedly at her.

"What are you doing here? I mean, shouldn't you be at your folks' place, carving turkey or something?" Her voice sounded hoarse.

"I asked you a question first." He waited with arms crossed.

"Oh that! Mrs. Bishop's sister and her niece surprised her and came to take her to their family dinner. She invited me, but I didn't want to intrude. She was so happy, and I was happy for her."

"Mm-hm. So that leaves you completely alone."

"Yeah, but that's Ok. I have a lot of stuff I need to get done." She walked over to the couch, picked up a throw blanket, and began folding it.

"Like what?" he asked, still watching her.

"Just stuff I have been putting off."

"So, are you going to take time to eat?" he asked.

"Yes, of course. I have my, uh, meal planned," she said, not looking directly at him.

"What are you going to eat?" He knew she was getting tired of his asking questions, but he wanted her to realize that having dinner with his family was where she should be and not alone.

"Marcus! Why all the questions? I might have a date. I don't tell you everything, you know." She flopped down on the couch, still not looking at him.

He walked over and sat down near her on the couch and just looked at her. "I know you don't, but we will have that talk another time. I think right now, nothing would please me more than to have you as my dinner guest. But if you have a hot date, then I will understand."

"Thanks, Marcus. Now you need to hurry, or you will be late for your mom's dinner." Jill tried to inject some brightness into her voice.

"Who is the lucky guy?" He watched the guilty look that appeared on her face.

She could not look at him, but she took several deep breaths. "Marcus, what difference does that make?" She fiddled with the blanket that she had just folded.

"You know, Jillian, I have known you for a while now, and you have a hard time telling lies. This is one of those times. Now come clean. There is no date, is there?" He waited for her response.

"No," she admitted quietly. The next thing she knew, his hand was touching her chin and turning her to look at him.

"I will only go to my family's dinner if you leave with me; otherwise, you are having a guest for dinner."

"You cannot miss your family dinner! What will your folks think? What about your brother?"

He just shrugged. "It all depends on you." He took off his jacket, then loosened his necktie. He sat back down and stretched his arms out across the back of the couch. He leaned his head back and closed his eyes.

"You are so mean-spirited! You are just way too much, Marcus Jordan." She got up and as she walked past him and went down the hall, he could hear her mumbling. She closed her door more forcefully than what was needed.

He sat up, smiling, before stretching back out on the couch. Twenty minutes later, she appeared in a gold-colored dress with sheer sleeves and matching pumps. She had accessorized it with a pair of hoop earrings. She wore no makeup, but her lips had a natural color with a little glisten.

He immediately approved. "Wow, you look amazing, if I may say so."

She gave a little smile but cut it short and looked at him as if she did not want his compliment. "Ok, let's go to your dinner. Let the record show I am only going because I did not want your family pissed off with you for acting crazy!" She rolled her eyes for effect.

"Well, I got you to go, didn't I?" he teased.

"Boy! Come on!" She rolled her eyes again, but this time she tried to hide a smile as she grabbed her jacket as they headed out.

⌒

They arrived at his parent's house in no time. Marcus was in such a good mood on their drive there that his good spirits rubbed off on Jill. She too was now smiling and could not remember when the change in her mood had occurred. Once inside the house, she saw quite a few people. She was introduced to his father, an uncle, two aunts, and his grandmother on his father's side. Brice was there as well, entertaining a young woman who seemed to bore him to death, as his usual brightness seemed somewhat dim. When Marcus ushered her into the kitchen to meet his mother, he shared with her that Brice had been set up by his mother with the young lady. That was why his brother was not his usual life-of-the-party self.

"I feel sorry for Brice," Jill said. "A blind date is no fun."

Marcus started to laugh, then cut it off as they walked in the kitchen and saw his mother holding her head.

"Mom? You, ok?" Marcus asked.

She looked up and gave a small smile, but she obviously was in pain. "Just a blasted headache! Sorry, son—oh, you brought a guest. How nice! Sorry you had to see me not at my best," she said to Jill.

"Oh no, ma'am, you are fine. Can I help you in any way?" Jill came to stand by his mother, while Marcus stood there with a worried expression.

"Mom, this is Jill, a good friend of mine. Jill, my mother, Catherine Jordan."

"It's nice to meet you, ma'am," Jill said.

"Likewise, sweetie," Catherine Jordan said, but she still held a hand to her head.

"What can I get for you?" Marcus asked.

"I have some aspirin in the cabinet over there. Can you get them for me, son?"

"Sure."

Once she had taken them, she looked up smiling but still held her head.

"Mom, it's early yet. Why don't you go upstairs and catch a few winks?"

"But what about dinner? I haven't finished with the preparations for the final things on my list. Turkey is done, but I still have to make the gravy, the mashed potatoes—and you know how your brother loves mashed potatoes. I have one pie to finish, and the bread will go in the oven last. Oh my, I should not have taken on such a project with so many people to feed."

Jill caught Marcus's eye and pointed at herself, and he nodded in understanding.

"Mrs. Jordan, if you will allow me, I would love to finish your list for you while you lie down until your headache goes away. I am a pretty decent cook; at least, that's what I've been told. I often had to cook most of our family meals, so if you wouldn't mind, I would love to help you get it done."

Marcus's mother looked at him, then at Jill, smiling. "You know, dear, if it is not too much of a bother for you, I would appreciate it to the highest. Oh, Jill you would be helping me to save face. So yes! I would appreciate your help." Catherine smiled at Jill.

"Ok, then. Marcus help your mother upstairs so she can lie down, and I will get cracking. Don't worry; dinner will be just as you want it to be." Jill smiled as she walked over to the counter and read the list; she was already in the cooking mode.

Marcus's mother looked at Jill and then Marcus. Her face held a huge smile as she looked from one to the other. She wrapped her hand around Marcus's arm as he walked with her upstairs.

When Marcus came back downstairs, he found Jill fully involved. "How can I help you?"

"Can you hand me the cream out of the fridge? And where does she keep the whisk? Oh! I will need you to fill those pie shells with the filling in that big yellow bowl," she said, reading his mother's notes from a list.

Marcus put his jacket on the back of the chair and rolled his sleeves up. While he was filling the pie shells, Brice walked in.

"Marcus, you never looked better. All you need now is an apron!" Brice teased.

"You are so funny, man! What happened? You lose your other half?" Marcus laughed quietly.

"Now, that is not funny, Marcus. Where is Mom?" Brice asked.

"She had a headache, so Jill volunteered to help her out. She is taking a nap upstairs until her headache goes away."

"That is mighty nice of you, Jill. Hmm, beauty and she can cook. Why can't I ever find someone like that?"

Jill looked over at Brice with a smile, revealing dimples. He winked at her.

"Agatha seems pretty nice, Brice," Marcus said trying to hold a straight face.

"It's Tabitha! She and I like different things," Brice complained.

"Like?" Marcus asked.

"She likes nothing outdoors. She says her skin is too sensitive to be out in the sunlight too long. She says her mother says she is delicate. Now Marcus, you know me; what am I supposed to do with that, huh?"

Marcus and Jill tried hard to keep from laughing. Jill walked over to the oven to retrieve a pan. When she pulled it out, Brice became excited.

"Oh my God! What is that heavenly smell? Don't tell me it's cornbread! I love cornbread. Tell her Marcus."

Marcus nodded his head. "Jill, he loves cornbread."

"Did you make that or did Mom?" Brice asked.

"Sorry, but the rolls that were made did not quite make it, so I improvised. I hope she won't be mad and that everyone likes it."

Marcus and Brice look at each other.

"Woman! Are you kidding me? The way that stuff smells, everyone will like it!" Brice said.

Jill smiled at the eager looks on both men's faces. "Would you like to try it to see if it's, ok?"

The men nodded their heads like little children. "Sure!" they said in unison.

She placed a saucer in front of both men as they took a seat at the counter.

"Oh boy, just as I thought. Lady, this is delicious and moist!" Brice moaned.

"Yeah, baby girl, this is really good," Marcus chimed in.

"Thanks, guys. Now back to work. We have to get dinner ready for your mother."

Marcus got back to work, and Brice carried out the dinnerware to the dining room table.

Catherine Jordan came down just as Jill was putting the jellied cranberries into a dish. Between the four of them, they got the food set up in the dining room. Once that was done, Catherine turned to Jill once again, thanking her for being such a big help. The two of them went out to the living room where everyone was gathered, and Catherine invited everyone to the dining room for dinner.

They all enjoyed the food, and conversation flowed easily, as well as the laughter. Jill had never had such an experience. She was used to conversation that turned into arguments; and then the fallout. It was hard to remember the good times because they were outweighed by the bad.

The men began serving dessert to the women, another unusual event for Jill. Marcus asked her what she would like, and she tried the strawberry shortcake that his aunt had brought. Mr. Jordan served his wife the pecan pie, which was her choice; the loving way that they treated each other created a sadness within her. It was so nice to see the love between the two parents and the whole family.

Marcus's grandmother leaned over to Jill. "This German chocolate cake is delicious, Jill. Did you make it?"

"No, ma'am. I cannot take credit for that. It might have been Mrs. Jordan—I mean, Marcus's mother, sorry."

Marcus's grandmother smiled, and Jill saw the twinkle in the old lady's eyes. "That's quite all right, young lady. It happens all the time. You can call me Mae."

"Thank you, but—"

"I know it feels awkward for you," Mae said. "That tells me you were brought up to respect your elders and have manners. My heavens, that's so refreshing!" The older woman chuckled and then smiled again at Jill.

"Yes, ma'am, you are right about that. My mother would handle me good for speaking to my elders in any way other than what was appropriate."

Mae nodded her head in understanding. She and Jill talked for a little while longer, but when Marcus's father came over, along with one of the aunts, Jill quietly left the group and started to pick up the dishes. After several trips to the kitchen, Jill was emptying the food scraps into the trash when Catherine Jordan came into the kitchen. She set a tray down before turning to Jill.

"You are a guest," Catherine said with her hands on her hips. "I do not expect you to clean up."

"Mrs. Jordan, it's no bother, really. I love helping; besides, you provided such an amazing meal that it's the least I can do," Jill said, smiling.

"Thank you, I am glad you liked it, but honestly, I do not expect you to clean up after us. Esther will be in tomorrow morning to help me get things right. William and I can take care of the leftovers after everyone gets what they want."

"Are you sure?"

"I am. But thank you for everything you did tonight. I could not have done it without you," Catherine said with a huge smile.

"Ladies, it's time that Jill and I headed out," Marcus said. "Mom, save some of those leftovers for me. I'll be around tomorrow."

"Ok, dear, but do you have to leave so soon? I haven't had a chance to sit down and get to know Jillian. The only thing I seemed to have done was put the young lady to work. What kind of hostess does that make me?"

Marcus smiled at his Mom and walked over to kiss her on the cheek. He wrapped his arms around her in a brief hug. "I think you are simply the best!" Marcus said to her.

"You would say that!" she said, trying to appear stern. Then she smiled as she patted him on the arm. "But you will bring her back when I am not so busy," she told him, and he looked over at Jill.

"Of course, Mrs. Jordan. I would like that," Jill agreed, still smiling.

"Let's head out," Marcus said. "We'll say our good nights on our way to the front door."

"You all be careful out there. Good night!"

It took them another twenty minutes before they made it to Marcus's car amid a lot of laughter and jokes between the men. Jill smiled as they all joked with Marcus, but she could feel the love.

The night ended with a pleasant drive back to her place. He walked her to her door, took the key from her, as usual, and opened the door to make sure everything was ok inside. Then he gave her a hug before saying good night and walking back to his car. Jill locked the door and wore a huge smile as she cut off the lights and went to bed.

The next week, after a long business meeting, Jill sipped tea at a café, happy with the way things had gone, as she had picked up a new client. She was very proud of how well she was handling her job as an ad exec. Her life had completely turned around, and she sometimes had a hard time believing that she was becoming a career woman. The café was surrounded by gardens, but because of the time of year that area was closed. She had a table in one of the smaller, more intimate rooms, where she'd had lunch with the client. She'd stayed behind after the meeting to enjoy a nice cup of Earl Grey before heading home. She admired the fireplace on one side, which was opposite a beautifully decorated Christmas tree, which gave the room a pine scent. *The decorations are awesome*, Jill thought. She loved the holidays the best. Jill had just drunk the last bit of tea when she heard a familiar voice.

"I do not believe it; she is like a bad penny that keeps showing up! Joan, are you taking a break from being totally helpless? Surely you are having a Marcus attack by now, especially since he has been away so long."

Jill rolled her eyes. *What have I done to deserve the constant nagging from this she-devil?*

Sheree stood at her table, rolling her eyes at Jill. She was accompanied by her best friend, Renee.

"Look, Sheree, I am not in the mood for your childish behavior. Show some couth, will you? I am sure the public would appreciate it."

Sheree looked as if she was about to spit fire, but she lowered her voice. "I heard about your defenseless-maiden act at the club a few weeks ago. What's wrong? Can't keep your good-for-nothing man in check?" The look of surprise on Jill's face just fueled Sheree's drive even more. "Oh yeah, didn't think I knew, did you? Marcus told me all about it—how he felt he had to look out for you because he hated to see a man taking advantage of a woman. You need to stop playing on my man's sensitive side. I am not going to keep playing these games with you, Miss Wrong Side of the Tracks. Why don't you just go back to where you came from and stop trying to hang with those out of your league? You are only a cheap trick, and women like you are not keepers for men like Marcus. He is mine, and you should know this by now. Think about it, sweetie. Has he ever attended any of the society functions with you? Or should I say, has he ever asked you?" She whispered her venomous words, and Jill felt the darts from her poison.

Jill took a deep breath and then said, "For the umpteenth time, let me say it slower this time. First of all, my name is Jill. I am only his friend. Why would he ask me out on a date? Besides, I have a man. I don't need your man, Sheree!"

A sly grin appeared on Sheree's face. "The performance you gave the other night at the club is a good example of what you have with your man! You may throw yourself at him, but Marcus would never pick you"—she pointed to Jill—"over all of this." She pointed to herself."

Jill knew she should not poke the bear, but she was really tired of Miss High and Mighty, and the opportunity was too good to pass up. "Well, if all that is your secret weapon for keeping your man on a string, why are you hassling me? Guess you are not so sure of all that."

"Listen here, you cheap trick! This is my last warning—keep away from Marcus! Because if you don't, I will end you in this town!" And with that, she marched off toward her table.

Jill released a breath that she had not realized she was holding. She grabbed her purse, left a tip, and headed to the exit.

"Can you believe that wench, Renee?" Sheree exclaimed as she took a seat.

"Just calm down, Sheree. I don't know why you let that woman bother you," Renee said, trying to calm her friend of ten years.

"Bother me? Are you kidding me? Every time I look, she is finding a way to get his attention, and now she is playing Miss Abused with that outdated pimp of a boyfriend of hers. This is another way of getting Marcus's attention, acting as if she is a victim. She is so pathetic, and he is just like a man, falling for her act.

"From what I could tell that night, the guy was pretty rude, yelling at her; it was embarrassing. Marcus was just being himself; he protected her from that jerk, that's all. It was not as if she was fawning all over him. They were just dancing."

"Like they were when he got upset because he asked me to dance, and I told him we could dance on a slow song, and then she came over and asked him to dance, right in front of my face? Nah, Renee, I see what's happening, and I am not going to hand him over to her, not easily."

"Sheree, forget about it. The girl has a boyfriend, and you have Marcus. Sounds like you have the best prize."

"Yeah, and if I ignore her, she will just sneak in and get him. I think I really need to talk to Leon," Sheree said with a smile on her face.

"Who?" Renee asked with a frown.

"Her boyfriend, Leon," Sheree said, heavy in thought.

Renee burst out laughing as she shook her head. "Sheree, it's Tyrone, not Leon, silly. But I think you ought to leave it alone. Marcus would be really upset with you if he knew you were involving yourself with that crazy guy."

"Who says Marcus has to know? This will be our secret, and if I can get Tyrone to keep his woman in check, I will be satisfied because I will have Marcus all to myself, with no interference. Come on, Renee, I got a call to make." Sheree got up from the table.

"We haven't ordered, and I'm starving. I thought we were supposed to be having lunch," Renee complained.

"We will, and I will treat you to whatever restaurant you want. I just have to find a way to get in touch with this Tyrone person first." Sheree hurried her friend along as they walked out the door.

———

It was hard for Jill to believe that Marcus would talk about her to Sheree, but she seemed to know what happened, and that knowledge hurt Jill—that he would ruin her confidence in him. She was ever so glad that she was seeing Tyrone because at least when she said she had a boyfriend, she was not lying—at least, not totally. She also realized that Sheree must not have known that she had spent Thanksgiving with Marcus's family, and that was one thing she was glad about. But once again, she felt she needed to distance herself from Marcus because she was tired of being confronted by Sheree. "Jill, girl, it's for the best," she said to herself as she headed home.

———

It was seven thirty when Marcus returned to his hotel room. He had been out all day at the site and felt beat as he prepared to pack for his trip home. Marcus felt good about his trip. He had returned on Monday after the Thanksgiving weekend and had managed to get everything back on the right track. He liked John Jacobs and his wife, Alice. He would have felt more comfortable had they not tried to shove him and Eugenia, Alice's sister, together at every chance. Marcus heard his stomach rumbling and realized it had been a long time since lunch. He called room service to order something.

When he had finished working on the closing figures for the projects he was overseeing, he faxed them back to the office so Joe could have processing work on them. After the faxing was complete, Marcus decided to check his messages, which he had meant to do a few days ago. Most of his messages were of little importance, except for the message he got from Fonze, and he immediately dialed Fonze's number.

His friend picked up on the third ring.

"Hey, Fonze, what's up with you and your messages? You left me so many. What is going on?

"It was only two; besides, that was weeks ago. Where are you?" Fonze asked.

"New York," Marcus replied.

"Ah man! I didn't mean to have you, call from out of town. It could have waited until you got back. Man, sorry to put you to all this trouble and—"

"Ok! Ok! Just tell me what is up." Marcus said.

"Yeah, Marcus, I'm not getting in your business, but this girlfriend of yours got into some trouble about two weeks ago, and I left you a message, just wanting to let you know about it. I was at Winky's, checking up on one of my students who had some issues. I was there picking him up from his evening job. Anyway, I was there, I saw your girl. She came in with Tyrone. A little while later, cops started coming in, and the bartender, who is a friend of mine, told me to clear out because something was about to go down. I went over to her—she was sitting alone because Tyrone was in the manager's office.

"Tyrone?" Marcus exclaimed.

"Yeah, I'm talking about Jill. I thought you—oh man! Sorry about that; I was not talking about Sheree. Apparently, he picked up a side job recently, working at Winky's, but he's not a waiter or busboy, so just what he does is questionable. Anyway, I explained to her what the bartender told me and got her to leave with me since she had come over in his car. Man! We were coming out of the driveway when cop cars came streaming around the corner, lights flashing—"

Marcus once again interrupted him. "She told me—oh wait! She did mention that she had something to tell me, but it could wait 'til I got back in town. She told me that she wanted to see my face because she was sure I would crack up about it, just like she did. I do not find anything about what you've told me funny at all. That scumbag took her to Winky's, of all places."

"Well, you know it's his hangout spot, and maybe she is hoping you won't be mad about it."

"Maybe, or maybe she had second thoughts about telling me because she knows how I feel about him." Marcus gave his own interpretation.

"Look, man, I'm thinking she didn't want you to get involved with her troubles with that idiot Tyrone."

"Yeah, I know how she tries to handle him on her own, and I have told her she needs to leave him alone. What scares me the most is that he could really hurt her, not just his two-timing ways but his anger. He's a dangerous man. I have seen guys like him always ready to justify what they do, whether it's good or bad. Like I said, he is dangerous, and I know making her see this has proven to be something, but what can I say? So Fonze, have you heard whether he got arrested? I would love to know, and if so, what for?"

"Probably drugs, but this time I cannot say for sure. I have heard he does something on the side. He is small-time, and he is shady. But you need to step up your game and let Jill know where you want things to go between you two. I mean, you are into her; we all can see it," Fonze said.

"Yeah," Marcus replied, sounding irritated.

"Stop playing hard before the best thing in your life gets away. C'mon, man, you know what you gotta do!" Fonze pleaded with him.

Marcus remained quiet for a moment longer and then released a long, slow breath before speaking. "Yeah, I know. Man, actually, I have never been in a place like this. It's complicated. It's hard to even sort out my thoughts sometimes. I'm happy, then scared all at once. Fonze, man, you are a good friend. Thanks. If Jill had been hurt, Tyrone's ass would be mine. If I'm not around and you see her in a situation, make sure she is safe for me. About what you said earlier, the answer is yes! I am into her, I want her, but she has some stupid notion that she is not my type. It is hard to knock those walls down, but I'm gonna keep trying. I convinced her to have Thanksgiving dinner with me and the family."

"You're kidding—she had Thanksgiving dinner with you and the family? Where the hell was Sheree?" Fonze wanted to know.

"Apparently, her family was doing some Thanksgiving thing at a ski resort. I told her that I could not do that because I had made plans to be with my family since my father's mother was in town. She was disappointed, but she knew this was something that could not be helped. My situation number two—because I really need to call it quits with Sheree. I am no longer in it with her."

"Well, my friend, if I were you, I'd make sure I was in town by the

Christmas holiday, not to mention New Year's Eve, because knowing what I know about that fool Tyrone, Jill may need a helping hand, if you get my drift. Whose better than yours?"

Marcus could almost hear the smile in his friend's voice. "Yeah, Fonze, I agree."

"All righty then, so go handle your business! I'll talk to you when you get back to town, I'm out." The phone went dead, and Marcus hung up, wishing he were boarding the plane for home.

———

It was the week after Thanksgiving, and the holiday spirit filled the office. Jill could hardly wait for the week to end; she had yet to get Christmas presents for her friends. The office was scheduled to close two days before Christmas, and the next week, it would close for two days prior to New Year's Eve. Many people were talking about attending the New Year's Eve dance that was put on at the City Center. Jill was down about having to stay home for New Year's after the let-down with Tyrone, but she put it out of her mind for now. Cyn had called her earlier in the week; the coming Saturday was Jasmine's birthday, and they would be celebrating at the club. A cake had been ordered. Jasmine knew nothing other than that they would all go to the club. Once the club closed, they would all go to breakfast.

Jill got off work at 3:30 on Friday and did some shopping so that she could wrap Jasmine's present. She had called Jasmine that morning to wish her a happy birthday.

As she got out of the shower, the phone rang, and it was Tyrone. He had sent her flowers, but Jill had refused to see him. They talked for only a few minutes, as he kept asking for a chance to come over.

"There's nothing to really talk about," Jill informed him.

"Baby, can't we meet after the party? I want to get this cleared up because I got us tickets to the big New Year's Eve bash. I got to see you looking hot in a pretty dress. You know what I mean? Please, Jilly! You know I'm sorry. I'll do anything for you, babe. I just need to explain what happened at the club that night. Will you please just hear me out before you jump to any conclusions?" Tyrone asked.

"What happened with the police, Tyrone? That's all I want to know. I feel like I don't even know you." When there was silence from the other end of the line, Jill said, "I need answers, Tyrone, or maybe I don't need them because things with us are not going to work."

"Look, Jilly, you know I care about you, and I know you feel a little something for me so why don't we just get together? I will tell you exactly what happened, and then we can hash all this out." When she said nothing, he said, "Ah, come on, Jill girl. Haven't I already gone through enough? Ok, fine—I got locked up and had to get myself bailed out because my manager got caught up on some numbers thang he was doing out of the place. Somehow my name got put in it by some clown who didn't have all his information straight, and now my woman won't talk to me. How much can a man stand?" Tyrone hoped to sound like he was really stressed.

"That place is so shady, Tyrone. I know it's not a reputable place. You need to make better choices. I don't know if you are really hearing me. I don't think you take me seriously enough and—"

"I do take you seriously," Tyrone said. "Why do you think I sent you those flowers? Girl, you got me. You hear me, girl? You got the Big T. So please, can we meet and talk? After making bail, I'm broke, so I cannot afford to take you out at a fancy place, but maybe we can meet and talk."

"Ok, Tyrone, listen—I can't do this right now. I have to get to a party. We can talk tomorrow evening around seven. Can you meet me at my place? I'll call you around six to make sure the time is still good. Then you can tell me about what happened at Winky's, among other things."

"Ok, Jilly, I will talk to you then. Don't have too much fun tonight. I got to run. Be good," Tyrone said.

"Good night, Tyrone." Jill hung up the phone and pushed his craziness to the back of her mind as she hurried to get ready for Jaz's birthday celebration.

———

Yvonne picked up Jill around six o'clock. Jill was packed and ready to go; she would be spending the night at Yvonne's place. When they entered the club, a lot of people were there, and everyone was in good spirits. Jill put her bag down on the table as one of the guys from the office grabbed her hand, pulling her toward the dance floor. She smiled at Ron; he always seemed to find a way to engage her in a dance. Tonight, her soft black dress, which dipped so revealingly and swayed with her every movement, kept Jill pretty busy. No sooner had she sat down than she was asked again to dance.

"Jill, I think you need a double," Cyn said, "or maybe a stand-in or something. Girl, you are burning up the floor. If only Marcus was here … I just wonder what he would think of how busy you have been."

Jill rolled her eyes but then sent her a smile and a wink. Just then, a very tall and nicely dressed man asked Cyn to dance. Jill discreetly gave her the thumbs-up sign as Cyn left the table. Jill was heavy in conversation with Yvonne and Jasmine, but her attention was drawn toward a group of people who suddenly got really loud as they greeted someone. She looked over and saw that Marcus had been stopped by two women. Joe tried to get his attention as he slowly made his way through the tables and people.

When Marcus got to their table, everyone greeted him. Joe was so surprised to see that Marcus had made it back from New York that he spoke boldly to his friend. "Man am I glad to see you. We were getting tired of beating the guys off Jill. Now you can handle that job my brother."

Everyone burst out laughing except for Jill, who was trying to hide the embarrassment. The music suddenly started jumping again, and the partying did not stop until the early hours of the morning. Everyone sang happy birthday to Jasmine, and she was presented with a birthday cake and presents. The party continued as their group contemplated having breakfast together. Jill was feeling tipsy, but Marcus kept his eyes on her. Yvonne and Joe were experiencing newfound love, so Jill decided to scrap the idea of spending the night at her place. She would just go home. Marcus volunteered to take her home, not surprising anyone. They were surprised, however, that she refused the offer.

"Thanks anyway, Marcus, but I have a way home. Excuse me; I have to go to the ladies' room."

Everyone had stared at that strange exchange.

"What in the world has gotten into her?" Yvonne said to Joe.

Marcus answered before he turned around to walk after Jill. "I don't know, but I aim to find out." He stood outside the ladies' restroom, waiting for her, and when she did come out, he placed his hand on her arm, ushering her into a more secluded area.

"Marcus! What is going on? What are you doing?" Jill exclaimed.

"That's what I wanna know. Care to tell me what the attitude is about?" He stood in front of her with his arms crossed.

"What attitude?" she asked meekly.

"The 'I already have a ride' attitude," he said in a mocking tone. Jill tried to hide her smile at the way he sounded. "So, who is taking you home because no one seems to know? If something is wrong, tell me. Talk to me, or we won't leave here until we clear the air," Marcus demanded.

"Look, Marcus, I think it's best that we don't hang around each other anymore." She looked at him but quickly looked away as she waited for the explosion.

"Why?" he asked. One eyebrow was raised, accompanied by a frown.

"Well, you are in a relationship, and me—well, it's questionable. But I might give Tyrone another chance, or I may not. But it's beside the point, so I think it's for the best that you and—"

"Best for whom?" he said, looking directly at her. He placed one hand on the wall next to her.

"Your other half, Sheree, and Tyrone, that's who," she said timidly when she saw the anger on his face.

"Why would our being friends hurt either of them?"

She was uncomfortable under his scrutiny. *If he keeps that up, he will see right through me*, she thought. "I guess they might misunderstand our friendship."

"Do you think we are doing anything wrong?" he asked, still looking directly at her.

"Well, no."

"And when did you start entertaining or seeing Tyrone again?"

"I ... it's a long story. But Sheree—why did you tell her about your confrontation with Tyrone at the club a few weeks back?"

He frowned deeply and got quiet before slowly asking incredulously, "Say what now?"

"She told me that you said it was because of me that you got involved in an altercation with my boyfriend at the club, and it was out of pity for me. She felt that I was taking advantage of your sensitive side."

"You are kidding me, right?" he exclaimed.

"No, I would not kid you about something like this. As a matter of fact, she was very close to making a scene when she walked up to my table at the Bayberry Tearoom. She warned me to stay away from you. I am so tired of her causing a scene so for the sake of keeping peace, at least on one front, I am doing my best to stay away from you and her."

Marcus swore under his breath. Then he stared at her for several seconds before he reached up, gently touching her chin with his fingertip. He lifted her face so that he could stare directly into her eyes. In an almost whisper, he said, "Jill, I need your honest opinion right now, and when I say that, I mean forget about Tyrone for a moment and Sheree too. Just think about how we are and the things we have been through since you came to Philly. Now tell me, thinking about you and me and how good we have been together, do you really want us to stop being friends?"

Her expression let him know that she did not want to stop being with him. After moments stretched out longer than he wanted, she shook her head. "No, I don't want us to stop being friends," she admitted in a voice that sounded more like a whisper, as her need for him filtered through.

Marcus saw the smoldering look in her eyes, which just seemed to mirror the attraction between them. "I sure as hell don't plan on allowing that to ever happen, baby girl, but just so you know, I never had a conversation with Sheree about that night at the club. She didn't get that information from me. Do you believe me?" He took his hand off the wall and stood up straight, looking directly at her.

She knew the answer as she gazed back at him and nodded her head. "How could she lie like that to my face?" Jill asked in disbelief.

"I guess you make her feel threatened."

"How? She is your girlfriend, and she is rich with a fabulous career. What does she have to feel so threatened about?" Jill asked.

"Jill, you are so amazingly blind, about yourself. You are simply incredible, not only on the outside but the inside too. I find that totally attractive, and so do a lot of other people. Sheree has a problem with any woman who can hold her own and not even sweat it. You are in that category, and it's so easy for you that you don't even know it. She hates that you and I get along so well. She hates that you have my attention."

"How could a country bumpkin, a girl from the 'wrong side of the tracks,' as she is always telling me, make her feel threatened? That's such a crazy idea, Marcus."

"You really want me to answer that? Because I am not so sure that's a road we want to go down just yet."

When she looked up at him, the look in his eyes made something inside her burst with warmth all over. "Maybe you're right."

"Now tell me—who is this bozo who's taking you home?" he said, seriously wanting to know.

Jill just laughed and shook her head at him. He tried using a more serious expression, which only caused her to laugh more.

"Why does he have to be a bozo, huh? See, that's totally unfair, Marcus Jordan," she argued.

"Because I don't trust some of these guys around here, that's all."

"To be honest, I don't have a ride. I was just trying not to occupy your time," she admitted.

"So, you lied to me again. Jillian, what am I going to do with you? Perhaps you need supervision because it seems that when I leave town, you get caught up in all sorts of craziness. I, for one, am not having it, young lady. Don't let me take my belt off."

She laughed at him standing there with his hands on his hips. "Yes, Father! I will try to be better and stay away from bad influences."

"Now that's more like it. Let's go back to our friends, shall we?" He held out his arm, and she wrapped her hand around it, and they headed back to the rest of their friends with smiles on their faces.

When they returned to their tables, champagne was being poured, and good cheer and good times was still in full effect. Later, Jill, being slightly tipsy, was very agreeable to almost everything. Marcus thought, *If only I could get this on tape.*

When they got to Jill's place, Marcus had to help her find her key.

When that was unsuccessful, Marcus gave up and took her to his home, assuring her that they would check the club tomorrow to see if her keys had turned up. Jill was so tired by the time they arrived at Marcus's place that she went straight to the guest bedroom. Marcus supplied her with a huge T-shirt, and she quickly got into bed and fell asleep.

As Marcus went through his routine of locking up, he thought of how cozy his condo felt with Jill in it. When he entered his bedroom, he noticed the time on the clock—4:00 a.m. Although he was tired, the excitement of having her near filled him with energy.

Chapter
7

Only a few hours later, Marcus woke with a melody playing in his head. As he looked out his bedroom window onto the view of the bright sunrise, he got the feeling that today would be a good day. His tiredness from his travels to New York had started to catch up with him, and then Jasmine's celebration last night also was having an effect. Everything felt right. The party last night gave him more time with Jill and her friends. It was a different type of socializing for him. He felt genuinely connected to the people, more so than when he went out with Sheree and her friends.

He still was amazed by how *right* this feeling was that he had for Jill. Marcus had known for a while now that he was attracted to her but always felt that there was more to it. Now, he knew for sure that he had fallen in love with her. It was getting difficult to be away from her, and he found himself seeking her company more and more.

After rolling out of bed and trying to stop his thoughts from going any further, Marcus pulled on his jogging pants and tennis shoes. He decided to go for a run, thinking maybe this would calm him down and clear his head. He needed this time to figure out his next move while she was still sleeping. He hurriedly washed his face and brushed his teeth, then remembered something Jill said last night. Jill had told him about Sheree and her attempts to get her out of his life. That thought alone, made him very angry, and he planned to speak to Sheree about it soon. He straightened his bed covers, then went down the hall and peeped in on Jill. He decided to write her a note, just in case she woke up before he got back.

Marcus locked the door without arming the alarm as he headed out. A quick jog would help to satisfy his daily regime because while he was away, he did not get to do any jogging, and it sure felt good to have the breeze brushing his face and refreshing his mind.

When Jill awoke, all was quiet. At first, she did not recognize her surroundings, and then her memory kicked in. She smiled as she lay there, thinking of how they'd celebrated Jasmine's birthday—the togetherness of the occasion with friends and Marcus. Jill thought about how good it felt to be held in his arms. Jill felt if only she felt this way about Tyrone, she would not have to hide it. Becoming frustrated with herself, she decided to get out of bed and freshen up. After dressing, she entered the hallway; it was quiet. Jill thought that maybe Marcus was still asleep. She decided to surprise him with breakfast. Jill was setting the table when she heard a masculine voice say from behind her. "Good morning!"

Totally startled, she dropped all the silverware on the floor. "Jeez, Marcus! You scared the living daylights out of me," she exclaimed.

He immediately bent down and retrieved the silverware. "Sorry! Guess you did not see the note I left." Walking to the refrigerator he grabbed the note and showed it to her.

"No, I didn't, and I have opened that refrigerator quite a few times this morning! I was in a hurry to fix you some breakfast before you took me home. I guess I didn't pay attention to anything else. But breakfast will be on the table in ten minutes. I hope you didn't mind my taking over your kitchen."

"Oh no, by all means." He smiled as he leaned against the counter, watching her.

"I hope you are hungry," she said, looking over her shoulder at him with a smile.

"I am starving," he said out loud but thought, *Food's Ok, but I'd rather have you.* He rubbed his stomach, exclaiming, "It's nice when a guy can get home-cooking. Whatever it is, it sure smells incredible." Marcus took a deep breath as he looked under the lids of the pans on the stove.

Jill felt heat stirring in her lower region. Shaking this feeling, she said with a laugh, "Let me feed you before you pass out."

"I'll wash up quickly and then give you some help. Be back in a flash."

When Marcus returned from washing up, Jill had everything on the table. He looked around with a smile. "Jill, my girl, you sure give good service."

"Thank you, kind sir. Shall we eat?"

Marcus agreed. They both sat down to eat, but after only a few minutes, Jill saw that Marcus had his eyes closed and a satisfied moan escaped his lips. "Ooh! Jill, this is heaven."

Jill laughed and shook her head, thinking, *how wonderful he is for a woman's ego.* "My grandmother used to make these a lot for my grandfather. It's I guess what you would call a country breakfast—fried potatoes with onions, bacon and eggs, and biscuits, except she would make her own. I just used the croissants you had." When he looked at her with a blank stare, she smiled. "Don't tell me that you have never had country cooking before."

"Not like this."

Jill's smile disappeared, and she said, "Now you are starting to sound like Tyrone."

At the mention of that name, Marcus dropped his fork and rolled his eyes. "I was meaning to ask you why you took him back, but we will save that talk for later. I don't want to upset my stomach, but should you mention that name again, I will not be responsible for what I do. I may leap across the table and silence you with my lips. Got it?" he said as a mischievous glint entered his eyes.

Jill smiled and, with a devilish look, she said, "Promises, promises.

Ty—" She broke out laughing, but before Marcus could act on it, the doorbell rang and he got up, promising retribution.

I'll give whoever is at the door a few choice words for interrupting my quality time with Jill, he thought. Marcus swung the door open—and gave a shout as his brother grabbed him in a bear hug.

Brice Jordan stood six foot seven. His short dark hair was covered with a baseball cap, and he wore a Cowboys T-shirt and dark jeans. He gave his brother a hearty smack on the back. "Hey, little bro! Mm-mm! It smells good in here tell. Mrs. Esther that I'll have double of what you are getting." He turned around then, as if looking for someone. "Look who I ran into on my way up."

"Who?" Marcus said.

Brice walked inside. "Your girlfriend. She just pulled up in a taxi." He whispered.

Marcus rolled his eyes. "Damn! Jill is in the kitchen."

"Whoa, the fireworks should be a doozy! I'm heading up to see my girl." Brice headed up the stairs as Marcus closed the front door, waiting for Sheree to ring the doorbell.

When the doorbell rang, he waited until the second ring, before opening the door.

"Hey, Sheree, what's up?"

She flashed one of her overly bright smiles, sauntered up to him, and purred, "Hey, sweetie, I thought I'd never get here. I have really missed you. It's been over a month, but it seems like much longer than that!"

Marcus rushed on, only hoping she would leave because he knew Sheree would not appreciate Jill's being there.

"Well, both of us have our careers, and they are pretty busy ones," Marcus said.

Sheree pouted for Marcus's benefit, then replied, "I know, baby, but I did miss you."

Marcus asked her about her shoot in Brazil and spending Thanksgiving with family at the ski resort. Sheree loved to talk about herself and fell hook, line, and sinker for the delaying tactics. She elaborated on how she and her family enjoyed their stay at one of the most expensive ski resorts in Europe.

Jill heard Brice's voice from the doorway and immediately felt relieved that it was not Sheree. Jill's being there so early would definitely get on Sheree's bad side. *Then again,* Jill thought, *Sheree hates anything I do.* Jill saw Brice coming up the stairs, and when he reached the top of the stairs, he smiled—but then quickly he placed his finger over his lips. He approached her with open arms. Jill felt very much at home with him and met him halfway.

"Hey, beautiful!" he whispered. "This is a nice homecoming. It sure is nice to see you; unfortunately, Sheree is downstairs too." Brice groaned.

Jill's smile was quickly replaced with a frown. "Brice, you are a wonderful surprise, but this will not end well. Dang it!" she whispered. "She is going to pitch a fit and come to all sorts of conclusions. She will put one and one together and come up with me sleeping with Marcus, though she would be so wrong."

Jill, shaking her head, missed Brice's disappointed reaction; then she looked up and caught him in deep thought. "Oh no, you won't get me in the middle of this Marcus mess," she said. "I'm leaving. Oh gosh! Um, can you put my dishes in the dishwasher or just hide them?"

Brice grabbed her arm to hold her back, and she suddenly realized that Sheree and Marcus were coming upstairs.

"Brice, what am I to do? She can't see me here, or there will be hell to pay."

Brice looked at Jill said, "Listen, darlin', I do not like that pariah being around my brother any more than you do. But since you have no escape route here, leave Sheree to me, and follow my lead."

"I'm sorry, Brice. I can't do this anymore. She and I butted heads the other day, and it was not pretty. She threatened me about this, but I said nothing was going on. Imagine what this will look like to her. I'm going to the guest room until she's gone." Jill rushed from the room and down the hall.

Brice got up from the table and placed Jill's coffee cup and plate in the sink. He decided to make himself a plate just as Marcus and Sheree entered the kitchen.

"Marcus, man, you been eating like a king. You gotta tell Mrs. Esther that she can come and cook for me anytime. I will gladly hire her." Brice turned around, looking directly at Marcus, who had picked up on his brother's cues, as he loaded his plate.

"Hey! Save some for me!" Marcus yelled playfully.

"Looks like you have had your share. This stuff is great! Sheree, I would offer you some, but I don't want you to go off your diet, even though I think a model with a little more is better. Man can't survive off bones. You know what I mean? Yes sirree, buddy!" Brice said, not giving Sheree time to answer him.

"Who cares what you think? You simply have no taste!" Sheree rolled her eyes at him, then turned back to Marcus, who seemed to be deep in thought. "Marcus, are you ok?"

He gave her a slight smile and said, "Oh yeah, just thinking about how much time I have before Joe will be here. We've got to look at a possible acquisition this morning, sorry, I've got to run. Sheree, I don't have much time right now, but we do need to talk. Maybe later?" Marcus suggested.

"I was so hoping we could spend the day together. It's been so long since we spent any time together," she complained.

"Yeah, I know, but duty calls. You know how that goes—unless you want to stay here with Brice until I get back."

Brice frowned at his brother. Marcus had known that would not fly with either Sheree or Brice.

"I'd rather hangout in a freaking bat cave," Sheree said, "so darling, definitely not! When you get done with your work, call me, and we can make some plans that won't get interrupted."

Marcus nodded as she placed her arm through his, steering him back downstairs to the front door. She called the taxi service, and she and Marcus talked while waiting for her ride. The cab soon arrived. Kissing Marcus soundly, Sheree said, "I'll wait for your call."

Marcus watched as the cab disappeared around the corner, then went back into the house.

"Man! That was a close one! She's gone," Marcus said, coming back up to the kitchen.

"Yeah, but now you need to soothe things over with Jill. I'm sure this was not a good experience for her. Did you know that Sheree recently threatened her?" Brice asked.

"I found out last night. I'm going to talk to Sheree later today. I'm actually going to break it off with her. I'd better tell Jill the coast is clear and—"

"Yeah, well, I think she was a bit anxious when I told her Sheree was downstairs, and that's understandable. Who would want to run into the wicked witch? But this was unexpected."

"I'll have a talk with her before I take her home," Marcus said. "The interruption sucks. We were having the best time, just talking and enjoying our breakfast. I've got to reassure her that I'm not playing games with the two of them. Sheree and I are finished." Marcus looked over at his brother.

"For real?" Brice asked.

"Yes, for real. It's not only the arguments between us, but she has been threatening Jill. She has got into arguments with the Governor's daughter when they worked on the School Violence Committee. She recently came down hard on Sidney. She went to the office afterward, not being able to get in touch with me when I was in New York. I did text her, that I was in the middle of settling some issues and would call her back. Well, you know Sheree; she has to be the queen bee at all times, so she went down to the office and asked for Sidney, who told her the same thing but agreed to pass on her message to me. Obviously, Sheree misunderstood anything Sidney said, as well as Mrs. T. The whole office was upset. If I could have gotten to her at that moment, it would not have been nice at all! She's thinking we are going to spend some quality time together today, but I'm actually going to get on her about how she treated my staff. Then I'll break it off with her. I'm tired of cleaning up behind Sheree's messes."

"Glad to hear it. Now you just have to make good with the right woman, who is just down the hall. I'm going to head over to Fonze's and see what he is up to. When you are through mending fences, maybe later us guys can hook up. I will be around for a few days," Brice said.

"Ok, man. I'll catch up with you guys later," Marcus said as they bumped fists.

Brice gathered his dishes and dropped them in the dishwasher before he left.

Marcus went down the hall and knocked on Jill's door. "Hey, it's me."

The door opened, and Jill stood there, looking weary. "How are things?" she asked.

"She is gone."

Jill looked relieved. "Good. Can you take me home, or if you are busy, maybe Brice can?"

"I will, but we need to find your house key first. Brice has already left," Marcus said.

"I'm set to go so whenever you are ready."

"Let me change, and then we can go." Marcus turned, heading to his room.

When he came into the kitchen, freshly dressed in jeans and a T-shirt, instead of heading downstairs, he pulled out a chair and asked Jill to have a seat. "I need to talk to you," he said.

"We need to talk?" Jill asked. "Marcus, look, there is nothing to say. I know my being here caused problems for you. I should not have stayed; it was not a good idea. Although it was your idea, it won't happen again. I am ready to go."

Jill started to get up from her chair, but when Marcus said her name, he sounded as if he was under great strain.

"Jill, I see the look in your eyes, but first I want to apologize for the way Sheree threatened you the other day. I will take care of that. You are my friend, but don't feel it's just you. She is jealous of anyone who gets my attention. I am not committed to her, nor do I plan to be. I have found out that we are, like my brother says, oil and water. We want totally different things in life. I guess it is my fault that she thinks it's more than what it is. But that too will all be straightened out soon. I want to make sure that you are all right and not mad with me." Marcus looked at her and raised that familiar eyebrow, waiting for an answer.

Jill took a deep breath, then said, "Marcus, I just don't want to be the cause of any conflict between you and your girlfriend. I enjoy being with you. Sheree is persistent with the thought that I am trying to seduce you or somehow steal you away from her. I am not a homewrecker." Jill saw a smile appear on his face, but she continued. "I am not! I am so tired of explaining our friendship to her." Jill stood up and turned her back on him and threw up her hands in frustration.

Marcus could tell she was upset because whenever she was, she used her hands a lot. He wrapped his arms around her and said quietly, in an effort to soothe her apprehension, "Jill? Hey! Stop. Stop trying to explain our relationship. It's nobody's business what you and I are to each other. I don't care what Sheree thinks because the Lord knows I have put up with a lot from her, even her so-called admirers. This is really not what I wanted to talk about anyway. Now, are we clear on this mess with Sheree?" He stepped back, allowing her to turn around, and when she did, he made a pleading face at her, and she succumbed slowly with a smile.

"I guess I'm fine, Marcus. She doesn't get it. I'm no threat to her relationship with you."

Marcus grunted and then said, "Sheree is not important; let me worry about her. She thinks just because the tabloids make a big item out of my seeing her that the church has been reserved, but it's totally different for me. I have made promises to no one!"

"Ok, Marcus, I hear yah," Jill said.

Marcus threw his hands in the air. "Finally, she hears me. What I really want to talk to you about was the problem you had when I was away. You said you would tell me about it when I returned, so spill it. I have been waiting patiently."

Jill frowned; she didn't understand what he was talking about. Then it dawned on her that he was speaking of the incident with Tyrone. "Don't worry about it, Marcus. You have enough to deal with." She knew it was no use avoiding it because Marcus stood with his arms crossed and his eyebrow raised, waiting. Jill threw up her hands and said, "All right! If you must know, we might as well take a seat."

After they both were sitting at the kitchen table, she told him about the incident with Tyrone.

"It was weeks ago on a Saturday night, after he kept calling, that I decided to hear his explanation for what happened at the club, so I went out with him. We were supposed to go to a diner around the corner from my place, but there was such a waiting list that he suggested we go to Winky's. Have you heard of the place?"

"Yeah, it's a dump—lots of drug deals and prostitution, to name two of the unlawful acts that happen there."

"It was dumb of me to go there with him, but at first, everything was ok. Then he said he had to speak to the manager about getting more hours; he said that he worked there a few days a week to make ends meet. He was gone so long that eventually, this guy—he is actually one of your friends, Fonze—came over to the table, and Tyrone still had not returned, and Fonze told me that something was about to happen, and I needed to get out of there. Cops came in and went to the back office, exactly where Tyrone had gone. I was afraid at first for Tyrone, but then my common sense kicked in. I left with Fonze, and he dropped me off at home. Yes, Tyrone got arrested, and his explanation was that his boss was running some illegal gambling and got caught, and somehow his name got mixed up in it, and he was taken downtown."

Marcus quietly said, "So, what are you going to do about Tyrone now? I wanted to ask you about that last night when you were talking about you and me hurting Sheree and Tyrone. I guess you two made up?"

"Made up? No! I just gave him the benefit of the doubt," Jill said.

"I see. If you want my honest opinion, he is not going to change. You know that; don't you? Believe me, I should know, as much as I apologize for the stunts Sheree has pulled. I cannot count how many times I have been out with Sheree, and there was an altercation, and I ended up making excuses for her, but not anymore. She came to the office the other day when I was away. Somehow, we got our wires crossed because I was supposed to be back in town, but the project got held up, so I didn't make it back. Sidney tried to explain to her that I was not there, and she went off on Sidney and demanded to speak to Joe, but he was not there either. She did not believe Sidney and barged past her into my office and then Joe's. She could not reach me by phone because I was at a site and missed all twenty-seven of her calls. Evidently, she thought my office, especially Sidney, was intentionally covering up my whereabouts. I did not find out how bad it got with Sheree until I got back here. When I finally called her back, she played it cool, using that overly sweet tone with me. Then I found out how nasty she was to Sidney, as well as Mrs.

Thomas. I have a big bone to pick with her. It never seems to stop with her. I'm over it now. I'm not going to continue seeing her."

Jill nodded her head in understanding, then replied, "Good luck with that one because Sheree will not let you go so easily, but I know how you feel. I am going to have to face Tyrone sooner or later because he just keeps calling. It's such a pain but it's got to be done, and maybe tonight is the night. I think I'll call him back and see if we can talk tonight. I haven't seen him since the incident, but I plan to get things straightened out. That is what I wanted to tell you. Now, I must get home to call him about coming over tonight to talk If you are ready, can you take me home now?"

Marcus nodded. "You know my feelings on Tyrone. I know you feel you need to clear the air and to talk to the guy, but I just don't trust him. Please do me a favor and stay out of that part of town."

"Yes, I will, and I will be more careful from now on," she said reassuringly.

Marcus reluctantly said, "I'll let it go for now."

He grabbed his keys from the counter, and as Jill walked behind him, she once again admired his tight derriere; his blue jeans hung off his nice frame just so, and their motion definitely had her attention. Jill was so into watching the way he walked that when Marcus stopped at the door, she walked right into him.

"Oops! Sorry!" she said with a slight smile. "I guess I was not paying attention to where I was going."

Marcus stared at her suspiciously, then activated the alarm and locked the door. He looked as if he was bewildered by something, and then he smiled.

Jill finally found her keys after going from the club to Yvonne's and finally to Cyn's, which was where she found them. By the time Jill got home, it was almost noon. Marcus helped Jill with her overnight bag that they had retrieved from Yvonne's, and Jill poured them a glass of tea. They sat at the bar and talked some more.

"Christmas is just a few weeks away. What have you got planned? Are you going home for the holidays?" Marcus asked.

Jill suddenly got up to refill her more-than-half-full glass and fluttered with the sugar dish. "I thought I would just have a quiet dinner here since this is my first Christmas in my own apartment." She briefly made eye contact.

"So, your parents are not coming down to spend Christmas and see your place?" he asked casually, raising his glass and taking a sip while watching her.

"I'm pretty sure they are tied up with all the church stuff that usually goes on during the holidays. The Christmas dinner is another thing that keeps them busy, as relatives usually come over. I know my father wants me to come home, but I told him that I had planned to just celebrate Christmas here—maybe next year. I bet you have a big Christmas planned," she said with a somewhat nervous smile.

He continued watching her for a moment before responding. "I don't know if you'd call it big, but it's pretty traditional, as far as my family is concerned. Brice usually flies in the day before Christmas Eve, and he and I go shopping. We have a knack for being last-minute about the gift-buying thing. We then save Dad from having to do final touches to the Christmas tree after he has already made a thousand and one changes because Mom keeps coming up with a new idea. Christmas Eve, we get together with the guys and do a little partying, and the folks usually have guests over on Christmas Eve. I would have thought, since you have been here a while, that your folks would like to see your place, especially since you did not see them for Thanksgiving."

"No, not this year. They are pretty busy, with the charity that's run by the church. So, what about Sheree? And I know Brice has a woman or two at hand." She smiled, although she really did not want to hear about Marcus's holidays with Sheree.

"Sheree normally would drop in, but things will be different this year. Brice gets loads of invitations, but he basically just hangs around with the family for the holidays. Mother tries to hook him up, but so far, he has avoided her matchmaking efforts, except for Thanksgiving. That was a bust, as you remember. The plan this year is to have the guys stop by at the appropriate time and get him away from the situation." Marcus laughed, and Jill joined in.

"It sounds like you have quite a plan," she said.

"Yeah, and I wouldn't trade the craziness for anything," he said with a smile.

A sadness crossed Jill's face, but she quickly covered it with a smile and asked him if he wanted more tea.

"No, I'm good. Jill, I'm curious why you are so satisfied with spending Christmas alone. Could it be that old Tyrone is really the reason you want some alone time?" He watched for her reaction to his question.

"No. I need less drama in my life, and that is my resolution. Sorry to disappoint your creative thinking, Mr. Jordan, but I don't have to spend it with someone."

"The meaning of this particular holiday is togetherness, spending time with family." He looked into her eyes, and he didn't like what he saw. "You know, Jill, I have always found that you are easy to talk to and be with, and I feel close to you. It bothers me that you plan on spending Christmas alone. I sense there is more to this. Care to tell me the real reason you are not going home for Christmas?"

She fiddled with her napkin and then looked out the window before turning to look at him. He noticed a shift in her posture—her shoulders went slack, and there was a solemn expression on her face.

"I mean, if it's the expense, then I will give you the money," Marcus offered. "I would insist that it's a gift. I know how you hate anyone giving you anything, but it is Christmas, a holiday especially for family."

She was still quiet and then she spoke. "I don't really know where to start." She looked over at him as he patiently waited for her response. She looked down at her hands.

"Just start. I have lots of time," Marcus said.

She gave him a smile that did not reach her eyes, as if it was still a struggle to talk about her family or her life in Claremont. Finally, she said, "Remember when you asked me at the hospital about what brought me here, and I told you I had a job interview; then you later realized that I meant that I had come here before Garrett's company had even called me. But later, I told you that I needed a break because I had a fallout with my family?"

He nodded his head.

"The reason I came ahead of time was because I left home after a big fight with my mother. You see, I have a younger sister who has my mom twisted around her little finger. I'm the oldest, and I have two twin sisters. Tiffany and I get along well enough, but Traci is another issue all together. To make a long story short, I caught Traci in bed with my fiancé before I left Claremont. Mother thought I was being selfish to let something like that come between me and my sister. She and I got into a huge argument the day after I found them together. A lot of hurtful things were said. I was a wreck. Traci only laughed when I walked in on her and Phillip in bed. She said a lot of really cruel things to me, and so when I left his apartment, I just walked and walked until I was so tired. I walked around most of that evening in full evening dress because Phillip and I were supposed to be attending an awards ceremony for the brewery where he worked. Instead, I walked across town in high heels and a long gown. People were looking at me. I guess they were wondering what this crazy woman was doing, dressed like that, and to top it off, I was crying all the way to my best friend's house.

"I came home the next morning, and Mother was waiting. The end of the argument was when she told me to leave because I was only making things worse. She told me if I could not forgive my sister, then I could not be helped. She said I was headstrong and selfish. She wanted me out of her house. So, I left, just packed up all I had and left. I called my dad at work, just to let him know that I was traveling with a friend to Philadelphia, where we had a great job lined up, which was all a lie. He was shocked. He tried to talk me out of going. He tried to give me money, but I told him I was fine. I did not want my father's life to be miserable because of me, and if Mother found out that he was going to send me money or support me in any way, she would make life miserable for him. I did not tell him about the argument with Mother or what Traci did. I was sure he would find out. I wanted to be out of range when he did because I knew it would be bad; it always was, and I would still be blamed for whatever happened."

"That's your mother. Surely, she wouldn't ..." Marcus stopped speaking when he saw the look on Jill's face

"Oh yes, my mother would. So, I told him I appreciated the offer, but I had some saved and I would be all right. The truth is that I had very little, and Charlotte, my best friend—oh my God, she simply saved my life. I would not have made it here. She loaned me some money, which

I have been paying back. She told me not to worry about it, but I could not; *not* pay her back. She gave me reports on my father; she kept in touch with him and let him know I'm ok. He did not want me to turn his offer down, but I had to. In the beginning, I would call him once a week at his job, just so he knew I was all right. Yes, I even managed to pull it off when I was in the hospital. I never want to have him choosing sides. But I do miss him very much. He is like my only family. It's hard to grow up knowing that your mother hates you. Anyway, now you know why I do the solitary routine. It's better this way." Jill found it Hard to look at him after bearing her soul, so she reached for her glass and suddenly found herself fighting back tears. She had to put the glass back down on the table as her lips began to tremble. She fought back the tears and embarrassment.

Marcus looked at her, feeling miserable himself after hearing her whole story. He saw the shimmering eyes and pulled her into his embrace.

She took a deep breath. "I'm ok," she mumbled with her face against his shirt.

"I know you are. Things will work themselves out, and I will always be here, no matter what," he murmured.

Jill could not control her trembling and wrapped her arms around him even tighter. The warmth spread through her like lightning, soothing her. If only she could stay this way. It felt so good, so right. It even seemed to lessen the feeling of loneliness she felt.

He held her away just slightly so that he could look into her eyes. "The word *alone* doesn't apply to you anymore. I'm here. I will always be here for you, and since you desire to celebrate in your own home, we will. It will be just you and me. We could even do it right. How about we put up a tree on Christmas Eve. Knowing how my brother feels about you, he will want to be here too. Now, Christmas Day, I am extending an invitation to you to come and share with us. The invitation is one that you cannot refuse because it's a Jordan tradition."

Jill smiled at him through her red eyes but then took on a suspicious look. "A Jordan tradition? Sure, this isn't something you just made up? What exactly does that mean because I am not a relative."

"It simply means that once invited, you cannot say no."

"Marcus, I swear you are making this up. I don't think it would be right if I barged in again for the holidays on your folks, and I just cannot do another knock-down drag-out with Sheree, especially not in your parents' home. I think it's best that I just do my own thing. I appreciate what you are trying to do, though."

"Sheree won't be invited this year because she and I will not be seeing each other anymore. So now you have no excuses."

"You really make it hard for a girl to say no," she remarked with a slight smile.

"Then don't say no; say yes. Look, just repeat after me: 'I will be a part of your family's celebration, Marcus.' I would worry less if I knew you were safe and happy, and I guarantee both. Besides, Brice would kill me if he knew I had not invited you, especially since he will be squirming with whoever Mother has paired him off with for the evening, believe me."

"Poor Brice," she said with a smile, which turned to a frown after his next question.

"So, when are you cooking me dinner?" Marcus asked.

"Marcus! I just cooked your breakfast."

Marcus shook his finger at her. "That doesn't count. You agreed to fix me dinner because you wanted to repay me for fixing your car, as I recall." Marcus beamed at her, figuring that he had outsmarted her. Jill finally agreed, saying that she would cook after the holidays.

Marcus hated to leave but a little while later, he had run out of excuses for being there. He told her to call him on his cell if she needed to because he would be out with the guys after going to see Sheree.

"I won't need to bother you," she said.

"If you need to use my cell number, do so. I mean it, Jillian. Use it." After a moment's pause, he said, "I guess I'd better go and catch up with that brother of mine and keep him out of trouble. But I'm going to mark that dinner date on my calendar. I just can't wait to sample your cooking skills again, my girl." He smiled as he opened the door.

"I'll call you, Marcus, if I need to, but you guys have fun, and be careful out there because I know how you fellas are when you get together."

Marcus nodded his head in agreement. "I'll check in later. See you later, Jill."

After he closed the door behind him, Jill just stood there for a minute, wondering if she would ever get over her attraction to him.

———

When Marcus got into his car, he sat there for a few minutes. He hated to leave Jill to confront Tyrone alone. Maybe he would call Cyn and have her check on Jill this evening. He knew Jill would hate someone watching over her, and that Marcus had initiated this would get him into big trouble. Marcus put it on the shelf until later. He started his car and roared away.

———

When Marcus arrived at Sheree's place, he took in the quiet streets and the large gated community. The buildings were large in design but smaller inside. There were hardly any yards, mostly condos with balconies. When he got out of his car, he noticed how quiet the place always was, probably because children were not allowed. He pressed the doorbell, and she immediately answered. She pulled him inside, then wrapped her arms around him as she placed kisses all over his face.

"Hey, baby! It's been so long for us." When he did not reciprocate, she hesitated and looked at him. "What's wrong?"

"Sheree, we have to talk," Marcus said as he removed her arms from around his neck.

"Must be serious, from the look on your face. Would you like something to drink, maybe some coffee or some scotch?" When he declined her offer, she followed him to the couch in the living room.

Marcus sat down and she sat next to him and waited for him to start.

"Sheree, while I was in New York, I was told you came to the office and created quite a scene, just because you had not heard from me."

Before he could go on, Sheree exclaimed, "Are you freaking serious right now? That was weeks ago! What did the little peon say? I guess she came whining to you about your girlfriend, didn't she?"

"Sheree, stop the emotional trip, will yah? You cannot come into my office and rage, just because you cannot get in contact with me. You left me so many messages while I was in a meeting, trying to get a business contract finalized. I could not stop and talk to you at that moment. There was no need to blow up my phone. Tell me—what was the urgency?"

"Rage? I was not in a rage, Marcus. I had not spoken to you in days, and when you did not return my call, I went to the only people I knew would be in contact with you. I would have spoken to Joe, but he was not in the office, and that Sidney person was simply not going to lord it over me, telling me I could not go into Joe's office—this, that, and whatever she tried to tell me. That wench! She gets on my nerves, acting as if she runs things!" She got up paced back and forth, only stopping to look at him.

Marcus took a deep breath. "She is in charge of my office along with Mrs. T, Sheree. I did send you a text, but I guess you were so mad that you did not see it."

"A text? I did not want a text from you. I wanted to hear your voice. I mean, Marcus, you've got to admit we have not even been out in months! I wanted more! Lately, I barely see you if it's not at the club."

"It's kinda hard to take someone out who always makes a hassle out of everything. To prove my point, name a time we have been out in the last six months that has not resulted in an argument. Just tell me when that was because maybe my memory is wrong; I do not remember any!" Marcus let his anger get the best of him.

"It has not been that bad!" Sheree whined, seeing his frustration and trying to get them back to a better place.

"Oh yes, it has, at least for me. I'm tired of having to explain or excuse your tirades, Sheree, and it's mostly no big deal for anyone but you! Sidney helps to run my office, especially when I'm away. She is one of my best workers, and she has my confidence in office matters. You will not come into my office and offend anyone. This jealousy of yours is so self-destructive, and I cannot have that in my life. The drama you caused at the office was over the top. I think the best thing for us is to just quit, before things get out of hand any further than they already are. I'm tired of putting out fires. I do enough of that at work. I do not need to do it all the time in my personal relationship! It's best that we go our separate ways, especially since you seem to have an issue with anyone who's around me. I think it's the best thing to do, so take care—"

The doorbell rang before Marcus could finish.

She did not move to answer, and it rang again, but she just stared at him, ignoring the ringing doorbell. "Marcus, please just give us a chance."

Marcus walked past her to open the door. "Trey, hey, man," Marcus said, greeting Sheree's manager.

"Hey, Marcus! How is it going?" Trey asked.

"It's been rocky, but I'm hoping it will get better," Marcus said.

"Yeah, I know what you mean, man. So is Sheree around?"

"Yes, she is in the living room. Go on in; I was just leaving."

"No, Marcus, not like this!" Sheree exclaimed as she stood at the entrance to the living room.

"Yes, Sheree, it's for the best." Marcus walked out, closing the door.

Sheree walked back into the living room, and Trey followed her. Trey had been her manager for over five years, and he was very familiar with her moodiness. One moment she could be an uppity knob, and the other times, she would pitch a tantrum to get her way, but this was different. She was very quiet.

"Hey, you want to talk about it?" he asked.

Sheree started pacing. "There is not a lot to talk about. I allowed some whore to come between Marcus and me, and now he wants to break up! I guess all those times I was out of town just allowed her enough time to sink her hooks in. I should have been more active instead of taking him for granted."

"Ah, Sheree, I don't think you're remembering all the arguments between the two of you. I mean, some of them were pretty heated," Trey said, trying to get her to be reasonable.

"I know, I know, Trey! But Marcus was so good for me and to me. I have never had a man like that, and I remember when we were good. It was so good."

"Yeah, Sheree, but how long ago was that?" Trey said, as his efforts were ignored.

"I'm not going to give up that easily. He is mine, Trey! Now you need to help me fix this! Oh, wait a minute—I have just the plan." Sheree grabbed her cell phone. "Hello, Renee? Can you come over to my place right away? I need your help with something. Ok, bye!"

"What's going on, Sheree? I was hoping we could get dinner and discuss the next assignment." He looked at her expectantly.

"Oh, Trey, honey, we will, and it will be my treat. As soon as Renee gets here, we will go out to dinner, and I know just the place! I'm gonna go and refresh my makeup. If the doorbell rings, it will probably be Renee. Can you let her in?" Sheree said with a smile as she headed down the hallway.

Trey had a skeptical look. He felt uneasy because Sheree went from totally out of it, crying and sad, to perky and upbeat. He did not like the feeling he was getting and wondered what she was up to now. Marcus was a great guy, but Sheree was like a bulldozer. She could run over people and disregard their feelings. He had been through it with all of her fallout relationships, but he felt she really did want Marcus out of all of them. The one thing that was different was that Marcus would not put up with her manhandling him. He feared how this would end because of her inability to handle the truth.

———

Renee arrived an hour later, and when Trey let her in, she quickly asked, "What's going on?"

"Renee, I have no clue. When I got here, Marcus was leaving after breaking it off with Sheree," he said, shaking his head.

"Oh, no! How is she?" Renee asked, looking concerned.

"Now that is hard to tell because one moment we are down and depressed, crying and wiping our eyes, and the next we are smiling and looking as if nothing is going on," he explained.

"You know, a couple of weeks ago, she had a fit after we went to the Bayberry Tearoom. She went over to Jill—you know, Marcus's friend—at her table, and they got into their usual thing with Sheree threatening the woman. It was right after that she rushed me out of the place to look up this guy that Jill has been dating, Tyrone. There had been an altercation at the club previously, and he and Marcus got into it over Jill. Tyrone was thrown out of the club because of this fight. Sheree hired someone to find out all he could about Tyrone. I managed to get her to forget about it, and it seemed she did. But now that Marcus has called it quits, my fear is that she will use whatever information she has gotten on Tyrone to help her get Marcus back. That's my guess."

"What do you mean, information on this guy Tyrone?" Trey asked.

"Well, she asked me to pull up the article that was in the news about Marcus saving a damsel in distress. You know how the media always pumps a story up; only I was actually at the club that night, and it looked just like the story reported. This guy Tyrone, not only got into it with Marcus but with another guy over a different woman. So, Tyrone was not too popular with the crowd. When Marcus flattened him on the floor, people were almost clapping. Sheree was not there, and she had not heard any of it. When I told her, of course she did not like it, and she told Jill to stop getting her man involved in her messes."

"I meant every word. I'm so tired of her! I plan to use anything I have; to do just that. Now, are we ready for dinner?" Sheree entered the room in a red jumpsuit, big hoop earrings, and matching red pumps. Both Renee and Trey turned to see her standing there.

"Wow! I feel a bit underdressed," Renee said.

"You look amazing, Sheree. You certainly do not look like a woman who just broke up with her man," Trey said as he looked at her, assessing the smile he saw now compared to the way she had looked when he walked in earlier.

"Thank you both, but I plan to bounce back and do what I need to do." She continued to smile. "So, let's go get dinner because I know Trey is starving. Trey, do you mind doing the driving? Dinner is on me."

"I hope it's a place that's casual," Renee said.

"Renee, what you have on is just fine. Now can we go?"

"Sure, but where?" Trey asked.

"I will tell you once we are on our way," Sheree said, heading for the door as the other two followed.

Once they were in the car and after several turns, Trey reacted to the direction in which Sheree was taking them.

"Ah, Sheree, why are we going in this direction?" Trey asked.

"Yeah, Sheree, why are we heading downtown? We never go to this part of town."

"Because I'm looking for Mr. Tyrone Jenkins. We need to talk about his girlfriend."

"Sheree, you said you would let this go!" Renee said.

"That was before Marcus broke things off. Now it's every man for himself, or should I say woman?" she said, smiling.

"No, Sheree, you are heading for trouble if you are planning anything with this crazy man! Trey, talk some sense into her!" Renee wailed from the back seat.

"Sheree, I thought we were going out to have an early dinner. What's this about?"

"You guys need to chill. I'm just going to have a little talk to see if I can get Tyrone to rein his girl in and away from Marcus. I've got to protect what's mine, and I thought both of you would understand," Sheree exclaimed.

"We know how you feel about Marcus, but you cannot make someone stay with you just by plotting and scheming," Trey said, trying to make Sheree see reason.

"There is no harm in removing someone from the playing field, and if her boyfriend has no idea what she is up to—and I'm pretty sure he doesn't—then this can help him as well," Sheree explained.

"You have no clue about their relationship. He might not even care anymore. What if they have broken up and it's not his business? Then what?" Renee asked.

"Then my hunch was wrong, but I do not plan to just sit back and hand him over to her. So, either you guys are with me, or just stop the car and; put me out. I can catch a cab the rest of the way."

"This is unbelievable! Sheree, what about your career? Bad publicity will not be good!" Trey made one last feeble attempt, but she was way past thinking about herself.

"Like I said, I'm doing this, and you guys do not have to come along. I would like to have your support on this, but either way, I'm doing what I have to do!"

A few minutes lapsed in the car where there was just quiet.

"What and where is this place?" Trey asked, giving in.

"After the second traffic light, make a right, and Winky's is on the left," Sheree said, smiling.

"Winky's? What is Winky's?" Trey asked.

"A dump," Renee answered from the back of the car.

"Sheree, where are you taking us? Some dive?" Trey sounded very displeased.

"Yes, it is, but it's only for this one time! We will be in and out in no time," Sheree whined.

"Why couldn't you have just called this guy and set up a meeting somewhere?" Trey asked. "I just think this whole thing is a bad idea. Where am I supposed to park my car? I'm not leaving it in some back alley."

"Right down there, Trey, on the street. You will be able to see it from the restaurant."

When they got out of the car, they only had to walk a few feet away to reach the front door to the restaurant. Once inside, smoke was heavy in the air. When they just stood there, a man came from around the bar and greeted them.

"Welcome to Winky's! I'm D. Sorry for the delay, but as you can see, we are pretty crowded. I can seat you at a table and take your drink order. The waitress is busy with another table right now, but she will be with you shortly."

"Ah, that would be fine, but I have a question for you, ah, Mr. D. Do you know someone named Tyrone Jenkins? I know he was working here, and I came by to see him," Sheree said, giving the bartender one of her brightest smiles.

"Are you friends of his? I've never seen you in the place."

"We are friends of a friend of Tyrone's and were told we could find him here," Sheree explained.

D looked them over before he said, "Tyrone is supposed to be here in thirty minutes or so. Do you still want a table?"

"Yes, we do, and when he comes in, can you send him over to our table?" Sheree asked.

"I sure can. Now just follow me." He gave Sheree the once-over before he led them to a table on the far side of the room. He took their drink orders before leaving.

"I can't believe we are doing this!" Renee grumbled.

"Renee, you did not have to come along. I told both of you that I could do this on my own, and I'm gonna," Sheree exclaimed as she looked from Renee to Trey. He was just observing the room and not saying anything.

A few minutes later, a waitress brought over their drinks and asked to take their orders for food.

"Maybe later," Sheree replied.

It was almost two hours before Renee saw Tyrone come in and walk over to the bartender. She watched as Tyrone and D conversed for a few minutes before they looked in the direction of their table. Renee whispered to both Sheree and Trey, "Tyrone is headed our way."

Tyrone saw the two women and a man seated at a table. They did not look familiar, but they didn't look like police. *Probably someone wanting a hook-up*, he thought, but his curiosity was piqued. This was a different sort of customer, more of the classier clientele, which he could certainly use in his business.

"So, someone here looking for Tyrone?" he asked, looking from one to the other.

"Yes, ah, Tyrone. I'm Sheree, and these are my friends, Renee and Trey. I wanted to speak to you and offer you a proposition."

Renee's eyes got big as she listened to Sheree, and Trey suddenly frowned.

"Oh yeah?" Tyrone asked as a smile appeared on his face, as he looked from one woman to the other.

"Ah, well, let me explain. Won't you have a seat?" Sheree asked.

Tyrone once again looked at all three before pulling out a chair and taking a seat.

"You see, Tyrone, you and I have something in common. The commonality is Jillian Weston and Marcus Jordan. Are you and Jill still together?"

"Why do you need to know?" Tyrone asked.

"If you are, you need to check her because she is running around, trying to take other people's property," Sheree said accusingly.

Tyrone frowned as he watched Sheree. "Whose property?" Tyrone asked.

"Well, it seems your girlfriend and my boyfriend are getting a little too close. Your girlfriend is trying to break up my relationship with my boyfriend, and I need your help in solving this problem." Sheree suddenly felt nervous when the look on his face went from calm to something that was not pleasant.

"Look, lady, if you can't keep your man in check, what does that have to do with me?" he asked angrily.

"Tyrone, I do not want any woman messing with my man. I assumed you would not want to be made a fool of by your girlfriend, who seems to be getting too friendly with Marcus. I'm quite sure no man wants another man taking what is rightfully his."

"What do you mean, taking what is mine? What do you know about this? I warned him to stay away from her before!" Tyrone growled

"Yeah, I just found out what happened at the club. Marcus told me it was nothing, but I found out she is still after him, although she said she is not. Something is going on, and I believe that if we work together, we can put a stop to their sneaking around." Sheree watched his reaction; she seemed to have struck a nerve.

"So, this is your way of helping me? Maybe it's you who cannot hold onto your man," Tyrone said, looking directly at Sheree.

"Honestly, he is making a fool out of me; they both are. She keeps saying they are only friends, but I know there is something going on, and you know it too. That's why you and he got into it at the club. All I'm asking, Tyrone, is just put your girlfriend in check, and I'll handle Marcus. They have made a fool out of me, and I am not taking it lightly." Sheree had a fierce look, but she lowered her voice. "I do need your help. I can make it worth your while to help me. How about, oh, say, two G's?"

Renee gasped. "Sheree, are you crazy?"

"Sheree, stop it! This is crazy!" Trey said angrily.

Tyrone sat quietly, never taking his eyes off Sheree. A hint of a smile began to play across his face, and after a few minutes, he said, "How about we make it ten?"

Sheree shook her head, "As far as I'm going is five; that's all I'm offering." She met Tyrone's look. "If you don't accept my offer, then I won't waste your time any longer. Let's go, guys." Sheree looked over at Renee and Trey, who both had relief on their faces as they stood up.

"Ah, wait, wait, Chica, not so fast. I respect where you're coming from, and you are not alone. I accept your offer of five G's. You can consider them as no longer a problem for us. Just keep your boy occupied and out of my way," Tyrone said.

Sheree released a breath before nodding her head. She quickly sat back down, reached in her purse, pulled out an envelope, and slid it across the table to Tyrone, to both Trey's and Renee's surprise.

Tyrone stuffed the envelope in his jacket, then looked over at Sheree. "What exactly do you know about what's happening between Jill and Marcus?"

Renee kept making little annoying sounds as she listened to the two.

Tyrone reacted. "Ah, Sheree you need to check your girl cause she is really annoying me right now."

"Renee, why don't you and Trey wait for me in the car?" Sheree said, giving them a pointed look.

"Sheree, we are not going to leave you in here with this!" Renee said, totally disbelieving that Sheree would ask them to leave. She looked over at Tyrone, who was lighting up a cigarette and ignoring them.

"Look, Renee, let's just get out of here," Trey said. "There is no use arguing with Sheree. She seems to have made up her mind just how low she is sinking. Come on! We'll be right outside if you need us." Trey looked over at Tyrone and held his stare for just a few seconds before ushering Renee out of the club.

"Glad you got rid of them. I can't stand an uppity bitch! Now back to business. So, you think Marcus has moved in on my girl? Is that who is occupying all her time?" Tyrone asked as he turned his head slightly to blow out some smoke.

"Actually, I think she is the one who is distracting my man with all her problems. Her car is always breaking down, or there is always an issue that brings them together, and I want it to stop! She acts so pitiful all the time. They have been seen around town a lot, dining together or whatever. When I get back into town, he hardly has any time for us. He broke it off with me earlier, and I will not hand him over to that—well, I need your help. I figure that if you distract her enough, and I do the same with him, we can break up all this craziness!"

Tyrone studied her. "So, is she the reason he broke up with you?"

"Let's just say that if she were not in the picture, I do not think it would have happened," Sheree said, overlooking the real reasons for the breakup.

"Do you have a way for me to get back into the club? Do you have access?" he asked.

Sheree froze. She wasn't sure if she should give him access, but then again, what did it matter if she and Marcus were already broken up? She could always lie and say she was forced into allowing Tyrone access.

"Well, can you?" Tyrone asked, looking at her, thinking she was taking too long to answer his question.

"Ah, sure! Just let me know when you want to come to the club, and I will make sure you are listed under my name. I don't know if you know this, but the club is closed usually on Christmas Eve and New Year's to special reservations only. That's next Friday and the following week. I will have to get you access sometime in January," Sheree said, somewhat unsure but hoping it would not come back to bite her.

"Get me access on New Year's Eve. I know she was excited about going to a New Year's dance so that will be my choice. I expect you will cover the admission for both of us as part of a thank-you for me keeping Jilly busy. That way, I will have Jilly all to myself, and you can enjoy pretty boy. Yeah, this will work. She will be totally surprised," Tyrone said, thinking out loud to himself.

Sheree watched the look on Tyrone's face and began to question her decision to get involved with this man. He seemed to be in deep thought, and that put her on edge. She wondered just how far he would go and what his true plans were. She knew she could not back out now. He probably would not let her, especially after she had given him the money. She hoped and prayed that this would not backfire on her.

"I have to be somewhere," Tyrone said.

"Ok, then," Sheree said, but before she could say another word, he walked toward the hallway that led to the back of the restaurant, leaving her standing there.

Brice was steadily checking the time, wondering what was keeping Marcus. He smiled, thinking that maybe Marcus had struck pay dirt with Jill. He had the beer chilling and had brought bags of chips; nachos were sitting on the warming tray. Joe was bringing the pizzas, Fonze had the wings from Mable's, and so all he needed was for Marcus to get there and set up the card table.

Marcus arrived twenty minutes later.

"Hey, Marcus, I couldn't find the table so that needs to be put up," Brice said.

"We have to use the spare that I have in the utility room. Jake borrowed the table we usually use when he had his party. I will go get it out of the utility room," Marcus said.

As he turned to go, Brice halted him. "Wait—you gonna tell me what is bothering you now, or do I have to wait and endure your preoccupation during the card game? You know we got to beat Fonze and Joe, or we will never hear the end of it. Need I remind you of the last time they sent us to Boston?" Brice said with an expectant look.

"Jill is talking to that clown Tyrone tonight, and I hate that he is anywhere near her. The guy is bad news, Brice. But before that, I went over to Sheree's, and I got nowhere with our talk. She didn't hear me, as usual, and tried to brush all her mess under the rug. So, I told her I couldn't do this anymore, and I broke it off with her."

"Oh really? I see. Well, did things go all right earlier with Jill? Did you explain things to her, Marcus?"

"Yeah, things went just fine," he said with a smile.

"Then what has got you so worried? I mean, don't you think Jill has enough guts to tell Tyrone what bridge to jump off of by now?" Brice asked.

"That's exactly what is worrying me—her inability to do just that! So, for some extra caution, I called Cyn and Jasmine before coming here and asked them to check on Jill. They were more than happy to help me out."

"Now, that was a great move! But I think the girl has her limits, and just watch—Tyrone has used up his last turn. He will be out, and no one will be able to say that you had anything to do with it. Then again, I think you have a definite effect on her. That's why Tyrone can't even get past first base."

They both laughed, and then finished setting- up for their card game.

Jill opened the door to Tyrone at around seven thirty. Tyrone had to work late because they were short on help but made it up to Jill by picking up Chinese for them for dinner. Jill led him to the kitchen table and took out some plates so that they could eat while they discussed their issues.

"I hope you like what I brought, Jilly," he said. He stood there awkwardly, seeming not to know how to handle himself with her.

Jill relieved him of some of the awkwardness by saying, "It smells good! Thanks for picking up dinner. Would you like to eat while we have our talk? We can just sit here at the table." Jill felt a bit awkward herself.

Tyrone looked at Jill, then looked away, as if he was struggling with something. "Sure, we can eat now if you want to, but I got to tell you, Jilly. I'm in knots 'cause of what happened. I don't want to lose you, girl. You mean a lot to me. Dammit! Jilly, I didn't know what to do when you shut me out like that. It was as if you thought I was guilty of something."

"I really do not know what to do or say anymore, Tyrone. The cops came in, and there was no sign of you, so it did not feel right. I left not knowing what was going on. I heard different things, like drugs and illegal activity. Are you involved with illegal drugs, Tyrone?"

"No, Jilly! I told you it was the manager running numbers, but you still do not believe me! I know you don't. I feel it!" Tyrone said, watching her.

The room got quiet, and after a few minutes, she said, "This question has really plagued me since that night; it was scary. I'm not used to that kind of craziness!" Jill saw his reaction coming before it erupted from him.

Tyrone threw up his hands frantically. "I got caught up in what someone else was doing at the club. If I'd had drugs on me, do you think I would be free now, Jilly?" When she looked doubtful, he said, "Come on, girl! You got to know me better than that by now!"

"Tyrone, what do you expect?" she exclaimed.

"I expect you to have more faith in me than this! You are the only girl in the number-one spot! Don't be listening to those haters! Jilly, come on, if I were doing drugs, why would I be always busting my ass with some job at the car wash or these side jobs at the club? I even had to sleep in my car a few nights after being arrested! Come on, woman, think!" He got up from his chair and started pacing.

"Tyrone, you act as though my questions are outrageous. It's bad enough with the girl thing, but the drugs—that's my limit! This is the second time you have been thrown out or been in altercations when we have been in public. I mean, even the first time, we were at the movies, and you got mad when your friend mentioned how you guys share women. You cut him off, but I knew what he was talking about. Even then, you stopped talking to him, and he was simply wanting you to introduce me to him."

"Nah, Jilly, he was trying to get in your panties, that's what! So, what are you trying to say, Jilly? Did you want me to introduce him?" Tyrone asked, nostrils flaring.

"Not necessarily, but what would it have hurt? When we go out, you have all the fun. You dance with other people, but as soon as someone notices me, you get all bent out of shape."

"Bent out of shape? Ah! Here we go. It's about Pretty Boy. All I know is that a woman's place is with her man, not manipulating other guys!" Tyrone said angrily.

"Manipulating? What? Are you serious, Tyrone? I do not come on to other guys. But you, you come on to other women, and right in front of me!" Jill exclaimed.

"You were slow dancing, with the crown prince. At least I don't dance like that with other women."

Jill gave a short laugh. "That's not from a lack of trying. We were dancing almost at arm's length. You were like a cat in a mouse house, the way you kept asking other women to dance. Me, I just sat there for a long time before I got asked to dance, and when I did, you wanted to fight!" Jill exclaimed.

"No, no, the fight only started cause Mr. Prince man did not want me to interrupt y'all's dance. I did not see you making any moves to come with me!" Tyrone now was really angry, and his voice got louder.

"You know what? This is silly. This argument shows that we are not suited to date each other. Let's just chalk it up to poor chemistry and call it quits." Jill looked over at him and saw that he was struggling to keep his temper in check."

"I ain't calling it quits! You need to get off your high-and-mighty place and give me some; that will get us back on track. We spend way too much time fighting instead of making love!" he said, as a way of resolving their issues. He came closer to her and grabbed her hand, pulling her over to the couch with him. Tyrone tried to pull her close, but Jill pushed him away, got up off the couch, and then walked to the door.

"Tyrone, you need to leave. I am so tired of these same arguments. It's over between us!"

Just then, the doorbell rang. He motioned to her not to open it, but she did anyway. Cyn and Jasmine were on her doorstep.

"Hey, girl, Jasmine brought this dress, and she wanted you to take a look to see if you can take it in. It's just a little big on her, but we figured with your magic, you can alter it just a little to make it fit right," Cyn said.

Jill stepped back for them to enter. They both walked in and sat down, making themselves at home.

"Oh, hey, Tyrone. Sorry—didn't know you had company."

Tyrone just grunted.

"Well, I can look at the dress. Tyrone was just leaving," Jill said, looking pointedly at him.

Tyrone swore loudly as he walked to the door but stopped to look at Jill. "Jilly, this ain't over!" he said quietly.

Jill rolled her eyes. "Yes, it is. Tyrone, goodbye!" She slammed the door behind him as he walked out. Jill leaned on the door, then pushed away from it, taking a seat on the small chair opposite Cyn and Jasmine.

"Sorry you guys had to witness that, but that was the breakup

I needed. If it had not been for your interruption, I might not have gotten him out of my house. Can you imagine? He wanted to have sex, thinking that would make it all better. We had been arguing about all the low-down things he's done; then he wanted to throw Marcus in my face. I'm just over him."

"It's a good thing we came by," Cyn said.

"Jill, how about if we do the dress thing some other time?" said Jazmin.

"Why? I thought you needed it soon."

"Not really. I, ah, we just used that as an excuse because Marcus had texted Cyn earlier. He was concerned about you meeting Tyrone alone and asked if we wouldn't mind checking on you. So, here we are, and we are so glad we came," Jasmine said with a worried look. "Jill, do you mind spending the night over at our place? Then you can take a quick look at the dress. Please?"

Jill released a breath and said, "I know what you are doing, and I do appreciate it, but—"

"Look, Jill," Cyn said. "Not getting in your business, but did you not see the way the brother was looking when we interrupted you guys? He was so pissed when he left; he looked as if he wanted to throw us out for barging in here. He did not want to leave. He is not breaking up with you willingly. I would be careful, if I were you. Give him some time to cool off; and take yourself out of harm's way. We would love for you to stay with us for a little while. Poor Jazzy has been worried about you since Marcus called."

"I'm so glad we came over." Jazmin admitted.

Jill got up and walked over to the window. It was too dark to see, but she knew Tyrone would be back. "Give me a few minutes to pack a bag, and I will come with you guys. What you said makes sense, and I am so happy you came when you did. I'll be right back."

While she was gone, Cyn texted Marcus, letting him know they were taking Jill to their place because Tyrone was not ready for the breakup. Jill was all right, and she would explain more later.

On the other side of town, the card game was well underway as Marcus and Brice were up by two games. Brice pulled out a cigar and examined it slowly, inhaling its scent, taunting Joe and Fonze as Marcus looked on.

"Would you gentlemen care for a sampling of the finest cigar from a man of many talents? A brand brilliantly put together. A masterpiece fit, only for a champion. I will share my fine collection of Cuban cigars with you gentlemen because I am a true sportsman. It exudes great taste, and it is impeccable and belongs to a class all its own, sort of like me." Brice flamboyantly displayed a lighter and made exaggerated gestures but still didn't light the cigar.

"Brice, you are not going to smoke that thing in here, are you?" Marcus asked with a smile, trying to keep himself from laughing at his big brother's ridiculous pose.

"Sure, little brother, why not?" Brice said, giving Marcus a ridiculous look.

"The fumes from it alone may singe our otherwise healthy lungs," Marcus replied.

"Yeah, Brice. I didn't think rangers smoked. Smoking is lethal to your lungs, man. Wouldn't want you to get out of breath when you are chasing bad guys," Joe said. He couldn't hold back any longer and started to laugh. Fonze joined in, as Marcus sat back, observing the expression on Brice's face—he seemed to be contemplating what Joe said.

"Little do you know, but you are looking at a superb machine. A body like granite steel and so marvelous that the ladies can't keep their hands off, let alone stop staring."

The fellas laughed even harder when Fonze said, "Yeah, you keep puffing like that, and the hands that touch you will be more like a nurse as she helps you with the oxygen mask."

The laughter continued.

"Come on, Brice. We need you to deal the next hand and cut out the BS, unless this is your way of stalling the butt-whooping we are about to put on you. Right, Fonze?" Joe said.

"You know, Joe, now that I think about it, it sure seems like a stall tactic. Who could blame him? His minutes of fame are about to be over. Come on, man, let's play some more cards and watch your lead diminish. Joe and I are through letting you guys warm up. Now it's time to get serious. I got to leave and give my lady some attention. I can't stay here and watch Brice try to enlarge his already huge ego," Fonze complained playfully.

"Lady? What lady? You mean that blow-up thing you got in the closet?" Brice said as the guys all burst out laughing.

"Ah! Come on, Brice, you know that is for the CPR classes that we give at the center. But unbeknownst to you all, I do have a real date for New Year's, and I plan to see her later this evening, gentlemen. I think if anyone needs that blow-up, it might be you, Brice, old buddy!" Fonze said, and everyone sobered up at his announcement. Fonze stared at the look of surprise on all his friends' faces, especially Brice's.

"Well, I'll be damned!" Brice said out loud. "Now, Fonze, I will gladly share my best smokes with you. Congrats on the date, man!"

"I appreciate it, but no thanks, man. I'm good," Fonze said.

"Since you gentleman failed to recognize very good taste, let alone the finest smokes you city boys will ever see, I will keep my special cigars to myself. Now, let's get on with the beat-down." Brice flashed a smile as he stuck his cigar back into his mouth. "Just not sure which direction I'm gonna send you two; Boston is always a nice destination. I think by way of freight car would be fitting, especially since you guys can't appreciate a good cigar."

Two hours later. the cards were left on the table as they ate and drank while watching a fight on Pay-Per-View.

"Marcus, you should have gotten us tickets since you got connections," Fonze commented.

"Yeah, and then I could have given all those fine women with hardly any clothes on an up-close-and-personal treat—me!" Brice said thoughtfully.

"How does one man get so full of himself?" Joe said, shaking his head.

"I don't know, Joe," Marcus said, "but here is my theory. Mom is trying so hard to get her firstborn hitched that I think the fear of that alone has created this weird ego monster. He tries to make everyone think he is a player, when in all actuality, he can't even get a date."

They all laughed.

"Oh, little brother, if you only knew." Brice glanced at his watch. "But give it time; you all will see what old Brice has lined up for tonight." Brice winked as he drained what was left in his glass of scotch.

They thought Brice would say and do anything to make them think he was a chick magnet, but thirty minutes later, the doorbell rang. Marcus looked over at Brice, who wore a huge grin on his face. When Marcus opened the door, there stood a tall redhead with twinkling eyes, in a tight dress and stilettos.

"Hi there! I'm Cybil, and these are my friends. We are looking for Brice Jordan. Is he here?"

Marcus had to close his mouth in shock, as he suddenly noticed that Cybil was not alone. Three other women were standing behind her. All were nice-looking, if a tad bit too heavily made up. Marcus stepped aside, allowing the women to come inside. He then called out to Brice, who appeared with a huge smile on his face.

"Cybil! Hey, doll, glad you could make it. My, my, who all do we have here?" Brice said, looking at each one of the ladies.

"Brice, baby! I brought some company with me since you said the fellas would be joining you. We couldn't have the fun and leave them out, now could we, sugar? This is Angel, Crystal, and Joy," Cybil said.

"Welcome, ladies! I'd like you to meet my brother, Marcus."

Marcus gave Brice a funny look before plastering a smile on his face, and he gave a slight wave with his hand as he contemplated what kind of fun they were supposed to have.

"Now, come on in. Let's get comfortable and meet the rest of the guys," Brice said as he headed back into the living room with his arms around Cybil. The girls followed closely behind them, with Marcus bringing up the rear. Joe and Fonze were both sprawled out in their respective chairs. Upon hearing Brice's voice, they looked up and saw the girls. They both got up out of their seats, brushing themselves off as Brice and the four women came in, with Marcus following.

"Fellas, I'd like you to meet some friends of mine." After the introductions were made, Brice fixed the ladies a drink. He then asked Marcus to put some good music on, ignoring Marcus's gestures to have a word with him. Joe excused himself and Marcus, and he propelled Marcus out into the hallway.

"What in the hell is Brice putting down?" Joe exclaimed.

"I don't know, but it looks as if he has provided us all with a date," Marcus replied.

"Yeah, and once Yvonne finds out, she will have my head on a platter. I told her I had changed. This will not help. I mean, not that the ladies aren't fine, but how will this look? You know that once Brice gets around the girls, he will be bragging, and the girls will pump him for information, and he will cave, Marcus. You know this."

Just then, Marcus said, "Hold on. Joe. I just got a text. Jill is breaking off with that idiot tonight, and I told her, if she needed me to call. Or this could be Cyn. I asked her to go over to Jill's, just to make sure old Tyrone was behaving himself. Ah, it is Cyn. Jill's staying at her place for tonight, and she is fine, but Tyrone did not want to break it off. For tonight, at least, I can relax because she is fine with the girls. Now, back to the problem at hand."

"I'm glad that she is with the girls, but what are we going to do with this mess Brice has created?" Joe asked, really frustrated.

"I know, but how do we get rid of them without hurting their feelings? Why don't we all sneak out and leave Brice to figure the rest out?" They both smiled, liking that idea, but before they could get Fonze in on the idea, he was being manipulated by one of the girls as she slid closer to him on the couch.

Both Joe and Marcus looked at each other and decided it would not be a good idea to walk out on Brice and Fonze, so they stuck around, kept supplying the women with drinks, and played some pool, which took another couple of hours. Marcus and Joe managed to keep the women at bay, but the same could not be said for Brice or Fonze. It turned out, to Brice's dismay, that the women got so drunk that the men decided to put them in a cab and send them home around 2:00 a.m.

The next morning, while Brice was in the shower, shortly before he and Marcus were to head over to their parents' house, Marcus called Jill.

Jill answered on the third ring.

"Jill, it's me, Marcus. What are you doing?" He waited for her to fuss about sending Cyn and Jaz over.

Jill responded with a smile in her voice. "Marcus, I just had some juice, and I made the girls breakfast. I was thinking about doing my power-walk in the park. Wanna join me?"

Marcus moaned and said, "Girl, don't hurt me like that. The guys almost hung me out to dry last night. I don't think I can hang anymore. I must be getting old or something."

"Who's aging, you? I don't think so. You are the most active person I know."

"Not with that brother of mine around. He likes to party all the time. I feel like his parent, as much as I have to watch him. But that's beside the point. What happened with the cutting-Tyrone-out-of-your-life process last night?" he asked calmly. "Is Tyrone outside your apartment in the nearest trash can? Or did you work him over yourself, just for self-gratification?"

"No! Nothing that extreme. But he is gone. So how was your long night? Sounds like someone has a bit of a hangover."

"Just a little. So, tell me how it went last night." Marcus needed to know.

"Well, we had a talk, and it went well for like thirty seconds. Then he started talking as if he had done no wrong. I guess I lost it, and then he lost it, and I told him that this was not working and it's best we break up. He had a fit, but luckily, I had a guardian angel and the doorbell rang at that time—it was Cyn and Jasmine. He was so mad. But I told him to just leave, and he told me it wasn't over. So, then Cyn said that I should not take him lightly. Jaz was so worried about me. But thanks to your intervention which came at the right time; because Tyrone would not have left if the girls had not interrupted. So, I packed a bag and came home with them."

"Good! I'm so glad I intervened, and I know you are probably mad at me, but sue me. I was really worried, and I do not trust that clown!"

"I could not be mad at you for caring, Marcus, and I want to say thank you! Because he was not taking no for an answer," Jill admitted.

"There is no need for any thank-you. We are all glad you're ok."

"So, you guys tied one on last night. Had to fight the girls off or what? And where is Brice?"

Marcus smiled. "First of all, that meddling brother of mine is in the shower, since we just got up."

"Uh-huh," Jill said.

He rushed to let Jill know that Brice had surprised them all by inviting some ladies over for their men's night.

"Oh! I am not surprised, but please go on." She didn't really want to hear about his date with another woman.

He could not remember ever caring if a girl knew where he spent the night, but now it seemed important that he tell her what happened before anyone else did. He told about the card game and that the girls had come by, thanks to his brother. He finally ended the story but kept the details to a minimum.

"Joe and I figured if we prolonged the card game, maybe they'd get bored sitting around and leave, but the crazy thing was that the girls were already on the tipsy side when they got here. They continued to drink, and then they passed out—all of them. We put them in a cab and sent them on their way." He laughed. "Yeah, Brice was upset about it turning out the way it did."

"Wow! That was really crazy! Poor Brice. I know he was looking for a different ending," Jill said.

He could hear the laughter in her voice, which made him feel better. "Poor Brice? Joe and I had to clean up his mess, not to mention that poor Fonze was taken in by one of them, but she fizzled out too! So, what do you have planned for today?"

"Gonna do some adjustments to a dress for Jasmine and then, at some point, I will head home."

"How about I pick you up when you are done with the dress, and you, me, and Brice get lunch and take him to the airport?" He hoped she would accept, especially since he threw Brice into the equation.

"That sounds good. So, I will call you when I'm done here, no more than one or two hours. How does that sound?"

"Fantastic! We will see you then."

———

Marcus was still sitting by the side of his bed where he had been perched, talking to Jill, when Brice walked in and leaned on the door frame.

"I just finished talking to Jill. Remember I told you she was breaking it off with Tyrone last night? Well, she did," Marcus said, smiling as he looked over at his brother.

Brice gave a shout as he walked over to his brother, and they bumped fists. "Now that's what I'm talking about. So now you just have to let her know she is the one you want. Wine and dine her, man! You know what to do. You two are already the best of friends. Show her how much better it could be as a couple."

"I plan to, big brother! She did say Tyrone was not willing to do the breakup thing, but as far as she was concerned, it was done."

"It doesn't matter what he wants because she has made her decision. Sounds like you two are finally getting somewhere," Brice said.

"Yeah, it seems that way. Since Jill and I are going to take you to the airport, we need to get ready to go pick her up!" Marcus smiled as he headed for the shower, and Brice walked out to finish getting ready.

Chapter

8

Monday morning dawned bright and early. Jill turned over to silence her alarm. She disliked that Monday was here so quickly after such a wonderful Sunday afternoon, which had turned into a nice evening. Marcus had picked her up from Cyn's place, and they met Brice at Jake's Deli, where they shared a nice lunch before taking him to the airport.

The previous week had been very chaotic, which meant there were endless loose ends that needed attention. It took a lot of effort, but Jill finally got herself into the shower and then dressed before fixing a quick breakfast of juice and a bagel. Her quickie breakfast would not last long, so Jill grabbed a piece of fruit on the way out the door. She often wondered how people could starve themselves just to look skinny. Was it worth it? Jill thought not.

She walked into the office to find her boss, Garrett Rogers, looking up from the secretary's desk. "Good morning, Jillian. How are you?" he asked.

"I'm fine, Garrett. How are you?"

"I'm going crazy. All hell is breaking loose, and I need all hands-on deck. I will need to meet with you in the office because there is going to be an assignment change, and I need your help with this mess so badly. As soon as you have gotten settled this morning—maybe in thirty minutes or so? Will that work for you?"

When she nodded in agreement, he headed into his office, closing the door.

When Jill entered Garrett Rogers's office a little later, it was empty. She sat down and waited for him. He soon came rushing in, arms loaded with files. Garrett Rogers was a very high-strung man; he was average height and thin. He was a perfectionist, and when that wasn't what he got, he became agitated and highly excited. Although Jill had witnessed his change in attitude many times, his anger was never directed toward her. He made her feel like family. He knew this was her first time away from home, and with having his own daughters away, he seemed to transfer some of his affections to her situation.

"Jillian," Garrett said, "sorry to keep you waiting, but there is total chaos with two of the accounts that we closed on Friday. Gregg had the deal all wrapped up, only to find a mix-up on the agreed figures, and I got this email from financials this morning. Now I have to get back in touch with the client and try to explain the mix-up without our looking like bumbling idiots. I will have to see what assignments you can put on hold so you can fill in for me. I was supposed to have a meeting across town this afternoon at Wallington's corporate office. If you can do this for me, it will be greatly appreciated. Gregg left for vacation on Friday after we closed the accounts. I would have gotten him to rework this, but of course he is not here. Samuel's dismissal uncovered a lot of loose ends. How he managed to have so many incomplete assignments that weren't noticed, I do not know! Anyway, I am getting off course here. This other assignment I need you to take is a major acquisition for us. I know you did the prep work for Samuel, but now the clients need us to complete the presentation because there is another company offering them a quote for the assignment as well. You did the prep on Tivor; that is the account I will need you to close on. There is one snag, though—you need to be on a plane late this afternoon for Boston. You will need to do the presentation in two days. Here are both files, one for this afternoon with Wallington and this one for Tivor. If you need any additional notes, I can send them to you in an email attachment, but everything else is in these files. Now tell me, what do you think, and can you reschedule your appointments for today?"

"I only have two appointments that I need to reschedule; the other two were just some return calls where potential clients had questions. Other than that, I can make this work," she said, looking a little nervous.

"Jillian, I trust your ability. You are organized, and that is so much a part of what makes you so efficient. I have been pleased with your work over the last several months, especially with your stepping in and helping me with the two new accounts that needed attention when Samuel left us high and dry. You have proven to me that I can depend on you and that you are up for a bigger challenge. Finer Things will be your challenge, and I have this feeling that you are going to hit this one out of the park. Everything you'll need—plane reservation, hotel accommodation, and allowance—is all set by Sarah. If there is something else that you can think of, just tell her, and she will take care of it. Do you have any questions?"

Jill asked him a few more questions before leaving his office to make calls to reschedule her appointments.

Jill's two o'clock meeting that she attended downtown went very well. Jill managed to schedule an appointment for a future expansion project that the company was working on that day as well. Jill arrived home that evening feeling good about her workday. She was still apprehensive about the Boston trip. Yvonne and Cyn both stopped by to give Jill a ride to the airport. Cyn had gone to Boston on many occasions, so she advised Jill of some good places to eat and shop. The three ladies grabbed a quick bite to eat on their way to the airport, and after seeing Jill board the plane, they headed back to their separate homes.

The plane ride gave Jill plenty of time to think over her presentation and the upcoming holiday. The dilemma with Tyrone did not seem to carry much weight with Jill anymore. Since their breakup the previous week, she had not heard from him—although every time the phone rang, she got nervous in case it was him, trying to force her into taking him back.

The feeling of excitement and anticipation she felt about the upcoming meeting with the representatives of Finer Things began to resurface, making her nervous. When ten minutes later, those same feelings had not subsided, Jill decided to phone Marcus. If she talked to him, he could allay her fears, and she also had forgotten to tell him she would not be around for a couple of days. She smiled as she dialed his number, but she got his voicemail, so Jill left him a message.

Once Jill arrived in Boston, she retrieved her bags from the terminal and caught a cab to her hotel. While she was unpacking, her cellular phone ran, and she rushed to answer. "Hello!"

"Hello! Were you running?" Marcus's voice came over the line.

"No, I had to find my phone because I was in the middle of unpacking."

"I'm just getting ready to go out to dinner at a friend of my family's home tonight—Paul and Brenda Stevens, old business friends of my father. Did you say unpacking?"

"Yes. I meant to tell you when I left town, but I remembered on the plane, so I called you and left a message. I guess my mind was occupied with other things. There was so much to get done at the last minute and telling the girls. I was lucky they were all at Cyn's, and did you know—"

"What? Wait a minute, Jill! Where are you and what's going on?"

"Oh, yeah, I'm in Boston," she said.

"Boston? Why are you in Boston?"

"Garrett ran into a snag with some accounts and could not get away because he was needed to straighten out other problems with two major accounts. I got drafted to do the presentation for the representatives of a specialty store called Finer Things. And get this—it comes with a promotion for me if I can pull it off."

She heard the smile in his voice when he said, "Well! You are just the one to pull it off. I know you can do this."

"You really think so?" Jill said, sounding unsure.

"Yes, I do. Look, baby girl, stop doubting yourself. You have accomplished so much already in such a little time."

"I guess you are right, Marcus, but when I think of this company and its popularity and reputation—"

"Ooh! Yes! Yes, they are so good at what they do."

"I can see by your reaction that this account will not be hard to get a successful jingle. I doubt if the men will pay any attention to the actual slogan but rather what is in the lingerie, huh?"

His positive response on the other end of the phone made her laugh. Then suddenly, the nervousness she was feeling disappeared; just the sound of him put her in a different mood.

"I should have recognized that typical groans are pretty common, coming from a male," Jill joked.

"What can I say, Jill? I'm a man, and I appreciate the differences between a man and a woman. So, what are your plans? How long will you be away?"

"I return on Thursday. Tomorrow's the reception dinner, and on Wednesday I'll do some shopping for the girls early in the day, then the presentation that night. Cyn and Yvonne gave me some tips on good places to shop, and I want to bring them something."

"You all are really close, and that's good. If you didn't know it, you would think you all were sisters," Marcus said.

"Yeah, it's funny how that happened. But Thursday, I'll probably get to the airport in Philly around five. Hopefully, I can close out everything in time. Marcus, did you have problems when you made your first formal presentation?"

"I didn't do too badly, and Jill, you will do fine. You are a natural when it comes to this advertising stuff. You really like the work you do, and that makes a world of difference. You are a people-person, no matter if you think you are or not. I have seen you when you meet people. You are a natural for advertising. You have a certain charisma. You, honey, will blow them away. Trust me on this."

I do trust you, Marcus. I have to admit the reason I called you is because I needed your support. I was beginning to feel nervous, the fear of my backing out had me calling you for reinforcement. You know how I get at times."

"Yeah! I know, but I also know how you can talk yourself into bouncing back, so you don't need me to tell you. Jill, you can do it and do it well, even without my input."

"Yeah, but somehow it feels better just hearing your advice. So, who are you going to this dinner party with?"

"Well, I have no date, so it's just me. On Thursday, is anyone picking you up from the airport?"

"No, I had not thought that far ahead," she said.

"I could give you a call on Thursday morning to make sure your arrival time is still the same. I can pick you up, if that's ok with you?"

"It's ok with me." she agreed.

"Good."

"Ok, Marcus. We can confirm everything on Wednesday night. Thanks!"

"You are welcome. Stop worrying about everything. You will be fine. Take care, Jill. I know you will be great. Good night."

Jill hung up the phone with a smile, already anticipating the next time she would see Marcus. She had Marcus on the brain, and it seemed like no matter what was happening, her thoughts of Marcus never went away.

Being out of town on business could not have come at a better time. She needed to be away since her breakup with Tyrone. She was always on edge that he would show up on her doorstep. He always wanted to have the last word, and she knew it was probably upsetting him that he did not get it. She decided to close her mind to thoughts of Tyrone and return her attention to unpacking and then pulling out her notes for the presentation.

When Marcus arrived at the Stevenses' home, the butler showed him into a huge room where many people were already mingling. Paul stood on the far side of the room, talking with a lively group. He noticed Marcus and made his way over, extending a hand as he drew near, then embracing Marcus with a slap on the back.

"Marcus, my man, how are you?" Paul said.

"Paul, I'm doing fine. How about you?" Marcus said.

"Everything is great." Paul leaned closer to Marcus but before he could speak, a familiar voice loudly interrupted him. Both men turned to see Sheree walking toward them.

"Marcus! It's so wonderful to see you." Sheree dramatically wrapped her arms around him and kissed him on the lips.

Marcus quickly unwrapped himself from Sheree as Brenda, Paul's wife joined the group at the same time, "Why hello, Marcus."

"Brenda, you look beautiful as always. How are you?"

"Doing well. Paul and I had lunch with your folks at the club, and we had such a nice time. Your mother has been helping the agency and me with this outreach program for women's help. She is amazing, and everyone loves her."

"That's Catherine Jordan all right. She loves a good cause," Marcus said.

"She's such a great organizer," Sheree said, trying to be a part of the conversation. "It's been so long since I've have seen her. I will have to stop by and visit."

"Oh, Sheree, before I forget, I have someone I want you to meet. She is one of our organizers at the agency, and she needs to run something by you to see if you or your crew would be interested. I'm sure by now Paul would be overjoyed to get us out of his hair so that he can speak with his number one business adviser. Ok, darlin, Marcus is all yours. We will get out of your hair," Brenda said as she received a wink from her husband.

Sheree had to hide her disappointment as she looked back at Marcus as Brenda escorted her across the room.

Marcus expelled a sigh of relief as the two women hurried off.

Paul looked at Marcus with raised eyebrows before he said what was on his mind. "What's going on, ole buddy? The way Sheree was looking at you was really, ah, strange, and you were standing here like stone mountain." Paul frowned.

"There is nothing to tell. I broke up with her. End of story."

"I see, you broke- up? Well, does she know you are not still a couple? Because she does not act as if you two are broken up, my friend." Paul shook his head.

"I think she thinks we are going to get back together, but it's not happening." Marcus looked straight at Paul and then said, "She complicates my life, causing chaos everywhere we go, especially if there are other women around. When she went to my office, and confronted my staff because she could not get in contact with me, oh no, that was enough! Man, she even had Mrs. Thomas frustrated. You know I could not have that."

"Yeah, I remember how pissed she was when you were paired with the governor's daughter at the Planning Commission's luncheon. What a scene that was!" Paul said.

"Yeah, I ended up apologizing to the young lady and the governor, who was beside himself with Sheree. He told me—and I quote, 'Someone needs to get a handle on that young woman.' I took her home, and all she ever wanted to do was blame someone else. I told her to think about it when I dropped her off at her place," Marcus said, as Paul continued to shake his head. "She is trying to give me some space, so to speak, but for me, it's over! Now, what was that business Brenda hinted at that you were so excited to discuss with me?"

Paul nodded and led Marcus over to the bar, where they talked as the bartender prepared their drinks.

A little later, when Marcus was speaking to a couple of old business associates, Paul caught up with him again, but he was not alone. There was a lovely lady holding onto his arm as she smiled up at him. When they got to the group where Marcus was being lively entertained, Paul interrupted and made the introductions to the sexy lady at his side.

"Gentlemen, I would like you to meet a very lovely lady and friend to both Brenda and me. Chloe Mitchell, this is Marcus Jordan, John Scoffield, Marty Alexander, and Sid Brockwell. These guys are the best of the best when it comes to successful entrepreneurs."

"Young lady, the pleasure is all ours," John said. "Paul always seems to surround himself with the finest women. If we were only single again, but with Marcus here, it's a totally different story." John Scoffield was a tall, thin man with salt-and-pepper hair. He'd spoken first, but the others smiled, taking their turns to speak as the jokes continued.

Paul intervened, laughing, as he directed attention to Marcus. "Chloe, Marcus Jordan is an old friend of ours. We met through his parents, who are like family to Brenda and me. We have designated ourselves as his guardians. Poor boy can't seem to beat the girls off— poor, poor guy!" Paul hung his head, as the other guys joined in. "We often wonder what we'll do with him," Paul said, barely managing to hold himself together without laughing. He noticed the look of delight on Chloe's face.

Marcus did not miss the wink Paul directed at Chloe.

"Pay these old men no mind, Chloe. They are longing for their less mature years," Marcus said as another burst of laughter erupted from the circle of men. "This is a pleasure, Chloe," Marcus said as he looked over at the tall, slender, and shapely browned-skinned woman with short-cropped blonde hair. Her light-green eyes really made her stand out.

She returned his smile with a dazzling one of her own. "Very nice to meet you, Marcus Jordan. Can I call you Marcus?"

He nodded his head, and Chloe dragged her eyes away from Marcus just for a minute to look at Paul. "Paul, I think you have outdone yourself this time because the party just got *so* much better." Chloe continued to watch Marcus as he interacted with the other gentlemen; then she returned her gaze to Paul. The conversation flowed very well. Marcus, at his best, oozed with charm as his attention was diverted from the circle of men to Chloe. Somehow Chloe had managed to create some separation between her and Marcus, away from the group of guys. But across the room, Sheree watched as the lovely newcomer engaged Marcus's attention in a corner of the room. Paul had left them alone for some time now. Sheree just wondered what this woman thought she was doing with her man, although Marcus looked quite relaxed.

Paul walked up a little later, smiling and shaking his head at Chloe, as he said, "You still got this man cornered, Chloe. You had better be careful because I think you are being watched. I think you should give the man some breathing room. You may be attacked or something."

"Well, if you were my man, you would not be left alone, especially at a party where the women outnumber the men. Perhaps the women of Philly are all doormats, and the men just do as they please—something I totally disagree with, right, Paul?" she said with a mischievous grin.

"Chloe, I refuse to comment, for further implication may put me under duress because I happen to live in this town with these women. In Millsburg, they may do things differently, but here, you respect other people's property," Paul said, looking in Sheree's direction.

"Chloe certainly has a right to her own opinion, but for me, I'm my own man, and no one controls me. That's just not my makeup," John Scoffield said, walking up to them, his eyes sparkling as they latched onto Chloe.

Chloe looked directly at Marcus and said, "Although I love to be in control, something tells me that having you exerting your power over me would be quite appealing, not to mention hot! Furthermore, I do respect other people's property, but if it is unclaimed, then I think it should be up for grabs. Don't you, Marcus?" Her smile turned into a full laugh, which Marcus suspected was just for show, which included Sheree, who was staring them down from across the room. Suddenly, Sheree appeared, and Chloe saw a need to place her hand on Marcus's arm.

"What was that about other people's property? Would anyone care to enlighten me?" Sheree said. The group seemed to have gotten quiet. Sheree placed a hand on Marcus's arm, staring directly at Chloe before her gaze moved to Paul and then Marcus, who expelled a deep breath. Chloe stared at Sheree and raised an eyebrow.

Paul rushed in to make the introductions. "Sheree Davis, Chloe Mitchell is a friend of ours from Millsburg. Chloe, Sheree is one of the best models in the business. She is an international icon. We have known her for quite some time."

Marcus, hearing Paul trying to unsuccessfully soothe the waters, knew it wouldn't be long before Sheree jumped in with both feet. The ringing of the dinner gong interrupted what would have become a slow meltdown. As Paul ushered Chloe and Brenda toward the dining room, Marcus and Sheree trailed behind them. Marcus knew Sheree was like a ticking time bomb. She was very watchful, like a hawk, but for now, small talk helped to fill in the gap.

When they entered the dining room, it was to Sheree's chagrin that their seating arrangements were not together. Initially, he thought Sheree would explode, but she managed to keep her temper in check, even when she saw who Marcus was sitting beside. Dinner went well, as far as Marcus was concerned. He and Chloe talked about her work and interests. Each time they laughed, or Chloe bent closer to tell him something, he could feel Sheree's eyes on them. Marcus knew Chloe was trying to get on Sheree's nerves, and he tried not to influence her in any way.

The drama was much too much for him. Neither woman seemed to interest him. His taste in women had changed, all because of Jill. He could not live his life being shadowed by a jealous woman. After dinner was over and everyone had adjourned to another room, which was set aside for dancing, Sheree was drawn into conversation with one of the promoters for one of Philadelphia's large charity functions. Marcus continued to mingle, although he was ready to call it a night; maybe he would stay for another hour or so.

One hour later, Marcus found himself deep in discussion with Liza Bowman about the upcoming bachelor auction, which was to benefit medical research for the children's hospital. He was laughing at Liza, who was remembering the previous year's benefit auction, when he noticed Brenda coming down the stairs with a worried look on her face. She seemed as if she was looking for someone, and when she spotted Marcus, she looked relieved. Marcus, sensing something was wrong, excused himself from Liza and met Brenda halfway across the room.

"Oh, Marcus! I need your help. Well actually, Paul needs your help in breaking up what I guess you could call a fight." Brenda looked bewildered.

"A fight?" Marcus said. "What do you mean by *fight*? Do we need to call the police?"

"Oh! No! No! I hate to ask you this, but can you take Sheree out of here now? It seems she followed Chloe into the ladies' room and started questioning her and threatening her. Well, knowing Chloe, she did not back down, so they got into a struggle."

Marcus quickly followed Brenda upstairs. Once they reached the landing of the second floor, Marcus could hear Sheree's voice, swearing every other word that came out of her mouth. When Marcus walked into the room with Brenda on his heels, Sheree's disposition changed from that of a she-devil to that of the victim. Rushing over to Marcus, she quickly began to defend herself.

"Thank God you're here, Marcus. This poor excuse for a woman attacked me!" Sheree yelled.

"You, lying little bi—" Chloe replied.

Marcus intervened before things could get more out of control. He threw out his arms, holding both women back. "Everyone chill! You are both too old to be acting like this, no matter the reason and especially not in Brenda and Paul's house. I think both of you owe them an apology."

Chloe was first to offer Brenda and Paul an apology, immediately followed by Sheree, who had the ability to look as if she really meant it.

Marcus added his regrets, along with the ladies, followed immediately by announcing that it was time he and Sheree took their leave. Sheree slid her arm through Marcus's and eyed Chloe with a big smile, as a sign of victory.

With that gauntlet thrown down, Chloe said, "I will talk with you soon, Marcus, and we can finish the conversation we had earlier. By the way, you can reach me at any of the numbers I gave you. I look forward to hearing from you." Chloe sauntered past, but she stopped and blew a kiss at him. Suddenly, Sheree lunged and shoved Chloe, who stumbled and fell against the wall. Marcus pulled Sheree back and sent her into the hallway; then he helped Chloe up. Brenda stood there in shock but Snapped out of it and hurried over to Chloe to make sure she was ok Marcus escorted Sheree down the stairs as he kept a viselike grip on her arm.

As they were getting Sheree's wrap, Chloe came down the stairs with Brenda and entered the room where the rest of the party guests were. Sheree stared at her and then mumbled, "She thinks she got one up on me. That no-good whore! I could absolutely ring her GI Jane–looking neck."

Marcus ushered her toward the front door as he told Paul good night.

The ride to Sheree's home was made in silence. When they reached her front door, Marcus took the keys from her hand to open the door.

"Good night, Sheree," Marcus said as he grabbed her hand and placed her keys in it. He turned to walk away.

"Wait! Marcus?"

"What, Sheree?" Marcus replied, totally upset with her.

"Aren't you gonna come in, and we can talk?"

"There is nothing to talk about. Whatever you do does not affect me anymore."

"But you took me away from that crazy woman to protect me."

"I took you away for Brenda. She and Paul have been very good friends, and she asked me to take you home. I did, end of story. You see, Sheree, one of the reasons I'm not with you today is because you always, have to act crazy and cause trouble. I have had enough. Goodbye, Sheree!" He walked back to his car, got in, and left as she stood there watching the taillights of his car disappear around the corner.

Marcus awoke to the rain pounding at his window. He got up, heading for the shower, but had to retrace his steps to the bedside table as the phone began to ring.

"Yeah?"

"Hey, man! I finally caught you. What's wrong with you? I tried calling you last night, but all I got was your voicemail. What's going on?"

"Hey, Brice. I thought you would be at work by now," Marcus said, looking at his bedside clock.

"I pulled a double, cause one of my men needed to be off, so I am off today. I was trying to get in touch with you because it seems our mother thinks I need home-cooked meals around the clock," Brice said with dismay.

"What did she do now?"

"She gave my phone number to this lady, who is expecting my call, and of course she has an available daughter." Marcus laughed, but Brice said, "Before you die from laughing so hard, I'm not finished yet. Listen to this—the daughter's name is Henry, which is short for Henrietta Henderson, and she is a chef. You know, I love our mother dearly, but she says she is sending me her own special fruitcake via airmail, just until Henrietta can take some time from work to come for a visit and let me sample her cooking. Marcus, my dear brother, you and I both have had her fruitcake, and it could choke a mule, and that is putting it mildly. How Dad eats that stuff I don't know."

"He doesn't.

"What?"

"You mean to tell me you didn't know that? He gives it to Harry to use as fertilizer on the lawn or gets him to carry it out with the weeds after he does the yard. I happened to sneak up on him one day and overheard him asking Harry to get rid of it, and then he gave him money as a tip. When Dad turned around, I was standing there smiling. He swore me to secrecy. Remember when he let me go on that spring break vacation? My grades were bad, and you thought it was strange. *That* is how I got to go."

"Yeah, yeah! He and Mom fussed about it. Son of a gun! I wondered how you pulled that off. So, you used blackmail."

"Yep! Sure did. But as far as our mother trying to play the matchmaker, just play along. You're so far away that you can come up with plenty of excuses, especially the job-related ones."

"I don't know. She's talking about this person named Henry, and I had to tell her, 'Mom, I'm not into men.' And she started to laugh; then she explained that this was the woman's nickname. But you may be on to something. I can use the distance to my advantage. Here I was, wondering, how in the world was I gonna get out of it. We will see how this works. So, tell me what's the latest update on romance central."

"You know I broke up with Sheree." Marcus heard a loud whoop from Brice, and then further elaborated on the events from the previous evening.

"Man! That is embarrassing! I just hope she gets your message because Sheree is determined, if nothing else." After a brief pause, Brice jumped in again. "So, what is happening with my girl Jill?"

"Unfortunately, she's out of town on a business trip this week. She left for Boston on Monday, and I'm hoping to pick her up on Thursdayy evening at the airport. Believe me, Brice, I am so hoping I get that chance."

"Why wouldn't you?" Brice asked.

"Tyrone," Marcus replied.

"Ump! He's still around? That's not good."

"Although she broke up with him, he was not ready to do so. The way I see it, that '70s reject is going to try something again. I just have that feeling. But in the meantime, I am going to be up close and personal with her as much as I can be."

"Now that's the way," Brice said, laughing. "That sounds mighty good, Marcus, mighty good. Now you just need to do what you do best—strategize your move. I'm glad you've figured out your feelings for Jill. It just took you so damn long. Fonze and I were wondering if we needed to find ways to make you jealous, just so you would realize what a knockout the lady is. So, this is progress in the right direction. Don't forget that I will be there for the holiday."

"I'm counting on you being here, especially since Jill will be coming also. She is not going to see her parents for the holiday, so I invited her to share Christmas with us. I want her to feel at home, so I'm counting on you to be here."

They talked for a little while longer before ending the phone call.

———

When Marcus arrived home from work, he ate a light dinner and checked his phone messages, but there was only a message from Sheree. He decided to ignore it and get ready for basketball practice. After practice, he thought about calling Jill, but then thought he should at least wait it out. Although it had only been a week, he felt as if Jill had been away for much longer. It felt great just looking forward to seeing her again. He suddenly realized that it had been a long time since he looked forward to anything with such eagerness.

Thursday morning, Marcus rose early; he'd been too anxious to get much sleep. He grabbed his cell phone as he was walking out the house and saw the message light flashing. He played his messages back; the second message was from Jill. She wanted to know if the offer of a ride home from the airport was still good. He immediately called her back, and just when he thought she wasn't going to answer, she did, sounding sleepy and wonderful, he thought.

"Hey, sleepyhead," he said, having a hard time containing himself; the sound of her voice did things to him.

"Marcus?" she said groggily into the phone.

"Who else would wake you up so early?" he joked.

"You are right; who else? I guess you got my message?"

"Yeah, I did, and I will be waiting on you. Just tell me what time."

"I should be there around 5:30 this evening, traveling on Eastern National. Will that time be, ok? If it causes a conflict, then I can take a cab."

"There is no conflict, Jill, really. I will be there," he promised.

"Thanks, Marcus," she said, still sounding sleepy.

"Everything ok?"

"Everything is going really good," she said, sounding more awake.

"How was the presentation?"

"Oh! Marcus, it turned out great! We got the account. Garrett was so happy when I called him. Yep, the account is ours, lock, stock, and barrel."

"You keep up the good work, and Garrett will have you running things," he said with laughter in his voice, and she loved hearing the sound.

"Yeah right!" Jill replied playfully.

"Do you need anything?" he asked.

She easily could have said, *just you*, but instead, she said, "Nope, I'm fine."

"Then I will see you in a little while, and I want a full report on your presentation."

"Ok, she replied and he could tell she was still smiling.

"Take care, Jill."

"You too, Marcus!"

Marcus arrived at the office two hours ahead of his usual start time to get a jump on his day because he would be leaving early in preparation for Jill's arrival. When Mrs. Thomas came into work, they sat down and went through Marcus's agenda for the day.

"Mrs. Thomas, once you have rescheduled my last two meetings for today, if you want to get off early, it's fine by me. There is not a lot going on for the rest of the day." Marcus, deep in thought, slowly looked up at Mrs. Thomas and slanted his head to the side, as if something had just occurred to him. "Mrs. Thomas, if you have a moment, I'd like to ask your opinion on something."

"Go right ahead," Mrs. Thomas replied as she put the final touches on her notes. She then put her pen down, giving him her full attention.

"I'm no longer seeing Sheree, and tonight I am picking up Jill from the airport. She has been out of town on a project for Garrett. I am planning on taking Jill out to dinner, only she doesn't know it yet. I had this thought for dinner as a celebration for her getting this new account. What do you think? Is it a good idea?" He wasn't sure if he saw a look of relief as she then smiled.

"Well, Marcus, first things first. I like your idea. The dinner isn't so much about her getting this account as the fact that you are falling for her—am I right?"

Marcus expelled a breath, then looked straight at the older lady, whom he respected. "Yes. Is it that obvious? If you can see that, I will probably have her running for the hills because she has this thing about, she and I being in two different worlds, and she does not fit in. Well, let me correct that just a bit—people have made her feel that way."

Mrs. T nodded her head in understanding, then replied, "I see the way you are together; you are good for each other. When I first met her here in this office, I felt the strong chemistry between you two. I don't know her that well, but from what I see, she appears to be very humble, gracious, and pretty. She has a genuine spirit, and that by itself is priceless. What you can offer a woman would probably be welcome to most you have dated, but for Jill, it might be a bit scary. But don't let that deter you; just have patience. She will come around."

"I sure hope so! The gossip around here and her continued battles with Sheree sure has not helped her confidence. She just thinks most of the problems between Sheree and me were caused by my friendship with her. Sheree and I were having issues well before I met Jill. Quite frankly, I'm tired of being cautious and going slow, but that is my brother's advice."

"Brice is always so lively, but he is a deep thinker. He will do well once he settles down. I think he is right—go slowly. I know you don't want to, but it's best for Jill's sake. I would not do an elaborate dinner tonight. I would change that reservation and make it something spontaneous. You know that way it won't feel to her that you have just dropped Sheree and now are doing exactly what Sheree has hounded her about—stealing her man. The thought of that by itself can bring a lot of guilt, especially for someone like Jill. She'll be more relaxed if it's not planned. It's all about making her feel comfortable with you and the change in your relationship. Timing is a very vital part in taking the next step. She needs the courting process because that makes the ease of getting to know you on another level so much better." When Marcus nodded with understanding, Mrs. T continued, with a smile, reminiscing about early days with her husband.

After his talk with Mrs. Thomas, Marcus's workday took on a faster pace. He had to get those loose ends taken care of dividing his time up, in order to get the right people in the proper places working in different areas that needed attention. Although he managed to get a lot done, it was three o'clock when he finally took a break. It was quitting time, so he gathered up paperwork to store in his briefcase and prepared to leave for the day. Marcus buzzed Mrs. Thomas to go over the agenda for Monday; Marcus would not be in the office due to visiting the worksites. He wished her a good weekend and said he would see her on Tuesday.

Marcus grabbed his briefcase and left the office. The car would be waiting for him out front. He caught the elevator down to the first floor, and as he stepped out, he met Yvonne heading toward the elevator.

"Hey, Yvonne! How is it going?"

She stopped, smiling at him in greeting. "It's going good; how about with you?" she said, suddenly smiling as if she knew something.

"Really good."

"I bet! Are you picking up Jill this evening?"

He tried to hide a smile as he figured she was gauging his reaction. "Yes, as a matter of fact, I am."

"Ok, I'm gonna shoot from the hip here. Are you guys gonna do something about this thing between the two of you?"

He gave a slight laugh. "We are friends, Yvonne, and that's it." Marcus tried to sound nonchalant but failed miserably.

She pointed a finger at him. "Don't you dare try to tell me the just-friends thing because everyone can see how you handle each other, and it ain't about friendship."

Marcus clutched his chest as if she had physically hurt him.

Her expression changed from a frown to a slow smile.

Marcus only shook his head. "Yvonne, honestly, we are just good friends. If you need further clarification, ask Jill." He smiled as she threw her hands up in the air.

"Marcus Jordan, anyone ever tell you that you are good at evasion? The worst part about this is that Jill is even better than you are at it. I am sure you and Jill will make a fine couple, if keeping things on the down-low is what you two are about." A few seconds ticked by with him staring down at her, not revealing anything but a smile, which only frustrated her more. "Fine! Don't tell me. I probably already know the answer. So what time is her flight coming in?"

"Around five thirty. I'm going to take care of a few things before going to the airport."

"Are you coming by the club Friday night with Jill?" Yvonne asked with a raised eyebrow.

Marcus felt like he was walking into a trap and tried to come up with an evasive answer. "I, um, don't think so. I have a lot to do this weekend before being away on business on Monday, so I'll probably catch up with you guys another time. I really don't know if Jill will, you'd better ask her. I guess I had better get going if I'm going to make the airport on time. I'll see you later, Yvonne." Marcus saluted as he turned to leave, but he turned around as she called out to him.

"Whatever you two are up to, have a very nice evening!"

He waved just before he went out the door.

It was 5:15 when Marcus's driver pulled the limo up to the arrivals pickup zone. After getting out of the car, Marcus waved to a couple of skycaps who were familiar with him because of his frequent flying. He walked through the automated doors and found the check-in desk for Eastern National Airlines.

"Good evening, I'm picking up a passenger from your 5:30 flight from Boston. Can you tell me if it has landed?" Marcus noticed that when the woman behind the counter looked at him, her eyes traveled from his wavy black hair to his gray suit, complemented by his green shirt and tie.

"I'm afraid that flight, has been delayed for about an hour. Would you like some coffee or tea while you wait? I'm Stacey." The woman extended her hand toward Marcus.

Marcus accepted the handshake and smiled slightly as her eyes continued to run up and down his body. He pretended to be interested in the flight schedules on the wall. He thanked her for her assistance and turned toward the waiting area. "I think I'll just have a seat over there. Thank you for your offer of coffee, but I'm fine." Marcus had only taken a couple of steps before he heard her speak again.

"Yes, yes!" she said as she stood watching him.

Marcus waited for another hour and fifteen minutes before the plane arrived. He saw Jill come through the entrance for the airlines. When she searched the crowd and saw him, her face lit up with a smile. He greeted her warmly with a smile of his own. Marcus immediately noticed the change in his body the moment he saw her. She also looked different. She was dressed in a two-piece tan-suede dress; a matching jacket complemented the dress. The hemline hinted at shapely thighs. The rest of her legs were covered in high-heeled suede boots that hugged the shape of her legs. He thought she looked amazing. The short skirt and the boots made him itch to feel the softness of those legs. Marcus had to get his mind onto something else before he blew a fuse, so he diverted his attention to her hair. It now seemed she had highlights in her hair and the slightly golden streaks looked incredible on her. Her curly locks looked even thicker, with lots of curls and waviness. She looked simply delicious to him, and he began to feel nervous with anticipation of the evening, hoping he could keep it light and not reveal his true feelings—she was not ready for that.

Jill waved as he waved back. She continued to look at Marcus, thinking how she had missed him. She felt her insides just quiver, remembering the few times she had danced close with him. When they finally reached each other after dodging around people in the crowded airport, they both stopped within a foot of each other, seeming to take a breath before either could speak.

"Hey, baby girl! You look amazing! I love the hair," Marcus said as he reached out, pulled her toward him, and wrapped his arms around her. He made Jill feel like she had just walked into heaven. It seemed neither Jill nor Marcus was in any hurry to let go but they gradually stepped back from each other. "I guess there is no need to ask, how was Boston? Because it seems to have agreed with you very well. So, how many hearts did you break while you were there?" Marcus said, as his eyes continued to closely examine her.

The way he was looking at her made her a little bit nervous. She covered up the nervousness by teasing him. "Maybe one or two," she said with a slight laugh. "I really enjoyed Boston. I got a tip about this great hair salon, so I indulged myself. I have always wanted to lighten my hair color, and the woman who did it was amazing. The trip to Boston was nice, but it's good to be home. Thank you for picking me up; that was sweet of you to offer."

"You are welcome. Let's get your bags, and then I can hear all about your presentation." Marcus placed a hand at her back as he guided her through the throng of people.

Once outside, Jill was surprised when he steered her in the direction of the limo. "We are riding in the limo?"

"Yes, we are, baby girl," Marcus said as the driver retrieved her bags and put them in the trunk. Marcus opened the door for Jill, then got in beside her.

"Wow! First-class service."

"Just what you deserve, since now you have a big client under your belt," Marcus said, watching her.

"Yes, I can hardly believe it myself."

Jill turned to look out the window. They were soon out of the airport traffic and onto the main highway.

"Are you hungry?" Marcus asked.

"Now that you mention it, I haven't eaten since lunch today. I guess I was anxious not to miss my flight. After wrapping things up in Boston, I just forgot about it."

"I have not eaten either. How about we find someplace to have dinner? We could just go straight to a restaurant from here; it would save time. What'd you say?"

Jill looked at Marcus, smiled, and said, "Sounds like a great idea! Thanks, Marcus, but you sure you don't have someplace else to go?"

He pressed a button on the console and a soft jazzy tune enveloped the car, making the atmosphere relaxing and cozy. "No place I need to be other than right here, right now with you. I hope you like jazz."

She nodded her head in approval, and he smiled, then picked up the phone and gave the driver instructions to stop at a particular restaurant. Then he sat back in his seat, asking her about her trip. They were soon turning into the parking lot of a small mom-and-pop restaurant. It looked more like an old house that had been nicely preserved. When the car stopped, Marcus helped Jill out of the car, and they walked to the door. The entrance was simply a front porch, and once they were inside, there was a living room with a fireplace, and each room was a like small dining room. He watched as her face lit up.

They were greeted by a tall, slender, brown-skinned older woman with salt-and-pepper hair worn in a small Afro. "Welcome to Dazzle. Will it be just the two of you?"

"Yes, and my driver," Marcus replied.

"We have several dining rooms; you can take your pick. If it was warmer, I would have suggested the back porch—it's surrounded by our gardens—but since it's chilly tonight, our front dining area is nice, and it gives you a little view of the city in the distance. My name is Camila, and if you need anything, there is a bell on each table, and I will come to check on you. So, what area would you like? You can take your time and decide." She gave them a warm smile.

"Camila, how about the front dining area?" Marcus asked, as he got a nod from Jill.

"Absolutely. Just follow me."

She led them to a small round table with an off-white linen tablecloth. The centerpiece was a small hurricane lantern, festively decorated with holly for the Christmas season. The table was in front of a huge bay window, and to one side was a seven-and-a-half-foot decorated Christmas tree. A fireplace complemented the room. *The atmosphere is very homey and cozy*, Jill thought. The room was only lit by the lamps on the tables, which gave the room a touch of intimacy. Jill loved it.

"This is such a creative idea. It has the *wow* effect. How did you know about this place?" Jill asked.

"Oh, Mrs. T talks about it all the time. It's a favorite of her husband, Frank's. They love coming here. They've come here so often that she says they've become friends with the owners, Camila and her husband, Douglas."

"It's easy to love this atmosphere. It's just like eating a meal at your grandmother's or something. The feeling is great."

"They make most of the food you will sample tonight, so I hope you have plenty of room."

"Suddenly, it feels like my appetite has come from nowhere. I guess this place has worked its magic," Jill said, as Camila brought over menus for them both.

They ordered a bottle of the home-brewed cider, and Marcus said, "To your illustrious career as an advertising exec, I wish you all the success!" They toasted with frost-coated–design goblets.

"Ummm! This is wonderful. It's chilled and taste so fresh, and the smell of apples tickles your nose."

Marcus laughed at her reaction.

"What?" Jill asked as she giggled at his expression.

"You know your appreciation for anything is priceless for me."

Jill blushed at Marcus's comment. She then gave Marcus the details of her trip, from the moment she left for Boston until she returned home. Their conversation went from Boston to the latest happenings in Philly, especially Marcus's dinner fiasco at Phillip and Brenda's with Sheree.

"I am sorry that the dinner ended so badly, but I am sure that Brenda and Phillip won't hold you responsible."

"I was pissed off about the whole thing. Phillip and Brenda were totally embarrassed, but they tried to keep the scene between Chloe and Sheree from leaking out into the party. I had to go up to the bathroom and escort Sheree out of the place. She looked like a mess. I couldn't believe that she was fighting some girl that neither of us knew. I was so embarrassed that I sent Phillip and Brenda flowers and tickets to a play to express my sincere apologies. Phillip called to say that I didn't owe them anything, but I told him that I really felt bad. If I had known that Sheree would be there, I would not have gone, especially given that our breakup was still pretty new."

"I would never have believed that she's that insecure. I just thought she loved shoving our different backgrounds down my throat, as well as that I was beneath her. But it seems she feels that way with anyone."

Marcus's response further surprised her. "You mean her cornering you in the bathroom at the club, as well as many other nasty things she has said to you from time to time." When he saw her look of surprise and then the slow nod of her head, he said, "Yeah, I was told about that too. I wish you had told me. Now that I know, I am so sorry that she harassed you. Brenda felt bad for me, but I told her that I was never in love with Sheree, which seemed to satisfy, oddly enough. I did break up with Sheree"—he looked straight at Jill. "And the rest, as they say, is history."

In that moment, for some reason, Jill found it hard to look directly at him. But he seemed to be waiting for some response from her, and she jumped in without giving it much thought. "Wow! It's funny, but I kinda feel sorry for Sheree—well, um, maybe just a tad," she admitted with a slight smile. "Breaking up is never easy. I know how that feels, but knowing Sheree, she will probably blame me for your breakup too."

"Why would she? Sheree needs to leave you out of what happened between she I. Besides, I don't think she will be troubling you anymore. I spoke with her yesterday when she called, trying to wrangle a lunch date out of me to discuss us getting back together. I told her to forget it—not in a harsh tone, but the words meant the same. So now, Jill, you are looking at a totally free man."

"I don't think you should count Sheree out just yet. She is a determined woman. She wants you so badly that she becomes reckless, and that can be scary."

"Yeah, maybe. She can try all she likes; my answer is still the same. Actually, I'm better off not having someone for whom I have to explain away her rudeness or make excuses because she puts down my friends. It was just not working for me at all anymore. It was just best for both of us that we called it quits. Ah! Good our food is here. I'm starving. Let's enjoy, huh?"

Jill, agreed. Marcus very nicely changed the topic of conversation, and soon Jill was laughing, as he found the funniest stories to tell her about Brice and the girl their mother had sent to visit. They continued to talk about the latest happenings in and out of the office. Marcus inquired about Tyrone and noticed how very quiet she was.

"So far, so good. Have not heard a word," she said.

"That's good. Hopefully, he stays that way."

Thirty minutes later, both were sitting back in their chairs, completely satisfied with their meal. Catherine reappeared and refilled their glasses. Jill felt so good and relaxed. Turning to Marcus, she said, "I'd like to make a toast—to the single life!" Jill held up her glass.

"To the single life!" he echoed as their glasses touched. His gaze never left hers.

Jill felt the intensity of his gaze, and it caused quite a craving inside her. She felt he was going to say more but had stopped short.

When Camila appeared with a dessert menu, Jill declined, but Marcus ordered the famous brown-butter apple cake. When he took the first bite, he made such a sound of appreciation that Jill had a hard time turning him down when he offered her a taste. When she finally grabbed the extra spoon he offered, she could not help the sound that came from her as she tasted the dessert. Marcus took a deep swallow; his mind loved the sound she made. They both had to laugh as Jill helped him finish the sweet treat. They were both so full and satisfied with their meal that when he asked for the check, they both raved to Camila about how much they enjoyed every bite. The smile that reached her eyes, told how much she appreciated their enjoyment of the restaurant's food. She asked them to return soon, which they promised they would.

Outside, the driver held the door as they got in. When Jill stepped into the huge vehicle, somehow, she slipped backward, but Marcus caught her and held her to him for the briefest of moments. Jill immediately tensed with the contact, but Marcus soon let her go. His hand grazed her backside as she sat down more firmly onto the seat.

"Hey, watch it, buddy!" Jill said playfully.

"Oops! My bad; sorry, Jillian. Just wanted to make sure you were safely on the seat," he said with a short laugh.

"And don't take that *Jillian* tone with me. I know when you are trying to rub me the wrong way."

"Jill, I wouldn't say the area I just accidentally touched would be called rubbing the wrong way. It seemed right to me. Mercy, girl." He rolled his eyes, and they both started to laugh.

"Jordan, you have got issues!"

His reply came in the form of joyful laughter, and she started to laugh herself.

The drive to Jill's house didn't take long, but they filled the time with small talk. The driver followed them with Jill's bags into her apartment, then turned and walked back out. Marcus walked through the apartment to make sure everything was ok and in order. Jill stood by as he inspected the apartment before giving her the thumbs-up sign. He looked at his watch; it was already after midnight.

"You haven't been here in a while, so I thought I would check it out. Happy to report, Captain, that everything is in order." He gave her a mock salute. "I hope that you enjoyed the evening as much as I did," Marcus said as he waited for her reply.

"It was wonderful. Thank you for making it such a great evening. With all that good food, I am sure I will be out before my head hits the pillow," she said with a little laugh.

"Oh yeah, me too. I'm glad you are back. Maybe I'll call you tomorrow or Sunday because I know I will be tied up on Monday," Marcus said as she walked him to the door.

"Thanks again for picking me up at the airport and feeding me. I really enjoyed myself tonight."

"Don't forget the bachelor auction afterparty. Remember, you said that you would help me out with that."

"Sure, Marcus," Jill replied, although it had slipped her mind.

"Well, I'll say good night cause your eyes are starting to droop." He walked over the threshold but turned back around with a smile, saying, "By the way, welcome home."

Before Jill knew it, his arms came around her and his lips came down on hers, soft and warm and caressing. Then he quickly released her, leaving only a trace of his cologne trapped in her lungs and lips that still sizzled. When the fog cleared, Marcus had already closed the door, and Jill rushed to the window to catch a glimpse of him striding toward his limo. It pulled off into the dark of night as she stood there smiling.

"Yes, it has been an exceptionally good night!" she said quietly.

Chapter 9

That Sunday, Jill and Yvonne attended church, which Jill felt always rejuvenated her spirit, thus giving her the energy to endure through the week. Jill had not heard from Marcus over the weekend, but she thought he was just being Marcus, and that was busy.

Jill went back to Yvonne's place after church; they had picked up something to eat for a late lunch. Afterward, they talked for a while, catching up on gossip. Yvonne commented that lately, Joe had been working a lot of hours, and she really missed him.

That was the opening for Jill to say, "It sounds like things are in a really good place for you and Joe."

Yvonne smiled at Jill as they cleared the table. "Well, right now, it feels really good. We are in a good place with our relationship. Who knows? Maybe all these months apart made us appreciate what we have. I know Joe had been playing the field for a long time, and I just want to be sure I'm what he wants before I get my hopes up. You know what I mean?"

Jill nodded in understanding. She grabbed some dishes off the table and followed Yvonne into the kitchen. "If you ask me, I say that you and Joe are just perfect for one another. It's hard not to see it, let alone feel it. He looks at you as if you are the stars and the moon, girl," Jill said with a smile. "But I also understand why you are being cautious. I really do."

"We had that rough start, but now I think he is a stand-up guy. It has taken us a long time to reach this point. We have had plenty of runs ends. His being jealous, and then me being jealous—all of that just did not seem to matter anymore. The time it took us to grow up was worth it," Yvonne said, and Jill nodded her head. "So now, how are things going with Marcus?"

Jill tried hard not to blush, suddenly discovering an interest in her nails. She shrugged her shoulders nonchalantly before replying to Yvonne. "Marcus and I are simply good friends. We enjoy each other's company. Just because we spend a lot of time together, everyone has formed this conclusion that we are involved, and it's just not that way."

"Yet!"

"Yvonne, no, it's really not!"

"Easy, girlfriend, this is Yvonne you're talking to. I know you are friends, but I have known you for a little while now, and you are very different with Marcus than the other guys, even Tyrone, heaven forbid!" Yvonne rolled her eyes; then she looked at Jill and said in a quiet and reassuring voice, "come on, Jill. We tell each other everything. If you feel a certain way about the man, it's ok. He is one gorgeous man. He's known to have women running after him, so I say it is no big deal if you like what you see. I have watched the man when you are around, and he always finds some way to occupy your time."

They both headed to the living room and took a seat on the couch.

"Right! Just get in line, or take a number," Jill muttered as she leaned back. "You see, Yvonne, I feel like a fool because all this time, I was telling Sheree that I wasn't interested in her man. Now it will seem like I was lying through my teeth. What kind of a person does that make me, huh?" Jill looked at Yvonne and then said, "Besides, I can't compete with the high-and-mighty women he takes company with. I am probably more of a charity case for him. I don't even measure up to any woman in his league, so there is no need for this discussion."

"If you think for one moment that Marcus Jordan is not the slightest bit interested in you then you are crazy, girl. Before you blew into town, when he and Sheree would come in the club, he would usually sit at his usual table; and once in a while, he would come up to our table and talk for a little bit. Otherwise, he would be too busy with Ms. Thang. I honestly think he was just trying to keep her from getting upset, so he didn't hang around us much. Now, the fact that Joe and I have become more involved, it's kind of gotten him to hang around more with a legitimate excuse. We all have become good friends and are at the club all the time. You are a new item on the food chain for the single guys. Now he makes a point of coming around, regardless of Sheree.

"When we are at the club, no matter who you dance with, Marcus manages to dance with you or be around you somehow. You talk to each other every day or almost. You have spent time at his place, for crying out loud, even if it's innocent. Joe says Marcus never takes a woman to his place, at least not for overnight. He has repaired your car twice without asking for anything in return. He picked you up from the airport after your trip to Boston and treated you to a celebration dinner at a cozy spot, and you think he is not interested. Tell me, Jill, when a man can have his pick of women anywhere, why do you think he spends so much time with you? He has plenty of charities he contributes to, and believe me, girlfriend, you are not one of them because he is giving you way too much of his personal time. It is also not because he has nothing to do or no one else who will spend time with him. Capisce?" Yvonne said with emphasis.

"I get your point, although I don't understand it. Just thinking about it scares the daylights out of me. He does not come on to me like guys normally do. He treats me more like a buddy."

"A buddy that he can't get enough of, is what you mean! Girlfriend, let me tell you, he has not taken another girl out since he broke up with the runway queen. I will even go one farther than that—once you blew into town, he lost total interest in Sheree, although they were already headed down breakup alley." Yvonne smiled at Jill. "This, I was told by a reliable source, my friend."

Jill's eyes became huge as she put her hand to her face. "Yvonne, are you serious?" Jill asked, eyebrows raised.

"I would not lie to you."

Jill was quiet momentarily, processing what Yvonne said, before speaking again. "Marcus moves differently with me than he does with those women who flirt with him. But he does make me feel special. The thought of him being, well, you know, into me—I can't even imagine such a thing." Jill became deep in thought as the room grew quiet. She marveled at the thought of something between her and Marcus. The thoughts that had suddenly appeared in her mind seemed to grow, just like a seed. "But then again, there was this one time," Jill said with a frown on her face; then a smile slowly emerged as she remembered but tried to hide her reaction.

A huge smile broke out on Yvonne's face until she saw that Jill was not going to elaborate. "Jill! You can't just stop when it looked like something good was going on in that mind of yours, so spill, girlfriend. I need details."

"It was nothing more than a good-night kiss, so don't mind me; it's nothing compared to what you have with Joe."

"Tell me what happened; then I will tell you if it's worth holding on to," Yvonne said with a smile.

"Marcus kissed me good night you know when he picked me up from the airport and we had dinner."

"Dang, girlfriend! Then again, it all depends—was it a kiss on the cheek or the lips?" When Jill's face broke out into a large grin, Yvonne said, "I would definitely say the guy is interested, and there you were with a new hairdo too—highlights looking all fresh and sexy, yep! He wants you. You need to stop doubting yourself. Only you and Marcus can sort this out. Girlfriend, let me tell you—I think you two have good chemistry. The problem is you both are fighting it. Take it from me; I know how that is. I always thought there could be more, right from the beginning when he helped you to get started in town. But I think when I saw you and him out on the dance floor for the first time, and he looked as if he had forgotten all about Sheree, that did it for me." Yvonne threw her head back and laughed, enjoying her thoughts very much.

"I don't know, Yvonne. I'm not the kind of girl who has all this confidence so I think I will wait for him to make the first move. Oh, Lordy! What am I saying? It scares the hell out of me just thinking about it. Besides, homeboy has got so many running after him that it's a wonder he can keep up."

"Isn't that the truth? When he comes in the break room, they watch him and plot the exact moment when he will be leaving so that they can bump into him or stop him about one thing or another." Yvonne looked at Jill with a smile.

"It figures, and I can't say I blame them," Jill said.

"Yeah, I know one particular girl who threw herself at him, but he didn't try to embarrass her, although her friends were watching. He let her down in a nice and quiet way, without embarrassing her. Made me admire him even more than I already do."

"What you just said made me think of what he told me when I felt I was not good enough to hang around him. He actually said it was refreshing to be with someone without an ulterior motive. He enjoys me because I'm not trying to get him down the aisle. Isn't that funny? I remember a time when I was much larger than I am now, and out of all the people in the world, he became my friend. I used to be so embarrassed when women in the secretarial pool would make vicious comments, especially when he would stop by to see how I was doing. I had low self-esteem and a bad hairdo when I first came to Philadelphia. I was silly and thought everything in this town was awesome. Little did I know this was everyday matter for everyone else. I was laughed at, put down, and degraded most of my life, until I got angry and tired of my mother and left home. Marcus was the first person I met when I came to town."

When Jill became quiet, Yvonne cleared her throat to break the depressing aura that suddenly lay heavy in the room. Thoughts of her friend having such a hard time in life seemed to lower the mood in the room, but she refused to let that happen. She reassured her friend, saying, "Whatever happens, you do have many friends, as well as Marcus now. All ladies need a friend like Marcus, though. He is everything rolled into one tall, gorgeous, smart, caring, not to mention loaded and a sexy piece of anatomy." Yvonne looked at Jill, and they both smiled and bumped fists. They continued to laugh and talk until around four o'clock, when Jill left for home.

———

Jill awoke early on Monday morning so that she could get a head start on cutting down on her workload before Thursday, when the office would shut down for the holiday—a short week with less staff, due to vacations and some taking leave to visit relatives out of town. Jill had planned to stay home and get some work done, but that was before Marcus invited her to Christmas dinner at his parents' home. She had tried to get out of it, but her one good excuse was useless now. She could no longer use Sheree as an excuse since Marcus had broken up with her. She couldn't use Tyrone either, as they were no longer dating.

By Wednesday, Jill's time had run out to think of a legitimate excuse for backing out of the Jordan family dinner so she decided to go shopping for gifts on Friday, when she would be off from work. Marcus called her on Wednesday evening, and she asked him for suggestions for a gift for his parents.

"You really do not have to buy any gifts, Jill. Your joining us is all that is expected."

"Well, if I'm going, I am bringing a gift. I insist!" she said strongly.

He gave in. "Ok, my mother loves collecting recipes, and she loves to read anything relating to gardening or history. My father is just a simple-gadget guy, or anything related to sports, especially the wrestling stuff."

"Really?" Jill said in surprise.

"Oh, yeah, he loved Dusty Rhodes, Randy Macho Man Savage, and now Cody Rhodes. He is known to attend the shows when they are in town. Brice and I both have gone to different wrestling events when they are in town. It's a lot of fun."

"Ok, great! That is helpful. It will make it so much easier to pick out a gift. Your folks are so cool and easy to be around," Jill said.

"Yeah, except when Mom is matchmaking; then it can get kind of dicey," Marcus complained.

Jill laughed. "Guess she has two to match up, now that you are a free man," Jill said, giggling.

"Oh, don't you start with that craziness. I prefer to do my own shopping. Oh hey, I got to take this call coming in, but I will pick you Up around 5:30 on Saturday, ok?"

"Ok, Marcus, see you then."

Later that night, Jill had just finished her shower when she heard the phone ringing. She rushed to pick- up before the caller ended the call. "Hello?" she answered.

At first, she barely heard the caller. Then he said, "Hey, Jilly, it's me. We need to talk. Can you spare time for old Tyrone? Please do not say no. Just hear me out, please?"

"Tyrone?" Jill said, sounding surprised; she hadn't heard from him since the night she broke up with him.

"The one and only! Sorry I ain't been in touch, but old Tyrone had to take some time to figure out how we could make this thing work. You know what I mean?"

"Work? Tyrone, what are you talking about? We ended it!" Jill said, quickly growing impatient with the conversation.

"We never got to finish our talk, Jilly. At least give me the benefit of the doubt here."

"Tyrone, I have always done that, and you just walk all over me. You dance with other girls and create such a scene when we are at the club, and you—"

"I'm not the only one dancing with other people! What about the rich playboy you were bumping and grinding with? And as far as the rest, that was me being old Tyrone, livening up the party. That's all that was, girl, but that ego-tripping pretty boy of yours—that's another situation. He acts like he is running things, especially my girl, and I ain't having that!" Tyrone still seemed very angry with Marcus for embarrassing him in public.

"First of all, Tyrone, we were simply dancing, not groping each other like I've seen you do with some of your dance partners! But you know what? This is why it's not working for me. We've different opinions on things. For whatever time, it was good; but I cannot do this anymore. Goodbye, Tyrone!"

"Jilly, listen to me. We can work this out! Give us a chance." His voice started to elevate.

"No, we cannot. Have a good life, Tyrone."

"Jilly don't do this!" he yelled.

Jill finally hung up the phone because he was not listening to anything she said, he just expected her to keep giving him chances, like she always had done, but she was tired of this situation with him. After hanging up the phone, Jill pushed all thoughts of Tyrone out of her mind and got ready for bed, looking forward to shopping with the girls the next day.

The next day, everyone met at Yvonne's before heading out to do their shopping. It seemed the girls had all finished their shopping, except Jill. They stopped for a quick lunch before continuing to help Jill find things on her list. It was almost six o'clock before they were done, just before the stores closed for Christmas Eve. When they got back to Yvonne's, they all pitched in and wrapped gifts, and later, they sat around, tired. Yvonne invited them to stay since the guys were having their night at Marcus's.

The next morning, Jill helped Yvonne with making breakfast, and the other girls came down, pitching in to set the table. They all discussed what they were doing since it was Christmas Day. After breakfast, they gave each other gifts before leaving to go to their various holiday celebrations with family. Jill was invited to join in with the others but declined, saying she was invited to Marcus's parents for dinner.

"Oh my, aren't you two something else? First it was Thanksgiving dinner and now Christmas dinner. Sounds like you two are becoming an item," Yvonne said, winking at Jill.

"Oh, it's nothing like that. He just did not want me to be alone on Christmas. He's thoughtful like that," Jill said.

"He has never asked any of us to spend time with his family," Cyn said, and the others smiled as they teased Jill.

"Ok, guys, enough of that. We're just friends," Jill said, but she felt uncertain because things had changed between her and Marcus; she kept that thought to herself.

"You know we're just teasing, but it's true, and we think it'd be wonderful if something happened between you two," Cyn said. "But anyway, merry Christmas, ladies. We will all see each other soon."

Everyone hugged each other.

"Hey, y'all, don't forget the New Year's dance at the club. I hope everyone has a reservation because you can only get in if you have one," Yvonne said.

"We got ours," Jasmin said, indicating herself and Cyn.

"What about you, Jill?" Cyn asked.

"I hadn't planned on going. I mean, after the expense of buying gifts and just getting ready for Christmas, my funds are running low. The New Year's Eve package for an evening at the club—I'm sure it's well beyond my budget."

"We could buy your ticket; but we have to do it quickly because it's only a week away. We had better call Rudy," Jasmine said, punching in numbers on her phone.

"Jaz, if you are calling Rudy, you can hang up the phone. The New Year's dance is sold out, but it doesn't matter. Jill has a reserved ticket. Her name is already on the list. Rudy told me that," Yvonne said with a mischievous grin, as she looked around at the stunned faces.

"And you knew nothing about this?" Cyn asked, looking at Jill.

"No one told me," Jill said with a frown.

"I guess it was meant to be a surprise, so act as if you don't know about it. He was probably going to surprise you," Yvonne said.

"Who? Rudy?" Jill said with a frown.

"No, girl—Marcus!" The girls all said his name at the same time, then burst out laughing. Jill only shook her head as a smile broke out on her face as well. Afterward, they gathered up all their things and headed out the door. Yvonne watched them pull out of the driveway.

Marcus arrived promptly at five o'clock to pick up Jill for his family's Christmas dinner. When they walked through the door of his parents' home, Marcus's paternal grandmother was there. He introduced her as Grandma Ginny. The conversation was great; they all talked while they enjoyed appetizers and drinks. Jill was initially a little tense, but after all the laughs and stories, she began to relax.

Shortly afterward, Catherine announced the exchanging of gifts. They did gag gifts, which only increased the fun. Catherine showed Jill how the dining room had been set up for dinner. She had arranged for a buffet-style dinner. The tables ran along the wall in the dining room, and everyone would eat at the huge table. Catherine also told her that her staff was always given the holidays off. She believed that everyone should be with their families for the holiday. The food this time was well organized, and they all pitched in to help.

Brice kept the conversation lively with his stories, even at the dinner table. Although Marcus and his father often shot barbs at Brice and then the whole table would start to laugh, even Brice himself. It gave Jill such a good idea of the Jordan family, and she found herself wishing her own family could be this loving.

Hours later, after helping with the cleanup, Marcus was alone with Jill in the kitchen.

"Hey, Jill, now that all the activity has calmed down, I wanted to give you your second Christmas present."

"What? Oh no, Marcus. That spa certificate you gave me was more than enough, especially since I can take the girls with me too. That was so incredible. I have never been to a spa, and I know that must have cost you."

"Ah, Jill, I do things for you because I want to. I think its way past time for you to be able to enjoy life; but getting back to what I started to say—better yet here." Marcus held out his hand to reveal a long, slender black box.

Jill slowly reached for the box. She looked up at him, and his eyes stared back at her as he raised his eyebrows. Jill removed the bow and opened the box to find a long gold necklace, and at the end of it was the letter J, trimmed in diamonds.

"Oh, Marcus! This is so beautiful!" she moaned and then her eyes began to tear.

"Whoa! I didn't give you this to make you cry," Marcus said, bewildered.

"Son, what are you doing to this poor girl to make her cry?" Catherine said, walking into the room. She saw Jill wiping her eyes, and then Catherine saw the box in Jill's other hand. She looked at the necklace. "Oh, that is so beautiful! I think the girl loves it, and I definitely approve!" Catherine said, hugging Jill and then Marcus before leaving the room.

"So, is Mom, right? Do you like it?" he asked, staring at Jill with his arms crossed.

"I do—I mean, I do love it. But Marcus, you keep giving me these expensive things, and all I gave you is a bottle of your favorite scotch! It's not equal by any means."

"Yes, it is equal to me because you gave it to me. Honey, listen, you have been through such a hard time in your life. I just want to do a little bit to help put a smile on that face. I know you don't like it when I do these things, but for some reason, I can't help myself. Its such a good feeling when your face breaks out into this huge smile. I simply hate it when I see that forlorn look in your eyes. I want you smiling and happy," Marcus said.

Brice walked in when he overheard Marcus and said, "I'll second that. Darlin', your smiles are like medicine, and when—"

"Brice! Do you mind?" Marcus exclaimed.

"Wow! Look at that amazing necklace for an amazing woman," Brice said, completely ignoring Marcus. He hugged Jill, then stepped back to walk out of the kitchen. "I have an errand to run. Catch you later, Jill. See ya later, Marcus."

Marcus responded with a grunt, then turned back to Jill. "I guess I had better get you home before someone else interrupts me." He didn't look so happy.

"I really do love the gift, Marcus, but tell me—did you reserve a ticket for me at the New Year's dance at the club?" she asked, hands on her hips.

"I did, not only for you but the girls as well. I would like you and the girls at my table as my guests. What? Did I do something wrong again?" he asked when she shook her head.

"No, you did nothing wrong. You are just an incredibly good guy. Thank you for always thinking of me, and I'm not going to spoil it with anything negative." On impulse, she stepped closer and kissed him on his cheek.

"Wow! Did not see that one coming," Marcus said, totally surprised by the kiss.

"You didn't, and I know I'm hard on you at times, but I honestly would not trade you for the world. So that's all the compliments I'm handing out tonight. Are you ready to take me home?" she said with a smile

"Ok, let's go find my folks," Marcus said, returning her smile as they walked out of the kitchen.

———

By the time Marcus took Jill home, it was well after eleven thirty. His parents kept them talking for a while, then Brice returned, extending the conversation. When they finally ended their conversation, Brice told Marcus that he would not be leaving town until the day after New Year's Day—he too was looking forward to the dance. Then he bid them good night.

———

Once they got to Jill's place, Marcus took Jill's key from her, and as their fingers touched, they both felt the energy from the force that seemed to always draw them together. Jill didn't know if he felt it too, as he did not seem to be affected by it. She followed him into her place. When he had checked the place out, he came back to the living room and headed for the front door, then turned to her before walking out.

"Hey, thanks for joining my family for Christmas dinner. It was nice having you there," he said, looking directly into her eyes.

"Thank you for persuading me to come because I'm so glad I did. You have an awesome family. I really do enjoy listening to them joking with each other. The way you and your dad are with Brice is so funny, but I can see the love there."

"Yeah, Brice is a handful, but we put up with him," Marcus said, laughing. "I guess I had better leave so that you can get some rest. It has been a night."

"Yes, thank so much for my gifts and this beautiful necklace." She looked up at him expectantly, but instead of kissing her, he drew her into his embrace for a few seconds. Then he stepped back, looking at her.

"Thanks, baby girl, for making it one of my best Christmases.

Good night!" Then he winked before heading out the door, to Jill's disappointment.

～～～

It was little after nine o'clock on New Year's Eve, as Tyrone sat with his friend Ray, drinking gin and juice, when his phone rang. "Yeah?" he answered, sounding mad at the interruption.

"Where are you?" Sheree asked excitedly.

"Chilling," he answered.

"Shouldn't you be at the club by now?"

"Oh, hey, Sheryl!" he answered, starting to smile.

"Sheryl? Who's Sheryl? It's Sheree, remember? Tyrone, are you drunk?"

"I'm feeling all right, Ms. Sheree."

"You need to get over to the club right now. I need you to show up before Marcus gets there," Sheree said excitedly.

"Woman, will you just chill? I will be leaving in a few minutes."

"You'd better not mess this up, Tyrone. You owe me!"

"Look, I told you I will have my girl in check. The rest is up to you. Now let me get off here so that I can take care of things."

"I'm counting on you, Tyrone, to take care of your girlfriend," Sheree said angrily, but he had already hung up. "Damn!"

～～～

Jill was ready early as she knew there would be lots of traffic and she did not want to have Cyn waiting on her. She took a last look at her shimmering silver dress with spaghetti straps that crisscrossed on the back of the dress. The hemline fell just below mid- thigh with matching silver pumps. Her sparling earrings dangled from her ears, and she chose a matching shawl as her wrap. Cyn picked Jill up on her way to the club, and Yvonne was to meet them there. It took them longer than usual because the traffic was so heavy. When Jill and Cyn got there, Yvonne and Joe were already at the table. The club was crowded so it was good that there was reserved seating.

"I'm glad you all made it," Yvonne said. "Jasmine called me before I left and said that a friend of hers from work named Craig had shown up at her door and that she would be around as soon as she got rid of him. She didn't want him tagging along with her, especially since she is supposed to meet a guy that she met in one of her yoga classes."

The girls all traded looks, hoping that this was not another health nut to deal with, and that meant usually just getting rid of him before he spoiled their evening. When a waiter appeared, they all gave him their orders. Yvonne noticed that Jill seemed a bit preoccupied. She kept looking toward the entrance, as if she was expecting someone, so Yvonne decided to tease Jill by talking in a low voice.

"Jill, you, ok?"

"Oh yeah, I'm fine."

"Well, if you are worried about Marcus—"

"Oh, no! He called and said he would be getting in late since he was out of town, but he would be here," Jill said with a smile.

"Great! It's going to be such a wonderful night. I love how Rudy and the crew decorated this place. It looks really festive, don't you think?"

"Yeah, they really did a great job. I'm so glad I came. I have always wanted to go to a New Year's Eve dance, this is great!" Jill said looking around excitedly.

"I sure hope there are plenty of single guys to choose from because I do not plan to waste any dances tonight!" Cyn said as she looked around.

Jasmine arrived twenty minutes later, just as the drinks were brought to the table. There were party favors on each table, and every table was now occupied. When the music changed, Cyn and Jill were asked to dance, as Jazmin and her date was not far behind as they all headed to the dance floor. Two pairs of eyes watched from across the room.

"We should have been at that table, not stuck here in the corner," Sheree said, fussing.

Renee tried to ignore her friend's sour mood as she swayed back and forth to the music. When Renee was asked to dance, she quickly got up, just as another gentleman approached their table—only Sheree turned him down.

Jill and the girls were on the dance floor awhile before Jill decided to take a break. When the others came back to the table, everyone seemed to have worked up a thirst. They ordered another round of drinks. Fonze was telling a joke, which had everyone laughing as the good fun was being had by all. Jill was reaching for her glass when she heard a familiar voice.

"Hello, Jilly." Tyrone stood by her chair.

Jill was totally surprised to see Tyrone standing there in a nice gray suit and tie, totally different from his usual fashion. She set her glass down, but before she could form words, Tyrone said, "Can I have this dance?"

She was speechless and felt that the air had just gone out of the room. Tyrone took her nonresponse as a yes. He reached for her hand as he pulled her up out of her chair. Jill looked around to find everyone looking at them, but she gave in and followed him to the dance floor. A slow song was playing, and he pulled her into his arms.

"Wow! Girl, you look hot! I'm so glad I came looking for you."

"How did you get in here?" Jill asked, coming out of the shock at seeing him.

"I have my contacts. I just could not let this night go by without seeing you. I have missed you so much, and I have so much to say to you, if you'd just hear me out," Tyrone said gently.

"Tyrone, we've already said all we need to say to each other." Jill tried not to draw attention to them.

"No, Jilly, I never got to finish speaking my piece. Girl, you have no idea how not seeing you—I mean, the effect it has had on me. I need you in my life."

"Look, Tyrone, I'm sorry, but you and I do not work."

"Can you at least hear what I have to say, please?" Tyrone said as he stared at her.

"What more is there to say, Tyrone?"

"I have lots to say. Just hear me this one last time, and if you still feel the same way, I will leave you alone." He waited for her answer.

"Ok, go ahead and tell me what you want me to know," Jill said, not feeling like going through this all again.

"Not here. How about we go outside and talk. It's way too loud in here."

"Fine, just let me get my wrap from the table." She walked to her table and saw the questioning look on the girls' faces. "Hey, y'all, I'm just going to step outside to talk to Tyrone for a minute. I will be right back. It won't take long; trust me," Jill whispered.

"Girl, it's freezing out there." Yvonne advised as she raised her eyebrows at Jill.

"I'll be fine; that's how fast this conversation will be over," Jill replied, then turned as she followed Tyrone out of the room.

"Something is not right, Yvonne. Jaz and I were there the night when he refused to leave Jill's place, but then he looked over at us and told her it was not over," Cyn said, looking at the door where Jill had just walked through.

"This is not good. Maybe I can get Joe to go check it out. Make sure she is all right. We'll give them five minutes, tops," Yvonne said, taking a sip of her drink.

———

Across the room, Sheree was wearing a big smile as she ordered a bottle of champagne. "Looks like everything is working out. When Marcus gets here, there will be no interruptions or distractions. I will just slide back in where I should be," Sheree said gleefully.

"I wouldn't count on it, Sheree. That bozo is no prize, and if I had the choice, I would certainly not pick him. Give the girl some credit. She is not dumb."

"Why are you always such a Debbie Downer? Tyrone will do his part. As you can see, he's already left with her. I told you the tramp was easy," Sheree said, laughing.

———

Outside it was cold, and Jill pulled her wrap more tightly around her. "Ok, Tyrone, what is it you wanted to say?" Jill asked.

"Jilly, we have a good thing going, and I need you in my life."

"Yeah, well, you messed that up with the way you acted whenever we were out. You ran after other women and whenever I danced with someone, it caused an altercation."

"All I did was dance and try to have fun. I tried to lighten things up a bit, and I think you misunderstood me, that's all. We can fix this. Don't make a small thing into something big."

"Are you kidding me, Tyrone? Let's not do this. It's over and done with. I'm going back inside. You obviously have a different opinion than I do about everything!" Jill said, really annoyed. She turned around to head back into the club.

"I wouldn't do that if I were you—unless you want me to get pretty boy involved, cause the way I see it, he is the problem I'm having with you!" Tyrone's calm voice suddenly turned threatening.

Jill froze when Tyrone mentioned Marcus without saying his name; she knew who he was talking about.

"Now are you prepared to hear me out, or must I stick around and take issue with *Marcus*?" Tyrone growled.

Jill tried to be nonchalant, but it was hard. She felt the fear of what he was about to suggest. "Tyrone, what more is there to say?"

"Lots more, and if I were you, I would be more understanding, especially in my case," Tyrone said angrily, losing patience with her. "Now I have a suggestion. This is what we are going to do. We are going to get in my car, go over to Winky's or somewhere I prefer, and talk this thing out. But if you are not willing, I will just have to stick around until Marcus arrives. This time, believe me, he will be the one carried out. So now, Jilly, what do you want to do?" Tyrone lit a cigarette as he waited for her answer.

After only a few seconds, Jill agreed. *I can't get Marcus into this mess with crazy Tyrone*, she thought. "Ok, Tyrone," Jill said, releasing a breath and sounding defeated.

Tyrone ushered her over to his car and held the door while she got in. He was just closing the door when Joe and Big Ben came out of the club. Tyrone hesitated before walking around to the driver's side of the car. When he put his hand on his door, he heard his name called and turned to look at them.

"Hey! Tyrone, man, we need to speak to Jill!" Joe yelled out.

"Later, guys. Right now, me and my woman got something pressing to do," Tyrone yelled as he jumped into his car and started it up. He quickly put the big car in reverse and backed up, almost hitting the two guys.

"Hey, wait! Stop! Jill!" Joe yelled out.

"Stop the car, Tyrone!" Jill yelled, but he ignored her. When she reached for the door handle, he grabbed her by the neck and pulled her closer to him on the seat. The door swung open, but he did not stop. The car squealed out of the parking lot, narrowly missing the two men.

"Tyrone, please! They have to know that I'm ok!" Jill said frantically.

"Oh? Are you really, Jilly?" Tyrone started to laugh as he increased the speed of the gray 1959 Deuce and a Quarter, which headed down the street into the night.

To be continued

Printed in the United States
by Baker & Taylor Publisher Services